Above the Clouds

As Latham's arms encircled Nikkola's slim waist, her head was magnetically drawn to his chest. Lacing his fingers under the curls at her nape, he pressed his lips to her temple. Wrapping her arms around his waist, she splayed her fingers across the strong muscles of his upper back.

Nikkola and Latham moved across the dance floor with grace and style. With each step taken, they melded themselves closer together, until they couldn't get any closer. Shutting their eyes, they blocked out the rest of the world. In perfect tune with the seductive rhythm of the music, they flowed together harmoniously. Both Nikkola and Latham were totally unaware that the music had stopped until Latham felt a tap on his shoulder.

BOOK YOUR PLACE ON OUR WEBSITE AND MAKE THE ARABESQUE ROMANCE CONNECTION!

We've created a customized website just for our very special Arabesque readers, where you can get the inside scoop on everything that's going on with Arabesque romance novels.

When you come online, you'll have the exciting opportunity to:

- View covers of upcoming books

- Learn about our future publishing schedule (listed by publication month and author)

- Find out when your favorite authors will be visiting a city near you

- Search for and order backlist books

- Check out author bios and background information

- Send e-mail to your favorite authors

- Join us in weekly chats with authors, readers and other guests

- Get writing guidelines

- AND MUCH MORE!

Visit our website at
http://www.arabesquebooks.com

Above the Clouds

Linda
Hudson-Smith

BET Publications, LLC
http://www.bet.com
http://www.arabesquebooks.com

ARABESQUE BOOKS are published by

BET Publications, LLC
c/o BET BOOKS
One BET Plaza
1900 W Place NE
Washington, DC 20018-1211

All Kensington Titles, Imprints, and Distributed Lines are available at special quantity discounts for bulk purchases for sales promotions, premiums, fund-raising, and educational or institutional use. Special book excerpts or customized printings can also be created to fit specific needs. For details, write or phone the office of the Kensington special sales manager: Kensington Publishing Corp., 850 Third Avenue, New York, NY 10022, attn: Special Sales Department, Phone: 1-800-221-2647.

First Printing: March 2005
10 9 8 7 6 5 4 3 2 1

Printed in the United States of America

A heartfelt thanks to all of the wonderful people below who've touched my life in a special way. Each of you has played a significant supporting role in my life during 2003 and into 2004.

Brenda Bailey
Judyann Elder and John Cothran
Reggie and Willie Mae Flood
Yolanda Renee Flood
Jessica Holcolmb
Torri Harris
Beverly Jimerson
Tiffany King
Kielli Lilvois
Charlie Brown and Sherra Miller
Art Nora
Willie Patterson
Mary Perez
Eugenia Washington
Luwalia King

An extra-special thanks to the wonderful book clubs who've offered me tremendous support:
   Girlfriend 2 Girlfriend, Phoenix, AZ
   Ladies Of Color Turning Pages, Los Angeles, CA
   Women In Sisterhood, Memphis, TN
   Amber Bailey and Friede Chevrolet (Thanks for getting me out of a real paper jam ☺.)

Chapter 1

Captain Latham Scott dropped off his flight gear in the cockpit of the fuel-efficient three-hundred-passenger-seat Boeing 777 before he sought out the purser, Nikkola Knight, to begin the first of his routine checks. Nikkola was the senior member of the seventeen flight attendants, ten females and seven males, assigned to Flight 126 leaving from Dulles International Airport outside Washington, bound for Heathrow International Airport in London, England.

Nikkola's heart never ceased to flutter wildly whenever the six-foot-three African-American aircraft commander approached her. Besides being extremely rugged, handsome, and buff beyond description, he was one of the kindest, nicest pilots she'd ever worked with. He'd been her fantasy since the first day she ever laid her hazel eyes on him. She felt lucky when she'd won her bid for one of the hottest routes around. But she felt extremely blessed after she'd met one of the airline's sexiest commanders, Captain Latham Scott. Several days of the month, Nikkola had the pleasure of serving Latham and his two first officers. Blaine Mills and Alexander

Streeter were the first officers for today's flight. There were always three pilots on flights over water.

Smiling broadly, Latham entered the first-class galley. "Hello, Nikki. It's nice to see you, as always. Ready for the preliminary flight check?"

"But of course, Captain Scott." The crew often called one another by first names, but there were times when Nikkola referred to the pilots by their official title. "I got my little pen and paper ready when I saw you coming down the aisle. By the way, it's always nice to see you, too."

Latham smiled. "For the bin order we'll need Evian water, orange and cranberry juices, Cokes, 7-UP, and of course a bucket of ice. Our flight time is six hours and twenty minutes. Expect some light to moderate turbulence approximately four hours into the flight." He then gave her the pass code to the cockpit, a new security measure adopted after the hijacking disasters.

Nikkola nodded. "Same choice in meals for you?"

"I think I might like a change. Make the hot meal vegetarian."

"Okay. The hot meal an hour and a half into the flight and the snack two hours later, right?"

"Right you are." Latham's expression turned somber. "I trust that you're emotionally prepared to deal with the passengers that are still fearful of flying through the not so friendly skies."

"I'm prepared, Captain Scott. It has taken me a while, but I'm starting to get back as close to what we'll probably consider normal. Though three years ago, the 9/11 tragedies changed everyone. We all knew at least one or two of the crew members on those doomed flights."

Feeling the same emotions as Nikkola did, Latham smiled with empathy. "Yeah, it's been tough on everyone. Keep your chin up, though. God is still in control. See you later."

Nikkola watched Captain Scott stroll the aisle greeting passengers and the other attendants. As he was known to always take time to make himself available to his crew and passengers, she thought he was really a genuine guy. She couldn't help wondering if he was as good to his women as he was to his crew and the passengers. The thought of his fingers and lips touching her intimately sent shivers of pleasure up her spine. If only she had a ghost of a chance with him.

Nikkola knew trouble was brewing when she first spotted Carmen Thomas, Latham's supposedly ex-lover, out in the passenger area. No doubt she was flying space-available to keep up with Latham. It had been rumored that the affair had been over for a couple of months, but no one knew for sure. Seeing Carmen today made Nikkola even more curious about their relationship. If they were no longer involved, she felt no shame in wanting to pick up with him where Carmen left off.

Nikkola spotted the ground crew as she looked out the window from her seat in the front of the aircraft. The tiny blue and white lights on the runway lit up the night's pitch-blackness, the glistening tarmac slippery wet from a recent downpour of heavy rain.

Bright lights from the inside terminals shone out into the darkness to the right and left of the runway. No silhouettes of hands waved enthusiastic farewells from the rectangular-shaped windows, since the tragedies in New York, Washington, D.C., and Pennsylvania had brought about drastic and badly needed changes in security services in and around national airports. No one other than ticketed passengers was now allowed into the boarding areas.

Air International Flight #126 inched its way onto the seemingly never-ending runway. The Boeing 777 jumbo jet taxied the tarmac, rapidly picking up speed. The ground crews stood by in silence, seemingly enchanted by the plane's slow but sure ascent into the diamond-studded night.

Thirty-five-year-old Captain Latham Scott manipulated the mind-boggling array of controls in an expert fashion. Empowered by confidence and vast experience, he could have masterfully flown the shiny silver and blue aircraft blindfolded. Latham had joined the Air Force at the age of eighteen. After earning a degree, he had applied to and was selected to attend officers' candidate training school. He later applied for the Air Force pilot training program and was readily accepted.

Winging its way east, the aircraft sloped upward, mounting the stairway to heaven with grace. After climbing thousands of feet into the atmosphere, Captain Scott smoothly leveled off the ascent. He then picked up the microphone. Speaking with a slight southern drawl, his bass voice greeted the passengers. His sexy voice had never once failed to mesmerize Nikkola Knight.

Soon after the fasten-seat-belt light was turned off, Nikkola and the other crew members leaped into action. Taking orders for beverage service would take place first. During the six-hour-plus flight, two movies and a hot meal and one snack would be provided. Passengers in first class had the luxury of selecting the movie of their choice from individual monitors. As one of many special features of the Boeing 777, the first-class seats also pulled out into beds.

In charge of the first-class cabin, Nikkola smiled warmly as she greeted her passengers and then wrote down their drink preferences. One of the passengers, an African-American male with dark piercing eyes, looked at her as if dissecting her shapely anatomy piece by piece. His concentrated gaze unnerved her somewhat. Her curly fiery red hair and hazel eyes often brought her attention and hard stares. Standing a statuesque five-feet-seven in her stocking feet didn't help matters either. Nikkola had dreamed of being a model as a small child, and on up through her teens, but she'd never even tried to pursue it as a career choice. By the time she'd reached adulthood she had developed interests that leaned more in the direction of social and public services.

Air International Flight #126, originating from Washington's Dulles International Airport, was now parked at Gate C-12 at London's Heathrow International Airport. Without incident, the flight had landed safely, right on schedule.

After a long, tiring flight, both the passengers and crew looked eager to deplane. But there was something else Nikkola had to do. As she had done so many times in the past couple of years, Nikkola picked up the microphone and began singing "God Bless America." Tears filled her eyes as all the passengers joined in whether they were American or not. Loud cheering followed the song.

As the passengers scurried about gathering their personal belongings, the clicking noise of overhead luggage compartments being thrown open was heard throughout the plane; other passengers stretched lazily in the aisles. The busy flight crew tended to the needs of their passengers while anticipating a much-needed rest.

Flight #126 had proved a horrendous one for Nikkola. Everything that could've gone wrong had. When the plane had flown into unexpected turbulence, even though she'd been warned, she'd spilled coffee all over the very passenger who had unnerved her. She had practically ruined his expensive tailored suit. While she was helping a young mother with her baby, the infant had become airsick and had thrown up all over Nikkola's cleaned and pressed navy blue and gold uniform. That mishap resulted in her having to make a quick change of clothing.

Grabbing her flight bag, Nikkola headed for the front of the plane. Wearily, she carried her tall, slender frame down the aisle. Visibly tired, she stepped into the cockpit.

Captain Latham Scott grinned broadly as she appeared in the doorway. In appreciation of Nikkola's curvaceous figure and flaming-red curly hair, tied back with a decorative band, Latham's caramel-brown eyes gleamed with interest as they came to rest in her hazel ones. Nikkola's heart fluttered like crazy, as Latham flashed her an even white smile.

Latham chuckled. "So, Nikki, I understand you had a time of it back there."

She lowered her lashes and smiled lazily. *Bad tidings travel as quickly as this fast-moving time machine.* "That's an understatement. I've never spilled anything on anyone until now. I apologized profusely, but the arrogant man in 2A was none too happy with me. In a very haughty tone, he accused me of ruining a perfectly good suit. He even asked me if my parents had ever sent me to charm school. I had to practice a lot of self-control to keep from asking him if he'd ever made a mistake before. The cold stare in those dark eyes of his, and, of course, my dedication stifled some of the retorts I briefly considered. I thought he was a brother. But he seems to have a slight British accent. He could've picked it up if he's been living in England for a while. Whatever nationality he is, I hope I never have to deal with him again."

Latham's laughter thundered as Nikkola's hazel eyes twinkled with devilment.

"He could've been extremely rude, but he didn't dare with all the strict airline policies in place now. People are really taking things seriously, Latham, as they should be."

Latham looked displeased. "You should've contacted me. I don't want my crew taking anything off of anybody, even though it looks like you handled it okay. But

I can imagine that you had a hard time holding your tongue. Since I've seen the temper matching that fiery red hair of yours, I'd say the chap got off lightly. Still interested in having a house full of kids?"

Nikkola knew Latham was referring to the incident with the baby. "I'm too numb to think about it. I'll tell you after I've had a long shower and several weeks of sleep."

Latham howled at her comment.

"What's so funny?" Carmen Thomas asked, hating the sensuous way that Latham always looked at Nikkola. Possessively, she looped her arm through Captain Scott's.

Latham looked surprised to see Carmen. "What are you doing on this flight? On vacation?"

"You were busy with the instrument check when I was cleared to board. I didn't want to disturb you. Just using my benefits. But I was hoping to get a chance to talk with you," Carmen said.

When Carmen smiled brilliantly at Latham, Nikkola's heart arrested. She couldn't stand the fact that Carmen was so overly possessive of him. Latham didn't look as if he liked it much either.

"We were just going over Nikki's flight mishaps," Latham responded, his tone dry.

While bending over Latham's seat, it looked as if Carmen were about to kiss him. Although she'd come very close to touching her mouth to his, instead, she ran her slender fingers through his tobacco-brown hair. Jealous and embarrassed, Nikkola quickly turned away, but not before she saw Latham's look of utter dismay.

Carmen was a pretty African-American woman: keen features, long jet-black hair, dark eyes, and a toast-brown complexion. Carmen was short compared to Latham's six-foot-three frame, but she had a great figure.

Nikkola had heard from many flight attendants that Carmen was hard to get along with and had a nasty attitude. Nikkola had not regularly flown with her, and hoped she never had to, especially if what she'd heard about Carmen were true. Nikkola usually formed her own opinions about people. But Carmen had rubbed her the wrong way the couple of times she'd been in her company.

"Nikki, I heard you were bidding on another route. Any luck yet?"

Nikkola easily recognized the malicious intent in her comment. *You'd love that, wouldn't you?* "I haven't a clue where you heard that! This route is pure gold. I'll see you guys later. I want to get through customs and get to the hotel. I'm ready to sleep."

Latham and Carmen waved good-bye as Nikkola went through the tunnel.

Dragging her flight gear behind her, Nikkola rushed down to the customs area. All the other crew members had gone, but she figured that she'd catch up with her best friend, Glen Taylor, before leaving the airport.

Having cleared customs, Nikkola boarded the crew bus. Throwing her flight bag under the seat, she stretched her silky legs across the aisle. As there were only a few crew members on the bus, she looked around to see whom she knew. Already moving in her direction, Glen Taylor had spotted Nikkola first. Plopping down in the seat in front of her, he turned around to face her. She could see that his sable-brown eyes looked tired when Glen pushed his sandy-brown hair back.

"You look as tired as I do, Glen. I thought this flight would never end."

"I know what you mean, Nikki. What are you going to do on our layover here in London?"

"I'm going to sleep until it's time to go back to the States. I'm bushed, Glen. If I don't see another aircraft for the next six weeks, I wouldn't be disappointed."

"Sleep! That doesn't sound too exciting, Nikki. You can sleep anytime." Glen gave her a boyish grin. He had a golden-brown complexion and Nikkola loved his beautiful eyelashes, which were so long that they curled upward.

"I've had all the excitement I can stand for one day, but we do have several days off when we get back home. I guess I could catch up on my sleep then. The weekends in London are always exciting times. Did you have anything special in mind, Glen?"

Glen stretched his arm across the back of the seat. "I was thinking about going to Soho to do some shopping. Afterward, we could take the tube to Covent Gardens and have some lunch."

Nikkola nodded, though his suggestion was their normal routine. "Sounds okay to me."

Glen Taylor was Nikkola's best friend and confidant. They lived in the same condominium complex in Virginia and were mostly scheduled on the same flights. The two friends took turns driving to and from Dulles International. As far as Nikkola was concerned, Glen was the most kind and loyal person anyone could ever have as a friend, but their relationship went so much deeper.

Due to a terrible experience she'd had with a so-called best friend, Nikkola no longer believed in the idea of building lifelong friendships. She now found buddy-buddy relationships too complicated and totally unpredictable. After she'd discovered that her best friend, Tammy Amos, was having a secret fling with her boyfriend, Cyd Ashford, the two had a bitter break in their friendship. The affair had also destroyed the relationship between Nikkola and Cyd. Even though it had happened more than a year ago, Nikkola had never allowed herself to forget the devastating betrayal.

Nikkola grabbed her flight bag when the crew bus pulled up to the magnificent St. James Court Hotel, located in the heart of Westminster and the most frequented hotel for the Air International crews. Glen took it gently from her hand and carried it off for her.

Inside the hotel Nikkola saw both of the first officers
from Flight #126. She nudged Glen. "I wonder what's
up with the pilots staying in the same hotel as the flight
attendants. Contractually that isn't supposed to happen."

"One of the other flight attendants told me that they'd
be staying here. The hotel they usually stay in is under
renovation. It's not as if the contract has ever kept flight
attendants and pilots from fraternizing. There are no
rules about us dating one another, so it makes no sense."

After Nikkola and Glen checked in at the front desk,
the bellboy took their gear up to their rooms. In parting, the two friends promised to meet up in a couple of
hours.

Nikkola briefly looked around the luxurious suite.
The elegant furnishings were very British, while the entire decor of the suite was warm and soothing. Pulling
back the heavy gold-brocade bedspread, she tossed her
luggage on the bed and opened it. After taking out a
pair of jeans and a sweater to wear, she removed a lightweight jacket. It was early fall, and the weather in
England was always hard to predict.

Moving into the spacious bathroom, Nikkola stripped
down and then hopped into the shower. The shower-
head sprayed out evenly as she stood under it, allowing
the water to run freely over her body. Her muscles began
to relax and she felt as if she could stay in the steamy
hot shower for hours. After washing her hair and then
wrapping it in a towel, she stepped out and pulled on a
soft terry cloth robe. Nikkola then moved into the small
living room.

Opening the doors of the Louis Philippe entertainment armoire, Nikkola turned on the television and sat
down on the traditionally styled burgundy-and-gold-

striped Nottingham sofa. The program was none too interesting, so she allowed her heavy lids to close shut. Latham Scott's sexy smile cuddled her heart as she fell into a dreamy state. The steamy crush that she had on the sexy aircraft commander was starting to drive her up the wall.

Unfortunately for her, Latham Scott saw her as nothing more than a fellow employee. She was more than willing to find out if there could be more. But he'd have to make the first move. She'd met him long before Carmen had ever come into his life. Although he didn't seem to see Nikkola as a potential lover, he was very protective of her, always taking the time to find out how her flight was going. He also seemed to be able to sense Nikkola's emotional state.

Latham was seven years older than Nikkola, yet they still had a lot in common. She had been a social worker before becoming a flight attendant, working for the Virginia Welfare Department. Because of all the bureaucratic red tape one had to go through to help the needy, Nikkola become frustrated, and began looking for a job as a flight attendant. Her love of travel had made her second career choice an easy one, but she was still actively involved with helping those in need by volunteering her services.

From their many conversations, mostly before and after flights, she'd learned that she and Latham had a lot in common. They both loved the theater, long romantic drives, exotic travel, the beach, most sports, and jogging. Each felt a deep compassion toward others and both were often involved in community services. Their biggest weakness was an incurable addiction to butter pecan ice cream and chocolate cake. She clearly remembered the day they'd discovered their mutual addiction. When Nikkola had told Glen that if she didn't get her dessert fix soon, she was going to flip out,

Latham had overheard the conversation. He'd then told them a great place to find the ice cream, and that butter pecan and chocolate cake were also his favorites.

Nikkola awakened and rushed into the bedroom to dress. After a quick run-through of her hair with the blow dryer, she ruffled her curls and let them fall naturally. Before she could finish buttoning her crisp, white shirt, Glen knocked on the door. Nikkola slipped on her jeans before running out into the hallway.

When Nikkola flung the door open, Glen nearly fell inside the room.

Glen smiled lazily. "I thought you'd gone off without me."

Slipping her hand into his, as they walked into the living room, Nikkola then pushed him toward the sofa. "Sit," she instructed gently. "I'm nearly ready. I'll be right back."

Laughing heartily, Glen wiggled his fingers at Nikkola in a farewell gesture.

After entering the bedroom, Nikkola sat down at the dressing table. Once she'd applied a small amount of blush to her cheeks, she dabbed her lips with a clear lip gloss. Happy with her appearance, Nikkola grabbed her jacket and reentered the living room.

"Ready!" Nikkola gave Glen a dazzling smile.

Whistling softly, Glen looked at Nikkola with obvious admiration. "Sweetheart, you are one beautiful woman! Too bad I've sworn off women for the rest of my life. I should've asked you to marry me a long time ago. Latham Scott must be blind, or maybe he's gay," Glen teased.

Nikkola felt a sudden rush of love for the man she loved like a brother. Glen was fun-loving, so sweet, but sometimes moody, especially right after he'd let some woman take complete advantage of his good nature. Standing on her tiptoes, Nikkola planted a kiss on Glen's cheek.

As always, Glen was touched by her deep affection for him. He kissed her back. Glen was tall with a solidly packed physique. Handsome, witty, intelligent, Glen always carried himself in a very dignified manner.

"I probably would've accepted your proposal, Glen." Nikkola smiled sweetly. "You are the most sensitive, caring man I know. But I doubt seriously if Latham Scott is gay."

Glen grinned widely. "You're probably right. Latham seems like the strong, silent type."

"I don't know about silent, but Latham is definitely strong. I'm not going to think about him. Despite the rumors, I think Carmen might still have him wrapped up. We better be going," Nikkola mumbled, hurting inside for what she wanted terribly and couldn't have, Latham Scott.

Nikkola linked her arm through Glen's as they exited the suite. The elevator doors were already standing open when they entered.

"Speaking of Carmen Thomas, I don't think she ever really had him. That woman didn't give him room to breathe. I don't know how he stood her hanging all over him. That perfume she wears would gag a hippopotamus." Frowning, Glen turned up his nose.

Nikkola laughed at Glen's comical expression. "What would a hippo be doing smelling Carmen's perfume, Glen?"

Glen put his hands across Nikkola's eyes in a playful manner. "You overanalyze everything, Nikkola Knight." Knowing Glen was right about her, Nikkola nodded in agreement.

*   *   *

The couple walked out the door and into the courtyard of the hotel. Nikkola loved the courtyard's huge sparkling marble fountain, lush greenery, and colorful flowery trees. At night the trees and shrubbery were all lit up. She loved to stroll through the yard and look down on it from the windows in her suite. They walked through the tall, black iron gates and out onto the street.

Hand in hand, strolling down Buckingham Gate to Victoria Street, Nikkola and Glen passed the New Scotland Yard. A few minutes after turning onto Broadway, they entered the St. James Park entrance to the Underground. As it was early afternoon, the couple purchased off-peak travel cards, which would allow them to make several stops along the way.

"How many times have we done this, Nikki?"

"I've lost count. I love riding the Underground, but the security alerts are rough on your nerves. Maybe we'll be lucky today and there won't be any. In the wake of the terrorist attacks in the U.S., that's just wishful thinking on my part."

Any unattended packages were an immediate cause for alarm in London. The rail systems would come to a screeching halt until the suspicious parcels were checked out thoroughly. Nikkola wasn't the least bit surprised when security was beefed up in the United States. With so many alerts still happening, it didn't seem as if anyone would ever feel safe again. But Nikkola had unyielding faith in the U.S. military. More than that, she had unending faith in God.

When the underground train came thundering through the tunnel, Nikkola was happy to see that it wasn't crowded. Once aboard the train, she and Glen easily found seats. The moment the doors closed, the train quickly pulled away from the platform.

After a couple of train changes, Nikkola and Glen arrived in west Soho. Having decided to just have lunch there and save Covent Gardens for another day, the two friends walked around for a short time before stopping to eat at Le Tire Bouchon, a busy café-style brasserie. The atmosphere inside the small restaurant was cheery and friendly.

After receiving their food orders, Nikkola and Glen found a table in the back of the room and sat down. Nikkola ordered a chicken salad and sweet corn sandwich on a French roll; Glen was having shrimp and crab salad on a kaiser roll. Both ordered bottles of mineral water.

While biting into her sandwich, Nikkola closed her eyes expressively. "This is heavenly. If I had to live over here, I'd be so overweight. I could eat these types of sandwiches daily." While noticing that Glen hadn't touched his sandwich, Nikkola also saw the worried look on his face. "Glen, why aren't you eating?"

"Nikki, I haven't been feeling well lately. I feel hungry, but after I get something to eat, I seem to lose my appetite."

Concerned for her friend, Nikkola put her sandwich down and curled her fingers around his. "You don't look any thinner. How long has this been going on?"

Picking up the plastic bottle, Glen took a long swallow of the water and set it back down on the table. "I only noticed it a couple of weeks ago. Surprisingly, I haven't lost any weight, but I haven't been able to eat all that much either. Do you think I should see a doctor?" Pushing his chair back from the table, Glen crossed his legs.

"Glen, is there something you're not telling me? You seem awfully upset over this. You know you can trust me with anything, don't you?"

Lifting Nikkola's hand, Glen placed a feathery kiss onto the back of it. "Nikki, I trust you with my life! We have grown so close over the last couple of years. I wouldn't keep anything from you. I just don't feel that well. There's nothing more to it."

The sincere warmth in his statement made tears come to Nikkola's eyes. She couldn't have loved Glen any more than if he'd been her very own brother. "That was sweet of you to say. Glen, maybe you should see a doctor. You were practicing safe sex before you took your hiatus from the entire female population, weren't you?"

Keeping direct eye contact with her, Glen gave her a surprised look. "Of all the things you could've asked, why did you ask me that, Nikki?"

"Sometimes people get too comfortable with their intimate partner. Then they stop feeling the necessity to be careful. I hope you never get that comfortable with anyone, Glen."

"Sweetheart, I've always practiced safe sex." Glen shared most things with her, but at times he still felt somewhat embarrassed, especially when their conversations turned too intimate.

"I'm glad to hear that." Nikkola hated to see him looking so worried. While she didn't ever want to lecture Glen about his personal life, she felt it was her duty to keep him on his toes.

Picking up his sandwich, Glen bit a large chunk of it. Nikkola sighed with relief, happy that his appetite had returned.

"Has Latham ever seen you with your hair loose?" Glen laughed. "You wear it pulled back, so severe and tight, that I fear your eyes are going to become permanently slanted."

Nikkola found Glen's statement amusing. "Now that you've mentioned it, I don't think he has. I try to be very conservative when I'm working. There are too many hungry wolves flying through the air. They can smell my tempting single status as soon as they come aboard. I often wonder if my marital status is tattooed on my forehead."

"There's a hungry wolf right across the room, but I can't tell if he's looking at you or me," Glen joked, laughing heartily.

While looking across the room, Nikkola met with a pair of dark, icy eyes. She nearly choked on the food in her mouth. She was unable to remove her gaze from the ruggedly handsome man across the room. Their eyes burned into each other's. It was the same man who'd been seated in 2A on Flight #126. He didn't look any gentler or any less rude than he'd looked earlier. Only when Glen called her name was Nikkola able to take her stunned look from the man's cold, dark eyes.

"Do you know him, Nikki? You've turned pale, girl-friend."

Nikkola swallowed her food before it could get caught in her throat again. "It's the same man on the flight. The one I spilled the coffee on." She looked nervous. "His eyes are colder than a winter in Alaska. I wonder if his heart is just as cold?" Nikkola suddenly felt bewildered.

When the man stood up, Nikkola found her eyes being drawn back to him. She didn't seem to have any control over her eyes. As her gaze traveled upward, his legs seemed without end. He had broad shoulders and his smooth, shiny hair was a dark golden-brown. Turning away from him, Nikkola reached for her drink, but she knocked it over when her shaking fingers couldn't get a good grip on the slippery bottle.

Glen jumped up to keep the cold liquid from spilling all over him.

The man wired her an amused smile. She gasped loudly. His smile gently softened his features, chasing away the darkness from his eyes. As he started toward her, she gripped the edge of the table. As he neared, Nikkola reached for Glen's hand, only to find that he wasn't there. She could only imagine that Glen had gone to get some-one to clean up the spill. The man stopped in front of her, his eyes suddenly cold again. Nikkola shivered in response to his icy stare.

The stranger chuckled under his breath. "I see that you haven't taken my advice regarding charm school lessons. Are you always this clumsy?"

Nikkola returned his cold, arrogant stare. The fire in her eyes told him her anger was as red hot as the hair on her head. But to Nikkola he didn't look like the type to easily heed warnings. "Are you always this rude?" Putting her elbows on the table, she awaited his response.

"Always! And a proper lady never puts her elbows on the table."

Before she could even think about his remark, Nikkola had removed her elbows from the table. He laughed out loud, making her realize she'd responded to his command like a scared child.

Looking at him with irritation stirring in her eyes, Nikkola gritted her teeth, wanting to stuff her elbows into his big mouth. "Who ever said I was a proper lady?"

Glen returned to the table and sat down. He wrapped his fingers around Nikkola's trembling digits when she reached for his hand.

"Hello, I'm Glen Taylor." Glen extended a polite greeting to the strange man, but he ignored Glen's out-stretched hand.

Nikkola was outraged at his rude behavior. She could see that Glen's feelings were slightly hurt, but he smiled in amusement anyway.

"You stand there and talk about a proper lady, but you certainly aren't a proper gentleman." Nikkola's hard stare appeared to cut right through the stranger.

He seemed truly stunned by her angry remark. When he narrowed his dark eyes at her, they seemed to be warning her to hold her tongue. Turning to Glen, he gave him a half-smile. "I *was* rude, and I do apologize. I'm Mychal Stephen Forrester, investment banker."

Big freaking deal! Nikkola hadn't heard anyone ask for his name or his resume.

"It's nice to meet you, Mr. Forrester." Glen sat back in his seat to watch the fireworks.

Mychal Forrester remained standing. Then he turned his attention back to Nikkola. "Miss Knight, you should take the advice I've given so freely and graciously. Otherwise, you're going to have a lot of angry passengers on your hands. By the way, where are you staying? I'd like to send my cleaning bill around to your hotel."

At first Nikkola was stunned when Mychal called her by name, then she remembered how she identified herself to the passengers, plus the gold name tag always worn on her uniform. Glen was amused by Mychal Forrester's arrogance, but Nikkola didn't share in it at all.

Reaching into her purse, Nikkola pulled out several Euro dollars and stuffed them into Mychal's hand. "That should take care of your cleaning bill. And there should also be enough to pay for your lunch, Mr. Forrester."

Mychal Forrester was obviously perturbed by her sarcastic response, but it didn't stop him from shoving the money into his pants pocket. "That still doesn't answer my question about where you're staying." The look Mychal gave Nikkola was daringly challenging.

"You *do* have a nasty mouth, but I'm pleased to learn that you at least have clean ears," she retorted. Standing, Nikkola grabbed Glen's hand and walked away. Turning around, Glen waved good-bye to Mychal. Glen's friendly gesture toward Mychal irritated her to no end. She squeezed Glen's hand tightly, showing her irritation at his response to her newfound archenemy.

"Now there's chemistry and there's chemistry," Glen teased. "You both had your Bunsen burners sizzling. No telling what you two could have cooked up together."

Nikkola shot him a scathing look. "The only thing I'd like to cook is his goose. He's arrogant beyond belief, but he did have a great set of buns." Nikkola stifled a giggle.

"Well sweetheart, maybe his buns could stand to cook a little longer. I'm sure you wouldn't mind buttering them up once they came out of the oven."

"I should've known that you would run away with that statement! I was just making an honest observation. If he's as cold as he is rude, butter wouldn't stand a chance of melting anywhere on his anatomy. In fact, his eyes would probably freeze butter solid."

After laughing about Mychal Forrester for several minutes, Nikkola and Glen agreed not to talk about him anymore. For the next few hours they walked around Soho window-shopping. Turning onto the famed Carnaby Street, the couple headed for the unisex clothing store, Awards, which carried both casual and smart day or evening clothes for all ages.

Shortly after entering the store, Glen purchased two shirts, matching them with two smashing silk ties. Nikkola tried on several outfits, but she came out of the store empty-handed. She later purchased a pair of jeans at the Grip, a store that carried a variety of designer jeans and other unisex casual wear.

While sailing in and out of the many shops in Soho, Nikkola and Glen laughed and joked about the many unusual fashions found in this trendy part of town. In spite of the many times they'd shopped in this area, they always saw something that kept their sprees full of fun and surprises. The punk rockers were abundant in this area. Their spiked and neon-colored hairdos never ceased to leave Nikkola and Glen shocked and gaping wildly.

On the way back to the Underground, they stopped at Dunkin' Donuts to purchase doughnuts to take back to the hotel. After arriving in front of the London Palladium, the couple checked out the schedules for the shows and all the advertisements for other upcoming events.

Chapter 2

The hazy morning sun streamed in through the opened draperies. Still dressed in her nightclothes, Nikkola stood at the window looking out over the courtyard. There were many people who leased apartments in the St. James Court Hotel, and while watching the passersby with interest, Nikkola tried to guess their profession by the way they were dressed. One of the security guards looked up as he passed by and Nikkola waved happily. He waved back even though he didn't know her.

Nikkola had gotten a good night's rest, but dreams of Latham Scott had intruded on her sleep. Now, she had a new *midnight marauder*, Mychal Stephen Forrester. Mychal's cold, dark eyes had tortured her throughout the first part of the night and then they'd turned soft and seductive. He had swept her into a world of make-believe and she'd tried without success to return to the real one.

Moving away from the window, Nikkola went into the cheerful compact kitchen. After plugging in the electric teapot, she popped a slice of bread into the toaster. Reaching into the cabinet, she pulled out a coffee mug. The prior evening she and Glen had stopped at a local grocery store to pick up a few items before returning to the hotel. Glen had broiled shrimp for them in his suite. Later in the evening they'd watched several hours of television before Nikkola returned to her own room.

Nikkola poured her tea. Sitting down at the round table, she propped her feet up on another chair. Sipping tea while eating her toast, she thought about her parents and how much she sorely missed them. She hadn't seen them in a couple of months.

Nickolas and Ethel Knight were both retired government employees who now lived in Orlando, Florida. They had both worked for the State Department in Washington. During that time they'd lived in Maryland. Nikkola had gone to the University of Virginia in Charlottesville, but moved to Alexandria after graduation. Nikkola had been named after her father. Often, they'd both answer when one or the other's name was called.

Nickolas Knight was tall and well built, while her mother, Ethel, was petite and very slender. Both parents had dark brown hair, but Nikkola's red hair was passed down from Ethel's side of the family. Nikkola's great-grandmother had been a fiery redhead with a temper to match.

Nikkola walked over to the sink and placed her dirty dishes under the faucet and turned on the water. After washing the plate and mug, she carefully placed them on the rack to dry. Housekeeping was responsible for this chore, but Nikkola hated to leave this simple task undone. After pulling the plug on the teapot and toaster, she escaped to the bathroom for her shower.

Now dressed in her new jeans, Nikkola carefully slipped on a white knit sweater. She experimented with her hair, but left it to fall in a riot of curls. After she put her blush and lip gloss on, her medium brown complexion glowed with health.

Nikkola then went into the living room, expecting

Glen to show up for their morning walk in St. James Park, located across from Buckingham Palace. As a quiet knock sounded on the door, she rushed down the long carpeted hall and swung the door open wide. Much to her surprise, Captain Latham Scott stood there, smiling sweetly. Her heart did a backward somersault.

Latham stared at Nikkola curiously. "Are you going to let me in, Nikki?"

While trying to catch her breath, she moved aside. Latham stepped into the suite and headed for the living room. By the time Nikkola caught up to her visitor, Latham was already seated comfortably.

"What's up, Latham?"

Latham encouraged Nikkola to sit down next to him, but she took a seat across from him.

"I came to see how you were doing, Nikki. You weren't quite yourself when you deplaned yesterday. I know the flight was a rough one. Are you okay?"

It was true that the flight had been difficult, but she found his reason for being there hard to believe.

Latham could see the disbelief in Nikkola's hazel eyes. "I guess you don't believe my explanation."

Nikkola wore a puzzled expression. *Was my reaction that obvious?* "I'm just surprised by your coming here, Latham. Why *are* you here this morning?"

Latham laughed at her question, but Nikkola didn't see any humor in it. Then his caramel-brown eyes grew intensely serious. His sudden mood change made her even more nervous.

"Nikki, I did want to see how you were, but I have another reason for being here."

Nikkola suddenly looked frightened and Latham found himself wanting to hold her close. Her beauty sent off familiar signals, but he ignored the warnings as he marveled at the freshness and wholesomeness of her skin. Her hair was always tied up tight, but to see it flowing freely unexpectedly turned him on. Her hazel eyes had always intrigued him. Not a day went by that Nikkola had gone unnoticed or unthought of by Latham Scott.

"You have my attention, Latham." Her voice held a noticeable quake.

Latham twisted his watch around on his wrist. "I need to talk to you about your friend, Glen Taylor, Nikki."

The quietness of Latham's voice disturbed her. Hoping he wasn't going to ask her any personal questions, Nikkola became even more anxious.

"There are a few rumors flying around and I thought you could clear up a few things for me. Are you two romantically involved, Nikki?"

Nikkola swallowed hard, but the lump stayed lodged in her throat. "Why, Latham?" She fidgeted in her chair, gripping the arm of it tightly. *And I was almost willing to be stupid enough to think he came here because he was concerned about me.* She felt slightly disappointed.

"Nikki, I'd just like to know if you're involved with a member of my flight crew. Rumors are rumors, but I need to know the truth for myself."

"Latham, I don't see how my answering that question is going to squash the rumors. What Glen and I do in our private lives is our business. Even if it were true, I wouldn't tell you."

"I can see that I offended you, but that wasn't my intention. I thought you'd understand why I would want to know. As the captain of the ship, I just like to know what's going on with my crew members. I've heard several of the flight attendants gossiping about how chummy you two are before, during, and after flights."

"I *don't* understand, Latham. And our personal information is none of your business or that of anyone else. Glen and I are extremely close. He's my best friend and I wouldn't think of discussing our personal affairs with anyone. And I hope you understand that."

"What loyalty." Latham almost felt ridiculous for asking her personal questions, but he also felt jealous now that he knew how she really felt about Glen. His interest in their relationship had nothing to do with his command. It was his personal interest in her that had prompted the questions.

Ripping into the silence, the phone rang. Glad for the interruption, Nikkola jumped up to answer it. With her hands shaking badly, she picked up the receiver. "Hello."

Nikkola's voice was barely audible to Glen. "Nikki, it's Glen. Listen, I'm not feeling well. I'm not up to taking our morning walk. You go ahead and get going, but I'd like you to drop by here afterward."

Nikkola wanted to question him about his illness, but she didn't dare in front of Latham. "I'll see you as soon as I get back," she said in a whisper. Glen was puzzled by Nikkola's guarded communication, but he hung up without questioning her. She hung up and returned to her seat.

Wondering whom Nikkola had been whispering to, Latham was increasingly jealous of the person on the other end of the phone. "Do you have to go out, Nikki?"

"I'm taking a walk in St. James Park. Glen was supposed to go with me, but he has something else to do this morning. He won't be able to make it."

So it was Glen. "In that case, Nikki, would you mind if I walked with you?"

Latham surprised himself with that question. But Nikkola was more surprised than he.

Nikkola thought about how Carmen might react, but then she quickly decided that Carmen was his problem, not hers. "I'd love the company. I'll get my jacket."

As Nikkola walked out of the room, her heart suddenly felt light and breezy. She grabbed her jacket off the bed and slipped it around her shoulders.

The maid was about to knock on the door when Latham opened it for them to exit. He held the door for the maid and waited until she pushed her linen cart inside. Nikkola spoke and smiled cheerfully at the young woman in passing. She and Latham then headed for the tiny elevator. No more than four people could fit into the small car at one time. Oftentimes the ride in the lift left Nikkola feeling slightly claustrophobic. She had a tendency to feel that way when she stepped into the airplane cockpit too.

Once outside the hotel, Nikkola and Latham turned left on Buckingham Gate. At the end of street, the couple crossed the busy intersection in front of the palace and then strolled into the park. Looking across the sparkling lake near St. James Park offered a splendid view of the magnificent palace. Nikkola and Latham seated themselves under a large shaded tree, as the beauty of the park enchanted them both.

"Nikki, you should always wear your hair down. It's beautiful. I wonder if you're as untamable as your lovely hair seems." He wanted to lose his fingers in the array of curls, as he imagined how wonderful it probably smelled. Nikkola always looked so fresh and clean to him.

Latham's tender words made Nikkola's heart dance with glee. The strange longing she saw in his eyes excited her. "Thanks for the compliment. As for being untamable, I'm not so sure that I'm not. Maybe I just haven't found the right person to tame me."

Nikkola's answer stunned Latham. *Did it mean that she wasn't having a love affair with Glen?* Latham lifted his hand to touch Nikkola's hair but quickly withdrew it. "Are you still looking for the right person, Nikki?"

Nikkola had to wonder why Latham seemed to have a personal interest in her all of a sudden, but it made her feel so good inside. "Aren't we all, Latham?"

Latham nodded in agreement. "Yeah, Nikki, I guess so."

"Where's Carmen this morning?" Nikkola immediately wished she hadn't asked that question upon seeing the distant look in his eyes.

"Carmen mentioned that she was going off with some of her friends. She talked about visiting Harrods to do some shopping. I was surprised to see her on our flight."

"Was loneliness the reason you asked to come along with me?" It was another question Nikkola instantly wished she hadn't asked.

"I rarely get lonely, Nikki. I enjoy my own company too much for that. I asked to come along so I could enjoy *your* company." Latham finally found the nerve to touch her hair.

Nikkola closed her eyes and savored his tender touch. Leaning over her, Latham buried his nose in Nikkola's hair and deeply inhaled the fresh and flowery scent of it. Feeling nervous with the intimate situation, Nikkola got to her feet and walked onto the small bridge. Leaning on the black wrought iron railing, Nikkola watched the ducks swim lazily across the clear waters.

Enjoying the seductive curve of her hips, Latham sat quietly, in awe. Like Nikkola, he was questioning himself as to why he was finally acting on his longtime interest in her. But Latham knew perfectly well why he'd chosen to stay so detached from the stunning Nikkola Knight.

After getting to his feet, Latham brushed the dried leaves off his jeans and walked to the bridge. Standing behind Nikkola, he put his hands on her shoulders and then turned her around to face him. "Have I upset you, Nikkola Knight?"

Nikkola had never heard Latham call her by her full name. The seductive way in which he said it made her legs go weak. He was so close to her she could feel the kiss of his sweet breath. All he would have to do was lower his head a fraction of an inch and their lips would touch. If his intent toward her were clear, Nikkola would welcome Latham's full, sexy mouth upon her hungry lips.

"I'm not upset, but I know we shouldn't be indulging ourselves with any romantic notions. You belong to someone else. I don't want to interfere with any relationship you might have."

Latham tilted her chin upward. "I don't belong to anyone, Nikki. I'm my own man."

Not wanting to lose herself in the depths of Latham's soulful eyes, Nikkola turned back around and stared out over the water. She didn't know what his current relationship with Carmen was, but until he made it crystal clear to her she had to watch herself; she certainly wasn't interested in a rebound affair. Nikkola didn't want to be just a friend to him either. Latham Scott was the only man she'd ever desired as her lover, a constant visitor in her dreams.

Nikkola turned back around to face him. "I have to get back, Latham. I need to see Glen."

Latham hadn't allowed himself to believe the stories about her and Glen, but he was now wondering if Nikki and Glen were indeed in love with each other. They were definitely close, and she now suddenly seemed so eager to see Glen.

Taking her by the hand, Latham guided Nikkola out of the park and toward the hotel. She was nervous about his holding her hand, but it felt too good to raise any objections. This was something she'd wanted for a long time, but now she didn't know what to think or feel. Nor did Nikkola know how to handle Latham's sudden personal interest in her.

As Nikkola and Latham neared the hotel, without warning, she pulled her hand loose from his and ran through the gates and into the hotel. She knew that running away from him was such an immature act, but she couldn't help herself. Getting entangled with another woman's man was frightening to Nikkola, especially when she was already head over heels in love with him.

Punching the elevator button repeatedly, Nikkola prayed it would come before Latham entered the hotel. Feeling panicky, she headed for the stairwell and ran up the two flights of stairs to Glen's suite. Lifting the heavy bronze knocker, she let it thud loudly against the door.

Wearing a dark blue bathrobe and striped pajamas, Glen answered the door. He didn't look at all as if he felt well, his handsome face covered with an early morning shadow of stubbly hair.

Throwing herself into Glen's arms, Nikkola began to cry softly. Her tears had him stunned. After leading her into the living room, Glen sat down on the sofa and pulled her down onto the cushion next to him. For several minutes he just held her safely in his arms.

Holding her at arm's length, Glen looked into Nikkola's teary eyes. "What's wrong, Nikki baby?" Reaching into his robe pocket, he pulled out some tissue and wiped away her tears and the fluid running from her nose.

Nikkola laughed nervously, sounding as if she were laughing through her nose. "I just had a *close encounter* of the *romantic kind* with Latham Scott."

Glen looked genuinely surprised. "Run that by me again, Nikki."

Nikkola's tears continue to fall as she started the story from the beginning. "Latham came to see me this morning. When you couldn't go on the walk with me, he asked to come along. Once we were in the park, he started showing more than a casual interest in me. I don't think my imagination was playing tricks on me. He even ran his fingers through my hair and took the liberty of smelling it." She felt breathless when she finished explaining everything that had occurred in the park.

Glen raised his eyebrows with interest. "You mean Latham Scott has decided to take his blinders off?" Glen was amazed. "It's about time! I told you all along that Carmen wasn't going to be able to hold on to him. Did you play your cards right, Nikki? I hope you didn't expose your hand right off, because I've taught you everything that I know about what men react to."

Nikkola laughed. "I almost blew my cool. He was so close to me I had the urge to check out his tonsils. But I got scared. Before we reached the hotel entrance, I ran off with my tail tucked neatly between my legs. How immature was that move? The man must think I've lost my grip."

"Good for you! Make Latham chase you as far as his long legs will carry him. Then when you see that they won't take him any further, swoon." They both roared in laughter.

Nikkola's eyes clouded troublesomely as she remembered why Latham had come to see her in the first place. Rumors about her and Glen, indeed!

"What's with the troubled look, Nikki?"

Nikkola knew Glen was really sensitive about and very protective of her. He hated it when people did things to hurt her, but she felt compelled to tell him the reason for Latham's visit. "Glen, Latham came to see me about us."

Glen looked at her quizzically. "Us?"

Nikkola exhaled a breath. "There are rumors going around about us and he wanted to know if we're romantically involved. Glen, I'm really sorry about this. He says some of the flight attendants are talking about our being overly chummy with one another during working hours."

Glen's broad smile caused the corners of his eyes to crinkle. "Is that all? What did you tell Latham, Nikki?"

Nikkola lovingly traced the outline of his face with her finger. "I didn't tell him a thing. I told him it was

none of his business what we do in our private lives."
She still felt slightly irritated with Latham for even asking her about their relationship.

"It sounds like nonsense. But we are a little touchy-feely with one another. That's just how it is with us. We just happen to love each other very much."

Nikkola jutted her chin out in defiance. "We don't have to explain anything to anybody. I don't think anyone's going to ask you about us. I was simply the softer target. We shouldn't even worry with this crap. Flight attendants date one another, as well as the pilots, all the time. Look at Carmen and Latham."

"Sweetheart, people can assume anything they want. But my concern is for you, Nikki. What if Latham's questions came out of a personal interest in you? If he thinks we're having a love affair, he may not continue in his pursuit of you. Is that what you want to happen?"

"Not really, but it just might work in the reverse. He may see it as a challenge to win my heart from you." She cracked up. "Now that's a big assumption on my part. I don't even know if the man is trying to pursue me. Those little affections he threw my way may not mean anything to him. We shouldn't even be going over all this. It's crazy. By the way, how are you feeling now?"

"I feel better, Nikki. I really believe it's a stomach flu and nothing more. I took some Tylenol and stayed in bed. I feel much better than I did earlier, but I'll see my doctor as soon as I get back home. They have a walk-in clinic."

"Glad to hear it, Glen! Now shower and get dressed. We can go get some lunch."

Glen gave Nikkola a warm hug and a big smile before leaving the room.

Freshly showered and dressed in casual slacks and a navy blue sweater, Glen returned to the living room, where he found Nikkola curled up on the couch, with her red curls spilling out all over the loose pillows. He was glad that she was his best friend, and his heart warmed at the sight of her sweet face.

Glen nudged Nikkola gently and she opened her eyes and smiled. "How far had you and Latham gotten in your dream?"

Nikkola shook her head. "I wasn't dreaming of Latham. Believe it or not, I was having fanciful visions of Mychal Forrester. There's something about that rude gent that turns me on."

Glen wasn't surprised by her revelation. The chemistry between them had been undeniable. "Look out, Latham Scott. You just might have a formidable opponent!"

Nikkola laughed heartily. "No way! I'm going to wash my hands and then I'll be ready to go. Let's eat downstairs in the Inn of Happiness."

Glen liked Nikkola's suggestion for dining. "Sounds good."

The Inn of Happiness served Chinese, Szechuan, Cantonese, and Pekingese foods. Glen wanted Szechuan, but he feared that his stomach might not be able to handle the spicier foods.

Nikkola and Glen walked down to the lobby and entered the restaurant. The couple was immediately seated at a window table, which gave them a perfect view of the busy street front. After scanning the menus for several minutes, both Nikkola and Glen ordered Szechuan dishes, along with freshly brewed green tea.

The hot tea and egg rolls were served first.

Nikkola dipped her egg roll in the hot mustard and bit deeply into the appetizer. She winced when the hot mustard stung her nose and instantly opened her nasal passages. She quickly drank some ice water to cool her burning tongue.

Glen laughed. "Too hot for you, huh, Nikki?"

Nikkola smiled sheepishly. "It's not too hot for me, I just took in too much at one time. But it *is* spicy." She suddenly nudged at Glen's leg with her sneaker-clad foot. "Check it out."

Glen looked directly at Nikkola and then followed the direction of her eyes.

Latham Scott had just walked into the restaurant with Carmen Thomas hanging on his arm. The couple walked past the table where Glen and Nikkola were seated, but they didn't seem to notice anything or anyone. Latham looked rather grim-faced to Nikkola.

Nikkola raised her eyebrows. "It doesn't look to me like he's bothered by her being so possessive. Maybe they've patched things up, that is, if they ever broke up," Nikkola whispered to Glen. "I guess this morning *didn't* mean a thing to him. He was just yanking my chain for fun."

"They do look a little cozy. But I wouldn't worry about it if I were you, Nikki. I don't think Latham would've shown a personal interest in you if they're still romantically involved."

Nikkola scowled hard. "Why not? He's a man, isn't he?"

Opting not to touch Nikkola's sarcastic comment, Glen just shrugged his shoulders.

As the waiter appeared with the rest of their food, the two friends waited patiently until everything was set before them. Glen and Nikkola were eager to devour their food. Spearing a piece of plump Szechuan chicken with her fork, Nikkola popped it into her mouth. Glen savored his first bite of the Szechuan beef.

The Chinese dishes looked mouthwatering and each had been exquisitely prepared.

Nikkola and Glen entered into a light conversation about their flight back to the States. Both would be off for several days after their return home, discussing what they planned to do with their free time. Nikkola found herself stealing glances at Carmen and Latham, noticing how their heads were bent closely together, wishing she could hear their seemingly intimate discussion.

"Nikki, do you want to go down to the Olympian Health Club after we finish here?"

"That's a marvelous idea, Glen. I'd love to relax in one of the spas—my skin could use a good steaming. But I have no desire to work any muscles. I do enough of that at home."

Glen nodded. "I think I'll have a good massage. My muscles are really tight and my body could use a few minutes of total relaxation. I'll do the spa and sauna first."

Nikkola was momentarily stunned when Carmen suddenly rushed through the restaurant and out the door. Nikkola looked back at Latham, where he sat quietly with his head down. A desire to lift Latham's head and kiss his mouth thoroughly swept right through her. He looked so dejected. Scolding herself mentally, Nikkola swiftly turned her attention back to Glen.

Glen raised an eyebrow. "I wonder what that was all about. Carmen whirled out of here like a tornado looking for somewhere to happen."

Nikkola wanted to laugh, but out of respect for Carmen and whatever the situation was, she thought it might be in bad taste. "I don't know what's going on, but Latham doesn't look too happy either. I hate to say this, but maybe it's really ditch city. How I'd love to comfort him."

Glen shook his head and laughed. "Nikki, that doesn't sound like you. You're usually so sensitive. I know Carmen doesn't have a sensitive bone in her body, but give her a break this time. She really looked upset."

"I'd like to give her a break all right, but the kind of break I'm talking about she wouldn't be able to fly for years. You know how she's openly taunted me on the couple of occasions we've been in her company. She already knew I had a crush on Latham when she did it. She found out from one of the other crew members. I still don't like how uncomfortable she made me feel."

Glen laughed loudly. "What would we do without all the drama on air gossip! Let's go change clothes and get on with our plans."

Nikkola removed the linen napkin from her lap and stood. Once Glen put several euros on the black lacquered tray, he joined Nikkola, and they exited the restaurant.

As the elevator door was about to close, Latham Scott pushed the doors back forcefully. Upon entering the elevator, he curtly nodded his greeting to Nikkola and Glen, his mood turning doubly foul when he saw their hands entwined. Not a single word was exchanged on the ride.

Nikkola ached inside to touch Latham and soothe his hurt. Without thinking, she waved to him as she and Glen exited the elevator. Latham waved back without so much as a slight curve of his lips. His brooding eyes had stayed firmly on Nikkola during the entire ride. When the elevator doors closed shut, Nikkola was glad to have his gloomy eyes off her.

Nikkola entered her suite. Upon walking into the bedroom, she grabbed some items from the drawer and then slipped into a basic black one-piece bathing suit, deeply cut at the thighs. She finished dressing by putting on a white terry cover-up over her suit. In the bathroom she brushed her long curls upward and secured them on top with a decorative clasp and a few pins.

Her legs felt slightly hairy, so Nikkola sat on the side of the tub and lathered them with soft soap. After shaving off the unwanted hair with a disposable razor, she moisturized her legs with a lanolin-based lotion. Ready for a good soak at the spa, Nikkola grabbed her key card off the countertop, stuck it in the pocket of her cover-up, and dashed out the front door. Patiently, she waited for the elevator to take her down to the Olympian Health Club.

There were only two other people in the club when Nikkola entered, but Glen wasn't one of them. After walking over to the spa area, she removed her flip flops and stepped into the hot, swirling water. The rising steam swirled around her, immediately easing the tight feeling in her muscles. She'd just shaved, and the water stung her legs, but the discomfort only lasted a short time. She was completely relaxed within minutes.

Latham Scott walked into the health club wearing a pair of dark shorts. With a white towel thrown loosely around his neck, he stood in the doorway and looked around the vast room. His eyes smiled when they spotted Nikkola. Wasting no time, Latham headed straight for the spa area.

While wondering what was taking Glen so long, Nikkola had her eyes closed. Since she hadn't noticed Latham approaching her, he was able to install himself in the water without her being any the wiser. Appreciatively, he studied her gorgeous upper body. He then touched her shoulder.

Smiling broadly, she opened her eyes, expecting to see Glen. Her entire body turned into molten liquid as she flowed into the steaming water. Through the frothy, blue water, her wide eyes drank in the hairy expanse of his broad chest and the taut muscles of his strong thighs.

"You shouldn't be in the water alone, you know," Latham scolded Nikkola.

Nikkola rested her back against the tiled wall. "Thank you, Daddy, but I wasn't supposed to be here alone," she mocked him in a childlike voice. This kind of teasing was new for them, but Nikkola found it both exciting and exhilarating.

Latham's smile was soft and seductive. Using his toes, he rubbed them up the length of her leg. Nikkola quickly moved her leg from within his reach, but she hadn't acted fast enough. The heat from his fiery touch already had her intimate zones scorching. This playful little session had become more than just teasing.

"What's the matter, Nikki? You're sweating! Can't stand the heat?"

Nikkola glared openly at him. Latham found the look in her hazel eyes sweetly challenging, as his eyes teased hers in return, pleasurably so. She wanted so much to feel his lips on hers, to feel his hips grinding into hers, to have their legs entwined in a frenzied embrace, as they rode high upon the crest of passion. It was the same image she'd conjured up in her head a million times.

Nikkola smiled with sarcastic sweetness. "The only heat I feel is from the hot water. And it's relaxing. Maybe you should just be quiet and enjoy it." While Latham's eyes seemed to be calling her a liar, Nikkola could barely stand the probing heat they stirred in her.

"I think the kind of heat you're feeling has nothing to do with hot water," Latham challenged Nikkola. "As for being quiet, I've done that for far too long already." His eyes zeroed in on the droplets of water beading up on her seductively heaving cleavage. "I can help cool you down, Nikki," he taunted unmercifully. "Would you like to know how? Better yet, would you like to *experience* my cooling techniques?"

Nikkola closed her eyes and tried to ignore his erotic taunts. It was difficult at best.

"Nikki," he whispered, "are you shutting me out? That's not a good thing to do. I don't like to be ignored." Fighting hard the urge to kiss her delicious-looking mouth, Latham inched closer to Nikkola and lazily stroked his index finger down her bare arm. "Nikki, I'm putting you on notice today. I'm no longer going to deny the attraction I feel for you. It has become unmanageable. Keeping your beautiful mouth shut isn't going to stop me from trying to get next to you. Consider yourself forewarned, Nikkola Knight."

Latham's laughter was sensuously taunting, and Nikkola felt the heat burgeoning between her legs. The thought of making love to him right there in the spa had clogged her mind. Ignoring him wasn't possible. Denying what was happening to her anatomy was utterly hopeless.

Embarrassed by the visions of their making love dancing in her head, Nikkola stood up to get out of the water. Latham quickly curled his leg around hers, making it impossible for Nikkola to move. Like a small, unruly child, she reached down and splashed water in his face. The sting of the water in his eyes made him involuntarily release her leg. Stepping out of the spa, Nikkola grabbed Latham's towel. As she retreated to the door, Nikkola held up the large fluff of white, flashing him a triumphant smile.

"You may've won this battle, Nikki, but this is only the beginning of the war," Latham yelled across the room. "Don't say that I didn't give you fair warning."

"In that case, you may as well surrender. This war is unwinnable for you," she shouted back. *You've already won more than that! My lonely heart has become your prisoner of war.*

"You're the one that's retreating! Why don't you come back over here and see how strong your battle plans measure up against mine? I promise to fight fair."

"If I come back over there, you won't be able to handle my unbridled aggression. My war strategies will defeat you soundly and cause a major blow to your pride. You'll be begging me to have tender mercy on you. That, I won't be able to do!"

Boy, with what I have in mind for you and your fantastic body, you'll be begging me to keep you a captive for life.

Turning away from Latham's engaging presence, before she found herself running back to him and diving right into his arms, Nikkola rushed out the door.

Chapter 3

The engines of the large flying machine droned on and on in Nikkola's ears. Buckled safely in her seat belt, she patiently waited for the plane to land at Dulles. The aircraft wasn't as full as usual, but Nikkola had unconsciously anticipated seeing Mychal Forrester on this flight. She was surprised to find herself somewhat disappointed when he didn't show up for the flight. She'd only seen him on the airliner the one time, but she'd somehow guessed he was someone that flew frequently. Nikkola was familiar with many of the frequent flyers on this particular flight.

The last hours in London had been monotonous. She and Glen had traveled some of the same routes, doing many of the same things they normally did on a layover. Glen hadn't been feeling well on the last evening, so they'd stayed in and watched a lot of boring television shows.

After she walked out of the health club with Latham Scott's towel, he had shown up at her door later the same evening. When he didn't find her in, he'd left a note attached to her door, saying he'd come by to retrieve his towel. The towel actually belonged to the hotel. She'd found his excuse flimsy, but she had delighted in his attempt to see her. At the beginning of the flight, she'd noticed the tension between Latham and Carmen. Neither of them had hardly spoken to any of the other crew members. Even though Carmen flew as a passenger, she had mingled on the way over.

Flight #126 finally came in for a smooth landing at Washington's Dulles International Airport. Unbuckling her seat belt, Nikkola hurried to the microphone and began singing "God Bless America." Once the song and cheering were over, Nikkola moved right into her official duties.

Passing Glen on her way back to the front of the aircraft, Nikkola playfully swatted him on the behind in defiance of those who'd started the rumors about them. "That should give the gossip mongers something to talk about," she whispered to Glen.

Laughing at what she'd done, Glen smiled warmly at Nikkola. "Behave yourself now!"

Once Nikkola helped prepare the doors for deplaning, she then assisted several passengers in removing their luggage from the overhead compartments. Nikkola also helped the elderly patrons and those with small children, making sure no one left behind their belongings. As a wheelchair was brought on board to assist an elderly passenger, she made sure the lady was seated comfortably before being wheeled off the aircraft. Nikkola then gathered up her own gear.

As Nikkola passed by the door of the cockpit, Latham Scott poked his head out of the doorway. Nikkola had every intention of ignoring him, but it wasn't quite as easy as she'd thought it would be. Looming in front of her, Latham quickly blocked her entrance to the tunnel. She waas undeniably annoyed at him for making a spectacle of her, and her eyes bored into Latham's.

"You have my towel, Nikki! I plan on getting it back,"

he said menacingly. She tried to go around him, but Latham moved in front of her at each attempt.

"I could be mistaken, Latham, but I believe the towel belongs to the St. James Court Hotel."

"Maybe so. But at the time you removed it from the health club, I had it in my possession." His muscles rippled as he let out a bellow of laughter from somewhere deep in his stomach.

Nikkola spotted Carmen watching their exchange from near the middle of the plane. It looked as if the attention Latham was paying to her had Carmen fuming. Pulling her carry-on luggage behind her, Carmen advanced to the front of the plane.

"All ready to deplane, Nikki?" Carmen queried, giving Nikkola an insincere smile.

Nikkola had been enjoying the game between herself and Latham, but she wasn't about to let anyone know it. She smiled and nodded. "If you're ready, Carmen, we can walk together."

Nikkola flashed Latham a winning smile, as she stepped around him. His eyes narrowed, sending her a devilish warning, one that said the war between them wasn't nearly over.

The way Latham looked at her made Nikkola's insides turn to jelly. As Glen was also making his way up to the front, she was relieved to see that he hadn't left yet. Carmen looked as if she was glad to see him, too, but Nikkola was sure it was for a totally different reason.

"Nikki, you go ahead with Glen. I need to talk with Latham for a minute."

Latham scowled. He didn't want to get into another emotional scrape with Carmen, but he saw no way of avoiding it. Nikkola sensed Latham's discomfort, but she moved on with Glen beside her. As much as she wanted to look back, Nikkola fixed her eyes straight ahead.

* * *

Carmen sat down in one of the first-class seats after she looked around to make sure the plane was empty. Latham still had a scowl on his face, but he took a seat across from her anyway.

"What is it, Carmen?" His tone reflected impatience.

Reaching across the aisle, Carmen placed her hand on Latham's knee. "Latham, I'm trying hard to understand why you feel the need to break things off between us. But after seeing you with Nikki, I'm wondering if your decision has anything to do with her." Suspicion laced her tone.

"Carmen, Nikki doesn't even know things have ended between us. I've known Nikki a lot longer than I've known you, and I've never even asked her out. Nikki has nothing to do with this and you know it. But I'm going to be honest about something. I have a personal interest in Nikkola. I've always been very attracted to her." As tears came to Carmen's dark eyes, Latham placed his hand over hers to soothe her. "That wasn't meant to hurt you, Carmen. I was just being honest."

"Latham, you didn't ask me out either. I asked you out, if you recall."

How could I forget? You didn't ask me out. You practically demanded that I take you out. Thinking of past times in her company made him bitter. Carmen demanded everything she wanted.

"I'd like us to remain friends, Carmen, but we need to get on with our lives. We were never really compatible and we both knew it from the very beginning. I first told you my decision almost two months ago, but you still wanted us to keep talking. I get together with you every time you tell me you need to talk. That has to stop. It's not helping you to accept that it's over with us. I won't change my mind. I agreed to have lunch with you in London to settle everything once and for all.

Showing up on my flights won't change the way things stand. I just can't deal with your jealous obsessions. No man wants to deal with something like that."

"I know how I am, but that was in the beginning. I truly believe I've changed. I know I've made unreasonable demands on your time, but I am also working on that. I can see by the look in your eyes that it's going to be your way. If you ever need me, Latham, you know how to reach me. I'm still in the same place."

Pulling back her hand from Latham's, Carmen stood up. She looked at him thoughtfully for a few seconds. "It hurts me to know that you've always had a thing for Nikki," she said coolly. "I guess you were thinking about her the entire time we dated."

Latham didn't respond. He knew when he was being baited. If he didn't swallow the bait, he wouldn't have to worry about the sharp hook ripping him up on the inside, and neither could he be reeled in. Grabbing up her bag, Carmen said her farewell and then moved through the tunnel.

The cleanup crew made their way onto the plane just as Latham retreated to the cockpit. While gathering up his flight gear, he thought of Nikkola, hoping he'd see her before she got out of the terminal. He put on his hat and nearly ran through the tunnel, receiving several admiring glances from the many women passing him on his way to customs. Latham was always amused by the sultry looks women gave him. It was the uniform. They always seemed to fall in love with a uniform, without ever getting to know the person wearing it.

Latham grew uncomfortable as he reached the customs area and saw Carmen talking to Nikkola and Glen. Knowing that Carmen could be vindictive, he prayed that she wasn't taking her frustrations out on Nikkola.

As he drew closer, he could hear Nikkola's laughter. The musical sound of Nikkola laughing made him breathe a little easier.

On steady legs Latham approached the three gab-happy flight attendants. Avoiding Carmen's eyes purposely, he locked his gaze onto Nikkola. Latham's eyes fastened directly on her and the entire situation, making Nikkola uncomfortable. Short lapses in her conversation with Glen and Carmen became noticeable. Latham's steady gaze had taken away Nikkola's ability to communicate intelligently. Carmen and Glen immediately recognized the changes in her conversation, knowing Latham was the reason for her sudden difficulties.

Deciding to rescue Nikkola from making a fool of herself in front of Carmen and Latham, Glen slid his hand under her elbow and moved her toward the customs line.

Nikkola smiled gratefully at him. "Thanks, Glen. I'm so uncomfortable around those two. Latham and Carmen are acting very strangely with each other. Somebody has dumped somebody. I'd be willing to bet my retirement on it."

"I could clearly see your discomfort. I think Latham dumped Carmen. According to the rumors, he broke it off with her almost two months ago. Latham was openly flirting with you, and he didn't seem to care that Carmen was watching. I'm surprised by both their behaviors. Neither one showed any professionalism." Without commenting, Nikkola moved on through the line, waiting until Glen was processed. He joined her shortly.

"Glen, maybe Carmen dumped Latham, and he's flirting with me to make her jealous."

"I hadn't thought about it that way, but I doubt that's the case, Nikki. Latham would never use you like that. He's genuinely interested in you on a personal level. I'm sure of it. It seemed to me that he was letting Carmen know he's already moved on with his life."

Glen's statement prompted Nikkola to glance at him in a sympathetic way. "I know I agreed not to bring this up until you did, and only after you were ready to talk about it, but have *you* really moved on? Is it really over for you and Gennifer? You guys were together five years."

Glen stopped dead in his tracks. "Nikki, you promised."

Nikkola shook her head. "I didn't promise. I just agreed not to talk about it. I wouldn't break a promise to you. I think your silence about what happened has gone on long enough. Keeping things inside can't be good for you. That might be why you're not feeling so well."

"I know you wouldn't break a promise to me. But I'm sorry, Nikki, I'm just not ready for that discussion yet. Okay?"

"Okay."

"Thanks, Nikki. One day I'll tell you everything."

Upon reaching the outside, Nikkola and Glen hopped a shuttle bus heading for the employee parking lot. Nikkola grabbed a seat while Glen secured the luggage. The ride to the parking lot was short, but Glen's car was parked at the next to the last stop on the route. They'd done this routine so many times that Nikkola was sure she knew every make of car and license number in the lot. She used to love reading the personalized license plates, but now just the thought of it made her dizzy with boredom.

When the bus came to a smooth halt, Nikkola and Glen scrambled for the exit. Glen picked up the bags and carried them off the bus. He then handed Nikkola the long leather strap to her luggage. She pulled it along with ease. As they reached the car, Glen used the remote on his key ring to pop the trunk to store the bags. After opening the door for Nikkola, Glen walked around to the other side, opened his door, and then slid into the driver's seat of the late-model black BMW.

The drive to Alexandria was pleasant, but the feelings of jet lag made the drive less than restful. It was well after rush hour, which made it easy for Glen to drive at the speed limit. Normally he drove a lot faster, but he was too tired to risk it.

At the gates of the West Lake condominium complex Glen inserted his security card and waited patiently for the gates to open. Whisking the car through the entry gates, he drove to the secured underground parking area, where he used another remote control to open the gates. He then swung the car into its assigned space. After turning the engine off, Glen got out of the car and unloaded the trunk. Once Glen saw Nikkola safely into her own place, he placed a light kiss on her forehead and left for his own place.

Nikkola's two-bedroom-with-den condo was decorated in colors of ivory and gold. The French-style sofa, love seat, and chairs were fashioned in ivory with a button-tufted damask cover. Nikkola had purchased the hardwood, rectangular coffee and end tables carved in a southern chateau French style at an antique store. An ivory and gold hand-knitted wool rug made a lovely accent. A three-piece champagne-lacquer wall unit consisting of a glass curio bar and audio units took up an entire wall. The dining room was raised just above the living room and three hardwood steps led up to it. The transitional table, four side chairs, and the buffet were done in a champagne-washed finish. The chair cushions were fashion from a soft gold material made of pure cotton.

Walking into her bedroom, Nikkola sat down on the bed, putting her stocking feet up on one of the two gold velvet comfortable chairs right next to it. The entire room was furnished with ivory-washed pine furniture. The hand-stitched bedspread was ivory and gold;

the matching sheets were made of one hundred percent cotton. An ivory and gold luxurious velvet lounger sat near the sliding glass door leading out onto the balcony. The thirty-six-inch color television set, which could be viewed from the bed, was situated on a shelf on the video/music center.

Nikkola took her jacket off and then drew both her legs up. As she was searching through the mail she'd retrieved on her way into the condo, an envelope with a British postmark caught her eye. She opened it first. As she pulled out the inserted card, several Euro dollars fell onto her lap. Pushing the money aside, she read the handwritten card. A smile appeared on her generous mouth as she read the contents of the note.

Nikkola, hold on to this until you return to London. Meet me in the St. James Court Hotel lobby the day after your arrival at 1300 hours. You can use this money for the dry cleaning to buy me lunch.

Fondly, Mychal Forrester was signed at the very bottom of the expensive stationery.

The date mentioned in the note was the day after she was scheduled to return to London. She wondered how he knew her schedule and how he'd gotten her home address. "Mr. Forrester, I'm afraid you're going to have a long, lonely wait!"

Nikkola leapt off the bed and dashed into the bathroom. After removing her clothes, she folded her uniform pants and hung them along with her jacket on the back of the bathroom door. She stuffed the rest of her clothes into the dirty-clothes hamper. Turning around to face the mirror, Nikkola opened a jar of face cream and removed her already faded make-up. Upon opening the shower door, she stepped in and turned on the hot water.

Nikkola's shower was quick but thorough. Removing the gold towel she'd thrown over the shower bar, she rubbed herself dry and then dressed in a dainty blue, soft cotton gown and robe. On her way into the kitchen, she turned on the radio. Opening the refrigerator door, she pulled out a soft drink and reached into the cabinet for a bag of chips. Seated at the breakfast nook, she thought about the note she'd received from Mychal Forrester. While thinking of it, she realized she hadn't opened the rest of her mail. Putting the chips away, she took the soda into the bedroom with her.

Returning to a comfortable position on the bed, Nikkola set the soft drink down on a wooden coaster and then opened the rest of the mail. Most of it was junk mail and a few personal charge account bills. There was also a letter reminding her of her date with little Cydnee Harlan. Cydnee was the six-year-old child Nikkola sponsored in the Big Brothers Big Sisters of America program.

Nikkola smiled when she thought of the tiny girl with large, brown eyes and dark brown hair. Cydnee was orphaned at the age of three and had been placed at St. Anthony's orphanage by some distant relatives. Her parents had been killed in an automobile accident. She'd been an only child. Her relatives weren't in a financial position to raise her, but they came to visit her at least twice a month. Despite all the tragedy in her life, Cydnee was quite a cheerful little person.

Nikkola had been involved with Cydnee for the past two years. When she'd chosen Cydnee as a little sister to spend time with, she was dating Cyd Ashford. She had loved how close their first names were to one another. Cyd had accompanied them on many outings, but from the very beginning little Cydnee was none too fond of him. Nikkola never understood why. But after they broke up, Nikkola felt Cydnee had been a much better judge of character than she'd been. Young Cydnee had easily smelled the rat in Cyd.

Reaching for the phone, Nikkola picked up the receiver and dialed Glen's number. He answered right away, but it sounded as though he'd been asleep. Nikkola felt bad for waking him. "I'm sorry, Glen. I didn't think you'd be asleep this early."

"It's okay, Nikki. I'd only been asleep a few minutes. I won't have a hard time going back. I'd think you'd be asleep, too." His voice sounded drowsy.

"I'm about to go, Glen, but I wanted to share something with you. I got a note from Mychal Forrester. He returned the money I'd given him to have his suit cleaned and he also asked me out to lunch when I return to London. Glen, he knew the exact day we're scheduled to fly back to England. How he got my address has me concerned. What do you make of it? Oh, he knows where we stay, too," she added.

"Nikki, that sounds really strange to me. I can't imagine where he got your personal information, but with these darn computers anything is possible. I shudder to think how he managed this feat, but you need to be wary of this one. He said he was an investment banker, didn't he? Have you had any dealings with an investment bank lately?"

"That's what he said he was, but I haven't done any business with investment banks. I'll be careful, though. You go back to sleep. I'll talk with you in the morning. I love you, Glen Taylor," Nikkola crooned sweetly.

"Good night. I love you, too. Sleep tight, Nikki baby."

Nikkola hung up the phone, but she was really worried now. She wondered why the note hadn't really alarmed her from the beginning. *Maybe because he's there and I'm here.* Getting off the bed, Nikkola went into the room to turn off the radio, returning to her bedroom seconds later.

Latham was in the garage of his beautiful Alexandria, Virginia, home about twelve miles away from Nikkola's condominium complex. His head was bent under the

hood of his silver Saab convertible. He hadn't been able
to rest, so he'd been keeping busy cleaning the engine
of his car. Latham was very meticulous and orderly. He
kept his home and car spotless. After putting the hood
down on his car, Latham lowered the garage doors and
entered the house.

The house had four bedrooms, along with a spacious
game room with a wet bar. The furnishings were made
of various finished hardwoods and rich leathers.

After grabbing old newspapers from the last couple
of days, Latham went into the family room and situated
himself on the multipillow-styled sofa fashioned in awning
stripes of tan and ivory. The love seat, chairs, and ottoman
matched the couch. The room was accented with
southern-pine finish occasional tables and a southern-
styled armoire/entertainment center.

Latham read the business and entertainment section
of each paper before he tossed them aside. He mud-
dled through his umpteenth conversation with Carmen
about the breakup, relieved that he'd finally been able
to end it. He felt it was long overdue. They'd only been
seeing each other a few months, but they hadn't been
able to find anything in common outside of their jobs.

Latham saw that it was getting late. He'd already felt
the jet lag coming on. He'd welcome the chance to shut
his brain down for a few hours. He loved flying, but it
often left him mentally exhausted. He'd been an Air
Force reconnaissance pilot and had logged quite a few
flying hours through training missions. After several
years on active duty, he'd resigned his commission to
become a commercial pilot. At the time of resignation,
Latham had held the rank of captain.

On weary legs Latham moved into the master bedroom of his home, where he lay across the Shaker-style
bed designed from solid maple with a honey finish. The
set was made complete with mirrored dresser, armoire,
and nightstands. The heavy quilted comforter was done

in a selection of foulard and stripe prints in deep hunter green, burgundy, and gold. The decor was very manly.

Turning over on his back, Latham stared up at the ceiling. A vision of Nikkola dressed in a flowing white silk negligee suddenly appeared before his eyes. He blinked hard to dismiss the vision. *Too many hours in the sky.* As Latham thought about the main reason he'd stayed clear of Nikkola, he hoped he had it conquered. He was scared to death of beautiful women. Having been badly burned by one, he'd sworn them off. But the beautiful woman that he had once loved never possessed the inner beauty Nikkola Knight had going for her.

Since sleep refused to overtake his mind and body, Latham flipped the night-light on. Opening the night-stand drawer, he pulled out a soft leather-bound address book. He flipped through it and then picked up the phone and dialed the seven digits.

"Please don't tell me you need me to fly on my days off," she said in a husky voice.

The response stunned him at first, but then he knew exactly where she was coming from. "No, Nikki, your off days are safe." He laughed into the receiver.

"Who is this?" After sitting up in the bed, Nikkola turned on the light. She'd thought it was the airlines calling to ask her to come into work.

"It's your favorite night-flight pilot, Nikkola."

Nikkola's ears perked up at the sultry sound of the deep voice, with the slight southern drawl. "Latham, have you gone mad? Do you know what time it is?"

Latham turned the light off as he slid down in the bed. "Yeah, time for you and me to have our first official date."

Months ago Nikkola would've been thrilled to get this phone call, but now she was filled with apprehension.

"Nikki, have breakfast with me in the morning."

"I can't! I have a date with Cyd." She had purposely misled him by shortening Cydnee's name. It wasn't a very nice thing to do, Nikkola quickly decided.

"Cyd? I thought that was over long ago."

"So much for what you thought. I keep my private business private, Latham." She couldn't understand why she was fighting this, especially knowing she wanted Latham at almost any cost.

"Nikki, I'll be at Jenny's Café at seven-thirty A.M. I know it isn't far from your house. I do hope you'll show up. We need to clear the air between us. Good night, Nikkola Knight." He hung up the phone, fluffed his pillows, and turned up on his side. "Please be there, Nikki."

Nikkola stared at the phone, as if she expected the conversation to continue. Before hanging up the receiver, she checked to see if possibly he was still holding on; all she heard was the buzzing dial tone. *Seven-thirty. I could meet Latham for breakfast and still make my ten o'clock date with Cydnee.* Why did she always find herself in these impossible situations?

It felt as if she had known Latham Scott all her life and had wanted him forever. But it seemed as if he never knew that she existed, let alone existed as a desirable woman. *Why now?*

Nikkola had the urge to call Glen for advice, but since she'd already awakened him once she didn't dare disturb him again. He always gave her sound advice; they were always honest and up-front with each other. Deciding to play everything by ear, Nikkola turned out the light and once again settled in for the night.

Still unable to sleep, Latham dragged himself out of bed. Slipping his feet into leather slippers, he trudged out to the kitchen. He measured out enough coffee for two cups and filled the glass pot with water. After turning on the coffeemaker, he poured the water into the dispenser.

Seated at the dinette set, he waited for the coffee to brew. His sleepless night was caused by his inability to erase the memories of all the unpleasant things that had transpired with Carmen.

Carmen knew she was dominant and sometimes overbearing, but Latham had figured out that it was the only way she knew how to be. From what she'd told him, her mother was dominant and her father had jumped every time she cracked the whip. Carmen was an adult now. She should've been able to break the cycle. She knew her mother was wrong. According to Carmen, her mother had finally driven her father away with her unreasonable demands. Well, Latham thought, Carmen had certainly managed to push him away. *The apple didn't fall far from the tree.*

Most people drank coffee to stay awake, but it had the reverse effect on Latham. It relaxed him and made him very sleepy. Taking out a coffee cup, he filled it to the brim. The stronger the brew was, the better it was for his insomnia attacks, so he drank it black.

Latham had never allowed himself to spend the night with Carmen or her with him even on layovers; that always puzzled her. She often asked him if it was a common practice with him. He had to admit to himself that there were a lot of strange things about their relationship. He had been very affectionate with her in the beginning, but the passionate kisses and the warm hugs weren't over quickly enough for him. It was her big mouth that had cooled him off. He'd been irritated with her over the past several months. Their conversations had most always turned into vicious battles.

Latham liked sports; Carmen hated them. He couldn't put the top down on the car when she was with him, which bothered him to no end. He liked jazz and soft music; she loved loud, brassy music. He had often tried to come up with something they'd had in common, outside of their love for travel and flying, but he hadn't been able to. He wasn't even sure they'd been compatible in bed, since he'd never been fully satisfied. The fact that he'd never spent one entire night with her made him even more aware of the seriousness of their incompatibility issues.

Carmen would love to blame Nikkola Knight for the unrest, but she'd only be lying to herself. He had often thought of him and Nikkola getting together. He couldn't help noticing how relaxed he seemed and how much deeper his smile was when Nikki was around. But he had never been openly flirtatious with her until now. *Should he concede her love to Glen, or go down fighting?* Latham wasn't the type of man that gave up easily, especially when he wanted something. Nikkola intrigued him more and more each day. Her smile had a way of making his heart skip a beat.

Pulling the plug on the coffeemaker and his thoughts of Nikkola, Latham went back to bed.

The morning hours came much too soon for Nikkola. When the alarm clock went off at six-thirty, she groaned and moaned but rolled herself out of bed. After slowly making her way into the bathroom, Nikkola began her morning routines. Her shower was always last.

Dripping wet, Nikkola slipped into a thick robe. She then emptied the hamper and transferred the dirty clothes to a clothes basket. Lifting the basket, she carried it into the small laundry room located down the hallway. Without bothering to measure the liquid, she poured the laundry soap into the washing machine and turned it on. Once the water mixed well with the soap, Nikkola dumped in a small amount of nonchlorine bleach and threw in the white clothes.

Nikkola went about readying herself for the breakfast rendezvous with Latham, not daring to think of what it meant. She and Cydnee were going to the park later, so she dressed with that in mind, pulling on black denim jeans and a crisp, white shirt. While looking through her numerous pairs of shoes, she decided on a pair of black leather sneakers. Despite the comment Latham had made about how he liked her hair loose, Nikkola brushed it back and tied it up with a black bow.

On her way to the front door, Nikkola transferred the clothes from the washer to the dryer, throwing in a couple of fabric softener sheets and turning the knob to the delicate cycle. She hated to even use the dryer, but she had nowhere to hang the clothes outside. Her mother had always hung everything out to air dry. Nikkola loved the fresh smell of the clothes.

Snatching her purse off the hall credenza, Nikkola rushed out the door to catch the elevator.

In the covered parking garage area, Nikkola slid behind the wheel of her late-model silver Chrysler Sebring. The Virginia license plates read: RX4LOVE. After starting the engine, Nikkola pressed the button to open the moon roof and then drove out of the security gates.

The morning air was cool and crisp. This was the type of weather Nikkola liked to jog in—before the weather would become hot and muggy and the humidity would hang in the air like a stubborn enemy. There were days that she praised the mastermind behind the invention of the air conditioner. At times the artificial air caused her respiratory problems, but there were times that she knew she'd perish without it.

Jenny's Café was less than a mile from Nikkola's place. Latham's sports car was already in the parking lot when she arrived. Suddenly unsure of herself, Nikkola tried to will herself into turning around and speeding back to her safe haven. But her heart screamed out to her; it wouldn't be able to stand the disappointment.

Chapter 4

Latham was waiting for Nikkola at the entrance to Jenny's Café. She expected him to be smug, but instead he smiled cheerfully. His eyes seemed to tell her he was glad she came. Nikkola smiled back at Latham, but her face felt like plaster, threatening to crack if she smiled any wider.

Latham briefly took hold of Nikkola's hand. "Nikki, thanks for coming."

Feeling a little testy, Nikkola eyed Latham curiously. "It sounds as if you were pretty sure I'd show up." Instead of responding to her comment, Latham once again reached for Nikkola's hand and then guided her into the cafe.

The café was clean; the banana-yellow and tangerine-orange decor made it bright and cheery. The wallpaper boasted colorful slices of different fruits, along with other pictures of appetizing foods. Nikkola and Glen had eaten here a couple of times, but the delicious-looking wallpaper had made it hard for her to make up her mind as to what she wanted to eat. Glen had laughed when she'd told him the problem she was having. He'd found her difficulty in selecting from the menu rather absurd.

Greeting them pleasantly, a waitress dressed in a yellow and orange uniform directed them to a booth toward the center of the restaurant, where Nikkola and Latham sat directly across from each other. After handing them the menus, the waitress disappeared.

Latham peered at Nikkola over the menu. "Have you eaten here before, Nikki?"

It was apparent to Nikkola that Latham hadn't patronized the place before from the way he was surveying it. "Yeah, I have, and I don't know why they bother giving you menus with all this food plastered over the walls."

Latham noticed the amused twinkle in her eyes. "I see what you mean. It makes for a hard decision." As he looked around at the wallpaper, Nikkola laughed softly. He'd heard her laugh many times and it sounded like pealing chapel bells to him.

"What has you so amused, Nikki?" *It doesn't really matter, as long as you're happy.*

"I said the same thing about having a hard time making a decision. My date thought I was being absurd. Hearing you say the same thing lends my absurdity a dash of credibility."

Was Cyd Asford the date she'd spoken of? Next time I'll find a place that she's never been. "Tell me about yourself, Nikkola Knight."

The sudden change in the tone of the conversation made Nikkola nervous, but not for very long. "Not until you tell me why you asked me to meet you," she said.

Challenging him seemed to be the name of the game, but Latham was here to change all that.

"I want you to know that I'm free to pursue you and also to give you fair warning of my intentions."

Nikkola raised her eyebrows in response, her eyes

flashing with streaks of lightning. "And what *are* your intentions, Captain Scott?"

Seeing the thunderstorm brewing in her eyes, Latham hoped he could successfully dodge the threatening bolts cast his way. "For starters, I intend to become your friend. Once that's accomplished, hopefully we can set a solid foundation for us to build something stronger."

Nikkola was impressed with Latham's statement, eager to hear the rest of his intentions.

As the waitress returned to take their order, Nikkola felt that her timing was terrible. Knowing she wouldn't be able to do justice to a large breakfast, Nikkola only ordered toast and orange juice. Latham wasn't too happy with Nikkola's meager order, but he held his tongue, ordering pancakes, eggs, hash browns, and hot chocolate for himself.

"Dieting, Nikki?"

"Nope. Just not hungry."

Latham laughed at her terse but honest answer. "Good! Anorexia-nervosa-looking women turn me off."

Then how in the world did you end up with Carmen? She was a walking advertisement for anorexia. "And what type of women turn you on, Latham?"

"Do you have a mirror, Nikki? If you do, look into it. The reflection you see there will reveal the answer."

Latham's response left Nikkola momentarily speechless. The desire to kiss him had never been stronger than now. She could almost taste his lips on hers. Her eyes glazed over at just the thought of their mouths uniting in passion.

Latham narrowed his eyes. "I'm not a mind reader, Nikki. What are you thinking?"

Boy am I glad. "Wouldn't you like to know, but I'm not telling," she teased. Glancing at her watch nervously, she looked around for the waitress. This was taking more time than she had even if she was enjoying it. Little Cydnee hated for her to be a minute late.

"Is Cyd waiting somewhere in the wings? I ordered that huge breakfast hoping to make you forget about him."

"Well, it didn't work. Cyd is expecting me. I'd never think of canceling my date," she said emphatically, suddenly feeling guilty about keeping the truth from him.

Latham had heard about this Cyd, though he'd never met him. He couldn't understand how Nikki could still be interested in him after what he'd done. "Suit yourself, Nikkola Knight. Maybe your head wasn't bumped hard enough the first time. Seeing how hardheaded you are, I can see why it didn't make a dent." He sounded exasperated. She didn't know if he was angry or jealous.

The food was then placed in front of them, a welcomed sight for Nikkola.

Without uttering another word, Latham picked up his fork and started eating, but not before he closed his eyes in silent prayer. Nikkola sat quietly, watching him eat. The rate at which he was shoveling it in amazed her. Suddenly he looked up and caught her staring at him.

Latham smiled impishly. "If you don't eat that measly breakfast, I'm going to think you lied about dieting. But I can't say I blame you. It doesn't look very appetizing. Care for some of mine, Nikki?"

All of yours would be nice. Devilment sparkled in her eyes. "No thanks." Picking up the toast, Nikkola took a bite off the end and washed it down with juice. "I have a confession to make."

Putting his fork down, Latham placed his elbows on the table, eyeing her intently. "Confession, Nikki? Do I look like a priest?" He saw the flit of fiery temper cross her face. "Sorry, Nikkola. I shouldn't have been coy."

"Apology accepted. I *am* meeting Cyd, but it's not Cyd Ashford. I'm in the Big Brothers Big Sisters program at St. Anthony's orphanage. I sponsor a beautiful little girl named Cydnee Harlan." Nikkola then went on and explained Cydnee's plight to Latham.

Tears glistened in Nikkola's eyes as she told Latham the child's personal story. Her eyes expressed the many emotions she felt, while his heart was touched by her obvious compassion for Cydnee. She had totally disarmed him. He suddenly knew the war was not winnable for him, as she'd suggested earlier. There was no weapon anywhere in the world strong enough to win out against his caring deeply for Nikkola Knight.

"You astound me, Nikki! Do you think I could come to the orphanage with you? Maybe I can become a big brother to one of the male children there. I'd love to be involved in such a worthy cause. What do you think?"

Nikkola was overwhelmed by his request. "And I'd love to have you join me, Latham! Sister Ingrid can use all the help she can get. There are very few men involved with the children." Picking up her glass, Nikkola gestured a toast, and then drained it.

Hurriedly, Latham finished his breakfast and paid the check.

The two cars pulled out of the parking lot with Nikkola leading the way. She had given Latham the directions just in case he couldn't keep up with her. He thought she was teasing, but he soon found out Nikkola had a heavy foot. She was used to putting the pedal to the metal, but luckily she'd never received a ticket. His car was equipped with a turbo-engine; today he was glad for it. Keeping up with Nikkola was a challenge.

Nikkola wondered how Cydnee was going to react to Latham, when she remembered how she'd reacted to Cyd. But she couldn't turn down Latham's request. He seemed so excited about the prospect of joining her. She was just as eager to have him come with her. Slowing down as she neared the orphanage, she signaled for the right-hand turn that she was about to make. She pulled into the parking lot. After turning off the engine, Nikkola waited for Latham to join her.

Exiting his car, Latham strode toward Nikkola with an amazing smile on his face. "Are you sure you aren't a jet pilot? You sure were flying low, Nikki! How many times have you been ticketed for speeding, girl?" He grinned broadly.

"Never," she boasted proudly. "I'll have to find some wood in a hurry." Reaching up, she knocked on his head. They both dissolved into laughter. Without giving it a minute of thought, Nikkola slid her hand into Latham's. Gently, he squeezed her fingers.

The orphanage was a large gray-brick building consisting of many rooms and numerous corridors, yet it was homey. Nikkola stopped by the front office to register and announce her visit.

"Nikki, how good to see you this morning!" Sister Ingrid Schuller greeted her guest warmly in a thick German accent, hugging Nikkola tenderly. "Cydnee is as jittery as can be."

Sister Ingrid's cheeks were bright with color and her baby-blues were warm, loving, and kind. With the habit covering all of her forehead, her huge eyes appeared to take up most of her face. "Who is your handsome guest, Nikki?"

"Sister, this is Captain Latham Scott. He's employed by the same airline as I am. Sister, he's interested in sponsoring a male child. If you don't mind, you can fill him in on all the details."

"Good morning, Captain Scott! We are elated to have you visit with us." Taking Latham's hand, Ingrid shook it vigorously, her grip strong and sure. Latham smiled at the nun with open affection. "Nikki, you go ahead and see Cydnee. I'll bring Captain Scott along momentarily."

All smiles, Nikkola waved good-bye as she ran down the hallway.

Cydnee was in the spacious playroom playing with the doll Nikkola had given her last Christmas. Nikkola stood still and quietly observed her young friend from the doorway. One of the other children spotted Nikkola first and then loudly shouted out her name.

The small Cydnee sprang into action, rapidly covering the short distance to the doorway. "Nikki, Nikki," she shouted gleefully, flinging herself into Nikkola's arms. Nikkola wrapped her arms around Cydnee, as she hugged and kissed her tenderly. "I thought you'd never get here, Nikki. You're late."

Nikkola wasn't late; Cydnee was always early.

"When are you going to learn to trust me? Have I ever broken a promise or not shown up when I was supposed to, Cydnee?" Nikkola asked in a gently chiding way.

"No, never, Nikki. You're my best friend in the whole wide world," Cydnee said sweetly.

Cydnee was very articulate for a six-year-old. That worried Nikkola at times. She seemed so grown up. Nikkola hated that the tragic death of her parents might have stolen her childhood.

"And you are my best friend, Cydnee! Why don't we go over there and sit down so you can tell me what you've been doing lately?"

"Can we go out onto the playground, Nikki? We can talk better out there."

Nikkola nodded, laughing at her comment. Cydnee grabbed Nikkola by the hand and pulled her toward the door leading outside. Cydnee was dressed in pink pants, a white, frilly top, white socks, and tiny sneakers, and her long, shiny brown ponytail bounced as she skipped toward the playground. Most of her clothes had been donated to the orphanage. The playground was fully equipped and most of the recreational items were donated as well.

Cydnee plopped into one of the yellow swings. "Please push me, Nikki."

Laying down her purse, Nikkola walked up behind the swing. Gripping it tightly by the seat, she lifted it and let it go. As it swung back toward her, Nikkola gave it another push, repeating the movement over and over. "How are you doing in school?"

"Excellent! I like school, but I don't like it when Sister Maria cracks my hands."

"Why does she even have to crack your hands, Cydnee?"

"Because I lose my temper at times. If the other children make a lot of noise, it disturbs me, like when if I'm reading."

Nikkola frowned. "Then you'll have to learn to control your temper. I used to have a bad temper, too. I still have to work on control all the time. When we allow others to make us lose our temper, we are giving them control over us," Nikkola explained patiently.

"I know, but it's hard at times. I'll try to do better. Could you please stop the swing, Nikki? I'm tired of it already."

Nikkola did as Cyndee had requested, watching her closely as the little girl climbed down. Hand in hand, they walked over to the large tree, where they sat down on the grass.

"I brought a guest with me today, Cydnee."

"Who is it, Nikki?" Cydnee's eyes brightened as she questioned Nikkola.

As Sister Ingrid and Latham were nearing the area where Nikkola and Cydnee were seated, Nikkola pointed at Latham. "His name is Captain Scott. He's an airline pilot, Cydnee."

Cydnee's eyes grew somber. "I hope he's nothing like

that Mr. Ashford. I didn't like him. His eyes always told big lies."

Nikkola marveled at Cydnee's ability to read people at such a young age. She had read Cyd quite accurately. "Later, in private, you can tell me what you think of Captain Scott, Cydnee. I'll be interested in hearing your opinion." Cydnee nodded her okay.

Latham and Sister Ingrid stopped right in front of the large tree. Cydnee jumped to her feet, looking curiously at Latham. Her bright eyes traveled his length.

Latham smiled broadly. "Hi, Cydnee."

Cydnee liked Latham's smile, but she was reserved. "Hello, Captain Scott. Nikki said you're a pilot. I can't believe you can fly one of those big planes," she exclaimed happily. She then returned to her grassy seat, keeping her eyes fastened on Latham.

"You can believe it, sweetie! It's true enough. I've been flying planes for a long time now. I used to be in the Air Force." Latham sat down on the grass just as Sister Ingrid walked away.

A shocked expression came over Cydnee's face. "My daddy was in the Air Force, too," Cydnee said proudly.

"He was? That's great, Cydnee. What's your daddy's name?" Latham's heart fluttered with empathy as he watched Cydnee bravely brush the tears from her eyes. Latham helplessly looked over at Nikkola and she gave him a sympathetic smile.

"His name was Robert Harlan. My mother's name was Rebecca. Aren't those nice names?" Cydnee asked Latham.

"Very nice, indeed, Cydnee," Latham reassured her.

Cydnee scrambled over to Nikkola and sat in her lap, looking up at her adoringly. Then Cydnee's expression suddenly turned pensive. Nikkola couldn't begin to imagine what was on her little mind.

"Nikki, I really wanted to go to the park today, but I'm needed around here. Robbie Broder, a new boy, moved in today. He's six years old, just like me. He's probably going to need me since he doesn't know anyone."

Cydnee's little-miss demeanor and motherly aura never ceased to amaze Nikkola. "If Robbie is going to need you, Cydnee, then you definitely should be here. Is he cute?"

Cydnee pondered Nikkola's question. "He's cute enough already, but he's a little too chunky. He needs some exercise." Latham howled at her statement, causing Cydnee to turn her gaze on him. "Maybe you can give Robbie some pointers, Captain Scott. I can tell by your big muscles that you get plenty of exercise."

Latham couldn't believe how observant she was for someone so young. "I'd be happy to help Robbie. I'm going to sponsor a child, too. Maybe it can be Robbie."

"That would be nice, but Seth really needs someone more than Robbie. He's been here a long time and he doesn't have anyone to come to visit him. Seth is the boy on the slide, the one in the red shirt." She pointed him out. Nikkola and Latham looked in the direction of Cydnee's finger.

Nikkola was well aware of Seth's background. Seth Minter was a biracial child. His father was Caucasian and his mother was Asian. He had been left at a local hospital when he was only eight days old. He'd been in and out of foster care and had ended up at St. Anthony's only six months ago. Seth had dark hair and dark, almond-shaped eyes. His complexion was medium brown and his facial features were mostly Asian.

"Can you introduce me to Seth?" Latham asked Cydnee.

Wearing a huge smile on her face, Cydnee jumped to her feet. "I'll bring him over here, Captain Scott. Be right back."

Smiling at Cydnee in an endearing way, Latham

grabbed hold of her tiny hand before she could flee. "I'd really like it if you'd just call me Latham."

Cydnee turned her head to one side, staring at Latham for several seconds without any expression. "I could handle that, but I'd have to add a mister to it. Rules are rules." Cydnee giggled. Latham then released her hand and she took off running across the playground.

Latham smiled lazily at Nikkola. She returned his smile, but she felt more like weeping. Her heart broke every time she visited the orphanage. She wished there was more she could do for Cydnee and the other children, silently praying that they'd all find good homes one day soon.

"Cydnee is beautiful, Nikki, and she's so bright. She talks and acts too much like an adult. That concerns me. But I'm glad you let me come here with you today."

"I'm glad it worked out okay for you. Cydnee is highly intelligent, Latham. You haven't seen the half of her capabilities. They've done a wonderful job in raising her here. I wish every orphaned child could be so blessed to end up here. There are millions of parentless children, but very few are fortunate enough to be placed at a wonderful orphanage like this one."

Latham placed his hand on Nikkola's in a consoling manner. She acknowledged his kind gesture with a warm smile before they both turned their attention back to the children.

Cydnee returned with Seth and introduced him to her adult friends. Seth was quiet and withdrawn, but with Nikkola and Latham's friendly and gentle persuasion, they soon had him talking. Cydnee had also rounded up Robbie and several other children to bring to the tree.

With everyone vying for the attention of the airline pilot, Latham entertained the children with declassified mission stories from his Air Force career. They asked a lot of questions; he filled each answer with intrigue. Nikkola, too, was held spellbound by his exciting military tales.

An hour or so later, several of the children walked Nikkola and Latham to the front entrance. Cydnee wrapped her short arms around Nikkola's waist and looked up at her. Her large brown eyes melted Nikkola's heart. "When can I spend another night with you at your house, Nikki? I like our fun pajama parties."

Nikkola twirled Cydnee's brown ponytail around her slender fingers. "The next time I'm off duty, Cydnee, I'll arrange your overnight stay with Sister Ingrid. We'll do something really special. Now give me a big hug and a kiss!"

Nikkola bent down while Cydnee hugged her and smacked a sweet kiss onto her cheek. Though she acted shy with him, Cydnee hugged Latham too. The other children waved excitedly as the two guests exited the building.

As Nikkola and Latham walked to the parking lot, a quiet friendship appeared to have settled in between the two. They smiled their approval of each other as Latham saw Nikkola to her car. After walking away, he abruptly turned around and leaned his hard body against Nikkola's car door, barring her entry. "I don't want this to end right now, but I don't want to push my luck either. Thank you for a wonderful half-day." He looked down at her license plate and laughed. "What is your prescription for love, Nikki?" Latham appeared genuinely interested in hearing her response.

Nikkola looked at him thoughtfully, giving him a delightful smile. "The main ingredients are a solid friendship and loads of trust and understanding. But I haven't been able to come up with the rest of the formula yet," she said ruefully.

"Maybe together we can come up with all the right ingredients. Are you interested in trying, Nikkola?" While holding his breath, Latham looked hopeful.

Nikkola nervously scraped the bottom of her shoes back and forth across the blacktop. "I don't know, Latham. Earlier, you said you were free to pursue me, but you didn't say what you were free from."

The look in Nikkola's eyes was seriously sobering to Latham. "I'm free of the relationship I was in. I had to break things off with Carmen for both of our sakes. It's been over between us for a long time, but she can't accept it. We had nothing in common whatsoever. I don't know how it got as far as it did. From my past conversations with you, I know you and I have a lot in common."

Latham winced at the barely tolerant look in Nikkola's eyes. "Nikki, please don't think it was easy for me to end things with Carmen. It wasn't. In fact, it was very difficult. I respect her very much, but I'm not in love. I don't want you to think I used her and then dropped her. It wasn't like that at all. I can't really explain it to you. It just wasn't good between us."

Nikkola saw the sincerity in his eyes and she could also hear it in his voice. "Let's work on building a really good friendship first. Then we can see what comes next. Okay?" Nikkola's mouth had said friendship, but her heart was ready for a steamy love affair.

Moving away from the car door, Latham towered over Nikkola, looking down into her eyes. "To friendship, Nikki." He raised his hand in a mock toast, touching her cheek lightly before walking away, completely satisfied that he at least had some sort of chance with Nikkola.

Nikkola stood stock still, admiring the graceful moves of Latham's lithe body.

Before entering his car, Latham turned around and blew a kiss aimed right at her lips.

Nikkola found herself completely mesmerized by the sexy aircraft commander. Her head was way above the clouds as she jumped into her car and sped toward home.

The minute she parked her car, Nikkola headed for Glen's place. After ringing the bell several times, she accepted that he wasn't in. She felt disappointed, since she had so many things to tell him and questions to ask. Turning from his doorway, she hurried to her own.

Before going into the living room to sit down, Nikkola gathered her clothes from the dryer and impatiently shoved them into the laundry basket. She then carried the basket to the sofa. As thoughts of her day with Latham occupied her mind, she knew she wanted to see him again, but thoughts of Carmen's saddened face kept entering the picture.

The phone bell shattered the less than peaceful silence. In her frantic flight to answer the phone, she accidentally kicked over the laundry basket. Looking utterly confused, she didn't seem to know whether to pick the clothes up first or answer the call. The insistent bell quickly helped her to decide. "Hello," Nikkola said breathlessly.

"Hello again, Nikki. It's Latham."

The sound of his husky voice made the blood rush through Nikkola's brain. Totally winded, she gulped in some much-needed air. "Hi, Latham. What can I do for you?" She was surprised at how calm she had become so quickly. Her heart had been racing only seconds before.

"How about us rediscovering the sedating night-lights of the monuments after dusk?"

Nikkola's heartbeat quickened at the thought of being with him, sharing the spectacular views of nighttime

Washington. Instead of allowing her heart to soar to the moon, she gave herself a reality check. "Maybe another time." Her dry response lacked no conviction whatsoever.

"This is another time, Nikki. We're definitely in a different place with each other. Different from where we were only hours ago," he said softly.

Nikkola had to agree with him, since her heart had already yielded wantonly to his suggestion. Aware that she had no strength to fight her feelings for him, Nikkola looked over at the clock on the wall. "What time do you want me to be ready, Latham?" Nikkola asked, feeling both defeated and elated.

"I can be there at seven. If the lines aren't too long, we can watch the sunset from the top of the Washington Monument. I'll see you then, Nikki." Without giving her a chance to change her mind, Latham rang off.

His ringing off without further comment reminded her of how arrogant Latham could be, but she had to admit that his arrogance was one of the many things she found so attractive about him. After checking for the dial tone, she dialed Glen's number, hoping he was now at home.

Nikkola giggled nervously when Glen's voice came on the line. "Hi, Glen. Are you busy?"

"I'm always busy, Nikki, but never too busy for you. The truth is I just walked through the front door. What's up with you?"

"Can you come over? I need some advice, and I need it now!"

Glen grinned. "Be right there, my dear friend."

Nikkola thanked Glen and then disconnected the lines.

While waiting for Glen's arrival, Nikkola quickly folded all the clothes and put them away. She then went into the kitchen and made enough coffee for at least two cups each. Though she was expecting Glen, the doorbell startled her. She laughed out loud at the silly nervousness. She hadn't felt this giddy since her very first date. At the front door, Nikkola pulled Glen inside by his hands.

Glen actually felt the excited anxiety in Nikkola's touch. "Calm down, Nikki. What has lit a bonfire under your butt, girlfriend?"

"Come in the kitchen and I'll tell you all about it." Nikkola exhaled a deep sigh as they made their way down the hall and into the other room.

After pouring the coffee, Nikkola took a seat at the able. Patiently, she explained all the events that had occurred between her and Latham over the course of the day.

"I don't see the problem, Nikki. You've wanted to get to know Latham better for some time now. What has you so darn scared?"

"*Rebound tenderness!* Is he trying to get over Carmen by using me, or is he truly interested in me for me?"

"We've had this conversation so many times before. Nikki, life is one big risk after another. At some point, we all have to take risks. You might get hurt, or you could end up with the man of your dreams. It's up to you."

"I guess there's no other way to find out other than by taking the plunge. But I'm going to hold him to his promise regarding building a friendship first. Drat! How can I be friends with somebody I've made passionate love to in my dreams?"

"Very, very carefully, Nikki. And it looks like you'll have Forrester to fall back on if it doesn't work out."

Nikkola frowned heavily at Glen's suggestion. "Forrester is another of those risks you mentioned, a huge one, but I'll keep my options open."

With coffee cups in hand, Nikkola and Glen moved into the living room, and dropped down on the same sofa, where Glen told one of his best friends all about his day.

"I'm feeling like my old self again. I'm sure my illness was nothing more than a type of flu. But I still plan to see my doctor before our next scheduled flight."

"That sounds like a good plan to me. We can't ever be too cautious when it comes to our health." With her confidence wavering, Nikkola suddenly looked downtrodden.

Glen smiled softly at Nikkola. He could see by her demeanor that her confidence needed a great big boost. "Believe in yourself, Nikki. If there's anything suspicious in Latham's intentions, your natural instincts will sound the alarm."

Nikkola scowled. "I beg to differ. I remember how my instincts failed me in my relationship with Cyd."

"But, Nikki, you weren't truly in love with Cyd. It hurt more for Tammy to betray you than anything Cyd could've ever done."

"I've wanted so desperately to believe that Cyd knew I wasn't in love with him, and that's what had made it so easy for him to deceive me. But I'll never understand how my best friend could've been a part of it."

"That's not something easily understood. Just know that best friends don't do that to each other. You might want to reassess your so-called relationship with her." Glen got to his feet. "I hate to run, but I've got to get back to the house. I have lots of unattended chores to take care of. Are you going to be okay, Nikki?"

Nikkola sighed hard. "I'll be just fine, once I rid myself of all negative thoughts."

After Glen left, Nikkola washed the coffee cups and cleaned the coffeemaker. Moving into the bathroom, she drew herself a hot bath and settled herself in the tub for a long soak, hoping the water would ease the tensions of the day and temporarily lift the burdens from her heart and mind.

Chapter 5

As it was just before dusk, the grayish shadows of nightfall had just begun to cast their magical spell over Washington and the surrounding areas. The cool evening air blowing off the Potomac River had already crowded out most of the muggy, stagnant air of the day.

Nikkola looked refreshing and relaxed dressed in dark blue jeans and a crisp, white shirt. Over her blouse, she wore a navy blue V-neck cashmere sweater. Her red curls waved in the wind and her hazel eyes had come alive with golden flecks of glitter. Latham also wore casual clothes, dark and extremely neat. His black pants had a sharp crease and the black knit crewneck sweater caressed his broad chest. The wind wrestled with his hair as his caramel-brown eyes twinkled with joy and contentment.

Latham considered himself incredibly lucky to have Nikkola seated next to him—he was doubly lucky when he found a great parking space near the Washington Monument. After easing his Saab into the grassy parking spot, he put the top up on the car. Calmly, Nikkola waited for him to open her door.

On the walk up to the monument, Latham tucked

Nikkola's arm through his. The cool wind whirled around them menacingly. Latham's nylon windbreaker had a hood on it, and he offered it to Nikkola, but she declined his generous gesture. The lines were a little longer than he'd hoped for, but wanting so badly to share this special time with her, Latham directed Nikkola to the end of them.

Latham smiled sweetly at Nikkola. "I'm sure we'll get inside before the sun sets, but if we don't we can watch it from right out here."

The sun has already set in my heart, Latham. Each time you smile it arises anew.

"Nikki, you're shivering. I have a blanket in the car. Want me to get it?"

Nikkola shook her head in the negative. "Latham, really, I'm fine."

Latham looked closely at Nikkola to be sure she wasn't just being polite. Though he seemed satisfied with her response, he was still concerned about her trembling. Her shivering had nothing to do with the cold, but she would've gladly accepted his arms wrapped tightly around her.

The line moved rapidly. Then the couple was in the elevator being whisked to the top. As they exited the car, Latham took Nikkola's hand and directed her to the west-side lookout point, facing the Lincoln Memorial. Positioning her in front of him, Latham gently placed his hands on her shoulders. As they looked on, the sun curtsied in descent, illuminating everything in its path.

Nikkola unconsciously gasped at the beauty of the sunset. As she laid her head back against Latham's chest, the warmth of her closeness beat a steady path into his soul. Lifting one hand from her shoulder, he nestled it in among her thick, silky-feeling curls.

Acutely aware of the position she'd put herself in, she tried to move, only to find that she was helplessly riveted to her spot. Feeling his warm breath touching the nape of her neck gave her a strong yen to close her eyes and pull his mouth down against hers. She successfully chased away the urge to do so. Nikkola had set the rules, now she needed to play by them. Being just a friend to Captain Latham Scott was going to be very difficult indeed.

Once the sun had slowly set, Latham turned Nikkola around to face him. She could clearly see the stars shining in his eyes. If one fell out, she imagined how she'd catch it and lovingly return it to its resting place.

"Did you enjoy the fantastic sunset, Nikki?" Latham whispered.

"It was spectacular from way up here. I felt as though I could reach out and touch it. These last few moments have been surreal."

"Oh, Nikki! I felt that way, too. I'm glad you enjoyed it. Let's take a drive around the city, and then I'll take you to my favorite coffeehouse. It's a special place and I only take special friends there. No," he said, before she could ask, "I've never taken any other woman there."

Nikkola slammed her lids down over her eyes to punish them for betraying her. "I would've never asked you that." Yet she already knew that her eyes had asked the question for her.

"I know that, Nikki, but I felt a need to share the information with you." Latham wouldn't admit it to Nikkola, but he had seen the unasked question in her eyes.

The descent of the elevator was rapid and smooth. Without asking her permission, Latham tenderly draped his windbreaker around Nikkola's shoulders before stepping outside. Then his arm came to rest firmly about her waist. With an unaccustomed boldness, she allowed herself to lean into him. She then slung her arm loosely around his waist as they walked on. Tourists were still arriving in droves as the couple settled themselves into the car.

* * *

During the tour around the city, Latham and Nikkola were caught up in the array of sights bathed in soft lighting. At night, the White House looked like a picture postcard coming to life.

While staring out at the Lincoln and Jefferson Memorials, Nikkola looked as if she expected the two noteworthy men to deliver their famous speeches at any moment. She also remembered the city at cherry blossom time, an unbelievable sight. The flowery memory practically took Nikkola's breath away.

Dimly lit with colored lanterns, the coffee shop offered an electrifying view of the Potomac. The color scheme of the café was red, black, and gold. Several large Oriental fans adorned the glossy walls. The decor of the café instantly had a calming effect on Nikkola.

Latham strode to the back of the coffeehouse with Nikkola close by his side. When he heard his name called, he turned in the direction of the familiar voice. As he pointed out several of his pilot buddies to Nikkola, the group of men summoned the couple over to the table.

Nikkola was somewhat embarrassed when she recognized Blaine Mills, the first officer of their crew. Blaine stood as they neared the table. He was medium built with ash-blond hair and expressive baby-blue eyes, much like the color eyes Sister Ingrid possessed.

Greetings were passed among the group and then Latham guided Nikkola to a more private setting. She slid into the gold-leather booth with ease while he took the seat across from her. Latham ordered hot chocolate for Nikkola and himself.

Latham looked worried. "Nikki, I could tell you were surprised to see Blaine. I hope it won't cause a problem for you."

As his sweet sensitivity calmed her tortured nerves,

she forced a smile to her wind-chafed lips. "I hope so, too. I didn't intend for our friendship to be publicized like this. No doubt that our relationship will be misinterpreted. I could be blamed for the breakup between you and Carmen."

"No one is to blame for that. I'll handle things with Blaine. We aviators have a code of silence among us."

The waiter promptly delivered the hot beverages and walked away.

Using her spoon, Nikkola fished a plump marshmallow from the steaming chocolate and popped it into her mouth. Latham smiled at the soft childish expression on her face, imagining tasting the marshmallow on her lips. Without taking his eyes off her, he slowly sipped on his drink.

"Do you have plans for when we return to London, Nikki?"

The tentative date with Mychal Forrester came to mind, but Nikkola had no intentions of keeping it, immediately dismissing the handsome stranger from her mind. "Not yet, but I'm sure I'll find something to get myself into. I love London. Glen and I usually end up doing the same things, but I'm going to come up with a new itinerary for us."

Nikkola had spoken with a quiet confidence, which for Latham fostered further intrigue.

"Please, Nikki, pencil me in somewhere on your calendar. We like many of the same activities, so it should be easy for us to come up with something to do together."

Blaine Mills sauntered up to the table, interrupting Nikkola's chance to respond to Latham's suggestion. Sliding into the booth next to Latham, Blaine crowded him into the corner.

"I've been keeping my eye on you two," Blaine announced with a smirk. "When did you two become an item?"

Nikkola's cheeks quickly became flushed.

"We're not an item, Blaine. Nikki and I are friends. We're both sponsoring children who live at St. Anthony's orphanage. We ran into each other there." At the moment Latham felt fiercely protective of Nikkola. He'd felt protective of her before, but more so now than ever.

Nikkola felt bad that Latham had found it necessary to lie, but she was grateful for it.

"Okay, Latham, I get the picture. I read more into the situation than I should have," Blaine conceded. "Sorry, Nikki." She merely nodded her acceptance of his apology.

Latham ordered refills of their beverages, including a cup of coffee for Blaine. Then he and Blaine shared death-defying aviation stories with Nikkola. Silently, she wished they'd change the subject. The thought of something terrible ever happening to Latham made her shrink inside from the fear of it all.

"Hey, Nikki, rumor has it that you and Glen are madly in love. What do you and him do all that time together? I hear that you two have a wild and grand time in the sack," Blaine joked.

Nikkola's hazel eyes immediately turned into glaciers of steely ice. Ready, aim, and fire signals glistened angrily in her eyes. But the signal for calm was much stronger. She knew that if she reacted with hostility it would somehow add validity to his ugly statement—and she'd never allow that to happen. Still, she wanted to drench his ash-blond hair with her drink. Nikkola swallowed hard as she tried to come up with a fitting response.

"That's funny you should say that, Blaine. Rumors do float, even above the clouds. I heard through the grapevine that you were deep into cross-dressing," she countered with acid sweetness. Her statement seemed to shock his nerves—and she steeled herself for his retaliation.

Blaine wondered if she was just being coy, or if he was in fact the subject of malicious gossip that spread around among the flight crews. His baby-blue eyes stared openly at Nikkola, as he tried to discern the truth. But her eyes remained enigmatic and her demeanor was cool. He had no idea why Nikkola had gotten so riled over his joking around, since the crew joked all the time.

"It doesn't feel very good, does it, Blaine?" Latham asked in a chilling tone. "Rumor or not, that was a horrible thing to say to Nikki. You owe her an apology. I never want to hear you disrespect any of my crew members or anyone else, for that matter," Latham strongly warned. "Someone's personal life isn't something you should ever bring up for discussion."

Blaine looked ashamed of himself as he struggled to find his voice. He then apologized to Nikkola. From the ice dripping from her eyes he knew she wasn't at all receptive. Shortly afterward, Blaine excused himself from the table and walked away in a hurry.

Latham arose from his seat and moved over next to Nikkola. "I'm sorry about that, honey. I wouldn't have brought you here if I'd any idea something like this might happen." The ice in her eyes suddenly dissolved into burning tears. "Come here, Nikki," he whispered softly. "Don't cry."

Gently, Latham pulled Nikkola into his arms, as the tears continued to rush from her eyes. When her tears were spent, he quietly led her from the coffee shop. Nikkola looked relieved when she saw that the other aviators were gone, but she still felt desperately angry.

The drive home was awkward for both of them. Latham sensed that Nikkola was in no mood to talk, so he graciously respected her need for silence. He walked her to the door, hoping that she'd ask him in. But when it didn't happen, Latham tenderly kissed her cheek and left.

* * *

During the drive home, Latham's mind rotated like a windmill in a dust storm. That Blaine had dared to cause Nikkola such pain made him irate; he hadn't finished with Blaine yet. He knew the rumors about Nikkola were hurting her, but there was no way to protect her from them. He also was aware that it took an incredible amount of willpower for her to control her temper, but he wasn't so sure she'd continue to keep such a tight rein on her emotions. He was certain there'd be more rumors and speculation about her and Glen. He had seen in Nikkola's eyes how deeply sensitive she was about her relationship with Glen. Latham silently prayed that Blaine hadn't.

Lying with her left cheek pressed into the pillow, with another pillow hugged closely to her body, Nikkola thought about the things being said about her and Glen. It didn't seem to be an issue when a pilot was dating a flight attendant. But when it seemed that two flight attendants got into a personal relationship rumors started flying all over the place. She couldn't begin to understand the cruelty and unfairness that occurred when that happened. She felt certain that a lot of discriminatory acts were born of ignorance and intolerance. If people would only respect others' rights to choose and live their lives as they saw fit, a lot of hatred and animosity could be put to death.

Isn't that what freedom and equality were all about? Why even bother to have the Constitution if everyone could write a postscript to it whenever they disagreed with a group of people or a lifestyle or the way people conducted their private lives? Why did people choose to play God and pass judgment on anything or anyone they didn't understand? God commanded his people to love one another as they love themselves. Then again, that could be part of the problem. Many people didn't know how to love themselves, so how could they love anyone else?

Nikkola drained her mind trying to figure out who started the rumors about herself and Glen. She replayed all of her and Glen's conversations while they were working, but she couldn't remember either of them discussing anything about their personal affairs. They'd always been careful not to discuss anything personal at work, choosing only to talk things out in the privacy of their own homes. Was just the fact that they lived in the same complex and had become best friends at the root of the rumors? The things Blaine said disgusted her. She was happy she'd been able to successfully turn things around, but she didn't like making hurtful remarks to anyone. Even if they had deserved it. His remarks about their so-called rumored sex life had been downright malevolent. *Contrary to popular belief, a man and a woman could definitely have a close personal relationship in the absence of lust and sex.* She and Glen were living proof of that.

Closing her eyes, Nikkola allowed herself to slip into a darkened world with Latham holding her tightly in his arms. His peaceful eyes hypnotized her as they escorted her into a bottomless sea of tranquility. Indescribable fantasies washed upon the shores of her unconsciousness. While she and Latham were discovering the beauty of the English countryside, they drove through the lush green rolling hills of the Cotswolds. Late in the evening, they took up residence at one of the most romantic cottage inns.

From the window of their intimate bedchambers, tall beech trees were silhouetted against the dusky starlit skies. Magnificent stone dwellings, rippling ponds, and streams were in abundance. Tucked away in a cozy corner of the room, a blazing fire was alive in the hearth. While the fire between Latham and Nikkola was also being stoked to an alarming fever pitch, there, in the little cottage by the sparkling brook, they consummated all the undeniable feelings between them. Before falling off to sleep, Nikkola and Latham promised to dwell forever in each other's hearts.

The rest of Nikkola's time off was spent doing personal errands and chores. She cleaned her place till every room shone with brilliance. After writing checks for her bills, she left them outside in the mailbox for the postman to pick up and deliver. Glen had asked her to go to the doctor with him, and after the scheduled afternoon appointment they'd gone grocery shopping. In the evening hours, Nikkola, Glen, and Josh, another of Glen's best friends, ate their dinner together. The relaxing evening had ended after the three friends watched several rented video movies.

Nikkola had hoped to hear from Latham, but to her dismay the phone had yet to ring. Calling him was out of the question for her. Being old-fashioned, Nikkola liked to be pursued and would never think of becoming the pursuer.

During the early morning of her last day off, Nikkola paid a visit to the dental office, where she had her teeth cleaned and polished. Afterward, she made a transaction at the bank in Alexandria, and then drove to Washington for lunch. Once she'd purchased a turkey sandwich, chips, and a soft drink, Nikkola ate lunch at a secluded table on the grounds of the Mall.

The Mall was one of the oldest parks in Washington, nestled between the Capitol and the Lincoln Memorial; a secondary axis intersected the Mall at the Washington Monument, which extended it to the White House and the Jefferson Memorial. The Mall housed nine Smithsonian Institution museums, along with a host of other stimulating attractions.

* * *

The suite was different from the previous one assigned to Nikkola at the St. James Court Hotel, but the decor was the same. The hotel had several individually designed suites, but each was furnished with one of eight distinctive themes. It was rare that she got one overlooking the courtyard twice in a row, but she was delighted that it had occurred.

Glancing at her travel clock on the nightstand, Nikkola saw that it was a quarter after one, fifteen minutes later than the appointed time she was to meet Mychal Forrester. A powerful magnetic field seemed to draw her out of the safety of her suite. Deciding not to engage in a battle with the strong but insane attraction she felt for Mychal, Nikkola quickly slipped out the door and rushed to take the elevator down to the appointed meeting place.

At the entrance to the informal Café Mediterranee, Nikkola stopped for a brief moment, taking in a deep breath. She then stepped inside. Nikkola scanned the room for Mychal's dark head, but he wasn't anywhere to be seen. With a mixture of disappointment and relief, she turned to walk out. After taking only a few steps, she ran smack into Mychal Forrester.

His eyes dark and scolding, Mychal looked from Nikkola to his elegant gold wristwatch. He then brought his narrowed brooding eyes to rest in hers. "Yet another bad habit, Miss Knight?" Somehow, he made Nikkola feel that she deserved to be punished. "Clumsy, bad table manners, and no respect for time. Tsk tsk. All are very unattractive, especially for someone whose natural beauty is absolutely flawless."

Even though Mychal's tone was curt, his eyes were unusually soft, carrying a glimmer of amused mockery. Nikkola was so confused she didn't know what to do or say. When he stuck his arm out for her to take, she obediently slipped her arm through it without comment. They were seated immediately by a waiter and then handed menus.

"Miss Knight, what do you have a taste for?"

"I'm not hungry, but I'd like a cup of hot tea. Calling me Nikkola or Nikki is acceptable."

"Very well, Nikkola. You said you weren't hungry, but the ferocious-looking tiger I see in your eyes appears very hungry to me. How was your flight?"

Continue with the barbed criticisms, and you'll find out how ferocious this tiger can be. "Believe me, it's not hunger. My flight went well. Thank you. There wasn't a single rude passenger aboard."

Nikkola's exaggerated point hit its mark precisely, and with ease, but her statement regarding the flight had stretched the truth more than just a tad, since so many things had occurred. First, she learned that Carmen was trying to transfer to Latham's flight. Then, when she'd served the flight engineers, Blaine's cold staring eyes had shattered her calm. Latham hadn't bothered to acknowledge her at all, which further shattered her calm and her existence. Latham hadn't looked up from the controls and she'd been left to crave his normal enthusiastic greetings.

Like old times, she simply didn't exist for Latham. Just as Blaine had done at the café, perhaps she'd read more into their friendship than she should have. His lie to Blaine might have been a badly missed clue. Her eyes had erected a flood wall to keep the tears from flooding the cockpit. Throughout the flight Nikkola had remained nervous and upset.

"Would you like to go with me to the theater this evening, Nikkola?"

"No," she responded hastily, sharply.

The "no" was a direct hit to his ego. His eyebrows shot up as though they'd been grazed by the sharply spoken two-letter word. Mychal Forrester was not used to being turned down—never so abruptly. Nikkola stared right into his eyes, without flinching. The defiance burning in her lovely orbs knocked him off his high horse. Mychal's arrogance hit the floor with a deafening thud.

Mychal coughed into his white linen napkin to clear his throat. "I'm glad you didn't have to suffer through any mental strain to answer that question, Nikkola." Recovery and the chance to retrieve his arrogance hadn't taken Mychal as long as both of them had expected.

"None whatsoever!" It was several minutes before the hot cup of tea cooled sufficiently enough for Nikkola to drink, but it had seemed like an eternity.

No comeback was necessary from his lips; his eyes took care of it quite nicely. Mychal perused her face with piercing eyes, drying her skin with a heat intensely hotter than the tea. His close scrutiny was daring and unnerving. As he completely dissected her, she could almost feel the blood draining from her dying limbs.

"Since I can't convince you to take me up on my offer of the theater, can I be hopeful of seeing you again, Nikkola?"

Nikkola raised a perfectly arched eyebrow. "Let me sleep on it," she said, her tone surly.

Yet another answer that had taken Mychal by total surprise, only this time he was unable to hide from Nikkola his stunned expression. His unfathomable eyes tried to wage a war with hers, but her eyes shot him down before he could even load his weapon. He found himself digging into his endless repertoire of sarcasm to try to find a way to tilt the scales. Mychal Forrester wanted to knock Nikkola as off balance as she had him.

At some point the conversation between Nikkola and Mychal turned from a game of matching wits and barbed comments to a more personal one. When Mychal shared his business and personal aspirations with her, she was surprised how in depth he was about the personal aspects, learning that he was thirty years old and a graduate of Oxford University. He was from a wealthy African American family who owned many businesses throughout Europe. He was heavily involved in the management and investment end of the family's business firms. He'd never been married, and he didn't see that it was likely to occur in the near future. However, if the right woman came along, he wouldn't hesitate to propose. Mychal wanted a large family to spoil and pamper someday.

The mention of Mychal's family being stockholders in Air International sent Nikkola reeling, thankful that she'd kept her professional demeanor when they'd first met. That he could have her job stayed in the forefront of her mind, though it was an absurd thought. She took only one guess at how he'd obtained her personal information. Since Mychal's family owned stock in the airline she worked for, that bit of information somewhat explained things for Nikkola.

Over two hours had passed when Nikkola politely excused herself. He wrote two personal phone numbers on his business card and handed it to her. Armed with the knowledge as to how Mychal may've gained access to privileged information about her, she didn't see the need to offer anything more about herself; he probably already knew everything worth mentioning.

Rushing into her suite, Nikkola undressed and changed into a gold and forest green paisley print silk gown and robe. She then went into the living room. Picking up a white leather-bound book, she quickly became enraptured with the fairy-tale aspect of the lifestyle of the royal family. When she was halfway through the large volume, the brass knocker hit the door with an obtrusively forceful bang. The thought that it might be Mychal Forrester forced her to prepare for battle. She'd had enough of him for one day, even though, oddly enough, she was mildly attracted to him.

It was not Mychal Forrester but Latham Scott. His powerful sexuality and deep smile had Nikkola fighting for control over her desire to drag him into the suite and into her bed. As the svelte curves of her body were highly visible through the silk attire, he noticed the tautness of her nipples under the thin material. His light brown eyes roved her body hungrily. Nikkola prayed for a heavier robe to drop down from the ceiling to cover her up from his penetrating and obviously lustful gaze.

Latham's eyes were soft and bright. "Nikki, can we talk for a while?"

I'm glad to know you've found your tongue. Remembering that Latham hadn't spoken to her during the entire flight had Nikkola dying from curiosity to hear his explanation. She opened the door for him to come in. "You can go into the living room. I'll be right with you."

As Latham preceded her down the hallway, Nikkola dashed past him, and into the bedroom, where she threw on a pair of baggy sweats.

Nikkola returned to the living room. Latham was at the window, looking down on the York-stone courtyard. She sat in the winged-back chair, so he wouldn't be able to sit right next to her.

Latham moved away from the window and sat down on the rolled-armed love seat facing her. "I want to apologize for ignoring you at work, Nikki. I knew you were concerned about rumors of you and Glen. There are now rumors of you and me, so I didn't want to draw any unnecessary attention to us. Now I realize I drew more attention to us, but only after Blaine made a remark about my not speaking to you. Since we've always exchanged greetings and playful banter while on duty, we should continue to do so. I'm truly sorry. Am I forgiven, Nikkola?"

"Definitely, Latham. I had no idea what was wrong with you. I never would've guessed at your reasons for not at least saying hello to me, but I understand now."

Latham got up and moved swiftly across the room, propping himself on the arm of Nikkola's chair. Lifting her hand up, he pressed a moist kiss into her palm. Flashes of brilliant light exploded in her head as he continued to brush her palm with feathery kisses. Butterflies flew around in her stomach at breakneck speed; trying to calm them down was an impossible task. The lump in her throat bobbed up and down, making it difficult for her to utter a single word.

"Nikkola, I desperately want to kiss you. Is that okay with you?"

Latham's unexpected question drew a loud gasp from Nikkola's quivering lips. "I've heard of kissing cousins, but kissing friends?" Nikkola laughed nervously.

"We can be the first to start the trend," Latham suggested, laughing too.

Without uttering another word, Latham bent his head, tilting Nikkola's face with a finger under her chin. Looking deeply into her eyes, he tenderly covered her mouth with his. He'd only intended it to be a light airy kiss, but when the contact was made, the soft tantalizing sweetness of her mouth blew his good intentions into orbit. His mouth feverishly clamped farther down over hers, locking her lips into an utterly divine prison of heady passion. His tongue probed deeply into her receptive mouth, as his long muscular arms meshed her body tightly against his chest.

In the heat of the intense moment, Latham lifted Nikkola from the chair and situated himself in her spot. He then pulled her down onto his lap. After curling her legs up, she swung them across his lap and then over the arm of the chair. There was no time to think of the promises made between them, or to enforce any limits.

The boundaries of friendship had already been crossed, having been replaced with the deep emotional responses only lovers could lay claim to.

Nikkola's kisses were as intense and heated as Latham's had been, but she froze into a solid mass when he put his hand up under her sweatshirt. She found herself instantly thawing against him, as his hands only touched and caressed her back. Her hands drifted through his smooth hair with relaxed ease, his tender mouth tasting exactly as she'd dreamed. Realizing that she wasn't asleep caused her to murmur softly against his parted lips.

The passion dripping from Latham's glazed eyes was akin to hot, melting candle wax. His eyes burned into her flesh, leaving a blazing trail of wild-blue fire jetting through her entire being.

A distant rapping sound disturbed Latham's unhurried journey to ecstasy. Both realized at the same time that someone was at the door, but neither of them had the willpower to break the sweet enchantment.

As Latham's kisses grew more demanding, the person rapping at the door refused to be ignored. Nikkola gently pried her lips from his, but Latham hungrily recaptured them, before slowly releasing her from the irresistible bondage. Impossibly angered by the untimely intrusion, Nikkola smoothed her clothes and stormed into the hall.

Latham rested his head on the back of the chair to await Nikkola's return. Closing his eyes, he relived every moment of the tenderness he'd just shared with the red-haired beauty.

Standing ramrod straight, wearing a smelting gaze and a sardonic smile, was Mychal Forrester. The crisp, manly smell of his cologne wafted across Nikkola's nose. Momentarily forgetting Latham's presence, she stepped into the hallway. Mychal had that type of effect on her. Nikkola seemed to lose her sense of direction when she was face-to-face with the devil himself.

Cursing Mychal under her breath, Nikkola steeled herself for a clash with the arrogant, self-assured titan. As each blatantly sized up the other, their eyes met in a fiery collision. Nikkola cleared her dry throat, clasping her shaking hands behind her back.

"Are you going to be rude by not inviting me in, or are you entertaining a lover?"

Mychal's question incensed Nikkola. Her fingers itched to slap the cool, smug look off his face. "It would do no good to tell you it's none of your business, so I won't even bother to dignify your question with a response. But maybe you should tell me what the hell you're doing here?"

Nikkola's expletive amused Mychal. He especially enjoyed the fire in her eyes, which perfectly matched her hair color. His laughter was satanic in quality, which briefly gave her cause for alarm. "I came to persuade you to change your position on going with me to the theater. I have a hard time with the word 'no,'" Mychal boasted proudly.

"You're the most arrogant and incorrigible man I've ever come in contact with."

"That I am, Nikkola Knight. Now how about getting dressed up in your finest? I'll be back to pick you up about an hour from now."

Mychal's statement had come with way too much confidence for Nikkola's liking.

"What is it about 'no' that you don't understand, Mychal? Is it the *n* or the *o*?"

"I didn't say I didn't understand it, Nikkola. I just don't know how to accept it as an answer when I want something this badly," he said with candor.

"It sounds like a serious ego problem to me. I can tell

you're used to getting your way, but it won't happen with me. No means no—I don't use the word lightly."

"Nikkola, I *am* used to getting my way. In time, I'll have my way with you. I'll be looking forward it. Until then." Mychal quickly turned on his heel and strode down the hall.

Not knowing if she were coming or going, Nikkola stood rooted to the center of the floor. Her nerves twanged—she was practically overrun with trepidation. Mychal was a madman.

Latham was just making his way to the door when Nikkola stepped back inside. He'd heard the raised voices. Since she was taking so long, curiosity had gotten the best of him.

Concern was etched on his face. "Nikki, is everything okay? Who were you arguing with?"

Mychal's menacing aura hadn't worn off, and her brain had to strain itself to come up with an acceptable response. "My laundry wasn't to my liking and I had a hard time convincing them to take it back, but I managed," she lied. She hated the fact that she'd been reduced to such an evil deception as lying, especially to someone she cared so much about.

"That's surprising. I've always received my clothes back in impeccable condition. I guess everyone messes up once in a while. You should report it to the hotel manager so that it doesn't happen again."

Nikkola looked so distracted. "I will, Latham. Thanks for the suggestion."

Latham wanted to take up where they left off, but she seemed so disoriented to him. "Nikki, I have a few business calls to make, but I'll talk with you later." He kissed her on the shoulder and walked out. Her confused heart wanted him to stay, but her lips remained sorrowfully silent.

While sitting on the sofa, Nikkola reached for the

telephone and then began to dial Glen's number to his suite. She quickly hung up, remembering that he was spending time with friends. Her thoughts turned to Mychal's threats, and she couldn't help wondering why she let him get to her. Still, she had a strange whim to see him again. This was the strangest experience she'd ever had.

What about Latham? Nikkola had wanted him all this time, but perhaps he'd made her wait too long. His seemingly easy disposal of Carmen also had her worried. Would he dispose of her too, when he tired of the game? *No, he's not like that,* she assured herself, feeling as confused as the day was long. Latham didn't seem like the type of man who used women only to discard them.

The rest of the afternoon was eerily quiet, but Nikkola could hear the swishing water rushing from the marble fountain outside her window. Since sunset was still an hour or so away, she decided to jog in Hyde Park. After putting on a sports bra, she tied her hair back and slid into her running shoes. Nikkola grabbed a jacket and headed for the exit.

Outside the hotel, Nikkola broke into an even run, keeping a steady pace until she reached the massive park. Clean air filled her lungs, allowing her to breathe easily. Clearing the melee of thoughts running in every direction in her head was a different matter; Nikkola hoped running would take her attention off her troubles for now.

The park was crowded with people, but Nikkola liked the feeling of not being alone. It was a lot of fun to people-watch. London was an exciting place to be any time of the year. The British were an interesting group of people to observe. After jogging until her joints signaled to her they'd had enough, Nikkola slowly walked back to the hotel.

Chapter 6

The heavy rain pounding against the windowpanes awakened Nikkola from a dreamless sleep. As it was the best sleep she'd had in the last two days, she tried desperately to return to its depths. Reaching over to the nightstand, she flipped on the radio. Restful music drifted from the speakers. Although she couldn't go back to sleep, Nikkola decided to just lie in bed and relax.

Rainy weather in London was par for the course, but she was disappointed since she'd planned to go to Piccadilly Circus and to Harrods to do some serious browsing. Glen had called before she'd retired for the night to inform her that he wouldn't be back until late the next evening. She missed her faithful companion and would be glad for his return.

The brass knocker thudded against the door, causing Nikkola to sit straight up in the bed. Hoping Glen had decided to return early, she threw on a heavy robe and traipsed to the door.

Dressed in navy blue and white sports attire, Latham stood before Nikkola, smiling, his handsome face freshly shaven. Without uttering a word, Latham pulled Nikkola into his arms and then landed a kiss in her disheveled hair.

Nikkola's laughter carried a lilting tinkle. "Is telephone communication unfashionable these days, Captain Latham Scott?"

"Where's your key card, Nikki?"

Nikkola looked puzzled. "Whatever for?"

"Nikki, just let me see your key card. I'll explain later."

"Has everyone lost their darn minds?" Nikkola mumbled under her breath.

Nikkola went back into the bedroom, whisked the key card from its place on the mirrored dresser, and returned to the hallway. Reluctantly, she handed the card to Latham. After taking the key from her hand, he wrapped his other arm around her waist and pulled her out into the corridor. The door instantly slammed shut behind them. Though Nikkola protested loudly, Latham ignored her verbal resistance as he hurried her down the hall to his suite.

After sticking his own key card in the slot on the door, Latham swung it back, and then practically dragged Nikkola inside. He rushed her into the kitchen, where the table was already set, laden with an array of delicious-looking breakfast foods. The centerpiece consisted of a single red rose nestled in a dainty crystal bud base.

Latham grinned broadly. "All for you, Nikkola Knight."

Nikkola stared at the table in wide-eyed wonder. "This is wonderful, Latham, but I haven't even had a chance to brush my teeth or even wash my face. I can't eat breakfast in this state."

Latham ran from the room in haste, returning quickly with a brand new toothbrush and a set of linens, which he handed to Nikkola. "The bathroom is to the right in case you haven't had a suite designed like this one," he instructed softly.

Not knowing what else to do, Nikkola took the offered linens and went into the bathroom. She certainly
couldn't get back into her suite since he had the key.
Nikkola finally had to admit to herself that she was
dying to see what Latham had in store for her next.

Ten minutes later, when Nikkola returned to the
kitchen, Latham pulled out a chair for her and then
poured her a cup of coffee. Saving the best surprise for
last, he took the liberty of kissing her passionately. He
then sat down in the chair across from hers.

The turkey bacon was crisp and the eggs were softly
scrambled, just the way she liked them. Wheat toast was
piled high on a saucer, along with apple butter and jelly
spreads. A pitcher of cold, freshly squeezed orange
juice was in the center of the table.

"Did you prepare all this, Latham?"

"Room service, Nikki. But I did set the table." He
looked proud of his accomplishment.

Nikkola couldn't stop the huge smile from spreading
across her mouth. He seemed so tickled with himself.
"This was really a lovely thing to do, Latham. The table
looks divine. However, I don't agree with the tactics you
used to get me here. 'Please have breakfast with me,
Nikkola,' would've been a tad more appropriate."

"It may have been, but it's such a boring approach
for extending an invitation to such an interesting and
beautiful woman. However, I do have a flair for the dramatic."

Loving his style, Nikkola smiled generously. "For sure.
At any rate, thank you, Latham."

"You're welcome, Nikki. Thanks for being a good
sport."

As Nikkola and Latham eagerly consumed the meal,
their conversation was animated, and there wasn't any
shortage of laughter and teasing. After breakfast, Nikkola
helped Latham clear the table and wash the dishes.

During a playful escapade, they both ended up with soapsuds all over their faces and in their hair.

In the bathroom of her suite Nikkola showered and dressed in casual slacks and a black oversized hand-knit sweater. When Latham had found out that she was going shopping, and since the rainy weather had finally come to a screeching halt, he invited himself along.

In putting the finishing touches on her appearance, Nikkola added a rosy blush to her cheeks and dabbed on the usual clear lip shiner. After a quick appearance check, satisfied with her looks, Nikkola went into the living room to wait for Latham.

Mychal phoned while she was waiting for Latham. During the conversation, she turned down his offer of a late evening dinner. But he'd informed her that he'd keep on trying until she gave in. Before returning the receiver to its place, Nikkola found herself regretting her decision. Besides his dynamite masculinity, she didn't know what it was about Mychal that screwed up her decision-making capabilities and left her feeling like a bratty child in dire need of discipline.

Latham arrived right on time, wearing a black and gray sweater and gray light-wool-blended slacks. A light gray shirt was worn under the sweater and his dark gray leather shoes were freshly polished. The premature gray around the temples gave Latham an elegantly distinguished look.

Holding hands, the couple strolled leisurely to the closest underground station. The sun was hiding out, but as far as Nikkola was concerned Latham could easily command it to come out.

Piccadilly Circus was situated at the center of London's

entertainment area in the West End. The statue of Eros was also located there. Eros was fondly thought of as the god of love. At night Piccadilly Circus was a blaze of dazzling colored neon advertisement billboards. Tourists were mysteriously and eagerly drawn to it. It was once known as the "hub of the empire."

The pair excitedly browsed through numerous stores. Nikkola purchased some reading material and several postcards for her travel album. Because she couldn't always remember which ones she didn't have, she often ended up with duplicates. Harrods, their next stop, was one of the largest, busiest, and most exclusive department stores in Knightsbridge, carrying anything and everything one could imagine.

"Come on, Nikki, let's go to the fragrance bars," Latham suggested.

One entire room carried every type of fragrance one could imagine. Latham had fun spraying Nikkola with several samples. Before too long, she felt like gagging.

"Please, no more," she said in a choked voice. "I already smell like an expensive lady-in-waiting, Latham. My head is starting to kill me."

Nestling his nose in Nikkola's neck, Latham deeply inhaled the variety of scents. "Nikki, you smell good without wearing any fragrance. The perfume only adds an extra touch of intrigue to an already intriguing woman. Everything about you is so fresh."

"The flattery is good, Latham, good for my ego. What other wonderful things do you have to say about me?"

"Well, you're beautiful inside and out, you're charming, you have a great sense of humor, and you actually make my soul laugh uncontrollably. Should I go on?"

Latham's sexy smile had lit up Nikkola's eyes. "Please stop! I don't think I can take any more. If you inflate my ego any more, my head is going to burst wide open. That could be quite a gory mess for you to clean up."

His laughter at Nikkola's comment was loud and cheerful.

Grabbing him by the hand, Nikkola steered him over to the men's fragrance bar. She sniffed at several bottles, but only sprayed him with the ones she found to be sexy and manly. After being misted with several samples, Latham understood why Nikkola hadn't wanted him to shower her with any more perfume. His head was also starting to ache from the tangy-smelling colognes.

By late afternoon, Nikkola and Latham were seated in a small café having what was referred to as a "cuppa," a cup of tea in Great Britain. The British took their teatime serious, serving tea for each and every part of the day and evening. Nikkola's favorite was Earl Grey; Latham preferred De Ceylon orange pekoe. Delicious, hot strawberry-filled scones had been placed in front of them, along with hot tea.

"Are you enjoying the scones and tea, Nikki?"

Nikkola wiped her mouth with the corner of the napkin. "Everything is heavenly. Glen and I enjoy taking tea in different parts of the city. We've even done the dress-up routine required at the more exclusive hotels."

"By the way, where is Glen? I haven't seen him at all since the flight."

"He's visiting some old friends and is supposed to return to the hotel late this evening. I miss him. He's such a wonderful companion. He knows everything there is to know about this country. I've learned so much from Glen," Nikkola expressed with deep sentiment.

"Why don't you hang out with the other female flight attendants, Nikki?"

Nikkola's lashes lowered, veiling the raw pain in her eyes. "In plain terms, I have serious issues of trust. I know that sounds strange coming from a woman, but I have very good reasons to be distrustful."

"I'm surprised to hear you say that, Nikkola, but I'm sure your distrust is well founded. I don't trust many people myself, but I try to keep an open mind. Want to tell me why you feel the way you do?"

"I don't mind telling you. You already know that my relationship with Cyd ended before it really got a chance to get serious. I found out that he was seeing my best friend behind my back. I was devastated by the betrayal of both of them, but my girl's betrayal of our friendship was the hardest part to get over. I wasn't able to eat for weeks. I cried myself a river, and when I did get a grip on myself, I swore I'd never trust anyone. I know I shouldn't lump everyone into one category, but I've seen other things that people do to hurt each other and it makes me so sick."

Latham's smile was sympathetic. "I understand how you feel, Nikkola. I've been betrayed as well, but it wasn't by a friend, so I imagine your pain must run much deeper. Nonetheless, the betrayal hurt like hell. But I got over it. I now know that you have issues of trust, but what about trusting males, Nikki?" After making his statement, Latham realized that a friend had also betrayed him. He'd believed Morgan Carlton had been not only his lover, but also his best friend.

Nikkola eyed Latham with curiosity. "You seem to get over people rather easily. How do you manage to write people off without any regret whatsoever?"

Latham was stung by the barbed comment. "I don't think I deserved that, Nikki. I can only imagine you're referring to Carmen. I only did what had to be done."

Latham's bluntness had put Nikkola on edge. "I apologize. That was an unfair statement. As for the questions about males, I keep a watchful eye on them also. If I had truly been in love with Cyd, I might see things in an entirely different light, Latham. I was happy things were exposed before we had gotten any deeper into our relationship."

"You're fortunate, Nikki. My head was already covered with water, and I was drowning in it by the time I realized Morgan was a fantasy. I only have myself to blame. I ignored so many of the red flags she'd waved in front of me. One would've had to be blind not to see it. Even if I'd been sightless, I should've been able to sense it."

Since Latham hadn't said what the exact deception had been, Nikkola thought it was best not to press the issue. The mention of his ladylove's name was more information than she needed.

"Getting involved with someone is the risk we have to take, or end up being lonely. I'm glad I have such a loyal friend as Glen. He's helped me through a lot and he's always there when I need him, Latham." Nikkola's love for Glen was brimming over in her eyes.

"I'm glad you have him to look out for you. I hope I can one day become as good a friend to you as Glen obviously is." Latham leaned forward in his seat. "I'd like to take you to dinner tonight, Nikkola." He smiled charmingly. "We can also do the dress-up bit."

Nikkola's return smile dazzled Latham. "We have a date, Captain Scott."

Before returning to her hotel suite, Nikkola stopped by the front desk to see if she had a message from Glen. They were in the habit of leaving messages for one another if something unexpected would occur. There were none from Glen, but the clerk handed her two from Mychal. When she realized whom they were from, without reading them, Nikkola folded them and stuck them in her jacket pocket. Latham had already gone to his quarters. Before departing, he had asked Nikkola to be ready by seven o'clock.

* * *

The silent vacuum of the suite suddenly made Nikkola feel isolated and lonely. Normally she loved being alone and having time for herself, but the stillness seemed almost eerie. Walking across the room, she unlatched the windows and threw them open. In eager anticipation, she waited for the busy sounds from the street traffic to sweep into the quiet room. As Nikkola deeply inhaled the rain-washed air, the cool breeze tugged playfully at her hair and skin.

Nikkola went into the bedroom. Sensing that she and Latham might be out late, aware of their early afternoon flight schedule, Nikkola packed all the things she wouldn't need. Removing the plastic covering from her flight uniform, she hung it on the back of the door and laid out her clean undergarments. Once she pulled the two messages from her jacket pocket, she hung it up. While sitting on the bed, she perused the rather lengthy notes from Mychal.

As a flight attendant, Nikkola was always prepared for the expected and unexpected. Receiving numerous invitations to dinners and other gala affairs was almost an everyday occurrence for most flight crew members. While others saw it as a part of the territory and an extra- added benefit of the trade, Nikkola accepted very few invitations, yet she often brought along first-class evening apparel just in case a special occasion to her liking should arise.

Nikkola expected the evening with Latham Scott to indeed be special.

Nikkola greeted Latham at the door, wearing an elegant black French faille suit with a jabot-ruffled jacket, adorned with gold tone buttons; the skirt had a slight back vent. Her long hair was swept upward in a pile of loose curls, with a few soft tendrils falling smoothly around her face and nape. Just the right amount of blush and lip-gloss enhanced her natural beauty without disturbing the fresh, healthy glow of her skin.

Latham's eyes were filled with excitement. "You look beautiful, Nikkola. I've never seen you dressed up before. I can certainly see what I've been missing." Bending his head, Latham placed a soft, moist kiss onto Nikkola's slightly parted mouth.

"Thanks, Latham! You're looking mighty hot yourself. Your black suit is definitely working for you. I'll be the envy of every female." She gave him a dazzling smile.

The cab safely deposited Nikkola and Latham in front of the posh London Towers Restaurant. The decor of the five-star establishment was very old English. Each of the fine linen-dressed tables was intimate, softly lit with a single candle and lovely floral arrangement.

The waiter arrived almost immediately. Before long, a superbly prepared meal of roast lamb, new potatoes, and creamed spinach was placed in front of them. They also enjoyed very dry champagne along with the meal. For dessert, they devoured a mouthwatering English pudding.

After the second glass of champagne, Nikkola began to bubble over with effervescence, her eyes shining brightly. Latham was unequivocally under her enchanting spell. Each time he heard her effervescent laughter, he felt enchanted, bewitched.

Soft music drifted into Nikkola's ears. When Latham reached for her hand to dance, she floated from her seat and into his waiting arms. He then guided her onto the small dance floor. As he pulled her in close, her feet practically left the ground. She wasn't sure if the floating sensation came from the champagne or his close proximity. That she felt his heart beating through the material of her attire set sensual thoughts of him ablaze.

As Latham's arms encircled Nikkola's slim waist, her head was magnetically drawn to his chest. Lacing his fingers under the curls at her nape, he pressed his lips to her temple. Wrapping her arms around his waist, she splayed her fingers across the strong muscles of his upper back.

Nikkola and Latham moved over the dance floor with grace and style. With each step taken, they melded themselves closer together, until they couldn't get any closer. Shutting their eyes, they blocked out the rest of world. In perfect tune with the seductive rhythm of the music, they flowed together harmoniously. Both Nikkola and Latham were totally unaware that the music had stopped until Latham felt a firm tap on his shoulder.

Latham's eyes instantly narrowed and darkened at the tall, imposing man standing eye to eye with him. All movement was stilled. When Nikkola finally opened her eyes, she immediately forced them shut, praying that Mychal Forrester was only a mere vision of her champagne-saturated mind. But when she reopened them, Mychal's lazy smile openly taunted her.

"Old chap, would you mind if I cut in?" Mychal asked Latham in an acid-laced tone.

Latham looked questioningly at Nikkola, but she couldn't respond. Although he tried to read her near blank expression, he failed. "That'll have to be up to the lady," Latham responded icily. "Nikki, do you want to dance with this man? I'm sorry, I didn't get your name," Latham said to Mychal.

"How perceptive of you, since none was given," Mychal responded rudely.

Nikkola dug her nails into Latham's arm, vehemently shaking her head in the negative. She was in a state of turmoil, although she'd once again felt the need to be obedient to Mychal's wishes. Latham's presence had bolstered her courage, giving her the strength to deny Mychal's request.

"Please, can we return to the table, Latham?" Nikkola asked, her voice cracking badly.

Latham saw the turbulence in her eyes, wondering how Nikkola and this obnoxious man were involved. He noticed the odd chemistry between them. That totally unnerved him.

Pushing past Mychal without further comment, Latham led a stunned Nikkola back to the table. Both of them could feel the daggers from Mychal's eyes ruthlessly stabbing them in the back. Mychal was the last person Nikkola had expected to see and his presence had sent her into total shock.

Once they were seated, Latham covered Nikkola's trembling hand with his. "You seem so shaken by him, Nikki. Who is he?"

Nikkola stole a glance at the floor, but all she saw was Mychal's retreating form. Relieved that he'd decided to leave without further incident, she finally swallowed the lump in her throat. "He's the passenger I spilled the coffee on. His name is Mychal Forrester."

Looking enraged, Latham suddenly turned a pale shade of gray.

The anger in Latham's eyes gave Nikkola an uneasy feeling. "Do you know him, Latham?"

"No, but I've heard of him! He has quite a reputation as a ladies' man." *So, I've finally met the man that Morgan deceived me with.* The knowledge left Latham feeling awfully bitter inside.

The rest of the evening turned out into a big disappointment for Nikkola and Latham. He became moody and withdrawn, while Nikkola couldn't begin to think straight. She felt guilty for not having told Latham about Mychal sooner. Mychal had effectively and purposely destroyed the romantic aura between the two. And even though Latham had never seen Mychal, he had known exactly who Captain Latham Scott was from seeing him with Morgan.

Now that they were back at the hotel, Nikkola and Latham seemed to have recovered somewhat from the disturbing events at the restaurant. Nikkola invited Latham to her suite. Surprising her, he eagerly accepted the invitation.

In need of something to calm her nerves, Nikkola brewed a cup of coffee for herself and laced it with a generous amount of brandy. Knowing that Latham had to fly, she wouldn't think of offering him anything stronger than hot chocolate this late in the evening. As he was an extremely conscientious pilot, Nikkola knew he wouldn't have accepted it anyway.

Carrying the tray into the living room, Nikkola set it on the coffee table. She then handed a cup to Latham. Their fingers touched as he received the mug from Nikkola. His eyes turned soft and seductive. After taking one sip of the hot liquid, he returned it to the tray.

Gently taking Nikkola's cup from her hand, Latham set it down on the tray. He then pulled Nikkola into his arms. The fear of losing her to Mychal caused him to lose all thought of taking their relationship slow. Nikkola belonged with him, only with him. Latham's desire to completely possess Nikkola was compelling.

With steady fingers, Latham loosened Nikkola's hair, entwining them in its thickness. His lips trailed hot kisses up and down her throat. Taking her soft moans as encouragement, he pressed her back against the sofa, running his hands gently over her thighs and legs.

The heat in the pit of Nikkola's stomach flared wildly. Knowing that he could easily have his way with her was bothersome. The thought of protection was the next thing that came to her mind. The fear of destroying their friendship finally caused her to push him away. "We can't!"

Latham's eyes blazed with unsatisfied ecstasy. He felt as though cold water had been dumped on his head, but it did nothing to quell the heated hunger he felt for Nikkola's intimate touch. "Are you scared of me, Nikki?"

"No, but I'm frightened for myself. Neither of us is protected, not to mention that it's much too soon for us to be involved this way."

Nikkola's reasoning returned Latham's sanity, making him glad that it wasn't because she didn't find him desirable. "Are you telling me you're an old-fashioned girl?"

"I'm a responsible girl. And if we make love right now, that just might spoil our new friendship. We don't want that to happen. Do we?"

"No, Nikki, we don't want that to happen." His reasons for wanting to make her all his own skipped across his mind, making him feel sorry and a little bit ashamed.

"We should probably call it a night, Latham. We have a big day ahead of us tomorrow."

After getting to his feet, Latham pulled Nikkola up from the sofa. One long arm wrapped itself around her slender shoulders. "I'm going to leave at your request, but will you agree to see me when we're back at home? I'm free tomorrow evening and the evening afterward. You can opt for both." Burying his lips in her hair, Latham laughed softly.

"I'm opting for both, Latham. Now go and get some rest. Tomorrow my life will be in your capable hands!"

Tilting Nikkola's head back, Latham seared his lips onto hers. The passionate kiss lasted for several minutes, which nearly had Nikkola changing her mind about his leaving. She somehow managed to break their impassioned embrace and steer him out the door, watching as he crept down the hall toward his suite. After hearing his door open and close, she stepped back inside.

While stripping her clothes away, Nikkola entered the bedroom. Without turning on the light, she slipped between the cool, crisp linens. Though she had opted not to sleep with Latham, nothing could keep them apart in her dreams.

Chapter 7

The flight back to Dulles had been choppy with turbulence and the seat-belt sign had been on a good part of the way. Latham had grown weary from the flight, both mentally and physically. As soon as he'd landed the plane at Dulles, he had taken off without speaking to anyone.

While seated in the living room of his home, Morgan Carlton was heavily on his mind. He recalled how much he'd been in love with her and how he'd seriously thought she'd returned those feelings. Weeks before she'd told him it was over, he remembered how strange she'd been acting. Latham had questioned her behavior many times, but Morgan had put him off.

Morgan had refused to talk about their upcoming marriage and she'd refused to be pinned down to a specific wedding date. Then, she'd come to his home very late at night, to inform him that she was going to marry a man named Mychal Forrester. She told him how they'd been seeing each other over the past several weeks, and that she had already fallen in love with him.

Latham later learned from friends how Morgan had come to know Mychal Forrester. She had become so different after meeting him. However, Morgan had never told Latham any of the details about her relationship with Forrester. He hadn't seen her since that painful night. Now Latham wanted to know what really happened between Morgan and Forrester and why Mychal was now chasing Nikkola Knight. He reached for the phone and punched in the familiar seven digits. He then laid his head back against the cushioned sofa. When a deep male voice came over the line, Latham sighed, glad that his good friend, Joe Meyers, was not out on a trip.

"Joe, it's Latham. How's it going, pal?"

"Hey, buddy. I thought you'd fallen off the face of the earth. Long time no hear. What's on your mind, Latham?"

"Morgan Carlton," Latham said tonelessly. "Have you heard from her, Joe?"

"I've seen her a few times, but not since last year. I heard her engagement fell through and that she nearly had a nervous breakdown afterward. Why are you asking?"

"Why didn't you tell me this before?"

"I didn't think you would want to know, Latham. She hurt you pretty badly, you know. I was sure you wouldn't want to hear about anything that had to do with her."

"Wasn't Mychal Forrester the name of the guy she'd gotten herself so involved with?"

"Yeah, that sounds like the name. I never saw the guy, but Al Jennings saw them at a New Year's ball in Washington. He said the guy was really rude and stuck on himself. Al told me that he didn't know how Morgan was going to manage living with someone who thought he was prettier than she was." Joe laughed. "Are you still hung up on her, man?"

"Not in the least. It seems Mychal Forrester is interested in the girl I'm presently dating. I'm beginning to think we have the same taste in women. Nikkola Knight is as beautiful as Morgan, but she has a lovely heart to match. Nikki didn't tell me much about Forrester, but she seems intrigued with him. I felt outrageously jealous over it. I'm going to bring Nikki around for you to meet, then you'll understand. She's every man's dream."

"Be careful—and keep your shirt on, pal. You sound really excited about this Nikki. I'm looking forward to meeting her. What does she do for a living?"

Knowing Joe would find it amusing, his dating another flight attendant, Latham chuckled under his breath. "She's a flight attendant on my crew." There was a slight edge to Latham's tone despite the twinkle in his eyes.

"Oh! I hope you have more in common with her than you did with Carmen. I knew your relationship with Carmen was going to be disastrous from the start. I'm surprised it survived as long as it did. That is, if you can call a few months long."

"Nikki and I have a lot of things in common and I plan to explore each and every one of them. I didn't get into this relationship without much thought. Got to run. I'll be in touch."

Latham hung up the phone. As he thought of Nikkola, her smile lit a touch of warmth deep inside him. She was every man's dream, just as he'd told Al; she was certainly his dream girl.

How was it possible that she was attracted to both Latham and Mychal since they were total opposites? Latham was warm, kind, and sensitive; Mychal was cold, rude, and just plain impossible, yet she found his arrogance sexy and mysterious. Did she imagine more than just a little tension between Latham and Mychal that night, or was she just flattering herself? Latham had said he didn't know Mychal, but if Mychal's family owned a chunk of Air International it was possible Latham had heard more about Mychal than him just being a ladies' man.

Not having seen much of Glen during their layover in London, Nikkola turned her thoughts to her best friend. Glen had been preoccupied during the entire flight and on the ride home. She was worried about him. Feeling the need to find out what was on Glen's mind, she decided to pay him a surprise visit. Nikkola couldn't rest until she found out what was going on with her dear friend.

While standing at Glen's door, Nikkola seemed disinclined to ring the bell. Perhaps he had company. As she turned to leave, Glen's door was flung wide open.

"Nikki!" Glen yelled out. Nikkola turned around and smiled. "I was just coming to see you. Where you going, girl?"

"I thought I should go home and call first, Glen. I didn't know if you had company or not."

"Get in here, woman! You're always welcome here, whether I have company or not."

Glen hugged Nikkola when she came within reach. Leading her by the hand, Glen moved into the kitchen, where he pulled out a chair for Nikkola to be seated. Opening the refrigerator door, he pulled out a thermos of iced tea and poured his guest and himself a tall glass. Glen then set out some freshly baked oatmeal cookies.

"We've only been home a few hours and you've managed to bake cookies already! I wish I had as much energy as you do, Glen. I've been lazing around my place and haven't accomplished one solitary thing."

"Keeping busy takes my mind off of my troubles, Nikki."

Noticing the tiny stress lines forming at the corners

of his bright eyes, Nikkola eyed Glen worriedly. "What troubles, Glen?"

"Nothing serious, Nikki, but I've made a decision to return to reservations. I'm just not feeling well these days. Flying is taking a lot out of me lately. I don't know what's wrong with me, but I imagine the crew will start to speculate about that, too. You know that I'm a very private person, Nikki, and if I have a serious malady I won't feel comfortable sharing it with everyone." A pained expression crossed his face.

Nikkola reached for his hand and rubbed it soothingly. "You really are feeling bad, aren't you? When you told me you thought it was just a stomach flu, I didn't get all that worried. But now I don't know what to think. Are you sure about returning to reservations, Glen? I can't imagine flying without you, but I want what's best for you. Has something happened that you haven't told me about? Do you have a definitive diagnosis that you're not ready to talk about?"

Glen pushed his hair back from his forehead, sighing audibly. "No to both questions, Nikki. But I'm really concerned about my health, especially the unexplainable fatigue. Then there's a whisper here and there about you and me as an item, and Blaine has been looking at us with glaring resentment. I'm probably just being paranoid about everything. I've been racking my brain for days trying to figure out why all this is happening now. We've only been close for the past two years. And I've never felt sick like this before."

"Glen, don't let the crew get to you! As for your illness, I'm concerned, but you're strong, and I know you can handle anyone or anything that comes your way. However, you do need to closely monitor your health. Please give these things more thought before you go running back to a job that you hated."

Arising from his chair, Glen walked over to the window. Moving the curtains aside, he looked down on the flowery show of the complex landscaping. Walking up behind him, Nikkola put her arms around his waist, hugging him close to her. "Glen, let's just squash all the rumors and run away and get married. If it turns out that you're really ill, I can take good care of you."

Glen squirmed his way around to face Nikkola. With tears shining in his eyes, he pressed her head firmly against his broad chest. "Nikki, you're incredibly insane. And you're the most adorable woman I've ever known. The man who lands you will be inconceivably blessed. I'm rooting for Latham. I somehow sense that Mychal Forrester is not deserving of a precious woman like you. I promise to keep a close watch on my health, but I'd never let you marry me just so you could take care of me. I'm probably blowing the health situation all out of proportion. It might turn out to be nothing at all."

Nikkola lovingly stroked Glen's back, as she looked up at him with visible love and admiration showing in her hazel eyes. "I'd take care of you whether we got married or not. You got it like that with me. Besides, I was just talking from a sentimental place. A love affair between us might ruin our wonderful friendship. I'd never want that to happen. We're too much like brother and sister for us to take it any further than what we have now."

Glen grinned. "You're right, but I have wondered a time or two what it would be like if we fell in love with each other. I think it would be awesome if we didn't love each other like family."

Laughing at the absurdity of their conversation, Nikkola and Glen held each other in a warm embrace, happy and content in knowing that their backs were definitely covered by each other.

In the hallway, near the laundry room in her condo, Nikkola set up the ironing board. As it was only a few hours away from Latham's arrival, she had to rush through the few items of laundry that needed ironing. Compromising thoughts of Latham had her deeply mesmerized, causing her to burn the hem of the gold shirt she'd planned to wear. Angrily, she pulled the iron plug from the wall and then put the unfinished laundry away. She then wandered into the living room, where she sat on the sofa to give the torrid thoughts of Latham her undivided attention.

While dressing in dark brown dress slacks and the gold shirt she'd ironed, Nikkola shoved the burnt hemline deep into her pants, confident that Latham wouldn't see the bottom of it, *unless things get hot and heavy*. Laughter crinkled the corners of her eyes.

Arriving right on time, Nikkola opened the door to a smiling Latham. As he immediately sought out her mouth, her earlier thoughts sailed gently through her brain. As Latham crushed his mouth against Nikkola's, he could smell the sweet scent of her hair and the dangerously sexy perfume she wore. Her hands boldly roamed across his soft burgundy sweater he wore. Getting away from her control, her fingers worked their way down to rub the inflexible muscled thigh underneath the dark blue slacks. A shudder washed through him as her soft touch aroused him.

Once Latham was able to tear himself away from Nikkola, he steered her toward the living room and then pulled her down on the sofa next to him. "You smell wonderful, Nikki. I could lose myself in the sweet scent of your hair and body. How's your day been?"

As Nikkola suddenly began to withdraw into herself, she shook off the desire to do so.

Latham read the anguish in her lovely eyes. "What's wrong, Nikki?"

"It's Glen," she said hesitantly.

The sad expression on her face made Latham flinch in pain. "What's wrong with Glen?"

Picking up the picture of her and Glen off the end table, Nikkola stared at it with crystal tears in her eyes. As they were dressed in their flight uniforms, she recalled exactly when they'd taken the photo. The memory of that happy time forced a smile to Nikkola's turned-down mouth.

"I hope it's nothing serious, but he's not feeling a bit well. I'm as concerned for him as he is for himself. He hasn't even told me all of his symptoms, just that he has no appetite and that he suffers with major fatigue. All the rumors going around about us are taking a toll on him, too. Glen's really a sensitive guy. He's even thinking of transferring back to reservations, and I know how he hates that job." Nikkola took a deep breath to calm her jangled nerves.

"Nikki, I can see your being concerned about his health, but why are you and Glen really so concerned about these silly rumors? You shouldn't be, you know. They're just rumors. I'm sorry I even asked you about your relationship with Glen." Latham's words were so soft and kind.

"It's just that he's being hurt by the rumors. He's the type that is deeply affected over the least little thing. He also gets very hurt if someone does something to hurt me. I made the mistake of telling him what Blaine did at the café. Glen was really ready to take up arms over that one."

Latham brushed his hands down over his thighs. Shifting his position slightly, he moved closer to Nikkola. "Nikki, have you and Glen ever been emotionally involved? You don't have to answer, but I'm sure I already know the truth."

"And what truth is that?" Nikkola successfully hid the shock his question had produced.

Leaning over, Latham kissed the tip of Nikkola's nose. "It's not normal for a guy to be so sensitive about just a friend. Something tells me Glen is in love with you, and that matters a lot to me. Glen seems like a super guy, but if we're to continue in this relationship don't you think I should know if there's ever been anything romantic between you? I hope you know you can trust me with anything, Nikki. I have no reason to want to pull you and Glen's friendship apart if that's all it is. I just want to know that you aren't now or if you've ever had an affair with him."

Moving away from Latham, Nikkola looked at him incredulously. Her attempted laughter at his comments was fraught with anxiety. "This is an extremely interesting conversation we're having, since I asked Glen to marry me only a short time ago."

Latham stared at Nikkola with open skepticism. *Was she telling him that she and Glen were in fact in love with each other? Or had he just totally put both of his big feet into his mouth?*

"What are you saying to me, Nikki? Why would you do something like that? Are you really in love with Glen?" he asked with unduly curiosity. "What's up with us? Am I being played here?"

As Nikkola shrugged her shoulders, the Spanish Inquisition came to her mind. "That's not the case at all. Glen and I aren't *in* love either, but we do love each other very much. Just because a guy is sensitive to his best friend doesn't mean he's in love with her. My father is very strong and masculine, but he will cry in a minute, which makes him sensitive in my opinion. Despite his sensitivity, Glen Taylor is as much man as you are. So, are you saying that you're not sensitive?"

Latham looked deeply into Nikkola's eyes. "I'm sorry, Nikki. I guess I shouldn't have taken my curiosity there. I just don't understand all the hysteria over the rumors about you and him. That's what makes me continue to wonder if you're involved with him beyond friendship."

Cupping Latham's face between her hands, Nikkola

boldly assaulted his lips with a brutal but sensuous kiss. Pulling slightly back from him, she rubbed her thumb seductively across his lower lip. "Does that answer all of your questions, Captain Scott?"

Without directly answering all of Latham's questions, Nikkola was able to supply him with the response to at least the most important one. He knew she couldn't be in love with someone else and kiss him in such a passionate way. Groaning with pleasure, Latham gathered Nikkola against the strength of his chest. His lips found a way to tell her exactly how he felt about her. They were confident in their feelings for each other, and the evening began to bloom with unbridled passion.

Later, at Latham's request, Nikkola told him all that she knew about Mychal Forrester. He then told her the story about the demise of his love for Morgan Carlton, along with the reasons for his fear of beautiful women.

Nikkola and Latham had also shared stories of their families. Nikkola learned that Latham was an only child, just like herself. His parents were retired, like hers, and living in Europe. He had then kept her on the edge of her seat by sharing with her several more life-endangering military missions. Latham's love for flying was evident in the emotionally charged way he'd voiced his valiant stories to Nikkola.

Nikkola had found it easy to share with Latham her rewarding but often-troubled days as a social worker, speaking poignantly on the sad social and economic plights of her clients. Nikkola then shared with Latham her reasons for resigning from her position.

By the end of the conversation, the couple had found out that they shared a serious passion for many of the same things. They were both advocates for social reform. However, both kept a few serious revelations to themselves. Nikkola hadn't discussed the crazy attraction she felt for Mychal. And he'd held back the name of the person Morgan had become seriously involved with while they'd been engaged—Mychal Forrester.

Nikkola and Latham had also come to realize that they each had a lot of personal things to work through before they could move their relationship up to the next level.

It was three in the morning before Nikkola's and Latham's decision to part company had been made. They'd also set a time for later in the day to see each other again. Their evening had been filled with an incredible amount of straightforward conversation and had ended with strong feelings of trust.

Latham was on cloud nine as he sped toward his home. He had completely put Morgan Carlton and their painful separation from his memory, allowing only the memories of Nikkola to thoroughly saturate his mind. He planned to spend the upcoming hours, days, and weeks discovering the hidden mysteries locked deeply inside Nikkola. Latham desired to unlock her mysteries and hopefully allow love to flow over into each other's hearts.

Basking in the memories of the evening, Nikkola had decided to stay up for a short while after Latham had left. She could still smell his cologne in the air and could feel his strong, loving arms wrapped around her. She later slept with Latham tucked away peacefully in her heart, hoping to awaken with great anticipation and excitement of sharing the many hours that lay ahead. When the early morning brought the sunrise over the horizon, she hoped it would be a new day for them.

Thinking it was Latham, Nikkola ran to the door to fling herself into his arms. Instead, she landed in Mychal's.

With all the careful plans she and Latham had made for their day together, the one thing she hadn't planned on was for Mychal Forrester to show up at her place.

Mychal smiled brightly. "Now that's what I call a hell of a greeting. I have a sneaky suspicion that these aren't the arms you thought you were running into, but I hope to change all that in due time."

Nikkola's mouth was still gaping wide from the shock of seeing Mychal, which caused him to take advantage of her parted lips. Holding her head firmly in place, he continued to kiss her fervently, though she struggled to ward him off.

Finally managing to break free of Mychal's amorous embrace, Nikkola rounded on him with maddening fury. "You can't come in here and take advantage of me this way." She tried to push him back into the hallway and close the door, but he stuck his foot in its path. Massaging her bruised lips, she glared at him. "Just who in the hell do you think you are, Mychal Forrester?"

"You just answered your own question, Nikkola Knight. If you don't fully open this door, I'm going to set off the alarm for this entire building. What will your neighbors think of you then?"

Knowing exactly what type of trouble Mychal was capable of causing, Nikkola stood aside to let him enter. After strutting arrogantly into the hallway, he moved through Nikkola's place as though he owned it. As his sharp eyes took in the elegant furnishings, he seemed pleased with her excellent taste in decor. When he noticed the picnic basket on the dining table, he realized that Nikkola was about to have a lazy afternoon in the park with someone. Mychal easily guessed who that someone was.

Mychal turned to face Nikkola, unnerving her with the suspicious look in his eyes. "What time are you expecting him?"

Mychal's straight-to-the-point question caught Nikkola

off guard. If only she had the nerve to slap his arrogant face. Knowing Mychal would probably return the favor was what kept Nikkola's fists balled tightly at her side. "Who's him?" she asked, attempting to feign ignorance.

"Do I look stupid to you, Nikkola? On second thought, don't answer that. From the look on your face, I can see that your response is only going to get you into more trouble. I can also see that you already have plans. However, I expect to have dinner with you tomorrow evening. I'll pick you up at seven. If you aren't here, I'll camp outside on your doorstep until you have the good sense to return home," Mychal warned Nikkola unblinkingly.

Nikkola's jaw had long since dropped to the floor; she could think of no way to retrieve it.

Turning his charm back on, Mychal tossed Nikkola a bright smile. "May I use your phone, Nikkola? In private?"

With anger staining her cheeks, Nikkola spun around and ran into the other room.

Once Mychal located the kitchen-wall phone, he picked up the receiver and dialed. Minutes later, after finishing his conversation, Mychal went in search of the woman he'd set out to conquer. He found Nikkola seated in the living room.

"I'll see you tomorrow at seven, Nikkola." Without so much as a wave of his hand, Mychal turned on his heels and left.

Had it been anyone else Nikkola would've immediately called security. With Mychal, it wouldn't have done anything but cause her further embarrassment. She could only imagine the things he would've said to security, things that might be her undoing. It might've been hard for her to face anyone in the building ever again. Mychal's threats weren't to be taken lightly. His arrogance and selfishness were controllable by no one other than God.

Like a frightened child, Nikkola peeked around the

corner to see if the big, bad ogre of her childhood nightmares was really gone. Large tears slid down her face in relief.

Within minutes, Nikkola found herself laughing hysterically. In all Mychal's rudeness, he still found a way to be devilish and charming, all at the same time. She'd never been pursued in this manner, or ever by someone as powerful as Mychal Forrester seemed to be. Nikkola wanted badly to set up Mychal for the next evening, but she was afraid it would only backfire and that she'd become the victim of her own devilish schemes.

Walking into the bathroom, Nikkola wet a washcloth and washed away the evidence of her unsettling encounter with Mychal. After repairing the damage as best as she could, she returned to the living room and curled up on the sofa, her mind turning over and over like the blades of a massive fan. Nikkola suddenly smiled; she had figured out a way to beat Mychal at his own game. Picking up the phone, Nikkola began to put her shrewd plans into action.

With everything settled in her mind, her devious plans all worked out, Nikkola eagerly watched out the window for Latham to arrive.

Latham spread the large striped blanket under a massive oak tree located near the edge of the lake. Nikkola carefully placed the wicker basket down and reached inside to empty its contents. The menu consisted of chicken salad sandwiches on rye, macaroni salad, and cherry tomatoes; celery and carrot sticks were cut in thin strips. Latham had brought along a bottle of chilled white wine and Nikkola had prepared a cheesecake with lemon topping for dessert.

As Latham opened the wine, Nikkola pulled out the paper plates and plastic utensils. When she handed him the two clear plastic wineglasses, Latham poured a generous amount of wine into each one. After sticking a glass in Nikkola's hand, he lifted his in a toast. "To many more lazy days in the park and countless wonderful times in each other's company."

"Hear, hear," she uttered enthusiastically.

The smiling couple then touched the plastic glasses against one another. While staring at each other over the glass rims, they slowly sipped on the sweet-tasting liquid. Latham had also brought along a portable radio, which he turned on and then tuned to his favorite station, one that only played soft love songs. Latham desired to put Nikkola in a romantic mood.

The soft music, clear blue skies, a lake, and a cool breeze, accompanied with the delicious meal, were the ideal setting for sweet whispers and tender caresses to pass between Nikkola and Latham. When a slow song they both loved came drifting from the radio, Latham pulled Nikkola up from the blanket and nestled her safely into his arms, slowly dancing her about under the old oak tree. He buried his face in her hair, as her gentle hands tightened around his waist. The cool breeze sang a song of its own, gently strumming its tune through Nikkola's curly hair.

Latham kissed Nikkola's forehead. "I feel as though I've wasted so much precious time, Nikki. Time that I could've been spending alone with you," he softly whispered into her hair.

"It wasn't wasted, Latham. There is a time and a season for everything."

"Especially a time for love, Nikki. I can fall in love with you so easily. Do you think you can ever come to love me?"

Nikkola's hand moved from his waist, flitted tenderly across his suntanned cheek, and then moved upward through his wind-tossed hair. "You'll have to ask my heart that question, Latham," she whispered softly against his mouth.

Lowering his head, Latham asked the question of Nikkola's thundering heart. Smiling from the response he felt her heart had given him, Latham possessed her mouth with an erotic kiss.

Nikkola looked up into Latham's eyes. "What did my heart say to you, Latham?"

"Five loud thumps and a heavy sigh. The five thumps meant, yes, I can love you; the heavy sigh stood for forever."

"Hmm, I'm going to have a talk with that old heart of mine. Maybe I should listen to yours as well." She put her ear up to his heart; the steady beat quickly became hypnotic to her senses. She found herself wanting to stay in his arms forever. "Your heart is very encouraging, Latham Scott."

"Good! That must mean I'm in tune with it. Close your eyes, Nikki, and let love take us over. There's no one here but you and me."

Obeying Latham's request, Nikkola let her lashes sweep over her eyes. Simultaneously, she felt as though she were at one with the man holding her so intimately close. The romantic surroundings blotted everything from their minds, except summer days of glorious outings and warm, sensuous nights of passionate lovemaking and sinful thrills.

Returning to the blanket a short time later, Nikkola and Latham eagerly locked each other up in a tight embrace, searching for a place in each other's hearts. The sun later caught them sleeping as it swooped downward in a blinding array of dazzling colors.

Chapter 8

Nikkola had spent the better part of the morning putting her devious plans for Mychal Forrester into motion. She prepared a lovely dinner, baked a chocolate cake, and had iced it with creamy chocolate fudge. The table was set with fine linen, china, and crystal. A bottle of Asti Spumante was chilling in the refrigerator, along with a tray of raw, bite-sized vegetables.

After relaxing in a hot bubble bath, Nikkola dressed in one of her sexiest dresses. She then arranged her hair in a loose, sophisticated style. Humming softly to herself, she moved about her place with an enthusiasm she couldn't believe. Hoping to successfully set up Mychal Forrester was largely responsible for her excitable mood. She didn't know that deception could feel this good. She guessed that Mychal knew all about how good it felt since she believed him to be the master of deception. If Nikkola had her way, Mychal would get a good dose of his own bitter medicine.

Oh, he does make good on his threats, Nikkola thought, when the doorbell rang.

Inhaling deeply, Nikkola opened the door with a happy smile plastered falsely on her face. Mychal's eyes bravely, heatedly roved over her body. His cunning smile made her wish she'd never thought of trying to deceive the devil himself. Leaning forward, he kissed her glossy mouth. Mychal then handed her a lovely bouquet of spring flowers.

"Welcome, Mychal," she said enthusiastically. "Thank you for the beautiful flowers."

"You look gorgeous! Are you ready to go, Nikkola?"

"Mychal, I've taken the liberty of preparing a wonderful meal for us. We eat out so often, I thought a home-cooked meal would do us both good. We'll be more comfortable here."

Mychal looked genuinely pleased, yet he was wary of Nikkola's sudden change in attitude. After seeing him comfortably seated, she offered him a glass of wine before dinner, but he politely declined. Nikkola then excused herself to place the meal on the table.

Giggling to herself nervously, Nikkola placed the baked chicken and potatoes on the table. She then returned to the kitchen for the hot vegetables and bread. Once she'd looked over the table to see that everything was in place, she called her guest to dinner. As Mychal entered the dining area, Nikkola was just lighting the candles.

Mychal leaned a shoulder against the doorjamb, admiring the romantic setting. "You set a beautiful table, Nikkola. I like what I see so far."

Mychal moved farther into the room and pulled out a chair for Nikkola. Like the man of the universe he imagined himself to be, he sat at the head of the table. After handing him the wine to open, she handed him each glass to fill. When his hand briefly touched hers, she could feel the fire from his touch scorching her hand. Catching fire from the redheaded devil was a bit scary.

Right on cue, the doorbell rang again. Shrugging her shoulders, Nikkola smiled convincingly. Excusing herself, she started for the door. His dark brooding eyes followed her all the way. After she opened the door, Nikkola quickly turned to see the expression on Mychal's face when Sister Ingrid, Sister Maria, and Cydnee entered the doorway. She was not at all disappointed by the shocked expression he wore. Nikkola flashed Mychal a sarcastically triumphant smile, much like the one she'd given Latham at the health club in London.

Cydnee flew into Nikkola's outstretched arms. "I'm so glad you invited us to dinner," Cydnee screeched happily. I've been missing you."

"And I you," Nikkola responded cheerfully. "Sisters, I'm glad that you could bring Cydnee over." The two women smiled and kissed Nikkola's cheek. "Dinner is on the table already. I also have another guest dining with us this evening."

Nikkola led her company into the dining room. Mychal politely stood until all were seated. Once she'd introduced everyone, the hostess ran into the kitchen to get the other plates, praying that Cydnee wouldn't ask a single thing about Latham. Mychal was already far too annoyed with her.

All through dinner, Nikkola thought that Mychal Forrester was probably the quietest he'd ever been in his life. The formidable sisters in full habit were enough to quiet even the Pope. But she could tell that he was fuming inside. Nikkola imagined that he had already sworn to get even with her at least a dozen times, yet the expression in Mychal's eyes seemed to suggest that he was very impressed by the clever way she'd so thoroughly duped him.

The full meal and the dessert were eaten with a keen appreciation for Nikkola's culinary talents. Not allowing Mychal to hold his silence for very long, the sisters engaged him in conversation on a variety of subjects. Cydnee chattered on about everything. Nikkola was grateful that she hadn't yet mentioned Latham. However, much to Nikkola's disheartenment, Cydnee loudly made the announcement that she wouldn't be staying the night due to an unexpected field trip the following day.

Nikkola felt her heart sinking down to her feet. Taking full advantage of Cydnee's announcement, Mychal telegraphed Nikkola a sinister-filled warning message, which gave her some idea of what to expect from him later. Nikkola missed a large part of the rest of the conversation while trying to figure out how she could get Mychal out of her apartment before the rest of her company left. Her mind continually drew blanks under the dark scrutinizing eyes broiling her soft skin. Mychal's burning intensity kept Nikkola from thinking straight.

With Cydnee yawning every few seconds, the sisters felt compelled to immediately take their leave. After thanking Nikkola for a delightful evening of dining and conversation, the small group stepped into the hallway and closed the door firmly behind them.

Suddenly, Nikkola felt locked in the maximum-security prison of her glaring deceptions. Before she could sit down, Mychal loomed in front of her, taking her in his arms roughly. Her eyes became illuminated with fear as he hastily moved in for the kill.

Despite Mychal's rough handling of Nikkola, his kisses were butter-soft and moist. But she couldn't begin to relax in his too intimate of an embrace. She only now realized how much she was truly in love with Latham. No one could turn her on the way Latham Scott did. She'd been in love with him from the onset, but she'd been so scared to come to terms with it for fear of getting hurt. She was also aware that she'd been playing a dangerous game of intrigue with Mychal, but she didn't know how to end the out-of-control venture. When he suddenly pushed her down on the sofa, Nikkola feared that Mychal just might be capable of taking her against her wishes.

The unmistakable fear in Nikkola's eyes made Mychal

tremble with anguish. "Oh, Nikkola, please don't look at me that way! I'd never do anything to hurt you." His vulnerability frightened her even more than his menacing. Gently, he guided her head onto his chest. "I thought we were both enjoying this game of cat and mouse, but I can clearly see the fear in your eyes. I'd cut off my limbs before I'd take a woman against her will. For all my rude arrogance, beneath the hard exterior you'll find that I'm a very sensitive man. My bark is much worse than my bite."

Nikkola wept with relief against Mychal's broad chest, his sincere words helping to sweep the sheer terror from her heart. The fire in him was so hot, much hotter than what she was used to. Keeping herself out of the line of his blazing fire was a must.

Mychal was gracious enough to look chagrined. "Don't cry, Nikkola. I'm not here to harm you. I guess we've surprised each other with our equaled vulnerability." Taking a handkerchief from his pocket, Mychal wiped the tears from Nikkola's eyes and then tenderly kissed each eyelid. He saw that her hands were still shaking violently. To still them, Mychal clamped his large hand tightly around her fingers. "What did you think I might do to you?"

Nikkola really didn't want to tell Mychal what she'd thought, but she was sure he'd seen it in her eyes. "I don't know you very well, Mychal, and I thought of all sorts of things. I invited other guests to dinner to beat you at your own game, but deep inside I believe they were here as a safeguard against something happening between us. It started to look like I'd been caught in my own web of deceit." Nikkola managed a nervous chuckle.

"Don't you know not to play with fire, Nikkola?"

"Yeah, but I was already burned before I recognized it as something too hot to touch. I'll be careful not to make the same mistake twice. Thanks for being so understanding. You could've turned out to be Jack the

Ripper." Nikkola shuddered involuntarily, thinking of the awful things that could've actually happened. Her parents had definitely taught her better.

"Don't be too hard on yourself, Nikkola. If I had truly meant you harm, I think your instincts would've taken over long before now. And, at this moment, I wouldn't be sitting here with you in your home."

Nikkola wasn't so sure about his statement. Her instincts had a way of failing her.

As Nikkola and Mychal conversed late into the evening, she found out what a gentle and kind man Mychal Forrester could really be. Nikkola knew she could never fall in love with him as long as Latham Scott was in her future. From all indications, Latham Scott intended to be her future; Nikkola still promised Mychal to contact him when she returned to London. He'd promised to take her to lunch. Since she'd mentioned Jack the Ripper, he wanted to take her on the mystery night tour in the heart of the notorious killer's territory. She and Glen had planned to take the tour many times, but by nightfall they'd always been too tired to follow through.

Hours later, at the front door, Mychal had remained in control of himself and his emotions. Immediately following the light kiss to her mouth, he walked out of her apartment.

Just as Nikkola climbed into bed, the phone rang. Latham's deep voice instantly soothed her nerves as she relaxed against the pillows and allowed his voice to induce her into a delicious state of tranquility. Warmth spread to every part of her body as she listened to him talking sweet to her.

"I'm lonely without you, Nikki," Latham confessed. "I still can't believe it's taken me all this time to put myself in touch with you, your inner beauty. I can assure you I'll never allow it to be far from my mind and heart."

"I'm going to hold you to that assurance. Don't worry about the time we've missed out on. We've found each other now. I miss you, Latham. I have a few important things I need to tell you, but not tonight. I don't want anything to spoil this moment in time."

"Your comment just did, Nikki, because now you have me worried. You sound so serious. Is what you have to say about our relationship? Is there something wrong with us?"

Nikkola sighed hard, wishing she hadn't voiced her intent. "Nothing's wrong, Latham. I'd have to say that everything is right between us. I've come to realize quite a few things this evening, and I want to share them with you later. I promise it's nothing bad." *That is, if you don't consider my spending an entire evening, the majority of it alone, with Mychal Forrester as bad.*

Nikkola wanted to clear the air by being upfront and honest with Latham about the strange attraction she'd once held for Mychal. Discovering how deeply she loved Latham, and that he was the only man for her, was the most important matter for them to discuss. Nikkola felt that the timing was just perfect for her to now confess her undying love for Latham Scott.

Latham sighed with relief. "After hearing what you just said, I feel better now. I'll let you get some rest. I'll see you tomorrow. Sleep well, beautiful Nikki."

The phone clicked in Nikkola's ear, arousing her long enough for her to realize Latham had hung up. "I love you, Latham Scott," she whispered into the already dead phone line.

Seated at a corner table at Jenny's Café, sipping on a cup of coffee, Nikkola intently watched the front door. Though terribly nervous over what she was about to do, she felt that it had to be done. She had never stuck her nose in Glen's private business, but she had to know how much of his illness had to do with his breakup with Gennifer.

A five-year loving relationship had seemingly dissipated overnight. Gennifer was nothing like the women who had constantly taken advantage of Glen's generous heart, which was the main reason that it was so important for Nikkola to try and find out what had gone wrong.

Spotting Gennifer Ellis coming through the door, Nikkola stood up and waved her hand in the air for Glen's ex-girlfriend to see. Gennifer smiled sweetly as she started toward Nikkola. Gennifer was model-thin and beautiful from head to toe; her long, graceful stride brought her face to face with Nikkola in a matter of seconds. Gennifer worked at a local hospital as a registered nurse.

"Hi, Gen," Nikkola enthused, giving her invited guest a warm hug. "I'm glad you could meet me for breakfast. You look stunning, just as you always do." Nikkola took the liberty of pouring Gennifer a cup of coffee from the carafe, as the other woman took a seat. She then scooted the cup across the table in front of her companion.

Gennifer smiled gratefully, showing off her deep dimples and the sparkle in her amber eyes. "Thanks, Nikki, for both the compliment and the coffee. You look great, too. How've you been?"

Nikkola shrugged. "Couldn't be better. Life's been pretty decent these days."

Gennifer's expression turned somber. "Okay, now that we have all that out of the way, why am I here, Nikki? We haven't talked in a while. By the way, I've missed our friendly chats."

Nikkola felt ashamed of herself, though Gennifer hadn't called her either. "I know, and I'm sorry for that, Gen. There's no excuse for my not keeping in touch with you, so I won't try to make up any. I've missed our talks, too, though I asked you here this morning to talk about Glen."

Gennifer pushed her chair back and then got to her feet. "No can do, Nikki. That's not a discussion I'm up for. The topic of Glen is completely off limits."

Nikkola gave Gennifer a pleading look. "Please don't leave, Gen. Glen's been really ill, off and on—and I was hoping you could help me figure it out."

Gennifer looked both gravely concerned and distressed as she sat back down. "Ill. What's wrong with Glen, Nikki? Is it serious?"

Gennifer's love and concern for Glen showed in her eyes. Nikkola saw the look and had read it perfectly. Gennifer was still in love with Glen; Nikkola was pretty sure Glen felt the exact same way about the beautiful brown-skinned woman seated across from her. Then what was it?

"That's it, Gen. I just don't know. He thought it was the stomach flu at first. When he does start to feel better, the good periods don't seem to last for very long. Fatigue is a major problem for him. He's even thinking of transferring back to reservations."

Gennifer shook her head. "I hate to hear all this. I'm really concerned, but why do you think I can help you figure this out, Nikki? I haven't seen or spoken with Glen in over a month. You've always known way more about him than I ever did. I just don't see how I fit into the picture."

Nikkola recognized the hint of resentment in Gennifer's last statements. Was Gennifer jealous of her and Glen's relationship? Nikkola had to wonder. If so, there'd never been a drop of evidence or any feelings of envy coming through to her from Gennifer.

Wanting to be very careful how she presented her thoughts to Gennifer, Nikkola took a minute to think them through again. "Gen, I honestly think Glen's illness has to do with your breakup. He hasn't been him-self since you guys stopped seeing each other. The fact that he's sworn off women altogether has me worried. It seems to me that his heart is irreparably broken." Nikkola swallowed hard. "Was his heart broken by you, Gen?"

Gennifer looked shocked. "Me! I don't think so. I can see now that your best friend doesn't tell you every-thing, Nikki. For your information, Glen broke things off with me. And he didn't give me a single reason for wanting out. If anyone's heart is irreparable, I'm a prime candidate for a heart transplant. I haven't been able to feel anything but numbness in my heart and spirit since he walked out on me that devastating evening. I often feel as if I'm one of the walking dead, Nikki."

Nikkola felt sick inside. That Glen hadn't mentioned anything about his decision to end his relationship with Gennifer hurt her more than she could've ever imag-ined. *Hadn't he always said he trusted me with his life? If that were so, why hadn't Glen trusted me with the truth?*

Nikkola reached across the table and closed her hand soothingly over Gennifer's. "I'm sorry. I had no idea, Gen. But you're right. Glen obviously hasn't been very open with me, at least, not about this. If he broke up with you, why is he suddenly giving all women a bad rap?"

Gennifer shrugged. "Beats me. Nikki, I hope you don't get upset over what I'm about to say, but I need to get this off my chest. I really believed Glen left me for you. Since you're such a sensitive person, and when I didn't hear a word from you at such a difficult time in my life, I became sure of it. Now that I know differently, especially since you're here asking for my help, I'm even more clueless about his sudden disappearance from my life."

Nikkola looked deep in thought. She had heard

Gennifer's statement, but it hadn't fully registered with her yet. Glen's silence about everything had Nikkola completely stumped.

"Nikki, are you with me? What's going on?"

Nikkola looked up at Gennifer. "I'm sorry. I guess I'm still in shock." Nikkola then thought about Gennifer's last remarks. A look of discomfort crossed her features. "I feel so bad for not contacting you after Glen told me you two were over. I don't think it was a question of loyalty either. I just don't have an answer for my negligence. But I did feel awful about it. As for Glen and me, a lot of people think we're more than just best friends. We're not, Gen, nor will we ever be. We're just two people of the opposite sex who happen to love and respect each other as friends. Glen and I say silly things at times, but it never goes any deeper than that, never taken seriously."

Gennifer sighed with relief. "That's good to know, Nikki. Sorry I misjudged the situation. Now, tell me what you think I can do to help Glen. I'd love to be there for him, but just as a medical professional and his friend. I'm obviously not what he wants in a romantic partner."

"Gen, would you object to my setting up a dinner with you and Glen at my place? Of course, he wouldn't know until he arrived."

Gennifer looked skeptical. "I don't know about that idea, Nikki. If I knew why Glen had a sudden change of heart, I might be able to make a better decision. He'd more than likely see the dinner arrangement as deceptive on both our parts. You may also be putting your own relationship with him in jeopardy. Do you really want to risk that?"

Nikkola pulled a face. "I guess I didn't take time to consider all that. Well, with that in mind, do you have a problem with me suggesting to Glen that I invite you two to dinner?"

Gennifer shook her head in the negative. "That's a much better idea. That way, Glen can opt out if he wants. I think the other way would be terribly awkward for everyone."

Nikkola nodded in agreement. "You're right, of course. I'll talk to Glen and then get back with you. Are you sure you're okay with my sticking my nose into you and Glen's private affairs?"

A half-smile caressed Gennifer's mouth. "I actually welcome it. I think it's time I get to the bottom of Mr. Taylor's unexplainable actions. Did you know he'd mentioned marriage to me prior to the breakup? Not in any broad terms, mind you. Not long afterward he totally bailed out on me."

"I do recall Glen telling me he'd mentioned the M-word to you. He was probably looking for some sort of reaction from you. Maybe your response scared him. How did you react?"

"Since it wasn't posed as a direct question, as in 'Will you marry me?', I don't believe I responded to him one way or the other."

Nikkola laughed softly. "That might be the problem. If Glen thought you weren't receptive to the idea of marriage, and he really wanted that for you guys, he may've been hurt. I don't have to tell you how super-sensitive Glen Taylor is."

Gennifer chuckled. "Boy, do I know how sensitive he can be. However, I need closure. I think I can move on with my life once I find out Glen's real reason for ending it with us. Go for it, Nikki. You have my blessings."

Smiling broadly, Nikkola clapped her hands enthusiastically. "Consider it done. Since all we've had is coffee, what about ordering breakfast now? Are you hungry, Gen?"

"Starving is more like it, Nikki." Gennifer glanced down at her slim-banded diamond wristwatch. "I have about an hour or so to kill. Let's order."

* * *

Seated on the couch, with glowing candles as the only source of light, Nikkola and Latham were wrapped up in each other's arms. Having just finished dining on the superb pot-roast dinner she had prepared for them, both were full and feeling lethargic. A few sips of wine had helped them relax even more. The two half-empty crystal wineglasses were on the coffee table.

Latham's kisses were hot, making Nikkola's flesh sizzle beneath her silky evening lounging attire. Making love to him was at the very top of her list of things she was dying to do, but the timing was out of order. Nikkola still thought it was too soon for them to become that intimate, yet she had no doubt that it would eventually happen for them; *when* was the fifty-million-dollar question.

Latham rested his head back against the sofa, drawing Nikkola into the circle of his arms. "I sense we've gotten too hot and bothered for your comfort. Am I right?"

Nikkola laughed nervously. "Do you really expect me to answer that without being embarrassed by it? Am I acting too juvenile for you, Captain Scott?"

Moaning softly, Latham kissed Nikkola's forehead. "You don't ever have to feel embarrassed with me, Nikki. Juvenile? I think you're acting like a mature, responsible adult. You shouldn't rush into anything you're not physically or emotionally ready for. Are you feeling pressured by me?"

Nikkola shook her head from side to side. "No way." Feeling a bit shy, she lowered her lashes to half-mast. "The pressure I'm feeling is from my own burning desire to throw caution to the wind. You've been nothing but patient. That happens to astound me, since most of the men I've dated think sex should come on the first date or no later than the second one. Whether I was physically attracted to them or not never seemed to cross their minds. I've run into quite a few self-proclaimed studs. A complete turnoff."

Looking down into Nikkola's eyes, Latham gently outlined her mouth with his baby finger. "What about Cyd?"

Nikkola's eyelashes batted involuntarily. "What about him, Latham?"

Incensed with himself for even going there, Latham squeezed Nikkola tightly. "Forget that question, Nikki. It's one I shouldn't have asked."

Nikkola looked up at Latham, studying him closely. "Yet you asked it. Are you trying to find out if I'm a virgin or not?"

Surprised by Nikkola's bluntness, Latham jerked his head back. "Is that what you think?"

Smiling smugly, Nikkola reached up and tenderly glided the back of her hand down Latham's cheek. "Nice try at escaping that one, Captain Scott. Answering a question with a question is a good evasive tactic. If you want the answer to any personal questions about me, just ask. By the way, does it matter to you if I'm a virgin or not?"

Latham was once again surprised by Nikkola's candor about something so personal and intimate. This was the first time she'd opened up to him quite like this. He suddenly realized she had grown completely comfortable with him. That filled him up emotionally. "Not at all, Nikki." Latham's lips captured Nikkola's, locking them up in a riveting kiss, lasting for several moments.

With her heart beating way too fast, Nikkola took a second to catch her breath. "Glad to hear you say that, Latham. I'm more than looking forward to your finding out the truth for yourself, though. Just the thought of you deep inside me leaves me breathless."

The sparks of unbridled passion gleaming in Latham's eyes were not lost on Nikkola. To keep Latham from re-

sponding to her seductive remarks, she covered his
mouth with hers, their tongues instantly connecting.
Moaning and cooing softly against his lips, Nikkola lowered her head down onto his chest and closed her eyes.
Turning slightly onto her side, she slowly slid her hand
up under the front of his sweater, her fingers going
straight to his hardened nipples, squeezing tenderly.

Moving about until he was completely stretched out
on the sofa, with his long legs dangling over the other
end, Latham lifted Nikkola and then brought her down
on top of him. The rigid feel of his manhood throbbing
beneath her caused her to gasp with longing. Nikkola
seemed to have no control over her hips as they undu-
lated against his maleness with wild abandon.

As Latham's fingers worked the front zipper on her
silk lounging attire, Nikkola held her breath in eager
anticipation of feeling his heated hands on her bare
flesh. Reaching inside her gown, Latham's hand cupped
her full breast and freed it, his other hand frenetically
stroking her back as he brought the ripened mound of
sweet fruit into his mouth.

Minutes later Latham looked up at Nikkola, passion
burning fiercely in his eyes. "Don't worry, sweetheart.
I'm always in control of myself. You can trust me not to
let things go too far."

Nikkola lowered her head, her lips roving hungrily
over his. "I *do* trust you, Latham, with every breath of
my being. But I'd like to think I have the same sort of
control over myself." Although Nikkola was aware that
her control was rapidly slipping away, she believed
Latham to be a man of his word, a man of honor.

How deeply Latham felt about Nikkola's trust was re-
vealed to her in his hot, wet, sensuous kiss. "Don't
worry about anything, Nikki. Just lay here and bask in
the glory of our passion. I'm in charge of all the control
buttons, sweetheart."

Knowing that she didn't have a thing to worry about

with the man of her dreams, Nikkola kissed Latham back thoroughly, daring to massage with the heel of her hand his clothed stiffness. The passionate murmurings coming from Latham's lips excited her even more. She loved the fact that he was a man who seemed to have no hang-ups about audibly expressing the physical pleasures he felt. Nikkola could barely wait for the day to come when she'd hear Latham screaming out her name.

Nikkola's eyes connected soulfully with Latham. "You have my permission to be the sole commander of our exotic journey as we soar way above the clouds. My seat belt is fastened, but I'm afraid my no-smoking sign can't be turned off until after we've landed. My body is already on fire."

Latham smiled broadly. "It seems that we're both prepared for takeoff."

In no mood for further conversation, Latham claimed Nikkola's mouth in a passionate-filled kiss, ready to get back to the business of matching her heightened desires with his fervent need. Along with her arousing comments and the seductive way in which her sweet body danced atop his left him in no doubt about her deepest yearnings. Confident in his ability to completely satisfy Nikkola without crossing her boundaries, Latham set out to do just that.

Nikkola felt terribly anxious as she opened the door for Glen. Before she'd gotten a chance to call him about having dinner with her and Gennifer, Glen had phoned her telling her he had something important to say to her regarding his ex-girlfriend. The tension and impatience in his voice had put Nikkola on high alert. That Glen had learned about her breakfast meeting with Gennifer was the first thing to pop into her mind, though she was hoping that wasn't the case.

Before strolling into the living room, Glen kissed Nikkola on the tip of her nose. That caused her tension to ease up a bit. Perhaps his little display of affection meant that he wasn't upset with her. But then again, she thought, Glen was always warm and loving, even when he was put off with someone. His reaction to Mychal Forrester's rudeness when they'd first met in London was indicative of how easygoing Glen really was.

Looking a bit weary, Glen dropped down on the sofa, sighing heavily.

Very much atuned to Glen's edgy mood, Nikkola took a chair, clasping her hands together. "So, Glen, what's up with you? You sounded a little tense on the phone. Are you feeling ill again?"

Glen sighed hard. "It's Gennifer, Nikki. Have you talked with her since we broke up?"

Feeling a bit hot under the collar, Nikkola thought Glen had asked that question as if he already knew the answer. But since she couldn't be sure, she figured she'd better play it safe for now. "Why do you ask? More so, why do you even care?"

Glen looked abashed. "That's the problem. I do care. More than I've been willing to let on. I've never stopped caring. After you brought up the subject of our relationship the other day, I haven't been able to stop thinking about Gennifer, about how it once was with us."

Nikkola's relief came instantaneously. "Stop thinking and start acting, man. Call her!"

Glen shook his head from side to side. "It's not that simple, Nikki. My health is a big issue for me right now. I think I know what's wrong with me. I just don't know why this is happening."

Nikkola swallowed hard, moving up to the edge of her seat. "What is it, Glen? Please tell me. Is it something serious?"

"I think it is, Nikki. It's threatening enough to keep

me from living a normal life. I don't have a definitive diagnosis, but I definitely know the problem is a serious one. I just don't know if anything can be done about it."

"Glen, please tell me," Nikki shouted impatiently, nearly falling out of the chair. "The suspense is killing me over here."

Chapter 9

Dressed in a short yellow polka-dot sundress, Nikkola look cool and well rested. The beginning of summer sun had lightened her hair considerably and her complexion was now a deep golden brown. The air conditioner in her condo was running at full blast; it was ninety-five-plus degrees outdoors. The skies over Alexandria and the surrounding areas were shrouded with blazing sunlight, high temperatures, and heavy humidity.

While finishing up a special report for the orphanage, Nikkola sat at the small desk in the spare bedroom of her home. Having worked on her assignment off and on for several days, she was glad to finally have it completed.

Nikkola rested her head back against the chair, smiling at the sudden thought of how the love affair between her and Latham was going so strong. They spent nearly all their free time together and the bonds of friendship between them had also grown by leaps and bounds.

On many of Nikkola and Latham's days off, the couple involved themselves in several different social and economic projects. They had also taken many outdoor excursions, often taking Cydnee and Seth along. On the times alone, there'd been sunning by the pool, having picnics, and flying kites in the park, with long, romantic night drives around the city and along some of the enchanting waterways. Latham had taken Nikkola to his home and she had become familiar with all the rooms there, where he often felt her presence when she was away from him.

During the layovers in London, Nikkola and Latham enjoyed taking in the hottest West End plays and shows. Hanging out in the English pubs for hours on end, talking and sharing their life experiences, had become one of their favorite pastimes. Along with early morning and late evening drives through the English countryside, sunset cruises along the Thames were always a special treat. Many of the free hours had also been spent relaxing in the hotel spa and taking all of their meals together. Yet another of the favorite ways to reduce stress was to while away their time in the outdoor markets and the numerous London fashion venues.

Because his physical health had caused a slight decline in his emotional well-being, Glen was now working in reservations. He planned to return to a flight schedule within the next month if his overall health improved, but not on the night flight. A flight attendant slot had to open up on his previous route before he could return to the same schedule.

Breaking loose of her thoughts, Nikkola neatly folded her typed report, put it in the addressed envelope, stamped it, and then carried it out to the mailbox.

On Nikkola's way back from the mailbox, she heard someone shouting her name. Turning around to respond to the beckoned call, she spotted Carmen Thomas strolling up the sidewalk. Nikkola's mind spun into a tizzy at the sight of Carmen, who was all smiles when she asked to visit with Nikkola for a few minutes. Carmen then briefly explained to Nikkola that she needed to talk to her about something very confidential and extremely important.

Knowing Carmen's mission more than likely had everything to do with Latham, Nikkola politely welcomed her inside, though intent on keeping her guard up. It didn't surprise her that Carmen knew where she lived, since residential information was exchanged all the time among the different crew members. Someone was always looking for a referral to a nice place to live. Living in a gated community didn't always ensure security, not when visitors' cars could follow tenants right into the complex once the gate was opened. Carmen had to have gained access in the same way.

Once inside her place, Nikkola led Carmen into the kitchen. Before joining Carmen at the table to find out what was on her scheming mind, Nikkola first poured fresh lemonade over glasses of ice. After filling a bowl with chips, Nikkola placed the items on the table and then took a seat.

Carmen took a sip of the refreshing liquid and then smiled. "Nikki, the lemonade is great."

"Thanks, Carmen. I appreciate the compliment. How've you been doing with your new flight schedule? What route are you on?"

"That's what I came to talk to you about. I've taken several months of leave, Nikki."

Nikkola's curiosity was now deeply aroused. "What kind of leave?"

"Maternity leave. Nikki, I'm carrying Latham's baby," Carmen announced with an unflattering nonchalance.

Nikkola went pale as a sickening feeling of nausea swirled in her stomach. Unconsciously, she looked down at Carmen's stomach, but her loose-fitting attire covered any evidence of her shocking, bold claim of being pregnant with Latham's baby.

A quick recovery allowed Nikkola to look Carmen straight in the eye. "Why are you telling me this, Carmen? Isn't this something you should be talking to Latham about?"

Carmen was totally unaffected by Nikkola's intense gaze of disbelief. "Latham knows all of this," Carmen stated coolly. "I thought once he'd told you about the baby, you'd have the common decency to release him from any commitments he may've made to you. But I see you're still holding onto him," she accused blatantly.

This was the first Nikkola had ever heard about any of this. Carmen's accusations struck a disharmonious chord in Nikkola's heart, causing her to flinch at Carmen's accusatory tone. "First of all, Carmen, Latham hasn't made any commitments to me. If you're carrying his baby, that's between you and him." Nikkola was in no way prepared to let Carmen know that Latham hadn't discussed this serious matter with her, which was something Carmen would revel in.

Nikkola swallowed the bitterness she tasted on her tongue. "When's your baby due?"

"Around the end of December, first part of the New Year," she responded blandly. "Nikki, if you'll let go of Latham, I'm sure he'll see to his responsibilities toward this baby. I didn't want to come to you with this, but he's left me no other choice."

How noble of you! Burning agitation churned in Nikkola's stomach. "I'm positive that Latham will take care of his child regardless, but are you hoping for a marriage proposal, Carmen?"

Carmen's eyes sparkled with ridicule. "I'm hoping for us to raise our child together. If Latham proposes marriage, I'd accept. A child needs to have both parents. I'm a product of divorce. Only one of my parents raised me. I'd like much better for my child."

Nikkola was well aware of the hardships a single-parent

family had to endure. She'd seen so much of it when she worked in social services. She could truly sympathize with Carmen's situation. "Carmen, I wish you the best of luck. If there's anything I can do, please call on me."

Carmen narrowed her eyes. "Even if it means giving Latham up?"

"If that's what *he* wants." Nikkola was being as honest as she could without having the chance to think it through. Operating on nothing but emotions had left her mind unstable.

"Nikki, I'd appreciate it if you don't tell Latham I've talked to you. He wanted to handle this in his own way—from all indications, in his own time, too. He'd be furious with me if he knew I came here. If you really meant what you just said, you'll know the right thing to do." Carmen nodded curtly at Nikkola and then quickly made her way to the front door.

Nikkola didn't even bother to walk her uninvited guest out, wishing she'd never let Carmen in. Moving like a robot, she walked over to the sink, rinsed the dirty glasses, and then stuck them in the dishwasher. She then moved mechanically through the house and into the bedroom. Upon seeing her packed suitcase on the bed, Nikkola shoved it onto the floor with tremendous force.

For several hours, Nikkola had been huddled in the center of her bed, her emotions terribly shaken. Carmen's announcement had wounded her badly, had caused her emotional insides to bleed profusely. The phone had rung too many times for her to keep count of. Paralyzed by fear and pain, she hadn't been able to move a fraction of an inch. While staring at the clothes all over the floor, Nikkola was in deep agony. Her weekend trip away with Latham had just exploded into a ball of meaningless, unfulfilled dreams.

Knowing she had to get out of her place before Latham showed up, Nikkola dragged herself up from the bed. After picking up a few of the items from the floor, she packed an overnight case. Glen was at work, but she had a key to his place. She knew Latham would come there looking for her, but she also knew Glen would cover for her if she asked him to.

Before leaving for Glen's place, Nikkola called the airlines scheduling department to request a few days of emergency leave. Her request was approved without question.

The very next thing Nikkola thought about was trying to get her schedule changed to another flight. She then decided to worry about that later. Since Latham hadn't been man enough to come to her about his situation with Carmen, she wouldn't give his feelings any consideration whatsoever while making plans to completely avoid him.

Nikkola flirted with the idea of going to Florida to see her parents, but she was too upset. Besides, she didn't want to have to explain this ugly situation to her parents since she'd already told them all about Latham. Ethel and Nickolas Knight had hoped to meet him during their next visit.

Glen arrived at home late in the evening and found Nikkola curled up on his couch, which came as a big surprise to him. He only needed to take one look at her to know she'd been crying. The pain in her eyes was more than his sensitive soul could bear.

Throwing his briefcase on the table, Glen knelt down in front of the sofa and gently placed his hands on Nikkola's shoulders. "What is it, my dear friend?" he asked softly.

Tears swarmed in Nikkola's eyes as she hid her face in her hands.

Glen lovingly pried her hands loose from her face and then kissed her fingertips. "Nikki, you have to tell me what's going on. I'll give you more time to pull yourself together, but you have to let me in sooner than later."

Nikkola clutched at Glen's arm as he began to move away. "Sooner is better. I can talk to you now. I have to get rid of this incredible pain. Talking about it is the only way I know how," she sobbed brokenly. Nikkola sat up on the sofa and Glen sat down.

Nikkola's blood ran hot and cold as she thought back to the morning hours. While grinding her back teeth together, she laid out for Glen the story of Carmen's untimely visit. As she spoke, her hands nervously pushed back imaginary strands of hair from her forehead. Her nerves were as nakedly exposed as the pain in her eyes. Glen's face was blurred through her curtain of shimmering tears. While struggling tiredly to get the last sentence out, she had to pause several times. Nikkola's lips quivered as she ended her comments on a weary sigh.

Glen stretched his arm out along the back of the sofa. "I find it hard to believe Latham knew about Carmen and didn't mention it to you. Have you discussed things with him, Nikki?"

"No! And I don't intend to," she cried out in anguish.

Glen frowned, hating to oppose her unwise decision. "I think he deserves a chance to answer the charges made by Carmen. You and him have grown so close, Nikki. If he hasn't mentioned it, it's probably because he just found out himself," Glen said in defense of Latham.

Nikkola stood up and walked over to the window. The sedating sounds of wind rustling through the trees and the hypnotic swaying motions of the branches did nothing to drug the acute ache in her heart. A bird lit on one of the limbs, causing her to envy its freedom to take flight.

If she only had wings, Nikkola would've soared through the skies to find the fluffiest cloud in heaven to bury her sorrows in. Latham had the ability to fly his passengers around in more ways than one. Each time he touched her Nikkola felt as if she were soaring, floating high above the clouds. Now all she needed to learn was how to survive the crash landing.

"Nikki, go to him and ask questions," Glen said from behind her. "Don't assume what Carmen says is the gospel truth. Every human being is entitled to a day in court. You have already presumed Latham guilty. What if he's not even aware of the charges leveled against him?"

Glued to her spot, Nikkola couldn't turn around to face Glen. She had heard him, knew he was right, but facing Latham right now was impossible for her. Time was what she needed, lots of it.

A loud bang on Glen's door startled Nikkola. Mustering up enough strength, she turned to look at Glen, her eyes pleading for him not to give her away. She felt Latham Scott's energy from the other side of the door, and her heart was rushing into a headlong stampede to be near him. Nikkola sighed with relief. Glen's eyes had assured her he wouldn't give away her hiding place.

Rubbing his sweaty palms against his uniform slacks while waiting for Nikkola to disappear into the bedroom, Glen slowly opened the door to greet Latham. Right off, he noticed the worried look on the pilot's face, aware that he was facing an unenviable task. Lying didn't come easy for Glen, but he had to do it for Nikkola's sake.

"Hey, Glen." Latham looked anxious. "I'm looking for Nikki. Is she here?"

Glen swallowed hard, but the lump in his throat wasn't dissolvable. "She's not," Glen said, briefly glancing away. Glen's eyes had a way of deceiving him and he was very conscious of it.

Latham looked as though he had seen right through the deception. "I don't understand it." He shook his head. "We were supposed to go away for a couple of days. I've been trying to reach her for hours. If she's not here, I don't know where to look for her. Have any suggestions?"

It was getting harder and harder for Glen to keep up this charade. He was starting to get weak in the knees. "None, Latham. But if I see her, I'll have her call you. Will you be at home?"

"More than likely. I have a gut feeling that something unusual is going on here. Nikkola better have a good explanation for her strange behavior." Latham had spoken loudly, as though he knew Nikkola was there and could hear his warning message.

Nikkola *had* heard Latham. Her ear had been lodged up against the crack in the slightly opened door. Cringing at the thought of the unfair position she'd put Glen in, she felt deep sorrow for treading on the special bonds of their relationship by asking him to lie. Latham wasn't someone who would tolerate lying very well. She could only picture the fury he would unleash on her if he ever found out; *when* he found out was more like it.

After knocking softly on the closed bedroom door, Glen stood back to wait for Nikkola to permit him entry. As she opened the door for Glen, the expression on her face was one of shame and regret. Nikkola didn't have to voice her regret. Glen read her apology in her eyes.

Wiping his forehead with one large swoop of his hand, Glen entered the room. "I'm sweating pigs, Nikki," he joked, trying to put her at ease. "Captain Latham Scott knows you're here. If you don't think so, you're more naive than I've suspected. I'm sure you heard every word."

"Let him worry," she said obnoxiously. "I'll talk to him when I'm ready, not a second sooner. He may always be in command on the job, but he can't be in control of how I see fit to deal with this very personal situation."

Nikkola's rigid stance let Glen know any words of wisdom would be futile at this point, which caused him to drop the matter and change the subject altogether. "Are you hungry?"

"I'm not, Glen." Nikkola frowned. "Would you mind if I just went to bed?"

After gently smoothing Nikkola's hair back, Glen turned around and quietly left the room.

Dressed in pink cotton pajamas, Nikkola's still form was nestled in between the soft floral-printed percale sheets, as she listened to the night sounds wafting in from the open window. The breeze blowing across her fevered brow cooled the heated temperature of her body. Breathing easily had become a labored chore for her, as she sucked greedily at the fresh night air.

As Nikkola's arm fell heavily away from her eyes, she stretched it over her head. The shadows on the walls clearly showed the outline of the tree branches swaying against the window, which brought to Nikkola's mind the tree house in the backyard of her childhood home. She had spent countless hours in the midst of the thick branches of the old maple tree. When she needed to be alone, she would climb the rickety steps and seek solace from on high. Her secret place had been decorated with pictures of famous models and her favorite entertainers, and the floor had been lined with several blankets piled on top of one another. Her friends had wanted it to be a clubhouse, but she hadn't wanted to share her peaceful haven with a bunch of noisy kids. Few people had been invited into her wooded retreat.

Daydreaming of becoming a high-fashion model had

been Nikkola's favorite thing to do. She would often imagine herself wearing designer clothing and expensive perfumes while dazzling her audiences with seductive stances, flurried turns, and maniacal twists.

Her eyelids drooped shut with the desire to find peace in a sweet sleep, in a place where she could run free, where the wind and the sun would travel with her by day, and where the moon and the stars would guide her way by night. She dreamed of a place where peace, joy, love, and laughter were the supreme rulers of the land; pain and sorrow were prohibited by law.

No diseases, death, or war would ever render mass destruction in this magnificent place. Health, happiness, and well-being would be the rule of thumb. No hearts would be broken and no tears of sadness would be shed. Bigotry was forbidden. Discrimination against any individual or any particular group was disallowed. No homelessness, no orphanages, no hunger would be found there. Smiles, hugs, and kisses would be the only language spoken, while compassion, kindness, and genuine love would be the only emotions allowed to flow freely. That her dream place sounded like heaven was the last thing to cross Nikkola's mind before sleep claimed her.

In her dreams was the heaven that she would live in and love with Latham, where they'd bathe in blue lagoons, eat delicious fruits and berries from golden trees and bushes, and sleep in fields of perfume-scented flowers. As means of transportation, pure white unicorns would carry them throughout this glorious land.

Latham and Nikkola Scott would live happily ever after.

Shivering from the absence of the warmth Nikkola usually left him with, Latham pulled the spread up around the nude upper part of his body. Sleep wasn't coming naturally, and after countless times of ringing her number, he desperately needed to succumb to something other than his torturous thoughts of her.

There wasn't one valid explanation that Latham could come up with for why Nikkola had stood him up. He was exhausted from trying to make sense of her actions, and the words in his mind were all running together, making for one jumbled mess.

Nikkola, where are you? Are you running from me? Haven't you been as happy as I've been over the past several months? Does Mychal Forrester have anything to do with your sudden disappearance? Latham had asked the same questions of himself a thousand times, but no reasonable answers seemed forthcoming. Shutting his eyes tightly, he envisioned Nikkola blazing a trail of fiery kisses from his chest to the hardened flatness of his abdomen. Her small hands softly touched the insides of his strong thighs, the white heat emanating from her slender fingers igniting a fire deep in his loins. Her moist tongue teased his bottom lip. Then her mouth clamped down over his, her tongue probing deeply, producing the most sensational pangs of ecstasy he'd ever felt.

Sleep finally made Latham its own, but it was a restless night. As he tossed and turned in his bed, his body soon became twisted and tangled in the bedclothes. Along with his torturous night visions, hot, salty sweat poured from every pore on his well-toned body.

The plane was losing altitude rapidly, bursting into angry orange flames just before it hit the ground. Fighting to stay conscious while unbuckling his seat belt, Latham sat dazedly at the controls, waiting for the grayish nausea to pass. His ears were ringing loudly. Pushing the buzzing sounds to the back of his mind, he focused on his mission. After getting up from his seat, he stumbled out of the cockpit. Looking for his beloved Nikkola, Latham ran through the jumbo jet screaming her name loudly.

Finding Nikkola in the back of the plane, slumped forward in her seat, Latham carefully lifted her head. As he cradled her in his lap, the feel of her still warm breath on his lips caused him to cry out with relief. "Nikki, Nikki, please don't leave me. Our life together has just begun. We have so many wonderful days ahead of us, Nikki," he cried. "Don't go. Stay with me, Nikki," he pleaded.

Latham's eyes fluttered open slowly. Leaping upward and straight out of bed, he tripped and landed hard on the floor. Entangled in a web of sheets, frustrated and confused, he felt tears flow from his eyes. Realizing he'd only been dreaming, he cried out again from the relief. After untangling himself from the sheets, Latham slid back into bed.

Although it had only been a horrible nightmare, the startling events had seemed all too real, making Latham feel every emotion imaginable. He had to seriously wonder if Nikkola's sudden disappearance was an indication that their relationship might possibly be on a collision course with disaster. Then he thought she might've had an emergency of some sort and hadn't had time to call and cancel the outing. That Nikkola had walked out on their relationship was a premature assumption on his part, Latham decided, especially when he hadn't done anything to cause such an outcome. If only he knew all the answers. But he didn't.

Latham wiped the tears from the corners of his eyes. "At the first crack of dawn, I'll find Nikkola Knight," Latham vowed to the perpetual silence.

The crack of dawn came stealthily. Pastel colors swept across the shore of skies, as the amber sun sluggishly poked its head above the tinted clouds. Spilling its golden rays into the window of the bedroom where Nikkola lay, warmly kissing her face, causing her to awaken with a smile. Remembering her delicious, fanciful dreams, Nikkola crossed her arms over her chest and rubbed her hands up and down her arms. The dream and the sun provided warmth for her body, but there was a massive block of ice around her heart. The cold, empty feelings brought to Nikkola's memory the devastating reason for Carmen's unexpected visit.

Getting out of bed, Nikkola tiptoed to the door, opened it, and looked down the hall to see if Glen was stirring. The rooms were quiet and uninhabited and Glen's bedroom door was still shut. After collecting her things from the room, she packed them in the overnighter. She then sat down to write Glen a note. Once she'd propped up the note on the mirror, she tiptoed to the front of the house, where she quietly opened the front door. She then secured the lock and made her way home.

Inside her bedroom, with plans already formed in her mind, Nikkola busied herself making reservations to stay at a private bungalow on Chesapeake Bay. No sooner had she hung up the phone than she realized that running away wasn't the answer. She immediately called back the reservation clerk and canceled her reservations. The only place Nikkola wanted to run to was into Latham's arms, into the arms that had once held her future.

Even before the sun had appeared, Latham had already showered and dressed. Immediately afterward, he had begun his drive to Nikkola's place. But during the course of the drive he'd changed his mind. He hadn't chased after Morgan when she'd disappeared in much the same way Nikkola had. She'd come to him when she'd been ready to enlighten him, and he'd made the decision to give Nikkola the same opportunity. Since he still didn't know her motive for canceling their plans, his nerves were like jagged rocks cutting into his flesh, leaving him short-tempered and moody. Like Nikkola, he needed to get away. Latham had called on his friend, Joe Meyers, and they planned to go Jet-Skiing.

Latham was in the process of rigging his Jet Ski onto the back of the car when the phone rang. Hoping it was Nikkola, with some type of explanation, he ran into the house. He was bitterly disappointed when Joe's voice came over the line.

"Latham, I have to cancel our plans. Marilyn is not feeling well. She needs me to take her to the doctor. I'll call you later," Joe said calmly. "We can do this another time. Soon, I hope."

"Sorry, pal. I hope it's nothing serious. I'll check with you later. Give Marilyn my warmest regards," Latham requested, sending up a silent prayer for his friends.

Marilyn Randolph was Joe Meyers's longtime girlfriend. Latham knew Marilyn wouldn't interfere in Joe's plans without a good reason. He once again prayed that Marilyn would be okay, while his agitation with Nikkola was steadily growing.

As Nikkola reached the turnoff to Latham's house, her heart was beating rapidly. Beads of sweat had formed over her lips and her mouth felt dry as cotton. With trembling fingers, she wiped the moisture away. She then pulled the convertible into his driveway and cut the engine. Putting her head down on the steering wheel, she commanded her erratically beating heart to be still.

Nikkola's legs felt like lead as she walked to the front door. She rang the doorbell and waited, her breathing coming in short gasps. When Latham finally opened the door, the anger in his eyes made Nikkola wish that she hadn't come at all.

With his piercing brown eyes rapidly turning to dark pools of rage, Latham leaned casually against the doorjamb. "So, you decided to make an appearance after all." Frowning, he peered down at his wristwatch. "A day and several hours late—and not at the scheduled meeting place. But nonetheless, you've appeared."

Nikkola didn't make any attempt to move from her spot because she didn't think her motor skills would work. Latham couldn't have known that her legs were paralyzed by the rage she saw in his eyes. If she could've run back to her car, she would've done so. Instead, Nikkola stood perfectly still, hoping Latham's obvious anger with her would quickly subside.

"Are you coming inside, Nikki?"

"If it's okay," she said weakly, her voice barely above a whisper.

Using his right hand, Latham made a sweeping gesture for her to enter. Unsure of what she'd say to him, though she'd rehearsed her speech a dozen times, she slowly inched her way into the house. As Latham turned to walk away, Nikkola followed him into the living room.

Latham sat down on the sofa and invited Nikkola to sit next to him by patting the cushion beside him. "Let's have it! Why did you stand me up, Nikki? Didn't I at least deserve some sort of an explanation? I'm totally puzzled by your strange behavior."

Nikkola slowly exhaled a deep breath. "Have you seen or talked to Carmen lately?"

Latham shrugged, looking puzzled. "No, I haven't, not since she was on our flight to London. Why are you asking me that? What does Carmen have to do with anything?"

While twisting her thin gold bracelet, Nikkola was stunned by Latham's response. If he hadn't seen or talked to Carmen, then how could he possibly know about her pregnancy? And if he really didn't know, was it her place to tell him? A matter-of-fact voice in her head told her it was definitely her place.

"Carmen came to see me yesterday." Nikkola hesitated, drawing in a breath of air. "Latham, Carmen says she's pregnant by you."

Latham could've been knocked over with a feather. Nikkola could easily see that he hadn't heard the news before now. He wearily rested his hand on Nikkola's thigh. "I don't believe it, Nikki. Why would she tell you something like that without telling me about it first? Does she look pregnant to you?" Latham was having a hard time controlling his anger despite his attempt to do so.

Nikkola gave him a look of indignation. "Are you calling me a liar, Latham?"

"Oh, no, Nikki, it's Carmen that I don't believe. I know you wouldn't lie about something this serious. I'm sorry if I gave you that impression."

Taking his hand from her thigh, Latham tilted Nikkola's face at an awkward angle, searching her troubled hazel eyes with tenderness. As her long lashes swept downward, Latham's soft lips caressed her cheeks. "Nikki, sweet Nikki, we can't let Carmen come between us. I've fallen in love with you, Nikki," he whispered in a shaky voice. "I love you, Nikkola Knight!"

Nikkola's eyelashes darted away from her eyes, revealing pupils dilated with spellbinding astonishment. Taking the initiative to express her own feelings, she kissed his mouth slowly, deeply, kissing him as though she'd been waiting a lifetime to hear him confess his love for her. Latham's passionate response confirmed for Nikkola the magical words he'd spoken.

Sweeping himself into her arms, Latham nestled his head between her heaving breasts. She hadn't said "I love you, too," but he couldn't deny the corroborative language of her intoxicating lips, which had spoken volumes to his ever-listening heart. He needed to hear her say she loved him, too, but for now, Latham was more than content with the way Nikkola had physically and so passionately expressed her love for him.

Lifting Nikkola up from the sofa, Latham carried her into his bedroom and gently laid her down on the bed. He then fell down beside her, his hands spanning her waistline, anxiously molding her body fully against his own. The earth seemed to move as the two entwined bodies seductively swayed against each other. A sea of wavy emotions engulfed them, drowning them in steamy desire.

Latham removed Nikkola's sweater with one quick upward motion, as she nearly ripped the buttons from his shirt in her effort to free his broad chest. Attaining her goal, she slid her fingers through the thick trail of light brown chest hair. While his teeth nipped wildly at her engorged peaks, his strong fingers worked loose the zipper on her shorts, sliding them down over her lean, tanned legs.

As Latham's manhood throbbed against her bare thighs, reality checked in on Nikkola. She turned away from him in a jerking motion. "Oh no," she cried out, "this is insane. What am I doing? Latham, what *are* we doing?"

Latham looked perplexed. "Consummating our love for each other comes to mind, Nikki. I know what you're thinking about without asking, but I'm going to ask anyway. You're thinking about Carmen, aren't you?"

"So should you. Oh, Latham, what if she's telling the truth? Do we dare ignore her without knowing for sure? I just can't. I have to know the truth."

Shoving his hands through his hair, Latham sighed heavily. "I used protection, Nikki—each and every time. And she was on the pill. Nikki, it just can't be true!"

Nikkola caressed his cheek. "You know the only sort

of protection against pregnancy that comes with a guarantee is abstinence. You're too experienced in life to resort to that lame theory."

"That was a stupid response. I guess I'm not thinking as clearly as I normally do, Nikki."

After removing Nikkola's tightly clutched arms from around the pillow, Latham wrapped them around his waist and lowered his head against her chest, his tears falling onto her bare breasts.

Bending her head down, Nikkola traced the outline of Latham's tears with her lips, hating to hear the anguished sobs escaping from deep inside his throat. It seemed to her as if his world had been turned upside down. She'd expected Latham to show some emotion, but Nikkola hadn't expected it to come with such magnitude.

Latham lifted his head and looked up at her. "I feel so stuck, Nikki. What am I going to do if Carmen is telling the truth? I don't love her and I can't imagine being trapped in a loveless marriage. I'd love my child and take full responsibility for it, but I don't want to marry Carmen."

Nikkola released a frustrated sigh. "If it's true, I don't know what you're going to do, honey, but you have to find out. Maybe you should go and see her right now."

Latham shook his head from side to side. "No, not now, Nikki. I want to stay right here with you. If Carmen's really pregnant, everything is going to change all too soon. Nikki, stay with me tonight. I know we were going to have separate rooms on Chesapeake Bay, but I want you right here in my bed. I won't let anything happen to you. I promise."

Nikkola smoothed back Latham's hair and planted a kiss in it. She wanted to sleep next to him; she wanted all night with him, but she knew it would be taxing on both of them. She had already come so close to giving herself to him. Since there was nothing she wanted

more than for them to make love, Nikkola wasn't so
sure she could once again deny their physical and emotional needs if she stayed with him.

Nikkola finally agreed to stay with Latham, but only
if she could sleep in the guest room, to which he eagerly agreed. Latham didn't want to be alone. Just to
have her in the same house was a big relief for him. So
afraid they were going to be torn apart, Latham wanted
to keep Nikkola as close to him for as long as he could.

While Latham was out for hamburgers and fries,
Nikkola sat in front of the big-screen television, recalling the note she'd left for Glen. He wouldn't be able to
reach her with the information she'd given him, so
she'd picked up the phone to call his home. He wasn't
in, but she'd left Latham's number on his answering
service, promising Glen she'd check in with him later.

Seated on the floor in the family room, Nikkola
thumbed through Latham's CDs. Upon finding one
that she'd like to hear, she inserted it into the machine.
Kenny G's *Duotones* drifted into the room. The thrilling
notes reached into her torn heart with an offer of sweet
solace.

The music reached Latham as he entered the front
door. Since Nikkola hadn't heard him come in, he
stood in the doorway, watching the soulful movements
of her body as she swayed back and forth to the music.
The third cut from the CD, "Don't Make Me Wait for
Love," played softly. Latham knew that if Carmen was
carrying his child, he might indeed have to wait for the
one thing he so desperately wanted—Nikkola's love.

Feeling Latham's presence, Nikkola turned around
and opened her arms to him. He set the hot food on
the table and strode into her waiting arms. Holding
each other closely, they moved in rhythm to the music.

Into his ear Nikkola sweetly sang the words to the song. Every so often she drove Latham crazy by flicking her tongue in and around his ear.

"Nikki, Nikki, I don't have a crystal ball, but when you're in my arms, I can see into the future," he whispered into her ear. Catching her earlobe between his teeth, Latham gently sucked it into his mouth, causing Nikkola to gasp with pleasure.

Nikkola's body melted deeper into Latham's. "Latham, Latham, if we don't eat, our food is going to be cold, cold, cold," she mocked playfully.

Latham's soft, erotic laughter rippled through her ear, sending chills up and down her spine. A heat wave rushed in simultaneously, engulfing her most intimate body parts.

Comfortably seated on the floor, looking into Nikkola's eyes, Latham unwrapped all the food. He then plucked a plumb French fry out of the bag and fed it to her. Her mouth seductively drew his finger in with the crisp potato. Pangs of ecstasy shook his body as her warm mouth continued to close around his finger. Stripping two straws from their paper jackets, he stuck both in the cup of cola and then held the cup up to his and Nikkola's lips. The couple enjoyed feeding each other up until the last bit of food and drink was consumed.

The problems facing Nikkola and Latham were shut out for the remainder of the evening, as they talked and watched television for hours. Before retiring for the night, the couple ate one of their favorite desserts—a large slice of chocolate cake topped with butter-pecan ice cream.

A little past midnight, Nikkola showered and dressed in one of Latham's long-sleeve shirts. Emerging from the bathroom refreshed and relaxed, she went into the guest room, where the bedclothes were already turned back. A single red rosebud rested on one of the pillows. Happy tears swarmed in Nikkola's eyes as she picked up the flower and inhaled its perfumed scent.

Lying awake in his bed, Latham envisioned the expression Nikkola might wear on her lovely face once she discovered the rose. He had an idea that the loving gesture would bring tears of joy to her sentimental heart as he wished he could have her right next to him. Placing his hand over his chest, he tried to soothe the ache with his fingers. Nothing or no one, other than Nikkola, could remove the painful throbbing deep inside Latham's heart.

At two in the morning, Nikkola awakened from a troubled sleep, her face soggy with a mixture of sweat and tears. Sliding out of bed, she walked into the hallway, where she stood quietly for several minutes, staring at Latham's bedroom door. Without a thought to the consequence, she ran toward his room and entered the dark, cavernous space. Edging her way over to the bed on tiptoes, Nikkola slid in next to Latham.

Latham wasn't asleep. His arms immediately reached for Nikkola, welcoming her luscious warmth into his bed. He'd had the same thought earlier of going to her, but he'd made a promise. He was a man of his word. Although she was next to him, dressed in nothing but a thin shirt, he would keep that promise. But Latham's vow wouldn't keep him from making love to Nikkola with his tender mouth and hands; both were skilled in the art of lethal seduction.

Arousing and fulfilling her in ways that put her out of touch with the planet Nikkola resided on, Latham took her to heights yet unknown. He felt fulfilled just knowing that she was satisfied beyond belief. As Nikkola purred in his ear like a newborn kitten, each second next to her took him to a place he'd never been. The never-before traveled horizon brought to Latham's mind new beginnings and promises of forever after.

With his long legs curled tightly around Nikkola's sleeping form, Latham's mind planned forever with the woman lying next to him. Anything he'd ever felt for anyone paled in comparison to the way he now felt about Nikkola. He wouldn't rest until he got to the bottom of Carmen's accusations. All the while, he prayed it was just a terrible hoax. He saw it as a terrible trick for fate to play on him, for he'd finally found the woman he'd been looking for. But if the accusation were true, he prayed that Nikkola would not desert him—that she would stand by him. Latham couldn't begin to imagine his life without her in it.

Chapter 10

Awakening to find the spot next to her empty, Nikkola turned over and then pulled Latham's pillow into her arms. Burying her nose into the pillow slip, she deeply inhaled the sexy, manly smell of him. Hearing loud rattling sounds coming from somewhere in the back of the large house, she sat upright in the bed, stretching her arms high over her head. She crawled from the bed, went out into the hallway, and traveled in the direction of the noisy sounds, which seemed to come from the kitchen.

Standing over the stove, dressed in a dark burgundy robe, Latham was in the process of turning over two perfect eggs. Nikkola watched in silence as he made his way around the bright kitchen, giggling loudly when he flipped the eggs up and over in an expert fashion.

Turning around to face her, Latham smiled brightly, blowing a kiss to Nikkola from across the room. "Morning, love. Come on in here, Nikki. I could use some good company."

Smiling broadly, Nikkola blew Latham a return kiss. "Be with you in a second, Latham. I'm going to freshen up first."

Rushing across the room, Latham took Nikkola into his arms and hugged her warmly. As she turned to depart, he swatted her playfully on the behind. Laughing, she shook her fists at him menacingly. She then fled down the hall. Latham's eyes twinkled with love and adoration as he watched Nikkola disappear from sight.

Using the toothbrush Latham had given her the night before, Nikkola brushed her teeth vigorously and then gargled with peppermint mouthwash. Locating the fresh towel and washcloth he'd laid out for her, she turned on the shower and stepped inside.

The hot, pelting water brought warmth to her skin. Before getting out of the shower, she doused herself with a stream of icy, cold water, which brought her skin to life. Before drying her body off, she inhaled the fresh spring scent of the towel. Removing Latham's terry robe from a hook on the back of the bathroom door, Nikkola wrapped herself up in it and then headed for the kitchen, thrilled to life that she'd agreed to spend the night with the man she loved like crazy.

The food was already on the table. Seeing Latham seated there while sipping on a glass of orange juice gave Nikkola a tremendously warm feeling inside. Tucking the morning newspaper under her arm, she strode across the room and sat down across from him. As if she were in her own home, Nikkola opened up the periodical to take a glance at the latest headlines.

With breakfast on the table, Nikkola seated across from him reading the newspaper, both dressed in lounging attire, Latham felt that all the elements gave his home an aura of happiness.

The cozy feeling brought a hint of a smile to his lips. All that was missing was a couple of kids, he mused, the reality of such sobering him considerably. Although a kid might soon be added to his life, Nikkola wouldn't be the birth mother. That thought deeply saddened Latham.

Both Nikkola and Latham were embroiled in stormy thoughts. Though she seemed engrossed in the newspaper, the news was the furthest thing from her mind. He couldn't stop thinking about the imminent confrontation between Carmen and himself. Breakfast was eaten in a strained silence, with issues between them that neither seemed willing to address.

With both Nikkola and Latham sharing in the duties, the kitchen was cleaned in haste. He then went into the master bathroom to dress and Nikkola went into the guest room to don the same clothing she'd worn the prior evening. Once she'd quickly thrown on her clothes, Nikkola went into the living room to wait for Latham to make an appearance.

When Latham finally joined Nikkola, his hair was still damp with moisture from the shower. From across the room she could smell the lemony aftershave he'd generously splashed on his clean-shaven face. His hips were thrust into loose-fitting jeans and his broad chest was covered with a yellow shirt. Taking long strides, Latham reached the place where Nikkola sat staring into his heart, wishing she could discover within him the fate of their relationship.

"Penny for your thoughts, Nikki?"

Making direct eye contact with Latham, Nikkola cast him a bright smile. "Not sure they're even worth that much—my mind is so darn confused these days."

Plopping down beside Nikkola on the sofa, Latham slung his arm around her shoulders, drawing her in close to him. "Oh, Nikki, every thought you have is worth something, especially to me. I know things look pretty grim right now, but they're going to get better. I love you so much, Nikki, and I'll try my best to move heaven and earth to erase the sadness from your beautiful eyes. Trust me, sweetheart. I promise to guard your trust with my life."

On her drive home, Nikkola wanted so desperately to believe the assurances Latham had given her, but she was afraid to hope and dream about their being together eternally. He hadn't promised forever, but he'd certainly hinted at it. His going to see Carmen had her feeling so uptight and nervous. Nikkola felt as if her tightly wound heartstrings were in danger of snapping from the stress. The possibility of forever with Latham slipping through her fingers like tiny grains of sand was a reality she had to entertain but didn't ever want to face.

As though Nikkola's life depended on walking vigorously, she heaped miles of wear and tear onto the plush carpet in her condo. She paced back and forth through the rooms until she felt as if she were going stark-raving mad. The phone buttons also took a pounding, as she jabbed at them, dialing Glen's number relentlessly. Each time his answering machine came on, Nikkola gritted her teeth out of irritation.

After two anxiety-ridden hours with no word of any kind from Latham, Nikkola slipped into sweats and took the elevator down to the gym located in the basement of the complex. Once she settled into a workout routine, she took her frustration out on every piece of equipment available to her. After an hour-and-a-half-long, hard workout, Nikkola's strained muscles had started to rebel against her, so she took the elevator back up to her place.

The pain in Nikkola's legs was unbearable as she dragged herself into the bathroom, where she ran a hot bath. Sinking deep into the hot water, she totally relaxed and let the hot water soothe her tired, overworked body. When the phone finally did ring, Nikkola couldn't even move to answer it. Both physical and mental exhaustion had taken her completely over.

Placing the phone back on the hook, Latham ran his fingers wearily through his hair, wondering where Nikkola could be. As he thought about the possibility of a bitter end to the wonderful beginning he'd shared with her, his emotions swelled. Biting down on his lower lip was all he could do to keep from screaming out in frustration.

Latham dropped down heavily onto the sofa to think over his visit with Carmen. He first thought about the excellent case she'd made for herself and the unborn child, easily convincing Latham that she really was pregnant. She'd heaped so much guilt on him as she'd talked of all the horrible things she'd gone through growing up in a single-parent home.

Giving their child a chance at a normal, happy life was what both he and Carmen wanted most. However, Latham wasn't convinced that a marriage of convenience would necessarily provide such an outcome—not when he was in love with another woman. Latham was in no doubt that his life would be an impoverished one without Nikkola by his side.

Practically snatching the phone from its cradle, Latham redialed Nikkola's number. She answered on the second ring. Upon hearing her voice thick with anguish, his breath caught. "Nikki, I'm coming over. We have to talk."

"Okay," came her simple reply.

Nothing else needed to be said. Unwittingly, Latham had said it all. In her heart of hearts Nikkola already knew that it was over. She somehow knew that Carmen would be sharing his life and she wouldn't be. She could easily guess at what he was coming to say to her. Nikkola was sure she could recite his speech verbatim.

I'm sorry, Nikki, but I have to commit to Carmen and our unborn child. I love you, Nikki, but . . . Screaming out in anguish, she covered her ears from the loud, imaginary voices wreaking havoc inside her head. Life just wasn't fair, but no one had ever said that it was.

The large, saddened, tearful eyes of Carmen haunted Latham all the way to Nikkola's. The description of her childhood before and after the divorce of her parents was horrendous to say the least. Woeful tales of fighting, screaming, cursing, and master manipulation on her mother's part were the things Carmen discussed. A dam had burst in her eyes as she'd recalled the memories. There was no way Latham could've ignored her emotional state. Without holding Carmen in his arms, fearful of sending the wrong message, Latham offered her as much solace as he could.

Pulling up to the gate in Nikkola's complex and then lowering the car window, Latham punched in the code numbers to ring her phone. Without asking who was there, Nikkola immediately released the electronic gate from within her condo. In his haste to reach her, he forgot to activate the burglar alarm on his car. Once he'd set the alarm, instead of waiting for the elevator, Latham took the steps two at a time.

Nikkola was standing in the doorway when Latham emerged from the elevator. After tenderly kissing her forehead, he followed her inside, his fingers digging into her waistline as he guided her over to the sofa.

Nikkola could actually feel the slight tremors in his fingers, making her even more fearful of the outcome. *Latham Scott has walked into my soul and now he's here to strip it of his comforting presence.*

As he began talking, Latham's voice was low and sorrowful. Nikkola wished that she could silence him. She didn't want to hear the words that would wrench their love from each other's hearts, bravely steeling herself to listen to whatever he had to say. Nikkola would save her weeping for later; she'd have to mourn the loss of Latham for years and years to come.

"It didn't go the way I thought it would. I failed miserably at trying to move heaven and earth." Latham ran nervous fingers up and down Nikkola's arm. "Carmen *is* pregnant. She gave me the name and phone number of her doctor for verification. She also invited me to go along for her next appointment."

"So, you're here to tell me that you're going to make it work with her for the sake of the child, and that it's over between you and me," Nikkola stated with deadly calm.

Looking deeply into Nikkola's eyes, Latham could see the words "it's over" flashing on and off there. A sharp pain slammed into his heart like a speeding torpedo. *It'll never be over for me, Nikkola. How could it be? I love you.*

"Those aren't the exact words I would've used, but they'd have the same meaning no matter how I said them. Nikki, I haven't made any commitments to Carmen, but I have to commit to my child. A baby is a heavy responsibility and an even heavier one if only one person is willing to accept it. Please try to understand."

"I *do* understand." She looked dejected. *If only I'd let you make love to me last night, then I also would've had forever with you. The memory of you making love to me could've kept me company whenever loneliness paid a visit to my broken heart.*

"I set both you and me up, Nikki, and I did it without realizing it. I envisioned an entirely different outcome for us. I thought I'd be coming to you with happiness and relief written all over my face. I wouldn't let myself believe otherwise. And now, I'm here feeling a deep regret for hurting you this way. I love you, Nikki, and I'm deeply sorry."

"I'm not good at saying good-bye, Latham, and I won't say good-bye to you because you'll be in my heart forever. I understand that you're a man of integrity. I, too, had hoped for a different outcome. Unlike you, though, I tried to prepare myself for the worst-case scenario."

Nikkola stood up and reached for Latham's hands. She couldn't speak the words, but her soft lips smothered his, giving him an impassioned farewell. As the kiss grew in urgency, Nikkola reluctantly put distance between them and then quickly led Latham to the door.

"I love you, Nikki. I'll always love you." Gripping Nikkola's hair tightly, Latham covered her mouth with his, kissing her fervently. Their salty tears got lodged between their lips as the kiss deepened. Filled with raw emotion, he roughly pushed Nikkola away from him. Latham then rushed out the door and entered the exit stairwell, without looking back.

Stunned beyond belief, Nikkola closed the door. In a zombie like state, she slowly crept into the master bedroom. "Farewell, my heart," Nikkola cried into her hands. "I'm going to need an organ donor. My heart will never return to me, and my soul has been swiped right out from under me." *Is it possible to live without love? It has to be, because I'll never love another. I won't allow another to love me.*

"Heaven and earth, how dare you defy Latham! He commanded you to move, but you disobeyed. By doing that, you've sentenced me to a life of loneliness and uncertainty." *Someone else will share in his hope and dreams. Someone else will massage his weary shoulders while listening to how his day has been. He'll be the father of her children and she'll be the woman in his bed at sunset and dawn. She may have all that and more, but will she ever have his heart?*

Tears rolled down Nikkola's cheeks. "Impossible. Latham's heart belongs to me."

Glen still wasn't in when Nikkola phoned him for the umpteenth time. For a reason she didn't understand, or even bother to question, she found herself placing a call to London. When Mychal's husky voice finally came over the line, Nikkola practically shouted out his name.

"Who is this?" Mychal sounded puzzled.

Nikkola drew in a deep breath. "It's Nikkola."

Having a hard time containing his excitement, Mychal gasped loudly. "Ah, Nikkola Knight! I'm happy to hear from you, but you don't sound too happy. Is something wrong?"

"No, everything is okay," she lied. "It must be the connection. I hear a lot of static." There was static present, but she only used it as an excuse to cover up her lie. She needed to hear a comforting male voice. Since Latham and Glen were both unavailable to her, she had called Mychal. Although she was only conversing with Mychal to keep from thinking of Latham, knowing that it was dead wrong, Nikkola couldn't seem to help herself.

"I'm aware that you'll be returning to London in a day or so. I hope I can take you out to dinner, Nikkola."

Mychal's knowing her schedule still astounded Nikkola. She didn't feel as threatened by it now that she knew how he'd come by it. He probably hadn't checked recently since he didn't seem to know her schedule had been changed.

"That schedule no longer exists, Mychal. I had it changed. I had planned on taking some vacation time, but I'm starting to think it was a bad idea. I'm thinking of calling to cancel."

Work is the only thing that'll save me from myself and lone-

liness, even if I have to suffer through seeing Latham a bit longer.

"In that case, you can ring me from the hotel whenever you arrive. I hope it'll be soon. I'm glad you were able to forgive me for being so insensitive the last time we met."

"Me, too," she said somberly. "I'll call you when I'm in London."

Nikkola hung up without waiting for a reply, ashamed for what she'd just indulged in: false pretenses and blatant deception. Hearing Mychal's voice hadn't comforted Nikkola in the way that she'd hoped it would; maybe nothing would ever comfort her again.

Instead of returning to the house that he sensed would feel empty without Nikkola's presence, Latham drove around the city, stopping briefly at all the spots that he and she had frequented. The ambient memories were startlingly clear as they swept him into a time warp that he didn't want to return from. He vividly remembered the light in Nikkola's hazel eyes when they'd walked hand in hand while sightseeing, the sound of her exotic laughter, and the sensuous feel of her when she'd lain next to him.

Ending up at Jenny's Café, where they'd first met to discuss the possibility of entering into a meaningful relationship, Latham sat at the very same table. He then ordered hot chocolate from the waiter. Looking all around him, drinking in the sweetest of memories, Latham laughed quietly, recalling Nikkola's comments about the appetite-teasing wallpaper.

Drinking too quickly from the steaming mug of chocolate, Latham scalded the tip of his tongue. As his hand jerked the cup from his mouth, he nearly spilled the hot liquid all over himself. The near spill brought to his mind Nikkola's coffee mishap with Mychal Forrester, recalling how much it had upset her. Thinking of the disaster with his archrival left him wondering if Nikkola would now turn to the devil himself for comfort. Just the thought of that happening made him cringe with jealousy. Losing Nikkola to Mychal would devastate him.

How am I going to get through a life with Carmen when all I can think of is Nikkola? Although Latham and Nikkola had only built a few memories, those precious few had already had a profound impact on him. Their time together was all that he could remember, all that he wanted to remember.

After he'd drowned his sorrows in several cups of hot chocolate, the sugar had his nerves standing on end, and Latham knew it would be impossible for him to sleep. He paid the check and then strolled out into the cool night air, where the stars shone brightly overhead. Closing his eyes, he looked upward and made a wish on the brightest one. Not wanting to reveal his wish aloud for fear that it might not come true, Latham instantly put it from his mind.

With the top down on his car, the wind tackling his hair, the coolness of the night air chilled Latham to the bone. If only Nikkola were next to him, huddled against his body, their generated heat would've been more than a match for the cold.

While at home lying in bed, Latham switched the television on and turned off his mind. A variety of sitcoms entertained him for the next two hours. As soon as the shows were over, his thoughts of Nikkola magically clicked on. Although he fought the urge to dial her number, he couldn't stop her from appearing in his dreams, nor could Latham stop Nikkola's slender body from seducing him all through the night.

*   *   *

The sun was overpoweringly bright the next morning, but its powerful rays could not penetrate the thick
mountain of ice around Nikkola's heart. She awakened
with a start. The cold reality of the night before once
again broadsided her and sent her reeling. Putting the
phone into the bed with her, she dialed her employer,
making the necessary arrangements for her to return
to her regularly scheduled flight. Seeing Latham might
be difficult, but not seeing him would be worse. They
were both professionals and they'd just have to find a
way to make the best of a bad situation. It wasn't as if
they'd wanted this breakup. Besides, they should be
adult enough to maintain a working relationship and
put their personal feelings aside.

Just as Nikkola stepped from the shower, the phone
rang. She ran to answer it, water dripping from her
body as she gripped the phone receiver. Hearing Glen's
voice cheered her immediately, but Nikkola's joy was
short-lived.

"Hi, honey. How about having lunch with me today?
We haven't gotten together in a while. I miss you."

"Oh, Glen, I'd love to, but I have a few things to tend
to first. I can be ready by noon." Nikkola had forced a
bit of cheer into her tone even though the static on the
line unnerved her.

"I'll be at your door at noon. Until then, Nikki."

Before cradling the phone, Nikkola hit it with her
palm, trying to rid it of the static. She couldn't imagine
what was suddenly wrong with the phone lines.

Nikkola's chores were all finished long before Glen
was due to arrive. With too many empty hours to fill,
she felt at odds with being alone. *You've got to get used to
this*, Nikkola, she chided herself. *Crying over spilt milk is
definitely not your style. This spill is much too big to wipe up—
it's never going to evaporate on its own.*

While changing the linen on her bed, Nikkola had

wished the smell of Latham's aftershave was on her sheets, but it was safely embedded in her memory. Everything about Latham was imprinted in her mind, and she had no desire to erase a single detail. She didn't know if one was supposed to starve a fever or feed a cold, but she wasn't going to feed her insecurities or starve herself by denying his memory the chance to live inside of her.

After pulling from her closet a silk rose-colored tank top and a pair of white linen slacks, Nikkola laid them out on the bed. She then searched through the dozens of shoeboxes for her white sandals. Several of the boxes were labeled by color, but many were not, so she had to open quite a few before she finally located the desired pair.

At noon sharp, Nikkola and Glen left the building holding hands. He could feel the tension in Nikkola's grip, but he'd wait for her to tell him the reason for it. Sooner or later she was bound to open up to him. Glen opened the car door for her and walked around to the driver's side. It took them only twenty minutes to arrive at their destination, The Lobster Pot.

The restaurant Glen chose was bright and airy. A waitress showed them to a table that looked out onto the surrounding park. The lake could also be seen from their position. After their orders were taken, Nikkola watched the sun skimming across the water, aware that the silence would've been deafening had she not been in Glen's comforting presence.

The waitress quickly returned with their orders of crab and shrimp salads and iced tea. She placed the food down and strolled away.

Nikkola picked at her food, her appetite practically nonexistent.

Glen noticed right off that Nikkola wasn't her usual

animated self, as she stared blankly out at the water. He had to touch her to get her attention. "You looked spaced out, Nikki. What's going on?"

Nikkola looked at Glen through dulled eyes. "Latham and I won't be seeing each other again. He's considering working things out with Carmen. She really *is* pregnant, and he feels responsible for her, as he should."

Glen covered Nikkola's hand with his. Feeling sorry for her breaking heart, he thought of Humpty Dumpty. With the exception of Latham, he was sure that there wasn't a man alive who could piece her shattered heart back together again. "I'm sorry, Nikki. I know how much you love him. Will you be okay?" He already knew the answer. It was painfully clear in her eyes.

"I'll survive." She expelled a deep sigh. "I slept in the same bed with him the other night, you know."

Glen sharply raised an eyebrow. "No, I didn't know! And how did that come about?"

As Nikkola filled Glen in on the details, remembering every detail made her skin crave for Latham's tender, exciting touch. "I regret that we didn't make love in the true sense. We could've had all of each other, but what I felt with him was earth-shattering. I don't think I could've survived anything more, although I would've died happy and with a permanent smile on my face." Her hazel eyes filled with longing as a shudder of desire passed through her breasts, causing her to tremble.

Getting through the rest of the meal was difficult for Nikkola, but she managed to cope.

Shortly after consuming slices of apple pie à la mode for dessert, Nikkola and Glen walked down to the lake in silence, where they stood quietly for just a few minutes. Glen didn't intrude on her pensive mood during the drive home, but he was deeply concerned for her. This wasn't the Nikkola he was used to—Glen already missed his old friend tremendously.

Glen spotted Latham seated in his car outside the

complex gates and he immediately alerted Nikkola to Latham's presence. A dazzling light flickered in her eyes, but a tidal wave of raw emotions immediately drowned out her inner excitement. When the gates opened, Glen honked the horn at Latham, and then drove on through. Latham pulled his car in right behind Glen's and then parked in a visitor's slot.

"Hang tough, Nikki," Glen advised before leaving her. "You'll be okay."

Nikkola fearfully waited for Latham to reach her. Instantly pressing his body against Nikkola's, Latham crushed her lips under his. She clung to him with all her strength, as his hands roved across her hips, her body responding wantonly to his heated touch.

"My God, Nikki, I couldn't stand being away from you for another second. Nikki, I need you! Please don't send me away." Latham held her at arm's length to search her eyes for any sign that might suggest she needed him too.

"I need you, too, Latham. The hell with tomorrow," she whispered. "Let's go inside."

With his arm planted firmly around her waist, Nikkola and Latham entered the elevator. Once the doors closed shut, he pushed the red emergency stop button, and the elevator jerked to a screeching halt. Pushing her back against the far wall, he ground his hips into her body, causing her to gyrate wildly against him. Imprisoning her mouth, he stretched her reserve to the limit before he restarted the elevator. When the elevator came to a smooth stop on her floor, Latham lifted Nikkola up and carried her to the door.

After fumbling in her purse for her keys, Nikkola found them and handed them to Latham. She couldn't have gotten the door open with the way her hands were shaking. If she hadn't been in his arms, her trembling legs wouldn't have been able to support her either.

Inside the condo, Latham kicked the door shut with

his foot. He then secured the locks. Somehow she'd already managed to open most of the buttons on his shirt. As her hands sought out the smooth hair on his chest, she was highly aware that there'd be dire consequences for her actions, but she pushed every conscionable thought to the recesses of her mind.

Latham wanted Nikkola and she wanted him; that was all that mattered to her now. If reality checked in, just as it had before, she was prepared to cast it and any other doubts aside. A trail of clothes fell to the floor as the couple took flight to the bedroom. Pulling the linen back, he slipped into the bed and drew her in beside him.

Nikkola's hair hung between them like a glossy curtain and he reached up to push it away from her face. "Love me, Nikki," he whispered into her ear. "Brand me for life."

Nikkola's laughter pealed softly against his cheek. "You're the one with the branding iron, so you'll have to do the honors for both of us."

Latham muffled his laughter into her neck, causing a tingling sensation to ripple through her body. Pulling her on top of him, he looked questioningly into her eyes, where the windows to her soul were wide open. She heard his sharp intake of breath. "Are you sure?"

"Without any doubt." The engaging way in which Latham had looked at Nikkola left her feeling utterly breathless.

The brand of lovemaking he so willingly bestowed on her was slow, tantalizingly, deliberate, and strong. His hands stroked and caressed, rendering her powerless against his tender but forceful strength. His strong magnetism drew her into an atmosphere of colliding stars and shooting comets. Finding out that she too possessed magnetic powers over him, she drove Latham crazy with her own sweet brand of lovemaking.

In a blaze of mystique, Nikkola and Latham exalted

one another to a state of breathless wonderment. Thunder struck loudly in their ears as lightning flashed across the heavenly aura of their minds. The powerful effects of the sensuous lovemaking were staggering, leaving them with a fulfillment surpassing their loftiest and wildest dreams. Drunk with ecstasy, the happy couple nestled into each another, holding onto the precious moments that just might be their last.

Watching the changing expression of Nikkola's delicate features, Latham discovered they were even softer with the flush telltale signs of their arduous lovemaking. "Nikki," he whispered softly, "let's shower and then get dressed."

Squeezing her eyes shut, Nikkola hid the pain his statement had brought her.

Over much too soon, she thought quietly. Although she was in seventh heaven right now, she knew all too well that hell was soon to become her permanent residence . . .

Latham's lips pressed against her temple. She shuddered as the contact was realized. "Nikki, come home with me. I don't want to sleep without you tonight."

As Nikkola opened her eyes, the pain had completely dissolved. "Don't you think we'd only be prolonging the inevitable?"

The bewilderment in Nikkola's eyes charged the atmosphere surrounding his heart, engulfing him with an undeniable rush of yearning. "The hell with the inevitable. Tonight belongs to us, only us. I've never spent an entire night with anyone before you, and I'm not ready to spend another night without you. Somehow, someway, we're going to be together forever, Nikki. You can hold on to that promise."

Without responding, Nikkola climbed from the bed and dragged him into the bathroom with her, where they showered and made love until their legs felt weak and rubbery.

While packing a few things into her overnight bag, Nikkola was dizzy with anticipation of the magical night that lay ahead. Their flight wouldn't depart until midnight of the next evening; Latham planned on taking every moment Nikkola was willing to give him.

However selfish it seemed, Nikkola and Latham weren't ready to give up on each other.

Chapter 11

Executing her duties in a mechanical but cheerful fashion, Nikkola tended to her passengers' needs, aware that Latham was only a few steps away, but no longer accessible to her. Against his wishes, she'd decided that they shouldn't further delude themselves with any more fantasy nights. He was filled with apprehension over embarking in a loveless relationship with Carmen, but Nikkola had convinced him to give it more thought. In the meantime, Nikkola thought they needed to distance themselves romantically from one another.

Being in close proximity, and alone on the other side of the world, Nikkola and Latham knew it would be difficult not to indulge themselves in each other, but for the sake of argument, they were going to try and stay apart. Glen would have served as a safety net for Nikkola, but with him no longer a part of the crew she saw lonely days ahead. Latham hadn't spoken to Carmen since she'd given him her tale of woe, but he'd told Nikkola that he was aware he'd have to make contact with her fairly soon.

Busying herself with serving drinks, Nikkola pushed the serving cart down the first-class aisle. As Latham's sexy voice suddenly came over the loudspeaker, she nearly froze in her spot. Feeling as if she were suspended in midair, Nikkola couldn't help remembering a few delicious details of the last passion-filled hours she'd spent with Latham.

"Good evening, ladies and gentlemen. This is your captain speaking. We seem to be a little ahead of schedule, which means we'll arrive in London a few minutes earlier. Relax and enjoy the rest of the flight. I'll keep you informed of any new developments. Thank you."

"Miss, Miss," a concerned-looking passenger called out to Nikkola.

Nikkola's mind was lost in Latham's deeply tranquilizing voice and she had to shake her head to snap out of the trance. As she looked down at the woman, her smile came weak.

"Are you okay?" an elderly woman asked Nikkola.

"I'm sorry, ma'am, I was momentarily distracted. What can I get for you?" Nikkola asked, smiling a bit broader.

"I'd like another scotch and water. I'm scared to death of flying. I normally don't drink, but I might need a few more to completely relax me." She sounded as anxious as Nikkola felt.

Nikkola gave her a sympathetic smile and a few words of reassurance. She quickly mixed the drink and then handed it to the nervous passenger, hoping she wouldn't need another. Before moving on, Nikkola patted the woman's hand in a soothing manner.

Kneeling down in front of one seat, Nikkola smiled brightly at the little blond girl seated there. "What would you like to drink, sweetheart?"

The little girl put one tiny finger up to her temple in a gesture of thought. "I'd like a root beer! Can I have lots of ice?"

As Nikkola filled the child's order and handed it over, she couldn't help thinking of her too grown up, darling Cydnee.

For the duration of the flight, Nikkola was kept quite busy. When the seat-belt sign came on, signaling the time for landing, she sighed wearily. After making sure that all her passengers were properly secured, Nikkola took her own seat and buckled herself in.

The large aircraft was completely cleared in record time. Without bothering to make her usual visit to the cockpit, Nikkola hastily claimed her things and headed for customs. It felt strange not having Glen around. Loneliness came in to victimize her, but when she reached her destination, Mychal Forrester could be seen standing formidably on the other side of the baggage-claim line. Oddly enough, she was excited to see his smiling face. Nikkola wondered if his being there was just by chance, but she rather suspected that his presence was by design.

Mychal lifted his hand and waved at her enthusiastically. Nikkola's heart fluttered nervously.

As Nikkola easily cleared the customs line, Mychal strode up to her, grinning broadly. "Nikkola, I came to rescue you from the tedious travel to the hotel aboard the crew bus. My chariot awaits you, fair lady."

Nikkola smiled and then checked around for Latham. When she didn't see his tall figure, she handed her flight gear into Mychal's extended hand. "It won't do any good to protest, so I won't bother," she uttered in a resigned tone.

The jet-black Jaguar sprang to life with the flick of Mychal's wrist, purring softly under the highly polished hood. Unfamiliar with the route Mychal had taken, Nikkola relaxed and drank in the sights.

An extended time had passed before Nikkola began wondering where Mychal Forrester was taking her. With eyebrows furrowed, she gave him an impatient glance. She then looked at him with suspicion in her eyes. "We should be at the hotel by now, Mychal. What are you up to now?"

Mychal's expression was enigmatic. "I want you to see the house I lease when I'm here in London, Nikkola. I promise I'll be on my best behavior."

"I'm tired, Mychal! All I want to do is take a hot shower and climb into bed." Her challenge had come rather loudly.

"Calm down, Nikkola. We're almost there. You can lie down in one of the guest rooms."

Nikkola crossed her arms stubbornly, staring at him with angry indignation flashing in her hazel eyes. "I don't want to lie down. I want to drop dead asleep. With your slinking around, I'd never be able to do that. Your presence is unnerving to say the least."

Mychal grinned smugly. "I'm unnerving because you're so wildly attracted to me. Isn't that right, Nikkola?"

Mychal's arrogance grated on Nikkola's nerves.

"But know this, Nikkola, I never take anything not offered me."

"Is that so? I didn't offer to come to your home, now, did I, Mychal Forrester? You're so contradictory. I don't know why I bother to spar with you."

Mychal pulled the powerful car into the circular driveway of a large estate house. Cutting the engine, he turned to face his passenger. His eyes were soft and moist, which was even more disturbing to Nikkola as she recalled the last time those dark eyes turned soft on her.

"You never responded to my question regarding your wild attraction for me."

Incensed at Mychal's dastardly egotism, Nikkola turned away from him and stared out the window. The beautiful grounds quickly mesmerized her, brightening her dark mood. Though too stubborn to admit to it, she was eager to see the inside of this great gray-stoned house.

"Are you ignoring me, Nikkola Knight?"

Nikkola rolled her eyes. "By gosh, you've got it." Opening the car door, she stepped out and walked toward the huge garden right in front of her. The rich, green lawns were manicured to perfection while colorful flowers and shrubs guided her path. Indescribable scents wafted across her nostrils, as she took in a deep breath of the freshly scented air.

Walking up behind her, Mychal placed his hands on her waist, leaning forward to whisper into her ear. "Beautiful, isn't it? The flowers remind me of you. Softly colorful, willowy, yet so damn unbending and sweetly perfumed. You're indeed a wildflower. If wildflowers are not properly taken care of, they become unmanageable and start to run rampant. We can't have that, can we, Nikkola?"

The soothing tone of Mychal's voice sang tenderly near Nikkola's ear. Her heavy lids swooped drowsily down over her tired eyes. While guiding her head back against his chest, his hands gently massaged her temples. Too tired to fight the feeling, she gave in to the sweet feelings coursing through her trembling body.

Taking Nikkola by the hand, Mychal led her to the wooden bench positioned amid the massive shade trees. After seeing that she was comfortably seated, he sat down beside her and nestled her head against his muscular chest. With his hands gently strumming Nikkola's back, she was lulled into a semiconscious state. His hands were so therapeutic, relaxing her even more.

Completely enraptured with Nikkola's beauty, Mychal intently watched the rise and fall of her firm, perfectly rounded breasts, wondering if she knew just how beautiful and bewitching she was. Although he was falling hopelessly in love with her, he feared that she'd never feel the same about him. *If I'm a seasoned hunter, and you're the innocent game, then why do I feel so utterly trapped? If you find out what I've involved in, will you ever be able to forgive me?* Mychal felt guilty about playing Nikkola without ever giving her the rules of the game.

Awakening, only to drown in the depths of Mychal's dark probing eyes, Nikkola felt panic escalating in her breast. Wrenching herself away from his relaxed hold, she glared at him through hazy eyes, the passionate stirring in her breast belying the angry look.

"Let's go inside for tea. Then I'll return you safely to the St. James Court," he promised softly. "If you trusted me enough to fall asleep in my arms, you must indeed be tired. Or maybe your senses have taken leave."

Mychal's mocking laughter pierced the silence, forcing a melodic chuckle from Nikkola's throat. "Lead the way, you incorrigible brat."

Being in Mychal's company beats being alone with my own. Thoughts of the situation with Latham made Nikkola more determined to move forward. When she'd earlier told Latham that the war wasn't winnable for him, she hadn't meant it literally. His being married to Carmen wasn't what she'd had in mind. Not in the least.

Nikkola wasn't sure If Mychal was trying to play her or not, but if so, he was going to learn how it felt to get played. She merely saw him as a key to help her get over Latham, and she was going to turn that key every way but loose. Could she beat Mychal at his own game? Whether Mychal would emerge from this battle unscathed remained to be seen. It appeared to Nikkola that the hunter was already hopelessly caught by the game he'd so cleverly chosen.

The inside of the house was magnificently furnished with several exquisite antique and modern pieces. Each of the rooms represented certain periods of history, all of which were styled in elaborate furnishings relating to many different ethnic backgrounds.

Over hot tea and shortbread biscuits, Mychal entertained Nikkola with animated conversation. He was delightfully funny and she found herself laughing uncontrollably at many of the tales about people he'd met in his world travels. For a man who once looked so formidable, even at a distance, Nikkola found Mychal to be super charming and dangerously alluring.

Having set the tender trap, feeling that Nikkola was completely trusting and relaxed with him, Mychal decided that it was time to reveal his covert reasons for having brought her to the estate house. He eyed her intently as he thought of how to present his proposal.

"Will you be a guest in my home while you're here in London, Nikkola? You can have or do anything your heart desires. It's comfortable here, you know. I have so much more to entertain you with here than what that stuffy hotel has to offer."

Amazed by Mychal's generous offer, Nikkola dropped her mouth open, her eyes searching his for any underhanded motives. Finding only sincerity there, she toyed with the idea of accepting his hospitality. Perhaps staying far away from the hotel would keep her from fleeing to Latham's arms in the middle of the night. With that in mind, Nikkola accepted.

After showing Nikkola to an extremely large upstairs suite, Mychal made sure she was settled into the room before leaving to retrieve her travel bags. The massive canopied bed had her in awe, as the deep and lighter shades of rose accents induced a peaceful atmosphere. The sounds of a bubbling fountain suddenly caressed her ears. Running to the window, Nikkola looked down upon the most beautiful gardens she'd ever seen. Her breath caught.

With less than forty-eight hours before her return flight to the States, Nikkola's mind raced with thoughts of how she'd spend her time on this grand estate. She wished that she had a longer layover. Then it dawned on her that she wasn't in a hotel room, but in Mychal Forrester's privately leased home. He just might have something to say about how she'd spend her time there.

What he had in mind might not coincide with her plans—
a sobering thought for Nikkola.

A strong knock penetrated Nikkola's thoughts. She
whirled around to face the tall double doors. "Come
in," she called out, starting to feel a little intimidated.

Pulling Nikkola's flight gear behind him, Mychal entered the room, smiling. After helping her store the gear
in the spacious walk-in closet, he acquainted her with
the other areas in the suite, darting in and out of the
splendid rooms readied for her exclusive use. Though
intimidated by the expensive furnishings, Nikkola felt
more intimidated by the fact he'd obvioulsy been confident that she'd accept his offer.

Mychal left Nikkola alone while she showered and
changed into clean clothing. Sensing that he was hon-
orable, that he meant her no harm, Nikkola laid to rest
anxious feelings she'd begun to experience. A minute
later, a vision of Latham guided her thoughts elsewhere.

Under the gently spraying shower water, Nikkola
thought back to the last passionate night she'd shared
with Latham at his home, where they'd spent the entire
evening talking over their plight and making sensuous
love throughout the night and into the next day. Sending
him into the arms of another woman wasn't her idea of
nobility, but she felt that encouraging Latham to take
an active part in his future child's life was the right thing
to do.

Nikkola also felt if Latham really didn't want to be
with Carmen that nothing she could've said should've
convinced him otherwise. Latham had vehemently
protested the split at first. Then he'd begged Nikkola to
continue staying with him until he'd made a definite
decision as to what he should or shouldn't do. She'd
wasted no time in deciding that she wasn't going to be
an excuse or a distraction for Latham not to deal with
the issues at hand.

Imagining how worried Latham would be if he tried

to see her at the hotel, Nikkola felt pangs of guilt for being here in Mychal's home. But accepting that it was over between them was the best thing for everyone concerned. Putting Latham out of her mind, a difficult task, Nikkola began concentrating on getting dressed so that she could then find her way around the perplexing layout of the huge house.

Thirty minutes later, when Mychal appeared to escort her downstairs, Nikkola was happy that she wasn't going to have to navigate through the house on her own. She could see herself getting lost in the maze of rooms, which would've no doubt provided more amusing entertainment for Mychal Forrester at her expense.

The marble-stone terrace off the back of the house showed off a magnificent panoramic view of the vast grounds and the numerous lakes. Mychal pulled out a patio chair for Nikkola to be seated and then sat down in the chair closest to hers.

The heavy breeze coming in off the water felt so wonderful against her hot flushed skin. Nikkola knew that had her hair not been tied back, the wind would've blown her curls into a disheveled mess. On the other hand, Mychal wanted to see Nikkola's hair free and loose. Surprising her, he reached over and loosened the hair band, which gave the wind free rein in rearranging her curly style.

Nikkola gave Mychal an obstinate look. "Why did you do that?"

"Your hair is so beautiful. I can only imagine that you're even more beautiful with it wild and free. My curiosity got the best of me. It complements the free spirit inside of you, Nikkola. You look like an old schoolmarm when your hair is pulled back so severely tight."

Nikkola liked the reference he had made to her as being a free spirit, but she refused to show any signs of approval. His ego was big enough. "And you're a control freak, Mychal Forrester. I wear my hair strictly to please me, not for some egomaniac's pleasure."

Nikkola's words smacked of an attack on his character, but Mychal chose not to retaliate, mainly because there was a definite ring of truth to them. It hadn't taken him long to come to understand that he'd never be able to control the strong-willed Nikkola Knight. Moving his face very close to hers, he blew some loose strands of hair from her face, his fresh breath fanning her eyelashes. Backing away from his closeness, Nikkola gave him a boundary-enforcing glance.

Mychal grinned devilishly. "Don't tell me I've offended you, Nikkola. It wasn't my intention," he mocked with heavy sarcasm.

Nikkola's eyes softened as she flashed him a brilliant smile. "No offense taken, Mychal. You just have a way about you that irritates the hell out of me." *And, at times, thrills me to no end. What am I to do with all these crazy, mixed-up emotions—the direct result of Latham's future being so up in the air?*

"I do seem to have that type of effect on people. If it'll make you feel any better about me, I'll do my best to hone my skills in charm and grace and try to be more appealing to my most worthy opponents. Tell me about yourself, Nikkola. I'd like to learn more about the woman that truly fascinates me."

Narrowing her eyes, Nikkola looked at him with one lid closed. "That's a simple enough request, but since you seem to already know everything about me, why don't you tell me all about me, Mychal! Maybe I'll learn something new about myself. I suspect you even know exactly what time I was born."

"You have a very clever tongue, young lady. It could get you into real difficulty if you're not careful," he warned in a menacing tone. "I admit that I've done a little research on you, but I'm sure I've only scratched the surface."

"Since you're into researching my background, try digging a little deeper. Don't rely on me to tell you a thing. I'm an awful liar," she quipped. "I could sell you the Brooklyn Bridge if I put my mind to it. Then I'd later have you dying to present it to me as a gift."

"I like that you're not so easily intimidated." His face was alit with a mischievous grin.

Rising from the chair, Nikkola turned her back on Mychal and slowly walked from the terrace, feeling his dark eyes boring into her retreating back. His concentrated stare gave her the urge to run and never stop. Mychal Forrester was about as harmless as a keg of TNT. "I must be very careful not to light his deadly fuse," she muttered to herself.

The water in the lake was so clear Nikkola could see her reflection. Seated on the bench in front of the water, she removed her shoes and stuck her toes into the pool. The water was warm enough to take a bath in. If Mychal weren't present, Nikkola would've loved to skinny-dip.

As though he'd read Nikkola's mind, Mychal crept up behind her. Feeling his presence, she turned and looked up at him. "I'll turn my back if you want to get naked and swim in the lake. I do it often. Very stimulating."

"Desire or not, I wouldn't dare take my clothes off at your place, not unless I was sure you were stranded thousands and thousands of miles away."

Without warning, a heavy rain fell from the sky, causing Nikkola and Mychal to scramble for cover. Grabbing her by the hand, he pulled her back onto the terrace, where they watched the rainfall, each of them in wondrous awe of Mother Nature.

Mychal chuckled, breaking the silence. "Were you afraid you'd melt, Nikkola?"

"No, but I was terribly afraid of catching a cold and getting stuck here with you as a nursemaid. That's a fate I wouldn't wish on my worst enemy." She immediately felt ashamed of her churlishness. "I'm sorry. I don't know why I'm so testy. Flying all night might have something to do with it. I should probably take a nap. It might do wonders for my bad attitude."

"I know why you're so testy, as you put it. It comes back to what I said before. You're constantly fighting the wild attraction you feel for me. Giving in to your desires would also do wonders for your bad attitude, Nikkola."

Nikkola tilted her head to one side. "Mychal, you know, you just might be right, but I'm not willing to explore that possibility. You are way out of my league. Thank God I have sense enough to realize it. You're one extremely handsome man and your all powerful masculinity is something to be reckoned with, but I'm just not the one to do the reckoning."

"You're the only one that can reckon with it, Nikkola Knight." He kissed her forehead. "Come with me, it's obvious that you need a long nap."

Obeying Mychal was becoming second nature to Nikkola. Feeling completely worn out, jet lag robbing her of most of her energy, she wearily followed Mychal back into the house and up the stairs. For whatever reason, Nikkola still didn't fear he'd bring any harm to her. Mychal could be as charming as he was devilish. Keeping Mychal as a friend might not be such a bad idea, she mused, sure that nothing more than that could ever happen between them—not when Latham had her heart on lockdown.

Mychal was downstairs in the massive kitchen brewing a pot of tea. When it was ready, he placed it on a tray with two cups and carried it up the stairs. Not bothering to knock, he entered the room. Nikkola was lying in bed with her eyes closed and Mychal had to struggle to put a tight rein on his emotions. The soft, blue-satin night-shirt covered her endowments well, but his piercing vision and wild imagination allowed his dark eyes to easily penetrate the material.

After setting the tray on the nightstand, Mychal stood over the bed and tenderly stroked Nikkola's cheek. "I brought you some hot tea. It'll help you sleep. Do you take milk?" She shook her head in the negative. "I thought not. Some Americans have no class," he bantered lightly.

Nikkola's body was too drained to take issue with his crass remark. When he sat down on the side of the bed and lifted the cup to her lips, she willingly drank from it. As though she were a small child needing his direction, he fed her the tea until the cup was empty. Leaning forward, he placed a light kiss on Nikkola's forehead and then swiftly exited the room.

Upon entering his own suite of rooms, Mychal seated himself behind his desk and grabbed up the telephone. After dialing several numbers, he impatiently drummed his fingers on the hardwood, waiting for a response from the other end.

A sluggish male voice finally came on the line.

"Were you able to accomplish the mission, Rex?"

"It seems bloody impossible. That place is as secure as the Tower of London, Forrester. But don't worry, I'll keep working at it. I'll eventually find a way to get into that flat. Money has a way of working miracles." Rex gave an eerie laugh.

Mychal shuddered at the menacing sound of Rex's laughter. "Only use money as a last resort. The last thing we need is a paper trail. We're running out of time. She'll be returning home day after tomorrow. I'm counting on you, Rex. Don't disappoint me."

Mychal hung up the phone and then popped a cassette tape into the minirecorder. Using headphones, he listened to the tape recording. Frowning heavily, Mychal snatched the headset from his ears and turned off the recorder. The shame he felt was indescribable, but he was too deep into this project to desert it now. This was one damn job that he'd live to regret.

Frustrated and worried, after having stopped at the registration desk several times to see if Nikkola had checked in yet, Latham was seated by the window in his suite, running agitated fingers through his hair. Many troubling questions sped through his brain.

Where could Nikki have gone? Had something happened to her, or was she doing this on purpose to avoid him? Picking up his coffee cup, he took a long swallow and then placed it back on the small round table. *Yet we did agree not to see each other socially. Why did I go along with this crazy notion? Nikkola's in my blood and a transfusion would prove futile. How did he separate himself from someone he loved dearly, loved with an unyielding passion?*

It's impossible, a small quiet voice in his heart responded.

When Latham had reached customs earlier, he'd scanned the entire area, searching over everyone for a glimpse of Nikkola's fiery red hair. Rarely were they on the same crew bus, but after he'd reached the hotel he'd stayed outside to check for her on each arriving shuttle.

According to reservations, Nikkola had never checked in. He was aware that she and Glen knew several London residents, which had him hoping and praying that she was just off with friends. Though the man rivaling him for Nikkola's affection briefly entered his thoughts, it never dawned on Latham that Mychal Forrester would be someone she might choose to hang out with.

* * *

Hours had lapsed when Nikkola awakened confused as to where she was. Looking all around the room just to get her bearings straight, she slowly remembered the events that led her to the place where she lay. Hopping out of the bed, she headed for the window, where she was able to watch the birds winging their way to the massive trees to settle in their nests for the night. A dark shadow had already fallen across the blue skies, turning them a bleak gray.

As the sun had already begun the descent to its final resting place, Nikkola felt both blessed and fortunate to catch the still brilliant sun plunging downward behind the trees.

Magnificent. The awesomeness of God's beautiful tapestry nearly took her breath away.

With her last full meal having been eaten on the flight, Nikkola was ravenous and her stomach loudly protested the neglect. A light knock on the bedroom door turned her attention away from her growling belly. Slipping into a blue satin robe, she answered the door, coming face to face with a plump, brown-skinned woman with soft gray eyes and a pleasant smile, her dark hair evenly mixed with strands of silver.

"Miss Knight, I'm Olivia," the woman informed Nikkola in a thick British accent. "Mr. Forrester is requesting your presence in the formal dining salon. The evening repast will be served half past the hour. "Is there anything I can help you with?"

"No, there isn't. Thanks for asking. You can tell Mr. Forrester that I'll join him for dinner in the salon, Olivia. It's a pleasure to meet you."

Olivia thanked Nikkola and then sped away, as if she were on a burning mission.

So, Mychal does have staff. The knowledge somehow gave Nikkola comfort. She couldn't imagine him caring for this oversized mansion on his own, but then Mychal was probably capable of successfully managing just about anything he chose to take on, including her. That thought was a fearful one.

With formal dining in mind, Nikkola pulled out a dress appropriate for the occasion. It was a simple but elegant white-silk sheath. Upon glancing at the clock, she saw that she didn't have much time to get ready. Being late again would only infuriate Mychal.

As Nikkola enthusiastically set about the task of dressing and styling her hair, she felt completely rejuvenated by the cool shower. Brushing all her tresses to one side, she secured the mass of curls with delicately designed pins of ivory-colored seashells. She then sprayed a light fragrance behind her ears and misted a little in her hair.

Thoughts of Latham filtered through Nikkola's mind, but she fought hard to resist the temptation to lose herself in them. It would be so easy for her to climb back into bed and give in to the sensual dreams of him that she indulged in every single night. Not tonight, she mused.

Trying his hand at being the perfect gentleman, Mychal, dressed in dark, formal attire, appeared at Nikkola's door to escort her to the dining salon. His striking looks were overwhelming to her. The dashing tuxedo had him looking like royalty.

Mychal's eyes held a stunned expression as he raked in Nikkola's exquisite appearance, truly believing that he'd never seen a more beautiful woman than the one standing before him. He smiled brightly. "You look radiant, my dear Nikkola."

Nikkola smiled warmly at him. "Thank you. Royalty was the description that came to mind when I first checked you out."

Flattered by her comment, Mychal held out his arm

for Nikkola to take, and she took a relaxed hold of it. Placing his hand tenderly over hers, he carefully guided her down the winding staircase. Gasping loudly, as they entered the salon, Nikkola looked at the antique place settings, the softly lit crystal chandelier, and the Irish-lace linens. The highly polished wood slab could easily accommodate twenty people at once. With only two place settings laid out, the long table seemed to swallow up everything in sight.

Keeping his eyes fastened on Nikkola, Mychal lifted her hand to his lips and planted a tender kiss onto her. He then pulled out a chair for her.

Dressed in proper English butler-like attire, a tall man with thinning gray hair and lavender eyes entered the room. All he needed was a top hat, Nikkola thought with amusement.

Charles politely nodded at Nikkola and then turned to face Mychal. "Sir, shall I serve the appetizers?"

"That'll be fine, Charles," Mychal responded respectfully.

The fascinating man turned on his heels and disappeared from sight, only to return within seconds carrying two silver trays laden with petite sausages baked into puffed shells of thin pastry, peeled shrimp, cheese in a puff basket, and other assorted delicacies, of which he carefully placed at Mychal's side. Charles poured the wine into the crystal glasses and then stood by ready to meet Mychal's every demand.

After the appetizers were consumed, beef Wellington, grilled vegetables, and whipped carrots with ginger were served as the main course. Once several delicious-looking desserts were set on the table, the couple was left alone to enjoy an intimate evening of fine dining.

As the evening wore on, Latham became increasingly worried about Nikkola. He was about to contact the authorities, but he thought better of it. If Nikkola was away on her own accord, she would be furious with him for alerting the police; she'd also resent his interference. Upon dialing room service, he ordered a sandwich and coffee.

Just as Latham sat back to try and watch some television, the phone rang. Thinking it was Nikkola, he rushed to answer it. When Carmen's nerve-grating voice greeted him, Latham sighed with discontent, disappointment clearly showing on his face.

"Latham, I'm glad I was able to reach you. How are you?" she asked, her tone uncertain. She heard his deep sigh of disappointment and it stung her pride. "I've been waiting to hear from you," she continued. "Have you made any decisions about marriage yet?"

Latham's loud groan was unintentional. "There's still a lot to think about, Carmen. But are you going to be content married to a man who's madly in love with another woman?"

Latham's blunt question caught Carmen unprepared; his confession of love for Nikkola nauseated her.

Latham couldn't help wishing that Carmen hadn't called him because he didn't want to cause her pain, but he had no stomach for lying to her. Deception would only complicate matters even more. If things got any worse in his personal life, Latham wouldn't know where to turn.

"I'm not in this for love, Latham. My concern is for our unborn child. You should be concerned too," she hammered out. "Haven't you heard anything I've said to you?"

"Did I hear you? As loud as you were shouting, the entire world could've heard you. I hear you loud and clear, Carmen, but I don't see how our getting married can be good for the child. There'll no doubt be dissension between us. As the child grows up, he or she will feel the strain. I don't think it's fair to raise a child in an unhappy environment. It's just not healthy."

"It doesn't have to be that way, Latham. If we treat one another with respect, there shouldn't be any dissension. Please don't abandon your only child."

Carmen had successfully manipulated Latham into feeling guilty, which made him want to throw the phone across the room. "I'll be home soon, Carmen. We can talk then. I have to go. Take care of yourself," he said calmly.

Carmen had started to speak again when the phone lines disconnected. Latham had heard her, but he didn't want to listen and to be put on any more guilt trips. This was a nightmare. Even if he woke up, the problem would still be there. He definitely didn't want her to have an abortion, didn't even want to consider it, but he didn't want to marry Carmen either. The true victim in this situation, unfortunately, was the child.

Hearing the knock on the door, Latham got up from the sofa and answered it. After accepting his food order, he dug into his pocket for a few Euro dollars and handed them to the young man.

In the early hours of the morning, Mychal had tucked Nikkola into the huge bed, but she'd lain awake long after he'd gone thinking about the evening with Mychal, Latham, and how she'd gotten herself into an impossible jam. Mychal had been a perfect host, thus far, but she felt that it was a mistake for her to stay. He'd been sweet and charming over dinner and they'd even slow-danced and had a moonlit stroll around the grounds.

What had frightened her the most was when Mychal had kissed her—she'd responded rather ardently. She'd sent signals that she hadn't meant to send, and she was no longer sure she was just using him to get over Latham.

She loved the attention Mychal lavished upon her, but she'd also begun to question her own integrity.

"How can I be in love with Latham and respond even one iota to Mychal's affections?"

There was something about Mychal Forrester that she didn't trust, but she couldn't put her finger on any one thing. He also excited Nikkola but in a terrifying way. At times Mychal was so damn smug and overconfident. Then he'd suddenly turn boyishly charming, causing her heart to soften toward him. Mychal was a strange one. Then again, he could be so darn sweet.

Latham was even-tempered and Nikkola knew exactly what to expect from him. With him she felt safe and secure. However, it was no longer a matter of choosing one over the other. Latham simply wasn't available for her to choose him. Did she continue to hope for something to come of her love for Latham, something that didn't seem to be in the cards?

Though Mychal had promised to take her to the hotel at first light before she'd come back up to the room, Nikkola knew he'd do everything in his power to get her to stay with him for the remainder of her layover. She had gotten herself into an impossible jam by agreeing to stay over in the first place. Nikkola regretted that she hadn't demanded him to take her to the hotel when she first realized where he was taking her. Although it wasn't one she could now correct, the biggest mistake of all had been getting into the car with Mychal in the first place.

Before giving in to the sleep she'd been fighting so hard, Nikkola made the decision to return to the hotel at dawn. If she stayed on as Mychal's guest, Nikkola was concerned that the subsequent consequences might be terrifying. That was one risk she wasn't prepared to take.

Chapter 12

Not long after sunrise, breakfast was served to Nikkola in bed, much to her surprise. Olivia was the one who had awakened her, informing her that Mychal was on an errand and would return within the hour. As soon as Nikkola finished the well-balanced meal, she showered, dressed, and neatly packed her things. Telling Mychal that she wanted to return to the hotel was going to be hard for her. But she'd made up her mind, and Nikkola wasn't going to allow him to sway her carefully thought out decision.

Nikkola decided that a final walk around the grounds outside in the fresh air would help clear her head and assist her in mustering up the strength to do what needed to be done. After slipping on a lightweight jacket, she made her way to the garden nearest the entryway.

Once Nikkola had walked a good distance, she located the bench she'd sat on the previous day. After sitting down, she calmly drank up the magnificence surrounding her. The beauty of the place, alive with every color imaginable, absolutely mesmerized her.

"Good morning again, wildflower. Did you miss me?"

Mychal's sudden appearance startled Nikkola. She likened him to Houdini, capable of appearing and disappearing in the blink of an eye. "No, Mychal, I didn't miss you. And I'm ready to return to the hotel now," she stated willfully, all in one breath.

Nikkola's breathless announcement had stunned Mychal even as he remembered his previous night's promise to her. For once in his life he found himself darn near speechless. The thought of her leaving upset him more than he had imagined. "I had rather hoped you'd stay on here until your scheduled return flight to the States. I thought you were enjoying yourself. Is there anything I can do to change your mind, Nikkola?"

"I have enjoyed myself, Mychal, but it's time for me to leave. A lot of people are probably worried about me, especially since no one knows where I am. Staying at your home was never included in my plans. I had no idea you'd even show up at the airport, let alone that I would allow myself to be whisked away to your beautiful hideaway."

"A lot of people worried? Or is it Latham Scott you're mainly concerned about?"

A dark cloud crossed Nikkola's features, indicating to Mychal that he'd overstepped his boundaries. "You seem to have all the answers, so why don't you answer your own question? You know more about me than I'm comfortable with. I have no intention of giving you any more ammunition to use against me. Are you some sort of spy, Mychal, or just damn nosy? You must have quite a dossier on me."

Though Mychal hid the naked shame he felt inside, Nikkola's retaliation had winged him, but good. "If you insist on leaving, I'll bring the car around, but I'll be sorry to see you go. I've enjoyed your company tremendously."

"I insist, Mychal. Thank you."

Snorting loudly, Mychal abruptly turned and walked away.

Stomping her feet out of frustration over his arrogance, Nikkola felt as if she'd taken on the behavior of a spoiled brat. Mychal was so darn infuriating to her, she considered herself lucky to get away from him with her sanity intact. He had a way of driving her crazy. Mychal had more mood swings than a woman suffering from PMS. After his demise, Nikkola thought it a good idea for scientists to freeze him and do an in-depth study of his entire anatomy. Mychal would make one interesting scientific study. The man was the epitome of pure madness.

Nikkola's tremulous laughter floated on the air as she ran through the garden and into the house. Laughing felt much better to her than crying over the impossible situation she found herself in. Desperately in love with one man while using another to get over him was just as maddening. Mychal wasn't the only insane one. Nikkola entered the suite to gather her things, only to discover they'd already been removed from the room.

The drive into the city was deathly quiet. The tension between Nikkola and Mychal was undeniable. Without ever uttering a word to her, Mychal stopped the car in front of the hotel and got out. He then opened the door for her while waiting as the bellman removed her bags from the trunk. Nikkola wanted to at least thank Mychal, but the warning in his dark eyes kept her silent.

Overwhelmed by Mychal's awful attitude, Nikkola walked toward the hotel entrance.

"I'll be in the States in a few days. I have every intention of seeing you again. I know you'll be waiting for my visit with bated breath, Nikkola Knight." Grinning wickedly, Mychal winked at Nikkola as he entered the car, driving away with the speed of light.

Nikkola could only stare after Mychal in utter confusion, knowing nothing would stop him from seeing her, especially since he knew her address. Considering Mychal as a challenge was definitely an understatement.

Hurrying inside the hotel, Nikkola went straight to the front desk. After she signed the registration card, the desk clerk handed her her key card. Upon reaching the elevator, she pushed in the red call button and patiently waited for the car's arrival.

As the elevator doors slid back, Nikkola saw that Latham was the only passenger. Quicker than Mychal had sped away in his car, Latham had grabbed her roughly by the arm, pulling her and her bags into the lift. She'd never seen such raw anger from him before now.

"Where the hell have you been, Nikki? You have some tall explaining to do."

All but snatching the key card from her hand, Latham looked at the room number and punched in the appropriate floor. Once the elevator came to a halt, he grabbed her bags and practically dragged Nikkola out of the lift, steering her toward the assigned suite.

Upon inserting the key card, Latham pushed the door open and practically shoved Nikkola inside. He didn't look at her until they'd reached the living room. Pushing her into a chair, he knelt down in front of her. "Start explaining, Knight."

Angry as hell now, Nikkola shoved Latham hard, toppling him over.

Though stunned momentarily, Latham recovered rather quickly, bringing Nikkola down to the floor by her wrist. "I'm not leaving this room until you explain your actions, Nikki. And you're not going anywhere either. So give up the goods, or we'll be right here on this floor until you do. It might serve you well to remember that we still have lots of time left on our layover."

As Latham was practically up in her face, Nikkola wanted to slug him hard, but he easily read her intent, his eyes warning her not to even try what she was thinking. She quickly thwarted the idea of any physical retaliation, but that didn't stop her from glaring at him. "I was with a friend, Latham, but I don't understand why I have to explain anything to you. We did agree not to see each other again. Now you're acting like we never had such an agreement."

"No, Nikki, you agreed for us not to see each other. I only went along with it because I just wasn't thinking clearly at the time. You're the one who made all the decisions and laid down all the laws. I didn't want to agree to any of it!" he yelled. "I'm sick and tired of people manipulating me and trying to force their own will on me. I'm an adult and I know what I want. It's you that I want, Nikkola. No one but you."

Nikkola shook her head fiercely. "You can't have me, Latham Scott, nor can you have us both. You came to me saying you might have to consider trying to work things out with Carmen. Believe me, that conversation wasn't just a figment of my imagination. I've replayed those words over in my head a thousand times or more. I get the impression that you want me to sit the game out like some second-string quarterback until you make a definite decision. I'm a starter, Latham, never second to anything or anyone but God. I can't nor will I wait on the sidelines for you to decide if I'm in or out of the game. I'm also devastated by the whole thing, but I respect you and care enough about you to let go of our relationship so you can do whatever it is you need to do. You have a lot more at stake in this than I do."

"Nikki, that's not how I see you, and you damn well know it. You're number one—the only one for me. What in the hell do I have to do to convince you of that?"

Tears slid from Nikkola's eyes, her body trembling

with unleashed hurt and anger. "Are you forgetting that there's an unborn child involved in this crazy love triangle? I love and need you, but they're going to need you more. If you didn't want to agree not to see me again, you shouldn't have. I wasn't holding a gun to your head. Had you just waited until you were sure before announcing anything to me about Carmen I might see things differently. Now that you have your explanation, can you please get the hell out of here and leave me alone? Don't you see that this situation is killing my spirit, Latham?"

Latham instantly pulled Nikkola into his arms, cradling her like a newborn. "Oh Nikki, I can't stand to see you cry. I never wanted to hurt you. I don't want to fight with you, nor do I want to be without you. Nikki, there has to be a way for me to love you and be a father to my child without marrying Carmen. It's simply not going to work out between us. I just don't love her."

Holding Nikkola's face between his hands, Latham kissed her hard on the mouth, pressing her back onto the carpet. Her need for him was just as intense as his for her, but she somehow found the strength to push him away. Making mad, passionate love to Latham was what Nikkola wanted to do more than anything in the world, but it would be wrong for her to give in to her physical desires knowing he'd never be all hers. Number two wasn't a position she was willing to settle for. He had to come to that understanding. It had to be all or nothing.

Nikkola squared her shoulders, hating herself for what she was about to do. "It's not going to work out with us either, Latham. I've found someone that I might be able to have something solid with. He's not about to become a father, nor is he faced with the decision to marry someone else, and he's free to make a commitment only to me. You and I have had our few weeks of glory, but now it's over between us. I'm moving on. I've waited too long as it is. It seems as if I've been in love with you forever, long before you even noticed me. It's too late for us, Latham. I'm sorry."

Hurt beyond comprehension, Latham released Nikkola, and arose from the floor. His movements toward the door were laborious. Before exiting the living room, he stopped abruptly, looking down at Nikkola, as if he had something to say. With excruciating pain smoldering in his eyes, Latham only stared hard at her. He then walked down the hallway and out the door.

The devastation in Latham's eyes had taken Nikkola's breath away, making her want to run after him and kiss his pain away. But she had to let him go. She wasn't a bit confused about her love for him. Her feelings for him were abundantly clear. She loved Latham Scott more than anything, but she wasn't willing to share him with anyone, including his unborn child.

"Oh God, help me," Nikkola cried, wishing that she could be less selfish.

If Latham and Carmen's baby looked anything like Carmen, Nikkola didn't think she'd be able to handle it; she'd be plagued with guilt every time she looked at the child. Knowing Carmen as she did, Nikkola knew that Carmen would be in their lives at every turn should she and Latham stay together. Carmen was not above using her own child to blackmail Latham into doing whatever she wanted him to do. Carmen would see to it that they'd have no peace.

Pulling a pillow from the sofa, Nikkola placed it under her head, curling herself up on the floor. As she wept bitterly, the memories of their passionate nights engulfed her. Knowing there would be no more passion between her and Latham, Nikkola felt as if she'd already died a thousand deaths. A living hell had already welcomed her with open arms.

* * *

Alone in his suite, more emotionally upset than he'd been in his entire life, Latham refused to face the fact that it was over for him and Nikkola. He wasn't willing to let her go that easily, wasn't ready to have her walk out of his life, wasn't prepared to give up on what they had. As for her announced interest in someone else, Latham hadn't bought into it for a second.

Nikkola Knight loved him every bit as much as he loved her.

The city of Alexandria sweltered with heat. Humidity hung in the air like a heavy curtain, making for a muggy and unbearably sticky day. The air conditioner did very little to cool off the rooms within Nikkola's condo.

Tired from flying across two continents, frustrated and depressed, Nikkola sat quietly in her kitchen, drinking a cold beverage. The lack of sleep over the past two days was in part responsible for her irritable mood—not to mention that her heart was irreparably broken. Though she regretted what had occurred with her and Latham, she hadn't seen any other choice.

Discovering that Latham wasn't on the return flight to the States had rendered Nikkola shocked, worried, and humiliated. Too ashamed to inquire about his absence, she had come up with a hundred reasons as to why he wasn't in command of the aircraft. There wasn't any one reason that made sense to her.

If Latham was distancing himself from her, Nikkola couldn't blame him, since she had cruelly insisted upon it. But Latham wasn't the type to allow a broken love affair to interfere with his serious duties as an airline pilot. He was way too dedicated to his job for that. That his absence had to do with Carmen wasn't something Nikkola would even allow herself to entertain.

Feeling weak at the knees, Nikkola got up from the kitchen table and traveled the short distance to her bedroom. After going into the bathroom, she sat down at the mirrored counter and surveyed her looks: pale skin, swollen eyes, and unruly red curls. She stared at the barely recognizable reflection of herself. *You have to pull it together. You look as though you're on your deathbed.* All someone needed to do was pull the sheet over her lifeless body. Without question, she would be whisked away to a cold slab in a morgue.

Returning to the bedroom, Nikkola sat down on the bed and picked up the telephone. She sighed heavily, waiting impatiently for an answer from the other end.

Upon hearing Nickolas Knight's cheerful voice, Nikkola grabbed a tissue from the box. Dabbing at her watery eyes, she fought hard to compose herself. "Hi, Daddy. It's me."

Nickolas recognized right off the anguish in his daughter's voice. "Nikki, honey, what's wrong? Are you ill?" Only silence filled the void. "Nikki, are you still there?"

"I'm still here, Daddy. I'm having a few personal problems. I just needed to hear your loving voice. I miss you and Mom. Is she at home?"

"Your mom's out shopping, Nikki, but I expect her back shortly. What kind of problems are you having, honey?"

"Men, Daddy, what else? Latham and I have split for reasons out of our control. And I have another hot pursuer that drives me absolutely insane." Nikkola managed to laugh softly.

"Any man that didn't pursue you would be the one that's insane, Nikki. I'm sorry to hear about you and Latham. Ethel and I hadn't even gotten a chance to meet him yet. Why don't you come home for a while, honey? We'd love to see you. You could probably use a little parental pampering."

"I don't think I have enough gumption to pack and drive myself to the airport. I haven't slept in two days, Daddy. I wouldn't trust myself behind the wheel." She would love to feel her parents' arms wrapped around her, to have them indulge her with their pampering style of love, but just the thought of flying again so soon was too unsettling.

"Can't you get Glen to take you to the airport? Or better yet, get Glen to come with you. It's been a while since your mother and I saw him last."

"I just can't get on another airplane right now, Daddy. When you fly for a living, you just don't want to do it on your off days. The thought of flying again so soon isn't a pleasant one."

"Okay, Nikki. Once we hang up, I'll check on available flights. I'm sure your mother will want to come to Alexandria. Will our coming there to see you help out some, Nikki?"

"Tremendously, Daddy. I have a few days off and I can definitely use some pampering from two of the people I love most. We can just relax and catch up on things."

Nikkola's burdens seemed to lift at the prospect of having her parents visit. Before hanging up the phone, she asked Nickolas to let her know the arrival date and time. They always rented a car when they came to see her, so she didn't have to worry about picking them up. Passenger drop-off and pick-up had become a virtual nightmare at all major airports since the disasters of September 11. As part of Nikkola's job-benefit package, her parents also had low-fare and space-available flying privileges.

Excited about her parents' visit, Nikkola immediately went into the guest bedroom and started preparing things for their arrival, happy to have something to occupy her time. The linens on the queen bed were fresh, but the room needed dusting and the floor needed to be vacuumed. Deciding to do the carpet first, she pulled the upright vacuum from the closet.

Walking into the guest bathroom next, Nikkola

opened the cabinet under the sink and removed a dust cloth, furniture polisher, toilet and tile cleaner, and a bottle of Windex. She then returned to the bedroom, where she sprayed the wood furnishings with polish and rubbed it in until everything gleamed. Using the Windex and old newspapers, she cleaned the mirror on the dresser and then the large bathroom mirror. Although the sinks and toilet bowl had been recently cleaned, Nikkola wiped them down with a foaming tile cleaner.

Nikkola's next project was the kitchen. After cleaning it until it was spotless, she decided to make a list of all the things she'd need to pick up at the grocery store. Before writing down her list on paper, she ran about the room checking the contents of the pantry and the refrigerator.

A short time later, Nikkola looked all around her place, mighty pleased with her numerous accomplishments. Feeling as though she might be able to finally fall asleep, she went into the master bathroom to wash her hair while showering.

"Hi, Nikki. It's Glen. I can tell you were asleep. Want me to call back later?"

Nikkola groaned softly. "No, I'm awake now. I've been missing you like crazy. We haven't talked in several days. How are you feeling, Glen?"

"I'm fine, Nikki, baby, but you don't sound too swell. How was London?"

"You really don't want to know, but it'll help for me to talk about it. Mychal Forrester made another unexpected appearance, so that should give you some idea."

Glen frowned heavily. "What is all that noise I hear? Besides the static, the line keeps breaking. Is it your phone or mine?"

"I think it's mine. I've heard it before. I'll call and have the phone company check it out."

"Do that, Nikki. The sound is awful. Listen, Josh is on his way over. We're going out to eat somewhere. Want to join us?"

"Earlier I decided I was hungry for fried chicken, mashed potatoes, and gravy. I cooked the food before lying down, but I haven't eaten yet. I'm too tired to go out, but I'd like it if you and Josh came over here to eat."

"Sounds good to me, Nikki. You can tell me all about London and Mychal when I get over there. I have some good news to share with you, anyway."

"Okay, I have some happy news, too. I'll see you in a few, Glen."

A light sprinkle of rain began to fall, which Nikkola welcomed, hoping it would cool off the city. Raindrops gently hit against the windows in her bedroom, creating a musical pinging, which made Nikkola want to go right back to sleep. Instead, she forced herself out of bed. Pulling a multicolored caftan from her closet, she stepped into it and zipped it up. Nikkola then slipped her feet into leather slippers.

Nikkola trudged into the bathroom, where she brushed her teeth and gargled with peppermint mouthwash. After brushing her hair straight back, she attempted to braid the mass of curls, an unenviable task. Nikkola always had to use a light gel to help keep her braid in place.

Making her way into the kitchen a short time later, Nikkola turned on the oven and set the temperature on low. After removing the foil-wrapped pan of chicken from the top of the stove, she shoved it into the oven to warm up. She planned to reheat the mashed potatoes and gravy in the microwave once her company arrived.

The telephone rang and Nikkola swiftly picked up the kitchen extension. She could barely hear her father with all the static on the line. Nickolas had called to let her know that he and her mother would be at her place by noon tomorrow. Relief washed over Nikkola as she placed the phone back on the cradle. Seeing her parents was going to make things look a lot brighter. The idea of Latham never meeting her parents disappointed Nikkola. Before she could delve any deeper into her morbid thoughts, the doorbell grabbed her attention.

Holding the hands of her two handsome male friends, Nikkola led Glen and Josh into the living room, where they each took a seat. She was pleased to see them both looking so well, especially Glen, who appeared to have gained back some of the weight he'd lost.

Josh Townsend worked as a management-level accountant for Air International. He was very tall, with the magnificent physique of a bodybuilder, and his smile was sincere and angelic. Nikkola would've given anything to be born with straight hair like his, which was dark brown and cut close. Josh's warm, brown eyes had a way of sparkling when he smiled. He had the eyes of profound truth and warmth. Josh and Glen had been best friends since high school. The two men always made Nikkola feel very much a part of their lives.

"So what's your good news, Glen?" Nikkola asked, eyeing him curiously.

Shifting his position, Glen rested his back into the corner of the sofa. "I finally got scheduled back on the night flight with my best girl."

Nearly flying across the room, Nikkola pressed her cheek against Glen's, hugging him tightly. "I'm thrilled for you and me. The night flight has been a drag without you. Welcome back, partner. With you back in the jump seat, our shift is going to come alive again."

Josh looked on at his two dear friends in amusement, admiring each of them.

Nikkola gave Glen a high five. "Now let me tell you my news. My parents are coming here tomorrow! They'll be here for a week or so."

"Great, Nikki! I can't wait to see them. I'll invite you guys over for dinner," Glen said.

Nikkola got to her feet. "Speaking of dinner, let's go into the kitchen and warm up all the food. The chicken is already in the oven."

Glen and Josh followed Nikkola into the kitchen, where they'd eaten together on so many occasions. Glen warmed the potatoes and gravy, while Nikkola cooked some applesauce, spicing it up with cinnamon and sugar. Josh busied himself by brewing up pots of both coffee and tea.

"Nikki, do you want cream in your coffee?" Josh queried.

"I'd rather have the hot tea for starters. I'll get coffee later. Thank you, Josh."

"You're welcome. I'm glad Glen is back on your flight, Nikki. Our dear friend has been maddening since he took himself off the schedule. I'm glad we both talked him into going back to the job that made him the happiest."

Nikkola smiled at Josh. "He shouldn't have left in the first place. I don't like it when he allows others to push him around. People are always going to have something to gossip about. If they can't get any dirt on someone, they just invent it."

Glen laughed. "You two are talking about me as if I'm not even here. I made a mistake, so give it a rest. I left the flight because I was ill, not so much because of the gossip."

"You left because of both," Nikkola charged. "And we all know it."

"Well, when people go from thinking you and I are romantically involved to saying I may be gay, it won't be long before they start rumors about me having a serious disease. I did what I thought was best for me at the time."

Josh looked upset. "Who said you might be gay? I haven't heard this one before now."

"Latham asked me about it, Josh, but he'd heard it from someone else. We all know why people think that. And, Glen, it's time you do something about your situation. You're not the only man who has this problem," Nikkola remarked.

Glen looked embarrassed. "Could we not talk about this right now, Nikki?"

"Nikki's right, Glen. It's time you talk to your doctor about what's been going on with you for several months. It's nothing to be ashamed of, man. What if it's something that can be easily remedied? There are new medications out there that can probably help."

Glen sighed out of his frustration with his medical dilemma. "How does a man tell a doctor that he has experienced erectile dysfunction? He doesn't!"

"Get a female doctor," Nikki suggested, sympathizing with Glen, but only to a degree.

Glen looked horrified. "That would even be worse. I stopped dating Gennifer because of what's going on with me, and you want me to get a woman doctor! You must be crazy, girl."

"The rumors will keep on flying around about you because no one ever sees you with any woman but me. Once I got involved with Latham, the crew came to realize you and I weren't an item. At one time we purposely made everyone think that we were. All the gossip and your physical condition are killing you, Glen. You've admitted to us that you still love Gennifer like crazy, which is also eating you up on the inside. Yet you haven't done anything at all about trying to get her back. Do you want to go on like this for the rest of your life? You're only thirty. I've read that Viagra is helping a lot of men regain healthy sex lives."

Glen threw up his hands. "Okay, okay. I'll give your suggestion some serious thought, Nikki, but just thinking of sharing something so intimate with any doctor, male or female, is downright daunting. Can we change the subject now? It's not exactly dinner conversation to begin with."

Nikki leaned over and hugged Glen. "Okay, partner. Let's eat and then we'll play a game of Scrabble afterward. That is, if everyone is in agreement."

Both Glen and Josh agreed to Nikkola's plans by nodding their approval.

Full and satisfied from the delicious meal, Nikkola, Glen, and Josh had quickly engaged themselves in a game of Scrabble. Nikkola loved words, especially the big ones; she enjoyed breaking them down and researching their every meaning.

A lot of cheating was going on, but none of the friends seemed to mind; all were guilty of it. Nikkola and Josh often came up with words that none of them had ever even heard before. Glen constantly challenged each suspicious word, easily winning once he searched the dictionary to locate what nearly always turned out to be nonexistent ones.

Glen also kept the game scores, which allowed him to add a few unearned points to his tally every now and then. By the time the game was over, no one was really sure who'd won, though it happened every time they played. Just having fun was their main reason for playing.

At evening's end, upon Nikkola's request, Josh looked at her telephone to see if he could find the reason for the static. Josh was an electronic whiz, but he couldn't locate the problem with the equipment, believing it to be in the line. Failing at his mission, Josh advised Nikkola not to cancel her already scheduled appointment with the telephone service department.

Just a little before midnight, Glen and Josh helped Nikkola restore her kitchen to its original order. Once everything was cleaned and put back in place, Nikkola walked her friends to the door, where she kissed and hugged each of them good night.

As soon as Nikkola closed the door, loneliness rushed up to greet her once again. The phone rang, and she laughed, happy that the unwelcome solitude would just have to wait. Although Glen had just left, she expected him as the caller, based on the lateness of the hour.

"Nikki, how are you?"

Nikkola's heart throbbed heavily inside her chest at the sound of Latham's voice. *God, how I love and miss this wonderful man,* she cried inwardly. *Please don't let me make a fool of myself by saying or doing something stupid.* "I'm fine, Latham," she finally managed, lying to keep him from guessing at the truth. Fine she wasn't. "How about yourself?" *I hope you're as miserable without me as I am without you, Latham Scott.*

Latham sighed with discontent. "I guess I'll make it, Nikki. I miss you terribly. Do you miss me just a little bit?"

Do I miss you? How can I not miss my own heart? "I do miss you, though I don't see what good it does." She instantly wished that she'd left out the end of her remark.

Letting Latham know that she missed him was okay in Nikkola's estimation. At any rate, it was the honest to goodness truth. She didn't believe she'd ever stop longing to see him, nor did she think she'd ever fall out of love with him. Nikkola wanted to ask Latham why he hadn't been on the return flight from London, but she couldn't bring herself to do it. If his absence had anything to do with Carmen, Nikkola simply didn't want to know about it.

Latham decided to ignore that last portion of Nikkola's statement about missing him. That she missed him period was all he needed to know; he already knew that it wasn't doing either of them any good.

"I only called to see if you were okay, Nikki." Knowing that wasn't the main reason he'd called, Latham swallowed hard. "Sweetheart, I need to see you. We have to talk again. I can't go on with this lingering silence between us. If nothing else, Nikki, we should be able to remain friends. Although I want so much more for us, I know it can't be that way for you right now. I just hope and pray friendship is an option you're willing to explore."

Nikkola took a deep breath, fighting her heart's desire to take the lead on this one. "We are good friends, Latham. As far as I'm concerned, that doesn't have to change." Allowing her heart free rein over her mind, Nikkola inhaled another deep breath. "My parents will be here later this afternoon, Latham. I'd still like for you to meet them. That is, if you want to."

"I'd love to meet your family, Nikki. Will you call me when you want me to come over?"

"I think this evening would be a perfect time if you're free. Say around six o'clock?"

"No plans whatsoever. See you at six, Nikki. Sleep well, beautiful."

Before Latham hung up the phone, Nikkola held the receiver up to her chest, hoping he could hear her unyielding love for him within the melodic lyrics of her beating heart. Happy tears fell from her eyes as she cradled the receiver. Latham still wanted her as a friend.

Just as Nikkola stepped out of her caftan, she realized that the phone line had been static-free during her entire conversation with Latham, hoping the problem had finally resolved itself.

Without questioning herself as to why she had suggested that Latham come over and meet her parents,

Nikkola slipped between the sheets. In a matter of minutes, she fell asleep with a delicate smile pasted on her full lips.

Much like Nikkola, Latham hadn't slept very well since the night they'd had the disturbing argument in her London suite—the same night she had announced to him her interest in another man. Although Latham had temporarily taken himself off the flight schedule for Nikkola's sake, he constantly prayed that they'd one day fly together again. No aircraft was needed for the type of flying he had in mind; he and Nikkola knew how to make each other soar high above the clouds.

If nothing else in his life was a guarantee, Latham knew he'd sleep very well tonight.

Chapter 13

Just as the alarm clock wailed out a piercing wake-up call, in the distance, a horn repeatedly honked. Sticking her hand out from under the top sheet, Nikkola slammed her palm down over the alarm button and silenced the disquieting buzzer.

With no desire whatsoever to face the dawning of a new day, pulling the sheet up over her head, Nikkola buried her face deeply in the pillow, wanting to sleep at least another hour or so. A few minutes later, when the follow-up alarm sounded, she bolted upright in the bed, groaning loudly with dismay. Grabbing her robe from the foot of the mattress, she slowly swung herself out of bed.

Even before the sun had completed its ascent into the hazy skies, Nikkola could tell it was going to be another hot, muggy day. As she looked out the window, she saw that the tree branches were deathly still; no birds were flying around singing, and all the colorful flowers appeared wilted, looking as if they thirsted for the first taste of morning's fresh, sweet dew.

While heading for the shower, Nikkola looked over at the telephone. Calling Latham was at the forefront of

her mind. Just hearing his voice would start her day off
right. Instead of giving in to her desire, Nikkola tapped
into her own spirituality. Talking to and then listening
for the voice of God was the only conversation she
needed to help her start her day in perfect peace.

A hot shower washed away the last vestiges of drowsi-
ness. After dressing in clean jeans and a red-silk T-shirt,
Nikkola secured her place and headed for the underground parking garages. Shopping done in the early-
morning hours would help her beat the afternoon
heat.

The grocery store was only a few blocks away. With
very little traffic on the streets, Nikkola sped her car toward the shopping center. The parking lot was nearly
empty. Finding a good spot close to the exit doors,
Nikkola parked the car in between the white lines and
turned off the engine. After grabbing a shopping cart
on her way into the store, she placed her purse in the
child-carrier portion of the basket, steering the cart
into the nearly deserted store.

As Nikkola walked the aisles unmolested by reckless
driven carts and tag-playing children, the early-morning
hours proved to be a perfect time to shop. Pulling the
grocery list from a zippered compartment in her purse,
she perused it and began loading her cart accordingly.
Since her parents ate very little red meat, she mainly
stacked the cart with chicken and turkey-based prod-
ucts, but added a roast and a few choice cuts of steak.
She chose a variety of fresh and frozen vegetables and
then gathered all the things she'd need for making
spaghetti and lasagna.

Aware that her parents would only be in town for a
few days, she was careful not to purchase too many
items that possibly wouldn't be used, but she made it a
point to stock the things her parents loved. Her father
was a fanatic for Hostess Twinkies. Like herself, her

mother loved anything and everything made of chocolate. All three of them were crazy for butter-pecan ice cream. She smiled with knowing, remembering that it was Latham's favorite flavor, too.

The checkout line was a breeze to get through for a nice change. Removing the checkbook from her purse, Nikkola wrote a check for her purchases, along with an extra fifty dollars for cash, and handed it and her check-cashing card to the checker.

A young man in his late teens wheeled the bag-filled cart to her car. Fishing in her purse for a tip, she smiled brightly, generously rewarding his good deed.

At one o'clock in the afternoon, Nickolas and Ethel Knight rang Nikkola from the security gate. Excited to the point of giddiness, Nikkola opened the gates. Rushing out of the house to meet them, she quickly jumped into the elevator and took it down to the parking area.

Waving enthusiastically while directing them into a visitor's slot, Nikkola could hardly contain herself. Once Nickolas steered the late-model white Lincoln Town Car into the parking slot, Nikkola had her mother's door opened before he could cut the engine. Nearly falling into her mother's lap, she crushed her arms around the neck of the lovely, smiling woman.

"Mom, I'm so happy to see you! Let me look at you."

Ethel got out of the car, pivoted around, and then struck a modeling pose. Nikkola laughed with glee as Ethel gathered Nikkola against her warm body, hugging her daughter. Joyous tears slipped from both their eyes. Nickolas Knight hastily rounded the car, opening his arms wide, embracing the only two women for whom he lived and breathed.

"Nikki, you look wonderful, honey," he said, smiling broadly. "I see the sun's been playing in your hair. You're well-tanned too. We were on pins and needles while waiting for the plane to land, but now we're here. Seeing you looking so beautiful was well worth the wait."

Nikkola squeezed her dad, hugging him warmly. "Dad, I can't tell you how happy I am to see both you and Mom."

The luggage was removed from the trunk and carried inside, where Nickolas put everything into the larger guest room. Having spent much time visiting their daughter, the Knights knew Nikkola's place inside and out.

When Nikkola offered to prepare them a snack, the Knights declined since a light lunch had been served aboard the plane. However, they were more than ready for a cold drink and great conversation.

Within seconds Nikkola had poured iced tea into tall glasses garnished with lemon wedges. Placing the glasses on a plastic tray, along with the oatmeal-raisin cookies Glen had dropped by, she carried it into the living room, where her mom and dad were seated on the sofa.

Nickolas instantly removed the tray from his daughter's hands and set it down on the coffee table. Free of her cargo, Nikkola took a seat next to her mother on the sofa.

"Charles," Ethel summoned, "could you get me a couple of aspirin? My head is starting to ache." Charles was Nickolas's middle name. When they were all together, Ethel used it to keep her daughter and husband from answering simultaneously.

"Sure, honey," Nickolas sang out. "Nikki, aspirin in the medicine cabinet, right?"

"Yeah, I stock them in all the medicine cabinets. There's Tylenol in there, too."

Ethel gently pushed back a few unruly curls from Nikkola's forehead. "Have you been feeling any better, Nikki? Dad and I've been so concerned about you."

Nikkola lay down on the sofa and placed her head in

Ethel's lap. She then looked up into her mother's tender brown eyes. "I'm doing better than I was yesterday. I'm going to be doing even better now that you and Dad are here. When you were falling in love with Dad, did he ever hurt you?" Nikkola's question surprised Ethel, but she began to think back on those times.

Nickolas returned to the room with two aspirins and handed them to his wife. As she took them with her drink, he sat down in a chair. "What are my two beautiful girls talking about?"

Laughing softly, Ethel raised her eyebrows. "Nikki wants to know if you ever hurt me while we were dating."

Nickolas also raised his eyebrows, questioningly.

Nikkola turned her head and looked directly at her father. "Either of you can answer."

"Well, let me see," said Nickolas. "If I recall correctly, there was one time your mother really felt hurt. It was when she'd heard that I'd taken Marsha Burton to a college football game. I *had* taken Marsha, but not as a date. She'd needed a ride. Being the good Samaritan, I gave it to her. But it was blown all out of proportion. The next day your mother wouldn't even speak to me. So I guess the answer is 'yes.' But I didn't intentionally hurt her."

Nikkola looked at her mother to see if she agreed with her father's assessment.

Ethel frowned slightly. "I can think of another time I was none too happy with this handsome gent," she announced. "He was innocent of the Marsha Burton case, but he'd lied to me about something else far more serious. It hurt me badly."

Ethel intently eyed her husband to see if there were any sparks of recollection. He smiled sheepishly at her, knowing exactly what she was talking about. "Maybe you should be the one to tell Nikki what I'm talking about, Nickolas," Ethel prompted.

"That's okay, Dad. I don't want to hear any more. I don't want either of you to be embarrassed by something out of the past. I surely don't want this line of questioning to start World War III."

"Thanks, Nikki," Nicholas said with relief. "It's better to let sleeping dogs lie. But since you must have a reason to ask these kinds of questions, we'd like to hear what's on your mind."

Nikkola looked pensive. "I told you that Latham and I had split, but I didn't tell you the reason. I wasn't ready to then, but I am now. He was dating someone before me, and it turns out the woman is carrying his baby. He's thinking of marrying her. The thought of him married to someone else hurts like the dickens. So much so, that I can hardly bear thinking about it."

Ethel and Nickolas exchanged grave glances. Wishing she could ease her pain, Ethel ran her fingers through Nikkola's hair. Seeing Nikkola in obvious distress upset both parents.

Nickolas moved out of his seat and knelt down in front of his wife and daughter. "Honey, we're sorry. Now that we know the reason for your unhappiness, we certainly have a greater understanding and appreciation of what you're going through. What your mother was talking about earlier is sort of the same kind of situation we once found ourselves in. I now feel compelled to share it with you. While dating your mother, I was accused of impregnating another girl. I profusely denied ever being with her. By then I was so crazy in love with your mother, I knew if I'd told the truth I was going to lose her. I didn't realize there was another option."

Glad to have gotten his unsavory story out in the open, Nickolas inhaled a deep breath. Telling his daughter that he'd once been a cheater wasn't an easy thing to do, especially when she adored him and looked up to him as her hero.

Nikkola was stunned by her father's similar tale of

woe. It disturbed her that he'd cheated on her mother, but she was mature enough to understand that people simply made mistakes.

"Whoever said your sins will surely find you out, knew what they were talking about. Here it is nearly thirty years after the fact and I'm face to face with my past sins. However, I finally did tell the truth. It nearly destroyed your mother, but my honesty paid off, because we later learned that the same girl had also been with two other college students. One of them turned out to be the actual father," Nickolas concluded on a heavy sigh.

Ethel held her husband in high esteem. His courage was admirable, but she was regretting having brought up the long-ago indiscretion in the first place. Ethel would never want to do or say anything to cause Nikkola to lose respect for her father.

"Dad, how did you find out you weren't the father?" Nikkola sat upright on the sofa.

Nickolas moved onto the sofa beside his daughter and took her hand, taking a couple of minutes to try and remember the circumstances that had finally released him from blame.

"Since I started this, I'll take it from here," Ethel stated. "From what I remember, this girl told someone else that she'd been with the two other guys. She'd told the person she really wasn't sure who the father was. As rumors were spread around about campus, one of the other boy's parents got wind of it. They'd insisted on a blood test for proof to make sure."

"Back then blood tests were not one hundred percent accurate," Nicholas weighed in.

"But Nick has a rare blood type," Ethel resumed. "Because of it, he couldn't possibly have been the father. The lies and deceit had destroyed my trust and faith in him, but he was able to restore my belief in him by being sincere and honest from that point on. I can honestly say that he's never even come close to hurting me since."

"You two are incredible." Nikkola was awestruck. "You've been together all these years, and I never would've known this story if you'd not had the courage to tell me. It would be wonderful if Latham weren't the father, but I'm sure he was the only person she was involved with. By the way, he's coming over to meet you tonight. I don't want you to hold anything against him. I simply want you to meet him. Latham never would've hurt me knowingly."

Nickolas hugged his daughter. "Nikkola, we'd never hurt him or hold him responsible for your pain. This doesn't sound intentional on his part. These things sometimes have a way of happening. Life will never be perfect. We're just glad for the opportunity to meet him."

Ethel patted Nikkola's hand. "Dad's so right. While there are some things people say they can never forgive, forgiveness doesn't come with an option. We just have to live with the consequences of which of the two choices we make, to forgive or not to."

While Nikkola and Ethel planned a menu for the evening meal, Nickolas went down to the exercise room to work out and soak away the traveling wearies in the hot tub. The aspirin had taken hold of Ethel's headache, so she was in much better spirits. As she and Nikkola puttered around in the kitchen, they happily gabbed away while preparing the meal.

Ethel asked about Glen and Josh and then quickly suggested that Nikkola invite them for dinner. Nikkola thought it was a super idea. Her parents had been in a social setting with Glen and Josh on several occasions. When they got together, they were all like one big happy family.

Nikkola put a call through to Glen right away, and he eagerly accepted the invite, but would need to check with Josh regarding his schedule. Nikkola also mentioned inviting Gennifer along. Though Glen felt that he wasn't quite ready to come face to face with Gennifer just yet, he agreed to the idea. Seeing her in a social setting might be better than them being alone. It had been a long time since they'd last seen each other.

Two hours before all the guests were due to arrive, Nickolas and Ethel showered and went into the guest room to take a short nap, leaving Nikkola to handle the rest of the lighter chores. Deciding that she could use a nap herself, Nikkola decided that she should first ice the cake. She would then lie down on the sofa for a brief respite.

Although Latham had agreed to meet her parents— and he really wanted to—he was feeling very apprehensive, wondering if Nikkola had shared his present situation with them. He'd been hoping to meet them under happier circumstances. To be introduced as their future son-in-law would've thrilled him; he still had hopes of that happening. Though Nikkola only wanted them to be friends, never for a second did he believe she was involved with another man. But her angry outbursts in London had cut him down like gunfire. His near fatal wounds were still exposed, very raw, and tender.

Carmen had showed up at Latham's door earlier in the day. He'd let her in, but he'd been worried she'd find out about his plans for the evening and somehow find a way to ruin them. Fortunately, she'd been in a good mood, only wanting to talk about the baby. She had left of her own free will long before he needed to start getting ready for his dinner engagement.

Understanding of Nikkola's position and how much

she was hurting from all this, Latham couldn't let the anger and hurt stand between them. He loved her too much for that. If they could find some common ground, or only be friends, he was willing to accept that. But he couldn't accept her being cut from his life for good. If he married Carmen, she'd have to understand that. But he still hadn't warmed one bit to the idea of doing something as drastic as marriage, not when he was sure it would only end with bitterness.

When he'd felt that he was in no condition to fly due to the lack of sleep, he'd taken himself off the schedule. He then took a hop over to Switzerland to see his parents, Arlington and Portia Scott, but he'd only stayed overnight. His parents had met Carmen only once. It was when they'd come to visit him in London. Even then his mother didn't think Carmen was the right one for her son. When he'd told her Carmen was expecting his child, Portia had nearly fainted. Then a heated argument had ensued. Latham had left Europe in worse shape than when he'd first entered.

Portia had also been able to see right through Morgan. He trusted and believed in his mother's instincts about women since she was such a warm, loving individual, who rarely found fault with other people. She had never before interfered with his female choices. But she'd seen something in those two women that had set her tongue a-wagging. And she'd told her son in no uncertain terms how she felt. Laughing loudly at the things his mother had said to him, he realized she only loved him and wanted the best for him. He knew that if she'd met Nikkola, there would've been an instantaneous bond between the two women.

Nikkola was a lot like his mother. Though long-suffering, they had the same fiery temperament, but the purest of hearts. Both were effervescent and courageous, as well as advocates of justice for all. The women he loved were always the champion to the underdog.

* * *

The dining room table was nicely set with a small basket of yellow daisies gracing the center, along with fine bone china and crystal glasses. The sterling-silver eating utensils and the place settings rested on a beautiful ivory-damask tablecloth with matching napkins.

Since more people were invited than originally planned, in addition to the baked chicken, Nikkola had roasted a small, standing rib roast to ensure there'd be enough meat for everyone. Ethel had prepared glazed carrots, broccoli, and scalloped potatoes. Nikkola had purchased freshly baked dinner rolls to accompany the meal, and Nickolas had chosen very fine red and white wines. Chocolate cake and butter-pecan ice cream were on the dessert menu.

In her bedroom, Nikkola was finishing up with her appearance, looking lovely in a lightweight autumn-gold double-breasted coatdress. The soft, gold material highlighted her hazel eyes, sprinkling them with flecks of gold. The use of a warm bronze blush on her cheeks and a deep bronze gloss on her lips warmed up her eyes and complexion even more.

As Nikkola went into the kitchen to check on the roast, Nickolas entered the room right behind her. Taking the potholder from her hand, he gathered her into his arms, embracing her with warmth. His hazel eyes, which she had inherited, twinkled merrily.

As Nickolas tilted his daughter's face upward, Nikkola planted a soft kiss on his lips. "Nikki, you're gorgeous! I love the color of your dress. You take your impeccable taste in fashion design after your mother. I'm always eager to see what she's going to wear each day, especially when we're going out on the town. She never fails to astound me. After all these years, I still get excited when she enters a room."

Tears sprang to Nikkola's eyes. She had always hoped to have a relationship like the one her parents had. The things he'd expressed about her mother touched her profoundly. "Mom's a beautiful creature, Dad. You guys are blessed to have each other. You all keep your relationship so fresh and exciting. I see the way you two look at one another."

"It doesn't come easy, Nikkola," Ethel interjected from the doorway.

Nikkola heard her father's rough intake of breath as he marveled at his wife's gentle beauty. The genuine love her dad had for her mom came through with crystal clarity.

Dressed in a stunning, detailed ivory pants suit, a rich beige silk blouse and, with not a strand of her gray-streaked hair out of place, Ethel was the epitome of class. Her dark brown eyes were illuminated with the love and pride she felt for her family. Nickolas rushed over to embrace her. His dark tailored pants and shirt were in direct contrast to his wife's attire. Mixed-gray hair, a stately figure, and a bright sensuous smile all added up to a man of sophistication.

Pulling both women into the circle of his warmth, Nickolas kissed each one on the cheek. The joy of being together showed in their faces. The sound of the doorbell broke up the loving display of human tenderness at its best. Nickolas strode off to answer its beckoning call.

Latham stood at the door smartly dressed in a lightweight tan suit and a dark brown shirt. It only took one look at Nickolas Knight's hazel eyes for him to know that he was Nikkola's father. Latham politely extended his hand. "Good evening, sir. I'm Latham Scott! You have to be Mr. Knight. I see the family resemblance." Latham firmly shook Nickolas's hand.

"Nice to finally meet you, Latham. Come on in. Nikkola and her mother are in the kitchen." Relieved to have the initial introduction out of the way, Latham followed Nickolas into the kitchen, hoping Nikkola's mother would be as receptive of him as her father.

Nikkola's heart skipped a beat when Latham smiled brilliantly at her. His own heart was causing quite a stir inside his chest as he walked over to her and took her hand.

"Hi, Latham." Bending his head, he lightly grazed Nikkola's cheek with his lips. "Mom, this is the man, the night-flight pilot, Latham Scott. Latham, my sweet mother, Ethel Knight."

Latham found Nikklola's introduction sweetly endearing, though he heard the tremors in her voice. It seemed that she was as nervous as he was. "Hello, Mrs. Knight," Latham greeted warmly. "I know where Nikkola got her hazel eyes. Now I can see where she gets her beautiful smile." Ethel blushed as Latham squeezed her hand affectionately.

Ethel squeezed Latham's hand back. "I can see why my daughter finds you so charming. Thank you for your gracious compliments. It's a pleasure to meet you, Latham, though we feel as if we already know you. Nikki has had a lot to say about you, all of it good."

Latham grinned. "That's certainly nice to hear." Smiling at her, Latham playfully bumped Nikkola with his hip. Her sweet smile left him wanting more contact with her.

After Latham and Nickolas escorted the ladies into the living room, the group sat down to wait for the rest of the guests. Nickolas engaged Latham in conversation, and Ethel joined in, chatting up Latham with ease. The first topic of conversation was Latham's job as a pilot.

Nikkola was unusually quiet. All that she contributed to the conversation were a few monosyllable answers and a couple of nervous nods. Being so close to Latham had her unnerved, only because she wasn't able to show any affection toward him. During the course of the conversation, she found herself wanting to hold him and lose herself in his sensuous mouth. It was hard sitting next to the man she'd shared a bed with. All she could envision was them making love and later falling asleep wrapped up in Latham's arms.

Latham was very much in tune with Nikkola's feelings, since he felt pretty much the same physical tension himself. His thoughts had also taken him back in time to the nights when he'd held her closely beside him. Desperately wanting to feel her sweet lips against his had him moaning inwardly. It was hard for Latham to keep his eyes off Nikkola, the woman he loved.

When the doorbell rang, Nikkola snapped to attention, sighing with relief. She politely excused herself. On unsteady legs, her heart going berserk, Nikkola stepped into the hallway.

Glen and Josh were fashionably dressed. In Nikkola's opinion, both men could've easily been mistaken for male models. She'd love to see each of them featured on the cover of a BET Arabesque romance novel. Her gorgeous guy friends would certainly be a great draw for the African-American female reading audiences.

Josh kissed Nikkola on the cheek, handing her the flowers and the two bottles of wine he carried. "Hey, sweetheart. You're looking good. Thanks for the invite to dinner."

As she inhaled the soft scent of the colorful bouquet, Nikkola squeezed Josh's hand. "Thanks for the compliment and the beautiful flowers. As for the dinner invitation, you have my mother to thank since it was her idea. A pretty good one, I might add."

Laughing, Josh took the flowers from Nikkola's hand. "Sorry, but it looks as if I gave this bundle of scent to the wrong girl. But you get to keep the fermented grapes. Lead me to your beautiful mother."

The group of friends had a good laugh at Josh's comical antics.

Glen wrapped his arms tightly around Nikkola's waist. As if she were a part of his soul, he could feel the anxiety coursing through her slender body. To calm her fears, he whispered tender words of encouragement into her ear. Without her uttering a word, Glen already knew Nikkola was anxious about being so close to Latham under the strained circumstances.

After leading her guests into the living room, Nikkola nervously introduced Josh to Latham, wishing the trembling of her voice would go away. Watching the genuine love and warmth flowing among her parents and her friends made her heart soar. Nickolas had always wanted a son, but Ethel was seriously warned by her doctor not to have any more children after the birth of Nikkola. At any rate, Nickolas's daughter was nothing less than the apple of his eye. He absolutely doted on Nikkola.

While everyone got acquainted, Nikkola just got up and disappeared. Her tears gave way before she even made it to the kitchen, her hands trembling uncontrollably. *This should be the happiest day of my life,* she thought miserably. The man she loved was in there with her family, but he'd never be a part of it legally. Nikkola couldn't bear the thought of his being married to someone other than herself—not when Latham Scott's heart was already married to hers.

While working up false bravado, Nikkola put the food on the table, and then slipped into the bathroom to repair her make-up. No more tears. *This is a time for joy and celebration,* she told herself, not wanting to do or say anything that might spoil the evening for her guests.

Glen was waiting for Nikkola when she came back into the dining room, feeling better than she had a few minutes ago. He walked up to her and put his arms around her waist. "Everything looks so lovely, pal. You've done a superb job."

Nikkola twisted her body around until she was face to face with Glen, eyeing him with concern. "How are you really feeling about seeing Gennifer tonight? It's been a long time coming, friend. I hope I haven't pushed you into something you're really not ready for."

Glen shrugged. "There's no better time than right now. The family setting works better than a one-on-one situation. I did call her, Nikki, after I agreed to your suggestion of inviting her, so at least the ice has been broken between us. Getting it completely thawed has me a bit worried."

"Why's that?"

"I haven't decided to tell her about my physical problems yet. I don't know if I ever can. If I can't, there's no future for us."

"If you love Gennifer like you say you do, you'll tell her everything as soon as possible. If she loves you, and I think she does, she'll help you through this. Please don't underestimate her without giving her a chance."

"What if she rejects me outright, Nikki?"

"Cross that bridge when you come to it, Glen. Why borrow trouble? Tomorrow will take care of itself. You have to learn to deal with today and stop looking ahead."

"You and your 'live-in-the-moment' philosophy. Easier said than done."

Latham slipped into the room and Nikkola's face instantly lit up. "Are you two being antisocial? Everyone is wondering where you two are."

"Not really, Latham." Nikkola wished she had the nerve to kiss Latham gently on the mouth. With him standing so close to her, the desire was overwhelming. "Glen and I were just having a conversation about his seeing his ex-girlfriend, Gennifer, for the first time in a long while. I wanted to make sure he's okay with it."

Latham stroked his chin thoughtfully. "A little late for that since she's already been invited, don't you think?"

"You guys need to stop worrying about me. I'm going to handle everything just fine. This is your dinner party, Nikkola, and I don't plan to cry all over it," Glen joked. "There's the door. I hope it's Josh's Cindy. I'd get the door for you, Nikki, but in case it's not Cindy, I better let you answer the bell."

Nikkola shook her head in the negative. "If it's not Cindy, the only other person it could be is Gennifer. If so, it would be nice if you were the one to greet her. You can break the ice even more. Now scoot, Glen! We don't want to leave her outside too long."

"Okay, okay, Nikki." Glen reluctantly took off.

Latham laughed. "Kind of bossy, aren't you?"

"You men! Sometimes you need someone to tell you what to do. Glen is not going to work things out with Gennifer by avoiding her. He has to get back into the swing of things and stop wasting precious time. I know they still love each other."

Latham's eyes softened, his love for Nikkola shining. "Yeah, I know the exact feeling."

Nikkola heard the sorrow in Latham's tone and saw the love for her in his eyes. She knew the feeling, all too well. "Let's go back into the living room so I can announce dinner."

"Yeah, that's not such a bad idea." *For a number of reasons*, she thought.

As Nikkola returned to the living room, she saw that both Cindy and Gennifer were present and accounted for, thinking they must've arrived at the door at the same time. That Gennifer was seated right next to Glen gave Nikkola a warm feeling. She took a brief glance at Glen. The huge smile on handsome his face did wonders for her heart.

"Welcome, Gennifer and Cindy. You're right on time, since dinner is ready to be served."

Ethel's anxious eyes stayed on her daughter. From Nikkola's voice, when she greeted her newly arrived guests and announced that dinner was ready, Nickolas could tell his daughter had been crying. That caused him to swap worried glances with his wife. Nikkola had tried extra hard to hide her inner distress from everyone, but she could see that she'd failed.

Nickolas led the dinner party into the dining room. He then requested everyone to hold hands while he gave the blessing. Latham tenderly laced his fingers through Nikkola's, warming her through and through. When the blessing was over, they both found it hard to let go.

As the group took their seats, Nikkola sat on the same side of the table as Josh and Glen; Latham, Cindy, and Gennifer sat directly across from Nikkola and the guys. Nickolas was at the head of the table, with Ethel seated at the opposite end.

Hungry people quickly began to dig in and devour the delicious meal. Nickolas raved over the exquisitely prepared meal between bites. Over and over again, he complimented his wife and daughter. The other guests also gave a few hearty amens.

The group was just starting on dessert when the doorbell pealed unexpectedly. Not expecting anyone else for dinner, Nikkola shrugged her shoulders. Glen offered to get the door, and Nikkola nodded her approval. Pushing his chair from the table, Glen got up and walked from the dining room and out into the hallway.

Upon seeing Mychal Forrester standing at Nikkola's door, Glen gasped loudly. Without being invited inside, Mychal stepped into the hallway, smiling mischievously. "Hello, Glen," he stated coolly. "Is Nikkola in?"

Glen could've easily told this arrogant man a lie, but when Nikkola yelled out asking who was at the door, he no longer had a choice. The others passed through on their way into the living room, but Nikkola had already entered the hallway, stopping abruptly in her tracks. The filled wineglass she held crashed to the tiled floor as she gasped in horror.

Latham heard both the glass shatter and Nikkola's verbal distress signal. He immediately turned around and walked back toward the hallway. His face turned a chalky gray at seeing Mychal Forrester standing there.

Latham's and Mychal's fierce stares collided while Nikkola fervently prayed for deliverance from this startling turn of events. Glen nervously cleared his throat, tightly gripping Nikkola's shaking fingers.

"Is someone going to invite me in or is everyone going to just stand around and glare?" Mychal asked, his tone impatient.

"It appears to me that you don't need an invitation. You seem to already be in," Nikkola responded sarcastically.

"You mean to tell me that you don't remember my telling you I was coming to see you? I told you so when I dropped you off at your hotel."

Nikkola realized that her sarcasm had only served to further encourage Mychal's rudeness. *Another death,* she thought with irritation. "Mychal, since you're here, please join us."

"Glen, would you mind showing Mychal into the living room?"

Glen would've led the way, but Mychal needed to prove that he'd been there before. "I know the way, old chap. I've already been here a time or two."

With Latham suspiciously eyeing her, Nikkola looked directly at the man she loved. She saw that the color hadn't yet returned to his face and his eyes were a raging red.

"Is he the friend you stayed with in London, Nikkola?"

There was a disturbing calmness about Latham. His demeanor frightened Nikkola, since she feared there was a powder keg of dynamite inside him. It was obvious that it wouldn't take too much more to set off a powerful explosion. Getting caught up in such a fiery blast could prove fatal for her.

Nikkola's lashes lowered momentarily. She then looked at Latham through half-open eyes. "Yes, Latham, he is. If we could talk about this later, I'd really appreciate it. My nerves can't take much more of this."

Latham shuddered inwardly, fighting hard to remain in control of his temper. Biting his tongue was difficult but necessary. This wasn't the time or the place, but this little episode in their already strained relationship wasn't over by a long shot. "I have my answer, so there's nothing else to talk about," he responded with deadly calm. Turning his back on Nikkola, Latham strolled toward the living room.

Mychal was seated on the sofa with his legs crossed, thoroughly enjoying the unrest he'd caused. Nikkola entered the room behind Latham and sat down next to her mother, who could feel all the tense vibes in the room, but her daughter's state of mind was what worried her most.

While monopolizing the conversation, Mychal held everyone's undivided attention. Nikkola didn't know if he'd been properly introduced or not, but she really didn't care. All she wanted was for this night to end. Her discomfort waved in the air like a red flag.

"Your daughter is very special," Mychal droned on and on. "I plan on marrying her," he announced boldly.

The guests could've heard a pin drop had Latham's jawbone not cracked so loudly. If it had been a different set of circumstances, nothing could have kept Latham from breaking Forrester's nose and his jaw. Since he believed in peace at all cost, violence wasn't his forte, but

Latham saw how he could easily break the rules and cross the line when it came down to evil men like Forrester.

"That might be nice if Nikkola were in agreement," came Nickolas's surly interjection. "But somehow I get the feeling that she's hearing this for the first time."

"Sir, you're right, but I can't think of a better time to let my intentions be known. With her family present— and all her close friends—I couldn't have hoped for a more appropriate setting without planning it myself." Mychal shot Latham a look of triumph.

Nikkola was too mortified to respond. Since his daughter had made no attempt to intervene, Nickolas checked himself. He knew that Nikkola was being terribly upstaged, and he hoped he wouldn't have to step in between this arrogantly rude man and Latham Scott.

Glen then quickly changed the subject, tactfully so. By asking Mychal several personal questions about himself, Glen cleverly kept Nikkola's midnight marauder in check.

Although Mychal refrained from continuing to talk about marriage to Nikkola, he still managed to be in total control of the various conversations. Unable to stomach any more of Mychal's maniacal drivel, Latham gave his sincere regrets in taking his leave. Nikkola immediately got up to see Latham out.

At the front door, Latham stared at Nikkola through dark, questioning eyes. Nikkola's heart felt broken beyond recovery. She started to speak, but he silenced her by placing two fingers on her parted lips. "You don't have to explain, Nikki. Believe me, I understand. I'm sorry that the loudmouth in there ruined your dinner party. Be very wary of him, Nikki. He's not someone to be played with. Watch your back, sweetheart."

Upon opening the door, Latham turned to leave. Then he suddenly turned around and roughly pulled Nikkola into his arms. As his mouth clamped down hard and hungrily over hers, she clung to him as though her life was being severely threatened.

"I love you desperately," Latham whispered onto her lips. "It's not over for us, Nikki. Don't fool yourself into believing it can ever be over for you and me. Love is forever."

Latham was out the door before Nikkola could respond, but she rapidly ran down the hall after him and flung herself right into his arms. Thrusting her fingers into his hair, she desperately imprisoned his mouth with yet another seemingly farewell kiss. His mouth responded to hers with every bit as much fervor. Though fraught with intense love and passion, Latham's last sweetly torturous kiss had left her emotionally drained.

Weary beyond understanding, Nikkola let herself back into the house. No other words had passed between her and Latham. All they'd had was their demonstrative expression of unfulfilled desire to possess one another completely and irrevocably.

Glen was waiting for Nikkola in the hallway and she rushed into his arms. Massaging her back tenderly, he tried to soothe her jangled nerves. "You've gotten yourself into quite a mess," he whispered against her temple. "You need to corner that wild animal there in your living room. He's dangerous!"

Nikkola laughed softly. "I'm afraid he's too unmanageable for that, Glen. He needs to be put to sleep! Anything less than that would only make him more dangerous," she quipped.

"You've got a point, sweetheart. Josh and I are going to go. I'm glad you won't be here alone with Mychal and his rabid personality. I wouldn't think of leaving you by yourself with him if your parents weren't here."

After Glen, Josh, Cindy, and Gennifer said their

farewells, Ethel and Nickolas turned in for the night, but Nickolas planned on staying wide awake until Mychal Forrester had left his daughter's home.

Getting Mychal out of her house as soon as possible was at the very top of Nikkola's agenda. She entered the living room and sat down on the sofa next to her uninvited guest. "I'm ready for bed, Mychal."

Mychal grinned wickedly. "Is that an invitation for me to join you?"

Ignoring his boring comment, Nikkola got up and started for the front door. Much to her surprise, Mychal stood and followed right behind her. At the door, Nikkola turned to face him. "Good night, Mychal. I wish I could say it has been a pleasure. Drive safely."

Mychal snickered. "I don't know about you or anyone else, but it was a pleasure for me. Getting to meet my future in-laws was icing on the cake. Good night, Nikkola. See you soon."

"I hope not," Nikkola shot back, not caring that she'd been downright rude.

"Stop fooling yourself, Nikkola. You love being in my company. I keep you amused and on your toes if nothing else. Bye until next time."

Nikkola couldn't help thinking back to Latham's similar statement. Fooling herself wasn't easy. If only she could fool herself into believing that she and Latham still had a future.

Chapter 14

For the third day in a row, rain hurled itself against the windowpanes of all the rooms in Nikkola's condo. Nikkola, Ethel, and Nickolas sat quietly in the kitchen discussing the events of the past years and the episodes of the last evening.

Ethel smiled at her daughter. "I recall how shy you used to be and how you'd keep youself from getting too involved with boys because your studies had always come first."

"What I remember most is your dreams and aspirations," Nickolas added. "When I think about it, I can't help but laugh about all the times you modeled your mother's clothes even though they were way too big for you back then. I even recall the day you first tried on make-up. And you've always had some cause to champion. I remember how you defended your friends and others against those who tried to cause them harm." *Who was going to now defend his darling Nikkola from her recent troubles, from all of life's injustices?* Nickolas had to wonder.

Both parents remembered how hurt she'd been when Cyd and Tammy had deceived her. And now they were watching her go through another traumatic relationship with a man they believed she truly loved. Neither of them had any words to describe Mychal Forrester since he was utterly indescribable.

Trying not to glamorize herself, in order to match the feelings in her heart, dark and somber, Nikkola had dressed in baggy sweats and old tennis sneakers. Her face was as naked as her emotions. From yet another sleepless night, her eyes looked bleak and slightly swollen.

Nikkola attempted a bright smile for her parents as they drank their morning coffee. "I'm surprised that you guys remember so much from so long ago. Things have changed quite a bit for me since then. I wonder if I'll ever be that carefree again."

"Hold that thought." Nickolas jumped up from his seat and rushed over to the counter to pour another cup of the hot brew for himself and his wife. He returned quickly with the refills.

Ethel's smile was filled with sympathy. "Of course you will. Just give it some time." Nikkola mumbled an incoherent response. "That turned out to be some dinner party, Nikki. Mychal Forrester is something else! How did you ever get involved with him?"

Placing her hands under her chin, Nikkola sighed. "I didn't. He got involved with me. I've already told you about the coffee incident on the trip to London. If I'd known he was going to become this much of a nuisance, I would've poured the whole pot on him to make it worth my while. He is an insufferable psychopath. Glen thinks he needs to be committed—and I agree."

Ethel clearly heard her daughter, but she sensed that Nikkola was somewhat smitten with the haughty Mr. Forrester, or that she thought she could somehow use him to get over Latham.

"If you really feel that way, Nikki," Nickolas interjected, "why didn't you voice your objections to him last night?"

Nikkola gave her father an incredulous look, laughing out loud. "Were you listening to him, Dad? If you were, you would know it wouldn't have done any good. Mychal is inanely encouraged by controversy. I didn't stand a chance in hell of winning out over him last night."

Nickolas laughed. "I definitely know what you mean, honey. But something tells me you're more than a little taken with him. Am I right?"

Nikkola frowned. "You might be right on some level. If so, I don't have a clue why. He embarrasses me, infuriates me, and when I least expect it, he enchants me. He can be as sweet and as kind as he is insufferable. I seem to lose the ability to reason when he turns on the charm. Psychopath or split personality? You can tell me which one, but it all spells out insanity."

"You *are* faced with some choice," Ethel stated, feeling sorry for Nikkola's plight.

"Choice? If I had a choice, I'd choose Latham. But since I don't, there's a saying that goes, 'if you can't be with the one you love, love the one you're with.'" Though concerned for her slanted views, her parents laughed at the crude analysis. Nikkola couldn't help but join in.

Despite the heavy rainfall, the Knight family had decided to go out anyway, when Nikkola had suggested a trip to the orphanage to see the kids. Her parents had fallen in love with Cydnee the first time they'd met her a few years ago. Cydnee loved it when they visited and today was no exception.

Cydnee's large eyes brightened with wonder when she saw her surrogate family. Running into Nickolas's outstretched arms, she giggled when he lifted her high off the floor. He then passed her off to Ethel, who kissed and hugged her, making a big fuss over the small fry.

Soon after she received all the affection, Cydnee began to tug annoyingly at Nikkola's pants leg. Nikkola sensed that Cydnee had something important to tell her, but felt that the little girl wanted to do it in private. Excusing herself and her little friend, Nikkola took Cydnee into the playroom where they could talk more freely.

While Nikkola held Cydnee on her lap, Cydnee whispered into her ear, informing her that Latham Scott was in the building visiting Seth. That bit of news caused Nikkola to instantly look around her, willing her heart to remain calm.

"Captain Scott is up in Seth's room. I asked him about you and why you didn't come with him. He said you were entertaining guests, but he didn't tell me who. Now I know. He seemed so sad, Nikki. Do you know why? Do you have anything to do with his sadness?"

Cydnee often managed to catch Nikkola off guard with some of her pointed questions. And she'd done it again. "Captain Scott is having some grown-up problems. The problems are much too complicated for a little girl to understand."

"Try me!" Cydnee countered.

Laughing, Nikkola shook her head, burying her face in Cydnee's hair. "It's a secret, Cydnee. Latham wouldn't be too happy with me if I gave his secret away. Can you please let me off the hook this time?"

Pushing her hair back from her sweet face, Cydnee gave an intolerant sigh. "Adults!"

During the course of the visit, the Knight family played games with Cydnee and some of the other children. Sister Maria brought out refreshments and sat and chatted with the visitors for a short spell.

Nikkola enjoyed herself, but she kept a watchful eye out for Latham, hoping she didn't have to face him.

She wondered if he knew by now that she was there. It was difficult to concentrate on the games they were involved in, especially with Cydnee eyeing her curiously.

When the time came for them to leave, Nikkola was happy to escape without seeing the object of her affections. But as they reached the door, Latham and Seth came bounding down the stairs. Nikkola's heart made an illegal U-turn.

Latham politely greeted the Knight family, but his mind was involved in some illegal turns of its own. What he wanted to do with Nikkola was definitely against the law, especially since they were in public. Though they were able to get through the awkwardness of the moment, each wondered what would've happened if Nikkola had been there alone. Latham's mind instantly took him to the last passionate kiss they shared outside in the hallway of her condo.

Wanting to be close to Nikkola for a little longer, Latham risked asking if they could have lunch somewhere. When Nikkola seemed reluctant to the idea, Nickolas assured his daughter that they'd be okay on their own until Latham brought her home. Once Nikkola finally agreed, it was all Latham could do to keep from clapping his hands in celebration.

How am I going to get through life without Nikkola? he wondered as she settled into the passenger seat of his car. Deciding to go to the same café where they'd eaten their first breakfast together, Latham started the engine and pulled out of the parking lot.

Jenny's Café was nearly filled with patrons, since it was the beginning of the lunch hour, but a waitress was able to seat them immediately. After directing them to a booth near the back of the café, she took their orders right away. Nikkola only ordered a soft drink, but Latham ordered a burger and fries, since he'd worked up an appetite by playing football with Seth.

The minutes spent before the waitress came back with the orders were filled with nothing more than small talk between them, each asking how the other felt and how the visit had gone at the orphanage. Then nothing but silence ensued between the two of them while Latham devoured his meal. When he finished his lunch, he wiped his mouth, crumpled the napkin, and plopped it in the middle of his plate.

Latham then covered Nikkola's hand with his. "Thanks for coming here with me. I don't have the right to ask anything of you under the circumstances, but it's hard not having you in my life. Last night was the roughest yet." He blew out a ragged breath. "I miss you something terrible, Nikki. I still haven't made any concrete decisions regarding my responsibility to Carmen, but I will acknowledge and take care of my child. That's an absolute. What have you been thinking about this whole mess that I've gotten us both into?" He had made a silent oath not to talk about Forrester when Nikkola first agreed to have lunch with him.

Nikkola sighed. "I don't like thinking about it, but I do, constantly, wishing things could be different for us. But I do understand your wanting to take care of your responsibilities. If I were in Carmen's shoes, I'd want the father of my child to take his responsibility seriously."

"Would you want the man to marry you if he didn't love you, and then raise the child in a loveless environment?"

"I know where you're going with this, but, Latham, these are questions you should be asking Carmen. I can't give you the answers you're after. These are your decisions to make, not mine. I don't want to influence your decision one way or the other."

"Do you love me, Nikki?"

Nikkola cut her eyes sharply at him. "If you don't know the answer to that, you should. But this isn't about me, Latham. I won't let you make it so."

Latham swiped his hand across the back of his neck. "I'm sorry. I just feel at such a loss. Carmen is not someone I would've ever considered as a lifetime partner. It was never like that between us."

"I guess I need to ask the hard questions here. Why did you get involved with her in the first place if you felt that way? And why did you let it become a physical relationship?"

"Nikki, people don't go into every relationship with marriage on the brain. This may sound callous, but I wasn't even interested in a long-term or an exclusive relationship at that time. It hadn't been all that long since my engagement was broken off. And Carmen knew that."

"Did you tell her all of those things you just said?"

"Of course I did. I don't want to disrespect Carmen in any way, but she asked me out, and I went. I never even looked at her as someone to date exclusively. I didn't go out with her to spare her feelings or anything, but I didn't go out with her expecting to marry her either. One thing simply led to another. Have you thought about marriage with every man you've dated?"

"Don't be ridiculous! I know that men think that all women start picking out the engagement ring right after the first few good dates, but that's not always the case. And I don't think about having sex with everyone I go out with either, Latham. You had sex with Carmen and now she's pregnant. As we've already discussed, the only thing that's one hundred percent foolproof where sex is concerned is abstinence. Often the player becomes the payer."

"I'm not a player, and I'm not denying that I was with her, Nikki, nor that it could be my child. Right or wrong, people do have sex without being emotionally involved. I know that sounds heartless, but it's the truth. I just didn't fall in love with her. Is there a crime in that?"

"Not a crime at all. It's just that an innocent child may end up paying the penalties for adult carelessness." She rolled her eyes at him. "Don't you dare think it or even ask me if I thought it was reckless for us to make love. It was not only reckless, but it was irresponsible on both our parts. If I had it to do all over again, would I? Hell yes! How's that for recklessness?"

A huge smile spread across Latham's lips. "I don't think you intended to make me feel good with that remark, but you did. Knowing that you don't regret what we shared makes me feel damn good. Would you make love to me again if I asked you to?"

Latham had made her blush against her desire, but Nikkola couldn't be angry with him no matter how hard she tried. But the look on her face let him know that she wasn't about to answer his last question, which would've been a resounding yes. What had happened to Latham and Carmen happened to other casual couples all the time. Unfortunately, it happened all too often.

Nikkola sighed hard, thinking of what she had to say. "I need you to understand that I'd never intentionally try to make you feel bad. I didn't want you to feel bad last night either. I had no idea that Mychal Forrester would show up at my apartment during dinner. I'd never do that to you or anyone else. I need you to know how sorry I am for that, Latham—terribly sorry."

The expression on Latham's face turned grim. "I don't want to talk about that no-class clown, Nikki. Okay?"

Nikkola shrugged. "Okay, but I know it bothers you."

"Not at all, Nikki! Why would an egotistical jerk hanging around the woman I love bother me?" His sarcastic tongue and the darkening of his eyes showed Nikkola just how much the mention of Forrester really bothered Latham.

"Point well taken. If there isn't anything else you want to discuss, I probably should go. My parents' time here in Virginia is quickly running out."

"I understand that you have company, but there's one more thing. Could you give me a little more time to work these things through? I still want us to be able to talk and spend time with each other. I want us to hang in there together, Nikki."

"For how long, Latham? Until you decide to come to me and tell me that you have forsaken our love because you've decided to marry the mother of your child? How fair is that to either of us?" She got to her feet. "We really should go now. This isn't getting any easier for us."

After leaving on the table more than enough money to pay the check and a generous tip, Latham walked behind Nikkola as she strolled toward the front entrance. Outside the café door, he quickly took her into his arms. "I hate to keep repeating myself, but we aren't over yet, Nikki. Please don't continue to try and fool yourself into thinking we are. I still have plans for us to soar above the clouds." Before escorting Nikkola to his car, Latham kissed her hard on the mouth.

Nikkola knew that it would never be over for her, but what was she to do? It didn't seem right that they should continue in a love affair with so many problems staring them in the face. She then made a promise to herself to be available for Latham whenever he needed her, but she decided to keep it to herself. If he did come to her in need, she'd be there to comfort him until he made up his mind one way or the other. She needed him as much as he needed her.

* * *

268   *Linda Hudson-Smith*

The evening would've been quiet had Mychal Forrester not shown up at Nikkola's place. Everyone was tired from the earlier visit to the orphanage and a late-afternoon shopping spree. Soon after dinner was taken, the Knight family had settled in to enjoy their last night together. The Knights were departing the next day at noon, and Nikkola was flying back to London on the night flight the very same evening.

This time Mychal showed his sweet, charming side. He behaved like a perfect gentleman, but Nikkola was sure that his behavior change had a lot to do with the fact that he didn't have Latham as part of the audience. Nonetheless, she was grateful.

Surprising Nikkola once again, Mychal talked openly about his family, their numerous businesses, and the more intimate details of his life. He told them his father had started in business with a small loan, but within two years he'd become a millionaire. By heavily investing and reinvesting in stocks and bonds, he'd obtained enough success to purchase several businesses and loads of real estate.

By watching, listening, and learning, Mychal had followed in his father's footsteps. He had invested his own money in pretty much the same way—now he was a wealthy man in his own right. He even went so far as to tell the Knights that he had all he could ever want in life, all except a family.

After a couple hours of conversing with Nikkola and her guest, the Knights retired for the night. Nikkola didn't want to be left alone with Mychal, but seeing how tired her parents looked she kissed them good night, hoping Mychal would soon take his leave.

Relaxing on the sofa, Mychal looked as though he had no intentions of leaving any time soon. Nikkola offered him a hot drink and he enthusiastically accepted. When she departed for the kitchen, she turned around to find him following close behind.

A flyswatter would certainly come in handy, she thought, chuckling under her breath.

Along with the cup of coffee, Nikkola cut Mychal a big slice of chocolate cake. After making herself a cup of tea, she joined him at the table. As he sat staring boldly at her, with a brooking expression, she wished that he'd just say whatever was on his scary mind.

"You have a lovely family, Nikkola. You all seem very close. I can't wait to have a family of my own. Nikkola, do you want a family of your own?" His tone was soft and his eyes appeared sad with longing.

"Someday, Mychal. I used to want a house full of children, but now I'm not so sure."

"What changed your mind?"

"Life."

"What is it about life that has you so unsure?"

"I can't pinpoint any one thing, Mychal."

"Have you been disappointed in love, Nikkola?"

Nikkola didn't like the trend of the conversation. She shot Mychal an impatient glance.

"If you have, I can change your disappointment to utter satisfaction. I know exactly what a woman like you needs."

"And what's that, Mychal?"

Leaning across the table, Mychal began to whisper into Nikkola's ear.

Nikkola's face turned scarlet, suddenly making her feel the need to run away and hide from him and her own embarrassment. Besides giving her all the love and money she could ever spend in a lifetime, Mychal had had the nerve to tell her what he could give her in bed.

"Latham Scott can't ever give you what I can. If you'll let me, I'll prove it."

Nikkola swallowed the lump in her throat, caused by the embarrassment she'd suffered by his colorful remarks. "What does Latham Scott have to do with this?"

"Everything and nothing, depending on the choice you make."

"My choice is to change the subject," she asserted adamantly.

Arising from his seat, Mychal knelt down in front of Nikkola and stared up into her face. Spanning his fingers onto her waist, he pressed his face against her abdomen. A cold chill surged through her entire body, making her shiver. Lifting his head, he pulled her face down and covered her mouth tenderly with his own. Nikkola quickly pulled away, knowing the dangers of continuing to send mixed signals to an egotistical man like Mychal.

Mychal drew in a deep breath. "Nikkola, stop fighting what you feel for me. Let me give you the world. You've already become mine."

Latham was her world, but knowing it was a world she'd never live in with him, she insanely and not so carefully considered Mychal's proposition despite her earlier thoughts. She wanted to touch him, yet she stopped herself. She'd love to be able to run her fingers through Mychal's hair and lose all touch with reality, but just the thought frightened her. Besides, Nikkola couldn't fool her heart. It would never accept Mychal as a substitute for Latham.

Mychal studied her intently. The passion he felt for Nikkola flared in his mind and inflamed his heart. "Nikkola, you're as complicated as a first-time algebra problem. I can't seem to figure out the right equation. One minute you seem to detest me, and the next, you're as soft as a flower and as sweet as the purest honey. The one thing I feel sure of is that I love you. I'm convinced that you're the woman I want to spend the rest of my life with."

"Please, Mychal, let's not talk about love. That's not something I want to deal with at this moment. I'm sorry." Talking about love would only make her think about the love she'd lost. It was then that she realized she wasn't even taking Mychal seriously. How could she take him seriously, when the only love she was interested in having was Latham's?

"I remember feeling the same way about love. I met a special woman at a time in my life when the chips were all falling the wrong way. She'd thrilled me with her sophisticated style and her seemingly unmatched inner beauty. Before long the stars in her eyes were replaced with dollar signs, and she recklessly spent my money as fast as I could rake it in. From the beginning she never bothered to mention that she had a fiancé. I never thought something like that could ever happen to me. Not Mychal Forrester, not the man who had it all."

Mychal would never forget the day he'd found out about Latham Scott. The fact that the knowledge hadn't come from Morgan's lips had nearly killed him. His hatred for Latham had blossomed over time, growing strong and stronger, even after he'd come to realize that the person responsible for deceiving and hurting him was Morgan.

Nikkola actually felt sorry for Mychal. "How did you find out?"

"The bad news came from my best friend. The confrontation between my fiancée and me was sordid and ugly. It had come only a few days before our lavish wedding was to take place. It had caused me an unbearable amount of embarrassment, not to mention the unbelievable amount of money I'd shelled out for the ceremony and reception. I'm only telling you this because I want you to know everything about me. I need you to know that what I feel for you is so different from what I felt for the woman I was once engaged to. That disaster of a relationship happened such a long time ago. I'm glad that I found out before the wedding and not afterward."

Throwing her head against the chair back, Nikkola closed her eyes. While she tried to rid herself of all the confusion in her head, Mychal took advantage of her exposed throat, lining it with soft, feathery kisses, smothering her neck with the moisture from his soft lips. Following through with her earlier desires, she entwined her fingers in his thick head of hair, as his arms tightened around her waist. As Latham's image blossomed in her mind, Nikkola lost herself to sensuous thoughts of her night-flight pilot.

For the next few minutes, Nikkola played with the fire that Mychal had warned her about some time ago, but this time he wasn't sounding off any warnings. She knew that if she got burned, she'd be deserving of it. While Mychal pulled her from the chair and down onto his lap, Nikkola prayed that her body would prove itself fireproof.

Seconds later, breathing heavily, Mychal tore himself away from her and then looked deeply into her sparkling, hazel eyes. "Woman, I've got to get out of here now. I can't wait for our wedding night!"

Unimpressed with his flair for the dramatic, Nikkola laughed softly, watching after Mychal as he bolted toward the front door. The fact that he had actually run scared amused her. But the one thing that wasn't so amusing was how she had gotten so caught up in using him to get over Latham. She felt ashamed that she hadn't stopped things before they'd gotten to this point. It didn't make her feel any better about things, knowing that he'd been the one to douse the fire. The flame would've never gotten lit in the first place if she hadn't allowed into her mind the fantasy of her and Latham's first night back together again.

How was it that she could be in the company of one man and so easily indulge in erotic thoughts of another? The mind was as complicated as it was wondrous.

Summoned by an urgent call from Carmen, Latham was seated on the sofa in her apartment, listening to her hysterical explanation of why they needed to be together before the baby was born. None of it made sense to him—he'd already voiced his strong objections.

"It makes sense to me. I'm afraid of being here alone. Several times I've been so sick that I could hardly get out of bed. I don't want to suffer through this pregnancy alone."

Latham had grown impatient with Carmen, and the demanding tone in her voice severely irritated him. "But you'll have to be alone at any rate. I'm not in town that much. No matter what I do, you're still going to be on your own quite a bit. I can hire someone to come here and stay with you when I'm on duty," he tried to reason.

"Latham, you can have your flight schedule changed to a local route. You could be home most evenings," she challenged boldly.

"Is this about your being afraid or is it because Nikki and I are on the same schedule?"

Carmen made a false show of looking innocent. "I wasn't even considering Nikki in this," she lied. "It's over between you two, isn't it?"

Latham looked Carmen dead in the eye. "It'll never be over between Nikki and me, at least not in my heart and soul. I won't let you move into my house with me, but I'll consider spending more time here. That is, when you're close to delivery."

For the next hour, Latham listened to all the reasons why Carmen couldn't continue to live in her place. She complained that the apartment was too small, was sometimes awfully drafty, and had too many steps, along with a host of other trumped-up excuses flying out of her mouth. Her whining and complaining nearly caused Latham's brain to shut down completely.

Without giving in to her demands, Latham had left Carmen crying her heart out. These stressful scenes were increasing in frequency, and they had given him a preview of how life would be if he lived with her. Once the baby arrived, he would only expect it to get worse. Carmen's endless tirades helped him to see how unfair it would be to ask Nikkola to live like this. Until this very moment, he hadn't completely given up on the idea of their being able to work it out together and marrying someday. Now he was ready to concede defeat. That hurt to the bone.

Would the light in his heart become like a candle in the wind, completely snuffed out?

Latham was concerned for Carmen, even more so for the unborn child, but the raucous presentation of her numerous complaints and demands had left a lot to be desired. He'd tried using patience and understanding, but nothing had seemed to work once she'd already made up her mind. He saw a life filled with unreasonable demands and endless problems. With no intimate moments between them, doubting that there ever would be, Latham wondered how one made love to a continuous argument.

The night had been anything but peaceful. With the coming of dawn, Nikkola looked everything but fresh and wholesome. Her body felt tired and abused from the thrashing about in her bed as she tried to sleep. Like she used to do as a little child, she crept into the guest room and sat on the side of the bed where her mother lay. As though she'd been expecting her, Ethel moved over and drew Nikkola safely under her arm.

After turning over on his side, Nickolas reached across his wife and took his daughter's hand. "Did you sleep well, Nikki?" Nickolas asked, concerned for her well-being.

"Not so good, Dad. It was a rough night. As I lay in bed thinking, I remembered all the mornings I used to climb into bed with you two and how your warm receptions always left me feeling so loved and safe. On those unforgettable mornings the rest of my day seemed to go so much better. Why do we have to grow up?" She heaved a sorrowful sigh.

"Because it was designed that way by the Creator, Nikkola," Ethel softly responded. "What time did the incomparable Mychal Forrester leave?"

"Before midnight," Nickolas answered. "I know because I stayed awake until then."

Nikkola laughed at her father's response. "Not soon enough, Mom," she quipped. "And I didn't help matters by offering him something to drink. Really, he's not such a bad gent. I rather enjoy his company, especially when he's exuberantly charming. Last evening he exercised an overabundant display of charm."

"Does this mean you're getting over Latham?" Nickolas inquired.

Before answering, Nikkola seriously pondered over what she believed to be a reasonable and fair question. "I'm really not sure what it means, but I've sadly realized that I'm not above using Mychal to achieve my goal of getting over Latham. I don't think anyone can get over anything painful without something or someone to fill in the void. Being lonely is not my forte."

"Your slanted assessments concern me, Nikkola," Ethel gently scolded. "I fear that you're going to get badly hurt. You can't use people and not expect a severe backlash, young lady. In my opinion, Mychal Forrester is not the one you should be trying out this theory on. I shudder to think of the things he'd be capable of using against an adversary."

"Your mother's right, Nikkola. Reiterating your very own words, and Glen's, Mychal Forrester is dangerous."

"Yeah, I know. I haven't quite touched the flame yet, but I know it burns white hot. Latham asked me to continue to see him until he comes to some conclusion about his responsibility to Carmen. I vowed that I'd be there for him if he needed me, but I didn't tell him that. Is it right for us to do this with things so complicated between him and another woman?"

"Only you can be the judge of that, Nikkola. As your mother, I can only advise you, but the final decisions are yours, just as the consequences will be."

Nikkola sucked her teeth. "Enough of this, already! Let's fix breakfast." She forced a bright smile to her lips. Before leaving the room, she pulled her parents' heads together, kissing one and then the other. She then gave them a "not-to-worry" look.

The words of the elder Knights were not taken lightly. Nikkola was well aware of the way Mychal would react if he thought he were being used. *It's possible that he just might be using me. If he is, shame on him. I can also be quite dangerous when crossed.*

The time for the Knights' departure came quickly and Nikkola was saddened to see them leave. She'd escaped the menacing jaws of loneliness for days now, but she knew without question it would be coming back for her. The thought of Glen's being back on the same schedule with her somewhat uplifted her downed spirits.

Standing in front of the salmon-pink-washed complex, Nikkola tearfully watched the rented car ease through the security gates, as Ethel waved from the window. Disengaging her eyes from the parting car, Nikkola turned around and slowly walked back into the building and hopped into the elevator.

While she was riding up to her floor, it suddenly dawned on her that Mychal had been getting in and out of her building effortlessly. But how had he gained access? He kept her so off balance she hadn't thought to question it before now. She made a mental note to grill him mercilessly about it. Often, if the gates were opening, cars entered without using the security code. If that were the case, she wondered if Mychal sat quietly in his car just waiting for someone to stalk.

The thought left her with an eerie feeling. Calming herself, she entered her condo and quickly secured the locks, as though she expected someone was following her. She felt a sudden need to take extra precautionary measures.

In preparation for her late-evening flight, Nikkola set about the task of gathering her things for packing. After picking up the flight schedule off the nightstand, she checked to see the number of hours for the layover in London so she'd know how many clothes to pack. The schedule would vary upward from eighteen hours to several days. This time the layover was three days. Nikkola moaned over the lengthy stay.

With her bags ready to go and satisfied she hadn't forgotten anything important, Nikkola entered the guest bedroom and began stripping the bed. Carrying the bed linens through to the laundry room, she inserted the bedding and turned on the wash cycle. Grabbing the vacuum from the closet, she returned to the guest room to return it to its original state.

Once Nikkkola finished cleaning the bedroom, she did a once-over of the entire house, ending up in the kitchen, where she turned on the burner under the teakettle. During breakfast she'd had very little appetite, but now she found herself starving.

The hours raced by. After going through her usual routine, Nikkola took a nap before leaving for the airport, calling Glen before resting. The call found him eager and excited about returning to the night flight. He couldn't wait to get back to London. His enthusiasm was contagious. Nikkola immensely enjoyed the rebirth of Glen's excitement.

* * *

In all the excitement over Glen's return to the schedule, Nikkola had forgotten to set the alarm clock. Upon awakening, she discovered she had just a short time to shower and dress. Hopping out of bed, she ran into the bathroom and rushed through her toiletry routine.

The doorbell rang just as Nikkola finished putting on her uniform. Running to the door, she flung it open, telling Glen she'd be ready in a second. She then ran back to her bedroom. With no time to tie her hair back or put on a touch of make-up, she decided to do it at the airport.

Grabbing her flight gear, Nikkola wheeled it into the living room. "Ready, Glen."

After catching the elevator, the two friends descended to the parking garage, where Glen carefully stowed their bags in the trunk of his car and then opened the car doors. Sliding in the driver's seat, he started the engine and pulled out of the parking garage.

Chapter 15

On the way to the airport, the conversation was held at a minimum, but Nikkola did fill Glen in on the unexpected happenings at the orphanage and all the details of Mychal's last visit. She also informed him about how concerned she was that Mychal gained entry to the complex. Glen didn't think it that unusual since people trailed in behind others all the time, but he felt that Nikkola should confront Mychal about it if it upset her.

In turn, Glen touched briefly on how he and Gennifer were doing. Though he hadn't told her all about his physical issues, he had come to the conclusion that he'd do it as soon as he returned home from London. Their love for each other hadn't changed one bit, which had given him the courage to go ahead and be honest and upfront with the woman he loved.

Upon reaching the airport, with plenty of time to spare, Glen parked the car in the employees' lot and then he and Nikkola hopped on the first available airport shuttle. At this time of night, the terminals weren't nearly as full of passengers as in the light of day.

Nikkola left Glen and went into the ladies' lounge, where she fooled with her hair and put on her make-up. When she came out, Glen was waiting for her, and they walked through the security check and on to the departure gate. After showing their badges and passports, they boarded the aircraft.

Only a few of the crew members were already on board. Nikkola instantly noticed that Latham wasn't one of them. But Blaine Mills was there, smiling at her treacherously. He hadn't forgotten the retort she'd slapped him in the face with at the café that evening. He'd been waiting for an opportune time to get even with her.

"I guess you're wondering where Latham is, Nikki." Blaine's baby-blues sparkled with devilment as he eagerly awaited his chance to shoot her down.

"I'm not in the habit of keeping up with Latham's whereabouts," she retorted.

"I'm sure. At any rate, he's not going to be on this flight. He's taking some leave time to prepare for his and Carmen's wedding."

Nikkola was halfway down the aisle when he'd fired the fatal bullet into her back. Whirling around, she turned to face Blaine, a sugary smile on her face. "If you see him before I do, please give him my sincere congratulations."

The calmness about her was only a preamble to the stormy rage she felt inside, the smile a facade, but she managed to walk triumphantly away from Blaine, leaving him unsure as to whether he'd fulfilled his mission. In the back of the plane, she dropped down into one of the seats and let Blaine's comments really sink in. The area around her heart felt as if an avalanche had occurred.

Marriage to Carmen! Oh no, he's really going to do it.

But Latham's decision seemed so strange to Nikkola since he'd just made a speech only yesterday about it not being over for them. She just couldn't believe that he didn't care enough about her not to tell her his plan. But then again, she hadn't been very caring to him either. She'd been so busy playing Russian roulette with Mychal that she hadn't even given the bullets in the chamber of Latham's gun a thought. She felt as if grief and pain had totally ambushed her.

"Nikki, the passengers are boarding. We need you up front," Glen said. She heard him, but she couldn't see him through the blinding tears welling in her eyes. Seeing her tears, he dropped down in the seat next to her. "What's the matter, Nikki?"

"Blaine just informed me that Latham wouldn't be on the flight. He's taking leave to prepare for his wedding," she ground out tearfully, clenching her teeth.

"Oh honey, I'm sorry. But you knew it might happen sooner or later. You have to pull yourself together, or you'll just provide more fuel for air gossip."

Nikkola was stunned that Glen hadn't shown any signs of shock. Then she realized that what he'd said was for her own good. Heeding his advice, she stepped into the lavatory and quickly cleaned herself up. While walking toward the front of the aircraft, Nikkola warmly greeted the passengers in a friendly manner, helping out anyone who needed her services. Glen gave her an encouraging wink as she passed him. In return, she flashed him a reassuring smile.

If he hadn't been sitting in first class, Nikkola would've lost her shirt, since she'd earlier made a bet with Glen that Mychal Forrester would be on this flight. Totally ignoring his sensual smile, she quickly walked past him and disappeared into the cockpit, leaving him to question the mixed signals he'd received from her the past evening.

Smiling to himself, Mychal shook his head and opened up a magazine.

While giving the greeting and the safety information

over the microphone, Nikkola could feel Mychal's dark eyes trained on her, so much so that her face became hot and flushed.

Throughout the flight, Mychal had Nikkola waiting on him hand and foot. No sooner would she fill his glass with the requested refreshment than he'd quickly drain it, only to immediately summon her by ringing his call button. She'd even wondered if he had a flower-pot under his seat or if he was really drinking that much liquid. Tiring of the game, she prepared several drinks and set them down in front of him.

While she served the meal, Mychal gently touched her hand. Giving him an annoying glance, Nikkola forcefully pulled her hand away. "I'm working, Mychal," she whispered. "If you don't behave, I'm going to report you to the captain." Her tone was hushed but warning.

"Does that mean I can touch you after work?" he asked in a husky, playful voice.

"At ease, boy." Imagining what his response would be, she moved away before he had a chance to comment. Mychal knew exactly how to make her color rise, and enjoyed doing so.

Nikkola breathed easier when she later passed Mychal's seat and discovered he'd fallen asleep. She smiled at his sleeping form. His boyish looks made her heart thump erratically with compassion. Too bad he wasn't the one who made her heart soar.

Once the flight had terminated at Heathrow, and all the passengers had deplaned, Nikkola grabbed her personal items. Without any doubt, she knew that the impossible Mychal Forrester would be somewhere waiting to pounce on her. Knowing that friends were picking up Glen and that she was alone—and at Mychal's mercy—she ducked into the ladies' room. While hoping to wait

Mychal out, she prayed that he'd think she'd somehow gotten past him and give up the chase. Her tears were in dire need of release. Nikkola wanted to have one last cry over Latham, an uninterrupted one.

The strategy worked. Mychal was nowhere to be seen when she emerged from her hiding place, nor was he in customs. She finally boarded the crew bus without incident. The ride into the city seemed longer than it had ever before. Though angry, hurt, and terribly exhausted, Nikkola managed to deflect her demons long enough to take a short nap. The driver had to awaken her when the shuttle reached the hotel. Wearily, she dragged herself to the front desk, checked in, and fled to her suite.

The familiar surroundings temporarily calmed her down. After a long, hot shower, she gave way to all the pent-up emotions. Latham marrying Carmen aroused the type of anger in her that she wasn't aware she was capable of. It felt as though someone had dug a trench in her heart and that a jackhammer had boisterously transferred the sound of her breaking heart into her brain to echo inside her ears.

Tears, heavy sighs, more tears, and muffled screams echoed throughout the suite. She needed to be held, needed her tears to be kissed away, needed to feel special to someone, anyone. At this extremely low point in her life, Mychal Forrester would've been perfectly acceptable. She cursed herself for being silly enough to think that she could make it through the rest of this day and night all alone. She only wished that she had taken Glen up on his offer to cancel his plans so that he could see her through the raging storms of her bitter disappointment and hurt.

Back in the States, it seemed to Latham that all hell had broken loose. Carmen had been involved in an auto accident—the real reason he hadn't been able to make his scheduled flight to London. Pacing back and forth in the emergency waiting area, Latham was beside himself with worry as he waited for the doctor to give him a report on Carmen's condition. He'd been asleep when the emergency call had come through. Then he'd called the airlines to inform them of the emergency. Afterward, he had rushed right over to the hospital.

A short, stocky man with silver hair burst through the double doors, looking stern and businesslike. Spotting the white lab coat, Latham rushed up to meet the man, hoping he was the doctor in charge of Carmen's case.

"Are you the Mr. Scott that's here to see about Miss Carmen Thomas?" the gentleman asked. The doctor extended his hand as Latham nodded. "I'm Dr. Phillips," he informed Latham.

Latham looked terribly worried. "Is she going to be okay, sir?"

Dr. Phillips nodded. "It appears that she's going to be just fine. She's in a slight state of shock, but there's nothing broken, no serious damage whatsoever. However, she'll need a few stitches in her right hand."

"That's great news." Latham felt relieved. "Have you checked out the baby?"

Dr. Phillips looked surprised. "I wasn't aware that there was a baby."

"Oh yes, sir, there's a baby! She's due in six months," Latham insisted.

Dr. Phillips gave him a puzzled look. "Mr. Scott, I'm sorry, but I have thoroughly checked Miss Thomas over and there's nothing to indicate to me that she might be pregnant."

The look of horror on Latham's face caused the doctor grave concern. He was fearful that he'd broken the confidentiality of his patient, and the thought of a malpractice suit concerned him even more than the ghastly look on Latham's face.

"Are you sure about this?" Latham asked.

Dr. Phillips threw up both his hands. He wasn't about to give out any more pertinent information, especially after seeing that a measure of deception might possibly be at work.

Latham recognized the situation for exactly what it was. "I understand your position, sir, but I need to ask a few more questions. How did the hospital know to call me? Does Carmen even know I'm here?"

"From what I understand, the nurses used the information from the emergency card found in her wallet. She doesn't know you're here, or even that you've been called. Because she was in a slight state of shock, we didn't feel that she was capable of answering questions." Dr. Phillips looked anxious. "You can see her now if you'd like. I don't have any other medical information to give you. I'm sorry."

Latham remembered writing all his contact information down on a card and handing it to Carmen. He also recalled her putting it in her wallet.

After informing the doctor that he'd come in to see Carmen shortly, Latham sat down in the waiting area on one of the leather seats. Tears ran hurriedly from his eyes. *How could she? If she isn't pregnant, then why? Could the doctor be mistaken? Oh, God, was she that desperate to belong?* Only Carmen had the answers to these questions. And he'd damn well get to the truth.

Hurrying through the corridor, Latham entered the emergency room and asked a nurse where Carmen was. When the nurse pointed to a cubicle, he rushed over, parting the curtains as he entered. Carmen looked pale to him, but when she saw him her skin turned ghostly.

While walking over to the bed, Latham shoved his hands deeply into his pockets. "How are you feeling?"

Carmen turned away from him and stared blankly at the wall.

"Carmen," he said softly, "what's going on here?"

Still no response came from her. But he knew that she could hear him, though he knew the reason why she wouldn't answer him. Moving closer, Latham gently turned her head to face him. "I know what you've been up to, but I want to hear it from you."

"Go away, Latham! I have nothing to say to you," she said in a small but tight voice.

"You better have plenty to say to me, Carmen. You can start with why you lied to me about being pregnant."

"I didn't ask for you to come here and I want you to leave. Right now!"

"No, you wouldn't have asked me to come here. It seems to me that you never thought the emergency information would ever come into play. Because you knew what I'd possibly find out, didn't you? What were you going to do in the months to come, Carmen, when there was no visible bulge in your stomach? Or were you hoping I'd have married you by then and would've somehow fallen madly in love with you . . . that your deception wouldn't matter then? You've been living in a dream world, girl. And you've damn near destroyed mine. What really irritates me is that you can lie there so unemotionally, as if you couldn't care less. You don't even have the decency to explain your cruel actions. This is not a joke, Carmen. This is reality."

"All right, Latham, I deceived you! I lied to you, and I'm a terrible person because of it. Satisfied?" Carmen cursed herself for not taking the emergency information out of her wallet as originally planned. Had she done so, Latham wouldn't be here looking as if he hated her guts.

"Very satisfied! But I really feel sorry for you. You're rather pathetic, you know. You've hurt me. You've hurt Nikkola. Most of all, you've hurt and degraded yourself. I knew you were capable of a lot of horrendous things, but I never dreamed you'd take it this far. Carmen, I sincerely hope you get what you're looking for. I'm going to arrange for you to get home, but I'm not going to see you again. If you go near Nikkola, you'll answer to me. And, sweetheart, trust me, you don't want any part of that side of me," he whispered with deadly calm.

Carmen didn't take Latham's threats lightly, though she felt no shame in what she'd done. All was fair in love and war. Too bad she'd lost the battle despite her valiant fight.

The first sign of light peered through the windows in Nikkola's suite. Awakening to the loud thumping on the door, Nikkola rolled out of bed and donned her robe. Intuitively, she knew who was knocking out there without asking, but she opened the door anyway.

Nikkola gritted her teeth. "You are getting under my skin, Mychal Forrester! Do you always visit people this early in the morning? And without calling first?"

Leaning forward, Mychal kissed the tip of Nikkola's nose. "Early bird gets the worm, honey! As for getting under your skin, I plan on becoming your second skin. That's how close I'm going to stick to you, at least until you beg me to marry you and put you out of your misery. Now come here and kiss me, woman."

Nikkola turned to walk away, but Mychal pulled her into his arms and kissed her thoroughly. "Get your things together. You're coming with me. We're going to have a splendid day in this beautiful country."

"Yes, master," Nikkola responded with sarcasm. Mocking him, she curtsied repeatedly, backing out of the room. His loud laughter trailed after her.

The thought of having another horrendous night like the last one made her decision to go out with Mychal an easy one. After removing a change of clothing from her bags, she went into the bathroom, where she rapidly showered and dressed. Glen would be back later in the day. She would call him then to inform him as to her whereabouts. Since Latham was getting married, she wasn't going to have to worry another single day about him and what he thought.

The ride through the countryside was absolutely breathtaking. Lush, green-rolling hills were wet with the silky moisture of morning dew. A magical quality of mystique engulfed Nikkola as she got caught up in the rapturous beauty. A quiet peace permeated the atmosphere of the car. Mychal gently held onto her hand, as he cautiously steered the powerful car, but she couldn't help wishing that it were Latham beside her.

Nikkola was surprised that he'd once again ended up bringing her to where he lived.

The massive house was alive with fresh flowers and the sun streamed boldly through the numerous open windows. Mychal saw Nikkola to her suite. Then he left to run a few errands, promising that throughout the rest of her stay his time would be exclusively hers.

Standing at the window, Nikkola looked down on the colorful gardens, imagining that all this could be hers. She wondered if all Mychal was and had would be enough for her. Could she be satisfied being with someone she didn't love, or could she learn to love him? She was definitely intrigued with him, but was intrigue enough to consider a lifetime commitment?

Feeling the need to silence the voices in her head, Nikkola went in search of Mychal's music collection. Having become a little familiar with the layout of his home, she let herself into his private suite. While sitting on the floor in his den, she perused his vast music selections. There were so many choices she could barely make up her mind.

Walking over to Mychal's desk, Nikkola found some tapes out of their cases. Picking a couple of the cassettes, she carried them back to her suite, wanting to hear his music preferences. After popping a tape into the player, she positioned herself comfortably on the bed. When no music came forth, she rewound the tape and then pushed PLAY. When only voices came from the machine, she was shocked to hear her own voice. As she continued to listen, she heard the voices of both Glen and Latham. "What in the world is this?"

For the next several minutes, Nikkola was deeply immersed in the voices coming from the tape player. Hearing some of her and Latham's more intimate conversations made her head swim, her knuckles turning white from tightly gripping the edges of the bedspread. Pain gripped her heart when she heard Latham's deep voice telling her how much he loved her. Angry tears gushed from her eyes when she realized what the taped conversations meant.

"How did Mychal get these tapes and when?" She then recalled him asking her to use the phone in private. He must have bugged her phone then, she thought, recalling all the problems she'd had with static. She couldn't figure out why Mychal would do something like this. Jumping up from the bed, she went back into his suite and gathered up the rest of the loose tapes. After returning to her suite, she packed the cassettes safely away in her flight bag.

Arriving shortly after Nikkola had put everything away, Mychal entered her suite, smiling sweetly. Entwining his fingers in her loose curls, he tilted her head and gently kissed her mouth. She responded to his kiss, but it was difficult. Nikkola needed to keep her cool until she could find out what game Mychal was playing at—and why.

"I missed you, Nikki. Would you like to take a swim before lunch?"

"I'm not in the mood for swimming, but I'd like to take another tour of the grounds. There's a lot I haven't seen."

"I'd be happy to show you around. You should know every square inch of the grounds, since you could one day become the mistress of this mansion, should I decide to purchase it. We'd call it Forrester Pines Estates. Put on some comfortable shoes."

To Nikkola, he sounded so sure she was going to marry him that he almost had her believing it. She knew better, but she was going to enjoy stringing him along until she got exactly what she wanted from him—answers.

The stroll would've been serene had Nikkola's head not been spinning crazily with questions. In spite of her confusion, Mychal masterfully drew the laughter from her, hoping to kindle the light of passion between them. Seated beneath one of the large pines, she allowed him to hold and caress her tenderly, but all the while she imagined Latham as her suitor.

As he sat in his living room, Latham asked a lot of questions of his own. He wanted to know who the doctor was that had been willing to lie for Carmen and to help her in her deceptions. He'd practically torn up his den searching the room for the name and the number of the doctor that she'd given him earlier, even though he wouldn't be able to reach him this late.

Moving into his bedroom, he lay down, but the sweet smell of Nikkola wasn't there to caress his nostrils. "Oh Nikki, I miss you. I need you here with me," he whispered into the pillow. "I can't wait for you to get back here so that I can explain all this madness to you. I love you, Nikki. I just hope it's not too late."

No. Hope is only one notch up from despair. It won't be too late. It can't be too late. We love each other.

After undressing, Latham threw his clothes on the chair. Tired and emotionally drained, he climbed into bed and settled under the spread. Knowing Nikkola was in London and the possibility of her being with Mychal caused him a feeling of hopelessness. He should've told Nikkola about Mychal and Morgan from the start, cursing himself for having kept their affair a secret from her. Nikkola would've been more equipped to deal with Mychal if she knew the truth about him. Mychal was a devious character, but Latham had no idea how devious.

Turning up on his side, Latham embraced the sweet memories of his one and only love, Nikkola Knight, the most beautiful girl in the world.

Awakening Nikkola by brushing soft kisses across her lips, Mychal smiled as her eyes fluttered opened. She had fallen asleep on the blanket Mychal had spread out under the tree.

Forcing a warm smile to her lips, Nikkola sat up and crossed her legs under her. "I'm sorry I fell asleep on you. I don't know why I'm so tired," she said breathlessly. Her slender fingers haphazardly pushed her hair back from her face.

"You can fall asleep on me any time you feel the urge. I'd never do anything to cause you to mistrust me."

If those tapes are any indication of how much you can be trusted, Mychal, I dare not believe another word coming from your twisted mouth.

"I'm ready for lunch and a spot of tea, Mychal."

As Nikkola stood up, Mychal brushed the dried grass

and leaves from her clothes. Taking her hand, he led her into the house. Thinking it was strange that none of his staff was around, she inquired of their whereabouts. He told her that he'd given them some time off. She laughed weakly knowing Mychal had preplanned this visit, too, with his usual assured cockiness.

Attempting to please Nikkola, Mychal informed her that he'd made reservations for tea at a country inn not far from his place. When she smiled lazily at him, he hugged her and then told her to meet him in front of the house.

Seated on one of the large marble ledges in front of the house, Nikkola started biting her nails. While waiting for Mychal, she tried to come up with a way to get the matter of the tapes out in the open. She also hoped to be rid of her host very soon.

Just as Nikkola entered Mychal's car, the car phone buzzed. Reaching over to pick it up, he smiled at her before greeting the soft voice on the other end.

Mychal frowned. "I'm sorry to hear that, especially when I thought everything was just about finished. You need to sit tight. If confronted again, don't answer any more questions. If I win, there's still a chance for you to win too. I need a few more days to see my plans through."

Mychal's tone of voice let Nikkola know that something hadn't gone quite right for him. But what? Did the call have anything to do with the game he was playing with her? She couldn't help wondering what the stakes were and how high they were in his obvious game of deception.

"Keep me informed."

Nikkola eyed Mychal intently, now suspicious of his every move.

Mychal gave the caller's information a bit of serious thought. If he got out of this one alive, he wouldn't play at this game ever again. If their plans had fallen through, he could end up losing the only other thing he ever really wanted. He never dreamed that he could fall in love this hard and this fast once again.

Forrester, you've got to come up with some innovative thinking—and quickly.

All during lunch, Nikkola led Mychal up a primrose path. She smiled when she felt like crying and laughed at all his jokes, though she wanted to gag. She came off as a charming and loving companion, yet she wanted to scratch his eyes out. With him none the wiser, she had him believing he was capturing her heart and soul.

How he could be trusted came up too many times in his conversation, but each time she successfully squashed the urge to reveal what she thought about his so-called trust and what he could do with it. He wasn't the only one playing charades.

Mychal hadn't been aware that the beautiful woman in his company would enchant him to such a degree. He'd have to tell her soon about all the indiscretions, but he wasn't in any hurry to be leveled by her reactions. Having her by his side felt too good. Mychal suddenly feared losing Nikkola's respect more than he desired to win her love and affection.

In fact, Mychal had completely lost sight of his initial goal. He now thought himself utterly foolish for entering into such an unworthy cause in the first place. When he was first contacted to help out a friend in distress, he truly believed it was well worth it to get involved, especially after learning the identities of the other players in the game. His need for revenge began to take center stage.

Eating her lunch with forced enthusiasm, each bite tasting like burnt rubber, Nikkola couldn't wait until she'd swallowed a convincing amount of food to back

up her hunger claim. She'd been hungry, but the longer
she had to stomach Mychal's smiling and lying face, her
appetite had begun to diminish.

"Maybe you shouldn't try to force any more, Nikkola.
I won't be angry if you don't finish it all," Mychal assured her.

Knowing he'd seen through her made her blush
from embarrassment. Just to irritate him, she flashed
him a wicked smile and then crammed down every bite.
Then she quickly excused herself from the table.

Rushing into the ladies' room, Nikkola ran into a
stall, where she became violently sick. Unchecked tears
snowballed down her cheeks.

Placing the seat down, Nikkola sat on it and cried out
liked a wounded puppy. Feeling the same fears she'd
felt with Mychal before, she knew she had to get away
from him. Nikkola had to demand that he take her
back to the hotel. Her thoughts were fraught with anxiety, but she had to hold it together. Getting away from
Mychal was imperative.

Wanting Mychal to think she was more than just a little ill, Nikkola didn't repair her make-up, since her
cheeks were already deeply flushed from the upheaval.
With the gloss from her lips removed, along with the
luster in her eyes, she believed it was enough to convince Mychal that she was truly ill.

Returning to the table on wobbly legs, Nikkola stood
next to Mychal's chair. The look on her face caused him
concern. Lightly touching his shoulder, she attempted
a weak smile, pulling it off very nicely. He tenderly covered her hand with his.

"Mychal, I feel terrible."

As she faked a near swoon, Mychal was out of his seat
in a flash, his arm snaking around her waist to steady
her.

Nikkola rested the back of her hand over her forehead. "I must be coming down with something. Please, I'd like to return to the hotel as soon as possible."

For several seconds Mychal eyed her suspiciously. To heighten the dramatics, Nikkola squeezed a few tears from her eyes, and was immediately rewarded with a tender glance.

An Oscar-winning performance . . .

"You do look drained, Nikkola," Mychal conceded. Putting his hand on her forehead, he checked for any sign of a fever. To him she felt hot. He couldn't have known that sheer nervousness and willful determination had brought it on. "You can't possibly look after yourself at the hotel. I insist on taking care of you back at the house."

Nikkola suddenly saw the coveted Oscar being presented to Mychal instead, but she wasn't about to let it go that easily. "Glen will take care of me. We always take care of each other. I really do prefer it that way, Mychal."

After playing a few more sleeved aces while shedding a few more crocodile tears, Nikkola soon convinced Mychal to take her back to the hotel. Once again, the Oscar exchanged hands. In a last dramatic showing, she leaned on him for support as he guided her from the inn. If he could've seen the triumphant glint in her eyes, Nikkola was sure that she would've remained an unwilling captive at his place.

Fearful that if she went back into the house she'd never leave, Nikkola had requested Mychal to collect her things for her. But she was a nervous wreck the entire time he was away, fearing that he might find the tapes she'd packed away in her belongings. When he returned to the car and stowed her bags without incident, she expelled her pent-up breath.

The seemingly ever-falling London rain accompanied Nikkola and Mychal all the way into the city, as her mind raced along with the car. The desire to be away from Mychal, the need to hear all of the tapes, and the urge to put her foot on top of his to speed the car up were overpowering. Not wanting to appear too anxious, she calmed herself with many of her sweet memories of Latham.

Getting Mychal to drop her off in front of the hotel was as difficult as she'd expected it to be, but much to her pleasure, Glen was going into the hotel as she was about to give up. When she yelled his name from the open window, Mychal cursed under his breath, but conceded to her wishes. There was nothing else he could do.

Sweeping into the hotel suite, holding Glen by the hand, Nikkola, for the moment, was relieved to have rid herself of Mychal. He had given in to her wishes, but his eyes had turned hard and cold, which had brought back chilling memories of the first day that she'd met up with those dark, unfathomable eyes.

Wildly tossing clothes from her suitcase, Nikkola retrieved the hidden tapes. Pulling Glen down onto the sofa, she told him all the events leading up to now. Removing one of the tapes from her hand, Glen inserted it into the recorder and returned to his seat. Together, they listened to all of the tapes, both stunned by what they heard.

Glen was as astounded as Nikkola had been. Hearing some of the ones she hadn't heard, she found her blood striding toward boiling point.

"Glen, help me," she cried in anguish. "What are all these tapes about?"

Taking a deep breath, Glen pushed his hands through his hair. "Your phone has been bugged, Nikki. It rings of some sort of blackmail attempt to me. Whatever is going on here, Mychal Forrester is right smack dab in the middle of it. The man has proven himself to be as dangerous as we initially thought."

Nikkola looked at him in astonishment. Though she thought Glen was probably right, she couldn't come up with a reasonable explanation as to why Mychal would have her phone tapped. Her hand flew up to her forehead, a loud wail escaping from her tightly drawn lips.

Glen decided to spend the night in Nikkola's room. She finally cried herself to sleep, after several hours of wearing herself thin with angry outbursts. She couldn't believe she'd been so gullible where Mychal was concerned. Remembering that his family were major stockholders in the airlines caused her concern. She feared for her job, feared that she'd gotten in way over her head, and feared for her future now that Latham was off marrying someone else.

Around five in the morning, Nikkola screamed out at the top of her lungs, the nightmare she'd had still haunting her. Her body trembled with fear.

Glen tripped on the coffee table as he made his way into Nikkola's bedroom. After picking himself up, he rushed to her side. Gathering her into his arms, Glen encouraged her to calm down so they could come up with a way to handle the situation. With Mychal yet to discover the missing tapes, she knew they were in for a lot of serious trouble.

"We have to somehow stop Mychal, Nikki, stop whatever he's up to."

"There's no way to stop Mychal. In the short time I've known him, I know that he won't stop until he gets what he's after. If he's after me, I'm already had." As a loud knock came on the door, she tensed, reaching for Glen's hand. "Oh God, has he discovered the missing tapes?"

"I'll get it, Nikki." Unlacing her fingers from his, he went to answer the door. Pausing a moment before he opened the door, Glen reclaimed his usual cool, calm, and collected demeanor. He then bowed his head in silent prayer.

Finding Latham standing there was a huge relief for Glen, but he wasn't so sure about the effect it would have on Nikkola. Latham looked haggard and appeared agitated and restless. Unable to wait until Nikkola returned to the States, he'd been flying for hours as a passenger.

"It's good to see you, man," Glen greeted. After shaking Glen's hand, Latham followed him down the hall.

Nikkola didn't know why he was there, nor did she care. She was simply overwhelmed with joy at seeing him standing before her. Jumping up from her seat, she threw herself into his arms, tears streaming down her face. Molding her softness against him, Latham showered Nikkola's face and hair with hugs and kisses. Glen stood back, watching, smiling happily.

"Sweetheart, I've missed you! Oh Nikki, I have so much to tell you. We have to talk."

Glen was about to excuse himself, but Latham requested that he stay.

Everyone was seated when Latham outlined the details of what he'd discovered about Carmen. As he talked, expressions of pain, sorrow, disgust, and finally sheer relief crossed his face. Nikkola felt like she'd been put through the wringer during the entire ordeal. Like Latham, she was relieved when he finished, but it didn't appear to him that his statements had yet hit home with her.

Not ready to comment on his story, Nikkola rushed into her own story. After she finished, Glen put in the tapes for Latham to hear.

Latham's reaction after hearing the tapes was no different from that of Nikkola's and Glen's. When the last tape played out, Latham was spitting fire and brimstone. He then clued them in on some of Mychal's history with women, including the love affair that Mychal had had with his ex-fiancée, Morgan.

"Gosh, this entire scenario seems to be without an ending," Nikkola said wearily. "What are we going to do?"

"You aren't going to do anything, Nikki," Latham stated clearly. "Glen and I'll handle Mr. Mychal Forrester. If I'm correct, Carmen Thomas is a major player in this game. She may be the only other player."

"I have to agree with you, Latham," Glen pitched in. "Carmen has always been a vindictive witch. She's been responsible for most of the rumors spread around about the various crew members. I believe she's at the center of all this also, but I still have to wonder why she would take things this far."

"I think I know the answer to that one," Latham chimed in, looking at Nikkola with deep regret. "When Carmen was trying to convince me to marry her and raise the supposedly unborn child, she told me how her father had left her mother alone to raise her. Though there is no baby, Carmen is haunted by fears of ending up like her mom—alone and living in dark despair."

"So, the plot thickens," Glen asserted. "But what does Mychal Forrester have to do with all this?"

"I can answer that one, too," Latham interjected. "I have a feeling that Mychal's after my tail. Somehow, Carmen must have found out about Mychal and Morgan, and then solicited him to help her break up Nikki and me. After Mychal found out I was involved with Nikki, I believe he thought it would be fun to seek revenge against me. He found out that I was engaged to Morgan just before they were to be married."

Nikkola sighed hard. "Gee, this keeps getting deeper and deeper, but let's go back to the original question: What can be done about it?

"As I stated before, Nikki, Glen and I'll handle it. I

have a few ideas, but you're absolutely not going to be
involved in it. Mychal is too dangerous. Since Morgan
had deceived him in the worst way, and he now seems to
be pursuing you, he's a double threat. Glen and I are
tough. We can best handle our own gender."

"Guys, have at it! I have every confidence in you, but
what you've said still doesn't explain why Mychal would
tap my phone."

"I'm sure Carmen requested it. Though I'd agreed
to stick by her, she knew I loved you deeply. She probably wanted to find out if I had really broken things off
with you. She may have wanted proof to throw in my
face if I told her I wasn't seeing you anymore even
though I was."

"You two have a lot more to talk about. I'll let you two
catch up on what you've been missing. In fact, I plan on
staying clear of this suite. I want my friends to find all
the happiness you can. Your love has already been on
ice for much too long."

Glen smiled with knowing, warm thoughts of Gennifer
heating up his heart. With everything out in the open
between them, Glen thought of how Gennifer hadn't
even flinched when he'd told her the truth about his
sexual dysfunction. She'd been more hurt than anything that he'd felt he couldn't confide in her. Glen
had apologized and she accepted. While they planned
to take it slow, their relationship was definitely in the
healing process.

After kissing Nikkola and shaking Latham's hand,
Glen let himself out.

The door hadn't had a chance to close before
Nikkola found herself wrapped up in Latham's male
strength. She undoubtedly knew that it was right where
she belonged, never to stray again.

They were thrilled to be reunited, and for the next
several hours, pent-up emotions were set free, which

rapidly turned into pure ecstasy for Nikkola and
Latham.

Ecstatic to be safe in his arms, Nikkola allowed Latham's
flurry of sweet kisses and loving caresses to carry her
away. Lost in a magnificent world of their own making,
they talked over their problems and then came to the
conclusion that they wanted to be together for the rest
of their lives. Before their plans could be set in concrete,
they first needed to sever their ties to both Carmen and
Mychal.

Sorry for not having told her all about Morgan and
Mychal, Latham gave her a blow-by-blow description of
how his affair with Morgan began, how it ended, and
how Morgan had come to him to tell him she was marrying someone else. In response to his story, Nikkola
filled him in on the details of the times she'd spent with
Mychal, telling him how she'd even considered marrying him when she'd learned from Blaine that he was
going to marry Carmen. She assured him that nothing
physical had occurred between them, but she didn't lie
about her allowing Mychal to kiss and caress her a few
times too many.

Finding out that Blaine had lied to her about Latham's
marriage plans was seriously aggravating to Nikkola,
but nothing mattered as much as having Latham back
in her life. After promising to take care of Blaine in his
own way, Latham also promised her she'd never again
have to worry about Carmen and Mychal interfering in
their lives. He also knew how to shake things up—he
was hell bent on doing so.

Time seemed to stand still for the remainder of their
stay in London. Though he hadn't actually proposed
marriage, she felt sure that he would. They needed to
spend a lot of time discovering the mysteries they hadn't
yet unlocked in one another. It would take them forever
to unearth all they were, all they hoped to become.

Nikkola figured that hell having no fury would have nothing to do with a woman's scorn, not when Mychal Forrester ripped through his suite of rooms like a raging bull. Upon discovering the tapes missing, she guessed that he'd positively go ape. It wouldn't take Sherlock Holmes to figure out who had taken them. As far as she knew, she'd been the only visitor in his home. Once he'd calmed down, he might realize that he'd gotten exactly what he deserved. She had somehow managed to turn the tide against him. For that she was glad.

Mychal had schemed himself out of the one woman that he somehow believed could've really made a difference in his life. If his arrogance had allowed him to be honest with himself, he would've known that he never really had a chance with her. Mychal really wasn't all that bright, anyway, she now knew. If he were, he would confess his wrongdoing and move on.

But in all his irrationality, she was sure he thought he could still, to a certain degree, intimidate her. The phone had rung several times, and there was no doubt in her mind that it was Mychal. But a phone call would not suffice. He'd have to see her in person. She'd bet her last cent on that. She hoped that by the time he reached the hotel, she would've already checked out and be on her way back to the States.

There was nothing to stop Mychal from flying to Virginia. How many times had he already flown there? Too many to make Nikkola think any differently about his showing up again. Mychal was the sort of man who answered to no one.

Chapter 16

Although it was the middle of fall, the temperatures in the southern states had soared way up into the nineties. A blanket of unbearable humidity was hovering menacingly over Alexandria. Scantily clad, Nikkola sat in her living room, wishing she were in the cooler temperatures of London.

As she sat quietly, reading her mail, she wondered what Latham and Glen had up their sleeves. They were constantly having meetings, refusing to give her any details about the plans. She also wondered if Mychal had yet discovered the missing tapes, though she felt he had.

Nikkola was glad Mychal wasn't able to contact her. She'd changed her phone number to an unlisted one. Since she'd be off for several days, she hadn't given her new number to the airlines, but they knew how to reach her through Glen. With Mychal seemingly having access to her personal information, she thought it best to wait until everything was settled.

Stopping Mychal from showing up at her place was an entirely different matter, since he'd been able to gain access to the complex so easily. With no physical

evidence to prove there'd ever been a bug on her
phone, she couldn't help feeling that Mychal had also
found a way to enter her home. Latham and Glen had
checked out the phone as soon as they'd returned from
London, but nothing was ever found. Knowing Glen
would look after her, Nikkola had declined the invitation to stay at Latham's home.

The late evening rolled in, bringing with it a badly
needed cool front. After turning off the air conditioner,
Nikkola opened all the windows and deeply sucked in
the fresh, cool air. Standing still in front of the window,
she watched the events of the last few months unfold
before her very eyes. It was as though she were watching
a confusing movie, as each scene touched off a different emotion. So much had happened and so many
things had changed, but the one thing that would never
ever change was her love for Latham Scott. Their love
had taken many unexpected turns and twists. The
bumps and knocks had been hard, but she now realized
how much they'd remained steadfast in their feelings
for each other.

The insistent ringing of the doorbell startled Nikkola.
With uncertainty and fear written in her eyes, she turned
around to face the door, never expecting it to open
without her assistance. Her heart stopped when the
door flung open and Mychal stepped boldly into the
hall. Their eyes locked in a fierce battle, as they stood
perfectly still, sizing one another up. Her heart had
somehow started beating again. She heard the thunder-
ous pounding as it drowned out all the other sounds,
felt the adrenaline pumping wildly through her.

Willing her legs to move, Nikkola ran toward the telephone, but Mychal reached her before she could dial a
single number. Roughly grabbing the phone from her
hands, he slammed it back into its cradle. Snatching

her by the hand, he dragged her over to the sofa and pushed her down hard. As she looked around for something to defend herself with, his dark eyes warned her that it was foolish to even entertain the thought.

"I'm not here to hurt you, Nikkola," he thundered, "but we have to talk."

Although his eyes were now less threatening, her guard remained securely intact.

"Mychal, how did you get a key to my home?" Her voice had come out small and frightened, which she hated. Mychal shouldn't ever know how much he intimidated her.

"We'll discuss that later! You have something that belongs to me, Nikkola. I'm here to demand it back." His eyes had softened, but they belied the cold of winter in his sharp tone.

"I have no idea what you're talking about, Mychal. If you have any sense left, you'll walk out that door and forget you ever knew me."

Placing his hands on her shoulders, Mychal shoved Nikkola back against the sofa. Fear raced through her at top speed as she released angry tears from her eyes.

"Have you gone mad, Mychal? I want you out of here. Now!"

"You're in no position to make demands, Nikkola. I'm in control here! You lost control the moment you dared to step into my lair."

Now Nikkola understood what the fly must've felt when it dared to step into the web of the spider.

"The tapes, Nikkola. Hand them over."

There was no way Nikkola could've turned the tapes over to Mychal, since Latham had them, but she had no intention of telling him so. She sensed the need to change tactics rather quickly. "What's this all about, Mychal?" she asked in a soft voice. "Why is it so important for you to intimidate me? I know that you're intelligent, strong, determined, and very, very manly, but I also know that you can be sweet, loving, and considerate. If you'd be so kind, I'd like for you to explain all this madness to me."

The soft way in which she'd spoken had rendered Mychal speechless. He found himself wanting to take her in his arms and erase all the fear he'd placed in her eyes. He nervously cleared his throat, running his fingers through his hair. His jawbone jutted in and out as he wrestled with his conscience. "I had a job to do, Nikkola," he said bitingly, "but I never intended for you to get hurt. I simply fell in love with you as I was trying to do a friend a favor." While staring into space, Mychal seemed reluctant to explain any further.

Mychal's tone had softened and, unwittingly, Nikkola dropped her guard.

"Please, Mychal, continue," she gently prompted. "I have to know why you've involved yourself in whatever it is you're involved in."

In a barely audible voice, Mychal explained what his purpose had been and why. Just as Latham had said, Carmen had asked him to spy for her. When his old friend, Carmen, had come to him with her multitude of problems, he felt compelled to help her.

Mychal and Carmen had met when he'd been a frequent flyer on another route Carmen used to fly. They'd become fast friends. Although Carmen didn't know Latham at the time, Mychal had told her about his broken romance with Morgan. Much later, after getting to know Latham, she realized he was the same man that Mychal had told her about. Carmen never told Latham that she knew about Morgan and Mychal.

"Mychal, at one point I really believed you were a decent man, but I was dead wrong. Can you tell me why you felt the need to use me to help Carmen hurt Latham Scott?"

"Nikkola, the plan was for me to try to get next to

you so Carmen could win Latham back. I didn't count on falling in love with you, which complicated the whole scheme of things. Don't think my conscience hasn't attacked me over and over, but a man in my position knows how to overrule his conscience. I personally bugged your phone the first time I visited your apartment. I had it retrieved through one of my associates. Believe me, Nikkola, you were never in any real danger."

Nikkola stared at Mychal in disbelief. "Are you saying you had someone else come into my apartment, Mychal?"

"Like I said, you were never in danger. It occurred while you were in London. I didn't give anyone your key. Other proven methods of gaining entry were used."

Nikkola looked stunned. This was worse than she'd expected.

"As for Latham Scott, I saw him as a fatal enemy. He'd been engaged to the woman I once imagined myself in love with, and he's now holding the heart of the woman I'm truly in love with. It was easy to make the decision to destroy him in the process of winning you over."

The fact that Mychal didn't look ashamed of himself kept Nikkola from feeling sorry for him. But she felt sorry for the unexplainable intrigue and the undeserved respect she had held for Mychal Forrester because it now belonged to the past.

"Did you know about Carmen's fake pregnancy? If so, were you the one who put the doctor up to lying for her?"

Mychal expelled a deep breath. All the practiced deceptions swarmed around in his head like angry killer bees. "That came much later. If Latham had married Carmen, the path to you would've been cleared. I couldn't think of a better way to destroy Latham than to have him spend the rest of his life suffering through unbearable demands from Carmen while I slept every night in the same bed with the woman he adored. Although I didn't come up with the initial lie, yes, I arranged for the doctor. I guess you hate me, Nikkola?"

Nikkola shook her head. "I don't hate you, Mychal, but I certainly feel contempt for your devious mind. Any respect that I may've had for you has completely disintegrated."

"I'd feel the same way if I were in your place. I guess there's no chance of getting you to marry me now, is there?"

His cocky statement stunned her once again, but Nikkola couldn't help laughing. Mychal was already back at being as incorrigible as ever. His arrogance had already revived itself. Leaning into him, she put her lips close to his ear. "Not a chance in hell!"

Mychal was about to take Nikkola in his arms and beg for forgiveness, when, for the second time in one day, the door was flung open without her assistance.

Storming into the room like a rabid animal, dragging Carmen along behind him, Latham moved forward, taking long deliberate strides until he reached the living room. Coming to an abrupt halt, he practically pushed Carmen into a chair. Looking none too friendly, Latham then stood over Mychal.

Glen brought up the rear, looking as though he feared that a championship boxing match was about to take place right in Nikkola's living room.

Latham grabbed Mychal from his seat by the collar. "Forrester, we have a few things to discuss," Latham boomed. "I've brought your partner in crime along to make sure we keep the story straight and to the point. What the hell did you two jackasses think you were playing at? Are you two prepared to cut a deal? If so, we can get on with the negotiations."

Latham shoved Mychal backward and then pushed him in the chair next to Carmen. Latham sat down on the sofa next to Nikkola, who hadn't yet found her voice to speak. Glen sat on the arm of the couch and reached for Nikkola's hand.

"Ladies and gentlemen, let the games begin," Latham announced. Reaching into his pocket, he pulled out a tape and held it up in the air. "Here in my hand is something that can prove criminal intent on the part of two people in this room. Of course, we all know this isn't the only tape, but I'm sure everyone can guess which two people I'm referring to."

Latham turned to face Mychal. "Are you interested in negotiating for the possible return of your property?"

Mychal's dark eyes cut into Latham, but Latham's gaze remained both steady and challenging. Losing the battle of strong wills, Mychal nodded his head to Latham's proposal.

"Good, I thought you'd see it my way, Forrester," Latham triumphed, pulling out a sheet of paper and waving it in the air. "I'm willing to turn your property over to you if you're willing to give in to my demands. You both need to read and sign the paper they're written on. If not, I'll use your own property to file criminal charges against you."

Angry for getting him into this mess, Mychal glanced sharply at Carmen.

"Knowing tapes aren't usually admissible in court, I've gathered quite a bit of other evidence. A large portion of it is very incriminating. For sure, wiretapping is a federal offense. Maybe you should also know that the doctor you hired as a player in this game has already signed on the dotted line. The threat of losing your medical license works nicely as a surefire deterrent. With enough evidence to pull it off, miracles can often be performed."

When Mychal stood up, Latham rose too, his eyes daring Mychal to make one false move. He'd like nothing better than to outright flatten him.

"Listen, Scott," Mychal said nastily, "I've already told Nikkola everything. Could we cut with all the theatrics and get this mess over with? I don't plan on causing any more trouble for anyone. I realize I should've never gotten involved in this in the first place." Mychal shot Carmen another scathing look, but she only looked defiantly back at him.

"You're damn right you won't be causing any more trouble! While I can appreciate your telling Nikki everything, I insist that you read and sign my lists of demands. Then this boring party can come to an end," Latham remarked as a matter of fact.

In awe of the way Latham was handling Mychal, Nikkola flashed him a guarded smile. She thoroughly enjoyed Carmen's discomfort. She could tell by the look on Glen's face that he was more than just a little surprised at the powerful way Latham was running the show. Nikkola was grateful to have Latham sticking by her through this ordeal. Other than Nickolas and Glen, no one had ever come to her rescue.

After the papers were signed, Latham ushered their unwanted guests to the door.

As Latham started to hand over the tapes to Mychal, Nikkola grabbed them from his hand. "Mychal has something that belongs to me. He can have these tapes when I get it back."

Digging into his pocket, Mychal pulled out Nikkola's door key and handed it to her.

Nikkola crossed her arms in front of her. "I trust there are no copies?"

"Your trust is well-founded," Mychal responded. "I wonder if the same can be applied to the tapes," he said, eyeing Latham with cold suspicion.

"I always keep an ace up my sleeve, Forrester. You and your crime buddies are the only ones who can ensure that it'll stay there," Latham stated with confidence.

"You've proven to be a formidable foe, Scott. To know we have the same drive and determination frightens me into thinking you and I might have a lot more in common than just falling in love with the same women," Mychal openly taunted.

"Don't flatter yourself, Forrester. You and I have nothing in common. Nikki would have never gotten involved with the likes of you if she hadn't thought we were lost to each other. You and your scheming friend here deserve each other," Latham charged, pointing at Carmen.

Carmen had nothing to say, but it really mattered to no one. When Latham closed the door, the three friends screamed and shouted happily over the brilliantly executed triumph.

When they sat down to discuss what had just happened, Nikkola explained how Mychal had gotten into her place, and that he'd told her he'd made impressions of her keys when she'd been a guest at his home. Although Latham was happy the keys had been returned, he suggested the locks be immediately changed. Nikkola and Glen agreed wholeheartedly.

After handing a copy of the demands to Nikkola, Latham sat back and watched as she scanned the list of conditions. Once she finished reading, she smiled adoringly at her lover.

Moving toward him, she wrapped her arms around his neck. "You were brilliant! You would've made an excellent attorney. Besides the tapes and the doctor's signature, what other evidence did you have, Latham?"

Glen laughed, knowing there hadn't been any other evidence.

Latham smiled smugly. "I'm an excellent poker player! I'm damn good at bluffing, too. Those were also blank tapes I gave to Forrester."

Nikkola was astonished at Latham's revelations.

Latham turned to face Glen. "I don't think we're

312 *Linda Hudson-Smith*

going to have any more problems with the likes of Forrester and Carmen. We handled it perfectly, pal."

Glen smiled brightly. "I don't think so either. And I'm glad that Carmen agreed not to ever fly on a route that any of us might be on! This has been much too unsettling for all of us, especially for you and Nikki."

Nikkola smiled happily. "I guess it's back to business as usual for all of us. Back to the night flight, which will never be the same as it was. Thank God for that."

"Not for very long, Miss Knight," Latham chimed in. "I'd love for you to become my wife and leave the airlines altogether. As my wife, you'll still have your flying privileges. The choice about leaving is up to you." He smiled, winking knowingly at her.

Nikkola broke into a huge grin. "What about the choice to become your wife?" she asked haughtily.

Latham raised his eyebrows. "What about it?"

"I'll agree to become your wife if you agree to have your route changed to a local one," she stated emphatically.

"Then it's settled. Neither of us will ever again have to endure another night flight. Glen, I'd be honored to have you as my best man," Latham offered with sincerity.

Glen was truly flabbergasted. "My pleasure, Captain Scott." While hugging Nikkola, Glen whispered to her his congratulations. He then congratulated Latham, shaking his hand.

Falling into the arms of the man she loved and had just agreed to marry, Nikkola pressed her mouth against Latham's, kissing him deeply.

Smiling broadly, Glen slipped away without being noticed.

While returning Nikkola's kisses fervently, with all the love that was in his heart, Latham silently prayed that she'd never again leave him. Holding her away from him, he stared into Nikkola's eyes, happy to have her back in his life, permanently.

"Why," she asked softly, "didn't you tell me about Morgan and Mychal?"

For several long moments, Latham pondered Nikkola's question. "Because I didn't want to influence your decision. Since I really believed Carmen was carrying my child, I didn't want you to be caught in the middle. You also needed to see Forrester for what he really is."

Nikkola was somewhat impressed by Latham's answers, but not totally satisfied. "Is that all of it, Latham?"

"Basically. I knew that once you found out about Mychal, you'd have nothing to do with him. I ached for you day after day, longed for you night after night. I prayed repeatedly for this very ending. After I insisted on our staying together, I realized it wasn't fair to you under the circumstances. When I found out the pregnancy had all been a terrible hoax, I planned to wait until you returned to Virginia to tell you. Fearing that you might take up with Mychal is what drove me out to the airport to hop the first available flight to London."

"Your fears were well founded," she said regrettably. "I *was* considering a life with Mychal, knowing it was insane. And I did entertain the thought of trying to love him if I couldn't have you. As fate would have it, I discovered those tapes. Anything I'd thought I could feel for Mychal was simply lost."

Latham pressed Nikkola's head against his chest, stroking her back tenderly. "We're together now, Nikkola. We don't need to spend another minute regretting the past. Where's your phone book?" His tone was rather cool, but she had no idea why he wanted her phone book.

"Can you tell me what you want with my phone book? Don't you trust me to get rid of all the male phone numbers listed in my little pink book?"

Latham grinned lazily. "Sure, I trust you, but I need to get the phone number of my future in-laws. Woman, I need to ask your parents for permission to marry their beautiful daughter. We also have to get little Cydnee's permission. She'll make a beautiful flower girl. We can have Seth as our ring bearer. What do you think?"

Nikkola giggled, feeling happier than she'd felt in a long time. "I think you're the most wonderful man I've ever had the pleasure of knowing." She kissed him softly on the mouth. "Cydnee and Seth will be thrilled for us. As for my parents, we'll have to call them and see."

Latham kissed her back. "Ring that Florida number, honey!"

Reaching across his lap, Nikkola picked up the phone and dialed her parents' home number. Before anyone answered, she gestured for Latham to pick up the bedroom extension.

Ethel Knight answered the phone on the second ring.

"Mom, it's Nikki. I have to talk to you and Dad. Please have him pick up the other phone." Nikkola could hear her mother shouting for Nickolas. When he came on the line, she told them that someone wanted to speak with them.

"Good evening, Mr. and Mrs. Knight," Latham greeted, feeling excited. "This is Latham Scott. Not wanting to waste any time, I'm calling to ask for your daughter's hand in marriage."

Hearing her parents gasp in shock, Nikkola laughed. There was a long, pregnant silence. "I'm stunned, Latham and Nikkola." Nickolas finally spoke up. "Have you two worked out your problems regarding the woman and the unborn child?"

"Dad and Mom, there is no unborn child. Carmen was lying to him all the while. We have everything worked out. Latham simply wants your blessings."

"Son, you have both our blessings," Nickolas shouted happily. "Congratulations, kids."

"Have you two set a wedding date?" Ethel asked, shedding happy tears for her daughter.

"I'm afraid we haven't gotten quite that far," Nikkola responded.

"I can tell you this," Latham said, "we aren't having a long engagement. So get your fancy wedding attire ready. I'm not letting this woman get away from me again. We'll call you as soon as our plans are firm. Count on it."

"Congratulations, Nikkola and Latham!" Ethel squealed. "We'll look forward to hearing from you. We love you, Nikki. Latham, I know we'll come to love you too."

Latham and Nikkola shared another few minutes of their happiness with her parents and then signed off with the promise of keeping them informed of their plans.

Latham returned to the living room. After sitting back down on the sofa, he firmly positioned Nikkola on his lap. The phone rang before he could engage her in a lingering kiss.

"Nikkola, I know I'm the last person you want to hear from, but I had to tell you how sorry I am for everything. I hope you get all the happiness you deserve. Tell Latham Scott he's a better poker player than me." Mychal disconnected the line without another word.

Knowing how very hard it must've been for Mychal to call and eat crow, Nikkola smiled, feeling sorry that he'd reduced himself to such deception. After sharing the one-sided phone conversation with Latham, she snuggled up in his lap. "I love you, Latham Scott! I'm looking forward to spending the rest of my life with you. We may not fly together anymore, but we'll always reside *above the clouds*." Crystal tears of happiness slid from her eyes.

"Oh yeah, Nikkola, together for the rest of our lives. I love the sound of that."

After carrying her into the bedroom, Latham undressed Nikkola and placed her in bed, quickly sliding in next to her. Never again to be oceans apart, and never again to allow anyone to interfere with their love for one another, they passionately gave each other the love they both needed and had weathered the raging storms for. In their home, in their bedroom, and in their hearts, the impassioned nights below and above the clouds would live on forever.

Dear Readers:

I sincerely hope that you enjoyed reading from cover to cover *Above the Clouds*. I'm very interested in hearing your comments and thoughts on the story of Nikkola Knight and Captain Latham Scott, who share a romance far above the clouds. I love hearing from my readers, and I do appreciate the time you take out of your busy schedules to write.

Please enclose a self-addressed, stamped envelope with all your correspondence and mail to: Linda Hudson-Smith, 16516 El Camino Real, Box 174, Houston, TX 77062. You can also e-mail your comments to LHS4romance@yahoo.com. Please visit my Web site also and sign my guest book at www.lindahudsonsmith.com.

Linda Hudson-Smith

ABOUT THE AUTHOR

Born in Canonsburgh, Pennsylvania, and raised in Washington, Pennsylvania, Linda Hudson-Smith has traveled the world as an enthusiastic witness to other cultures and lifestyles. Her husband's military career gave her the opportunity to live in Japan, Germany, and many other cities across the United States. Linda's extensive travels help her to craft stories set in a variety of beautiful and romantic locations. She turned to writing as a form of therapy after illness forced her to leave a marketing and public relations career.

Romance in Color chose her as Rising Star for the month of January 2000. *Ice Under Fire,* her debut Arabesque novel, has received rave reviews. In 2000, the Black Writers Alliance presented to Linda the prestigious Gold Pen Award in the category of Best New Author. She has also won two Shades of Romance Magazine Awards in the categories of Multicultural New Romance Author of the Year and Multicultural New Fiction Author of the Year 2001. Linda was also nominated as the Best New Romance Author at the 2001 Romance Slam Jam Conference and won another Shades of Romance Magazine Award for Best New Christian Fiction Author of the Year 2002. Her name and novel covers have been featured in such major publications as *Publishers Weekly, USA Today,* and *Essence* magazine. Linda's debut inspirational, *Ladies In Waiting,* has appeared on several bookstores' best-seller lists since its release in August 2002.

Linda is a member of Romance Writers of America and the Black Writers Alliance. Though novel writing remains her first love, she is currently cultivating her screenwriting skills. She has also been contracted to pen several other novels for BET Books.

Dedicated to inspiring readers to overcome adversity against all odds, for the past four years Linda has served as the national spokesperson for the Lupus Foundation of America. In making lupus awareness one of her top priorities, she travels around the country delivering inspirational messages of hope. She is also a strong supporter of the NAACP and the American Cancer Society. She enjoys poetry, entertaining, traveling, and attending sporting events. The mother of two sons, Linda shares a residence in Texas with her husband.